THE
GREYZONE

A GLOBAL FEDERATION
OF NATIONS BOOK

THE
GREYZONE

JASON MCMILLAN

OMAHA, NEBRASKA

THE GREY ZONE

GLOBAL FEDERATION OF NATIONS SERIES BOOK ONE

Contact the Publisher at:

Rooney Publishing

c/o Concierge Marketing

4822 South 133rd Street, Ste 200

Omaha, NE 68137

rooney@conciergemarketing.com

402-884-5995

Paperback ISBN: 978-0-9993400-4-2

Kindle ISBN: 978-0-9993400-3-5

Library of Congress Cataloging Number: 2018951811

Cataloging in Publication Data on file with the publisher.

Revised Second Edition

Publishing and Production services provided by Concierge Marketing Inc.

Printed in the United States of America

First Printing 2018

10 9 8 7 6 5 4

AUTHOR'S NOTE

If you are reading this, I would like to start by saying: thank you. Your interest and support mean the world to me. I hope you have as much fun reading *The Grey Zone* as I had writing it.

I need to express some special gratitude to those people that helped me along the way. First off, my parents Michael and Karen McMillan could not have been more supportive. Since I was a child, they nurtured my desire to create. When I committed to writing a book, they did not hesitate to increase their support every step of the way.

To my family and friends and all those who talked with me during the process of creating this book, every comment and question gave me the fuel I needed to power through, even when I was stuck and frustrated. Know this—your words have power. The power to shape dreams and stoke the fires of creativity. Your words can empower someone to accomplish their goals. Though you may not recognize what follows, your words made this book.

A SHORT LIST OF ACRONYMS USED IN THE GREY ZONE

AFA: American Freedom Army
AFG: American Freedom Group
APD: All-Purpose Device
AR: Advanced Robotics
BHS: Basic Human Standard
BoLAS: Band of Latin American States
GFCoJ: Global Federation Court of Justice
GFN: Global Federation of Nation's
GSE: Global Stock Exchange
IWC: Implanted Wrist Chip
LGW: Liberation Grizzlies of the West
MAB: Media Accreditation Board
MOAT: Mobile Observation and Targeting
N.A.D.S.: New American Desert States
NASO: North American Security Office
O.o.B.:   Order of Bedlam
PPO: Prep Period Ops
SO: Security Officer or Security Office
SOHQ: Security Office Headquarters
STAB: Special Tactics for Advancing Border

PROLOGUE

3 May 2072

"And I'll have a club sandwich on rye with a kumquat spritzer. Thanks."

The man spoke to the waiter as he closed out the digital menu displayed on the table. He enjoyed the nostalgia of having a person come to the table to take your order. It added a touch of personal service he thought many eateries were sorely missing.

The man's companion, a brunette woman in her mid-forties, idly twirled the ice cubes in her water with her straw.

He watched her for a moment, then looked at the glass tabletop which now displayed the daily news. He tapped the table and a graph showing the weekly march of the Global Stock Exchange appeared before him. The GSE continued to climb, up a point and a half in the last twelve hours.

A gust of wind blew across the veranda and the man followed the current, then gazed across the street. It was a warm spring day in Oklahoma City—the sun shone above the restaurant's patio where some twenty-five other patrons enjoyed their lunch break.

"I think I'll go to the club after work. Get a swim in," the woman said as she continued to twirl the ice in her glass.

"Yeah?" the man asked absent-mindedly as his finger scrolled down the table and he changed graphs from one stock in his portfolio to the next.

"Yeah," the woman said.

She stopped twirling the ice cubes and let the straw settle in the drink. The water continued to swirl around the buoyed straw.

"That means you'll have to pick the twins up from practice."

"Yeah," the man said. His cheek rested on his hand and his eyes were cast down at the table top.

"David, are you listening to me? I need you to—"

"Pick up the twins from practice. I heard you, sweetie."

He closed out the graphs on the tabletop and the screen faded away, leaving only a faint reflection of David and the blue sky above. He looked up at his wife and gave her a smile.

She smiled back and returned to twirling the ice in her drink.

"Thank you. I just wasn't sure you were paying attention."

"I was," the man said, the smile still on his face. He studied her delicate fingers as they played with the straw. She made this childish motion look graceful.

A man sitting alone in the corner of the patio caught David's eye. Wearing a granite suit with a black shirt underneath, he blended into the shade. Only his right foot, crossed over his left knee, basked in the sun while the rest of him was covered by the restaurant's awning. David watched the man while his wife opened an app on the table and played drone footage of celebrities walking in and out of their massive homes. The man in the corner caught David's curiosity because instead of being entranced by the table screen or his All-Purpose Device the shaded man had a binder next to his plate filled with a few centimeters of paper. It had been some time since David had seen someone in public with so much physical reading material. He thought about how big of a hassle it would be to lug around so much paper.

"Linda said that their family is going to Havana next month to vacation."

"Yeah?" David watched the man lick his thumb and turn a page in the binder.

"I think it's time we start planning our next trip. The twins have their summer break coming soon and the only vacation we have planned is to see your parents in Kansas City."

His wife had stopped playing with the ice in her glass and was looking at David again. She removed her sunglasses and placed them on the table.

"What do you think about Kinshasa? The riverfront is supposed to be spectacular since the renovations. We haven't been to Africa in years, not since the safari. And the twins were just tykes then."

"I don't see why not," David said. He synced his APD to the tabletop and looked at his planner. "Why don't you book a flight for the third week of June, Christy?"

David's job in Sodium-Ion sales had provided the family with ample opportunity to travel the globe and see all the most highly recommended tourist sites—at least those located in the White Zone.

Christy finished tapping at the table, then took a drink of water and crunched an ice cube between her teeth as she put the glass down.

"Done," she said. "And I scheduled our vaccinations as well."

"Should be fun," David concluded duly. He hated when Christy chewed ice, but none of his previous efforts had impeded the quirk.

His eyes drifted away from his wife and into the restaurant through the opening to the patio. Among the crowd, he caught the gaze of a tall, well-built man. As recognition settled on both men's faces, David tilted his head back in acknowledgement. The man inside said something to the group he was conversing with, then strode through the rows of tables, out the opening, under the awning, and into the sunlight. David started to stand when the man was two meters away.

"David!" exclaimed the man. "No, no, keep your seat. How the hell are ya?"

David lowered himself back into his chair, then grasped the man's hand firmly. A broad smile spread across his face.

"Charlie, I'm great. Just great, my friend. How are you?"

Christy noticed her husband's sudden burst of energy and charisma. She turned her head to look at Charlie as she held up one hand to shade her naked eyes from the bright sun.

"And this must be your lovely wife. How do you do? Even more gorgeous than advertised," Charlie said.

Christy blushed and grabbed Charlie's hand, keeping the other cupped from her cheek to her forehead.

"Oh, I'm sorry. Yes, Charlie, this is my wife, Christy. Christy, this is Charlie Larkin. We met a few years back rafting with Conner. Shit, what was that now? Six? Seven years ago?" David inquired, bringing the conversation back between the boys.

"Seven years next month, if you can believe it. We need to get back on the Magpie soon." Charlie placed both palms on the table and leaned forward. "How *is* your brother? I haven't seen Conner in ages. You still hawking Sodium-Ion commodities? That's a dying industry with the new developments they're making with batteries, huh?"

David's face grew stern for a split second from the barb, but quickly regained its enthusiasm.

"Conner's fine. He was in town and we got together for drinks about six weeks ago. But yes, I'm still with NanClex. And those 'new developments,' as you put it, are still theoretical. Infantile. Sodium-Ion isn't dying. If anything, we're in our golden years. With the prevalence of—"

David's reply was cut short by the roar of a gasoline-powered engine.

The entire restaurant hushed at the rare sound.

Standing high above the shorter, electric vehicles, David eyed an ancient pickup speeding down the street. As it approached the corner and the couple's lunch spot, he saw three figures rise from the truck bed. The sudden burst of machine gun fire split through the air and was quickly joined by the sounds of screams and shuffles and crashing glass. David dropped beneath the table, shielding his head with his arms. He glanced at his wife and saw only her knees, shins, and stiletto-ed feet. She was still seated, exposed to the danger. David began to crawl, hoping to grab her ankle and pull her to the safety below. Then, in his periphery, there was a blur of movement. It was Charlie. He was on the ground; his eyes wide, his mouth agape, black blood bubbling down his cheek onto the cement. The visual terror was only overtaken by the unbelievable heat of an explosion. Then, David's world went blank.

CHAPTER ONE

3 May 2072

Natalie Kelley stepped off the railcar at the Metro Station in the Riverside District of Oklahoma City toting only a small overnight bag. The trip on the high-speed electric train from Chicago took a little over two hours. The ride gave Natalie a chance to research the terrorist attack that took place at The Bucket Bistro. The Global Federation of Nations, or GFN, had released a statement regarding the attack on one of its "White Zone" cities: sixteen people had been killed and another forty-one had been injured at one of OKC's busiest lunch spots.

Natalie covered acts of domestic terrorism for the *Chicago Tribune*. She focused on attacks by the American Freedom Group, or AFG, within the White Zones controlled by the GFN and in areas being transitioned into Federation abiding governments, or "Grey Zones". In the last twelve months, Natalie had published the details regarding eighty-two separate acts of terrorism directed by the AFG's military wing, the "American Freedom Army". Over the past year, she had grown accustomed to traveling to these communities at the far reaches of The Federation. She even spent a week in one of the areas completely devoid of Federation influence designated as a "Black Zone" pocket around Butte, Montana, interviewing supporters of the crude government run by AFG President John Hill.

During Natalie's research on the train she deduced that today's attack was unlikely to be orchestrated by Hill or any of his cronies. It was too sloppy. The ex-United States military officer's strikes were delivered with more precision and they generally focused on Federation infrastructure and employees, not civilians. Still, as attacks committed by the AFA became more infrequent, Natalie did not want to miss out on this breaking story if she happened to be wrong.

Natalie, a short, pretty, olive-skinned 32-year-old woman, bounced out of the station. She was happy to be out of the Chicago office and in the field. It had been nearly two weeks since she had been on the road. She was dressed casually, wearing a moss-green jacket over a white T-shirt, grey jeans, and white sneakers. She wore her dark brown hair pulled back in a style that showcased her round face, emerald eyes, and ski-jump nose. In her left ear, above faux-diamond stud earrings, a small, circular device called a "Reader" fed her the latest news from her APD regarding the attack. Natalie let the information from her Reader flow but absorbed little as she turned south on Robinson Avenue toward The Bucket Bistro. A block ahead she saw several local Oklahoma City Police cruisers blocking the street, as well as four black Federation Security Office SUVs parked behind them. On the outskirts of the perimeter cleared by the authorities, couplets of broadcast news teams stood around, waiting for more information so they could record and upload their latest segments. Drones circled overhead, capturing aerial footage of the barricaded area without flying into the restricted space.

Natalie turned off the newsfeed from her Reader and addressed her APD: "Call Cooper Gates."

The phone rang back in Natalie's ear as she stopped at the edge of the perimeter. The Bucket Bistro was two blocks past the boundary. Natalie scanned the faces of the authorities beyond the barricade. She didn't see Cooper among the personnel on the street, nor did she see any men or women wearing the familiar GFN Field Patch which signified that the individual was a Federation employee, or Federationist as they were commonly known.

The patch was a symbol overlay of geometric shapes. The base layer was a blue octagon. The eight sides of the octagon stood for the seven branches of the GFN and the eighth for the still yet to be incorporated lands beyond Federation influence. Inside the octagon was a green rhombus which represented the four major "Hubs" of each branch. Finally, at the center of the symbol was a yellow circle which stood for the fifth Hub and Capital of each Federation branch. The blue of the octagon symbolized the planet's water, the green of the rhombus symbolized the planet's land, and the yellow of the circle symbolized the planet's cities. This final, circular icon became known as the "*Anneau de Lumière,*" or "Ring of Light". An ever-shrinking globe to a single, unified halo, it only took a few years for the GFN Field Patch to become the most recognizable logo on Earth.

The line stopped ringing and a voice prompted Natalie to leave a message for the number or send a text message to Cooper.

"Cooper, it's Natalie. I just got here. Let's get dinner tonight. Give me a call back."

Natalie ended the call and walked across the street to get a different angle down the avenue to see if she could spot the man she just left a message for.

Natalie had been sleeping with Cooper Gates for close to a year. They met in San Clemente after a desalination plant was bombed by the AFA. Gates was a retired Security Officer for The Federation and was currently the Assistant Press Secretary for the North American Security Office. His good looks and charisma, in addition to his combat experience, made him an ideal face of the GFN military arm, as well as an ideal sexual partner for Natalie when they happened to be in the same city.

Satisfied that Cooper wasn't at the scene, Natalie turned around and started for the nearest Metro light-rail station. Once there, she walked through the security gates and the station's electromagnetic sensors read her Implanted Wrist Chip, which gave her clearance to board and started her travel fare. She boarded the Metro, found a window seat, and headed north to the Plains Hotel in Midtown. On the way, the Metro passed St. Joseph's

Old Cemetery and the Oklahoma City National Memorial and Museum. The memorial, built at the turn of the century, was constructed on the former site of the Alfred P. Murrah Federal Building. The Murrah Building was bombed on 19 April 1995, by Timothy McVeigh and his truck full of fertilizer. Natalie recalled reading about the seventy-fifth anniversary of the tragedy not long ago. The death toll of one hundred sixty-eight had topped the list of the deadliest domestic terrorist acts in America at the time. Now, after fascist and counter-fascist attacks as well as attacks against The Federation, it didn't crack the top twenty.

Natalie was only a block away from her hotel when she deboarded the Metro. Walking off the platform, she saw a signboard reading "Plains Hotel" running down the length of the twelve-story glass building. The exterior glass of the building rippled from left to right and the brash golds and crimsons of the setting sun reflected off the glass panels of the hotel.

Natalie reached the lobby of the hotel and checked in to room 923 at the digital terminal. She walked past the elevator bank and found the stairwell. At home in Chicago, Natalie worked out six days a week to keep the athletic frame she had sculpted when she played lacrosse at Northwestern. On the road, she had to get creative to reach her exercise goals.

As she entered her room, Natalie checked her heart rate and oxygen levels on her APD. The program told her that her aerobic activity was adequate, but that she was behind on her daily strength training. That would have to wait. Natalie sat down at the desk, maximized the APD's screen size, rolled out the keyboard, and began typing her preliminary notes as footage from the local news station played on the television. After twenty minutes of work, a message from Cooper was displayed on the screen. He wanted to meet her for a late dinner in Bricktown in an hour. She considered taking a quick shower, decided against it, and continued tapping away. Thirty minutes later, she jogged down the stairs and headed for the Metro Station.

Natalie walked into The Mantle and immediately saw Cooper sitting at a table in the low-lit restaurant named after the long-deceased New York Yankee great. He already had a Scotch sitting in front of him and one waiting for her. She beamed as she took off her jacket and tucked it under her arm.

Cooper slid out of his seat and met her, crouching between the bench and table without leaving the booth. He gave her a light kiss on the cheek, then sat back down and directed Natalie to sit across from him. Natalie hesitated briefly at the lack of warmth in Cooper's greeting but quickly obliged and took her seat. She took a drink from her Scotch and placed her jacket in the corner of the booth.

"Nice to see you again, stud. It's been a while since we've been able to get together. Thinking about you on the train made me wish I had a private compartment," Natalie said as she winked and took another drink.

"Natalie, this will need to be a, uh, strictly professional meeting," Cooper replied. "Jenny's parents live in Edmond, so she came with me."

Natalie looked at Cooper, then glanced down at his left hand which cupped his Scotch. His wedding ring ticked against the side of the glass. The ring flustered her. Of course, she knew that Cooper was married; she had just seldom seen him wearing his matrimonial band.

"Okay," she said, disappointed. "No problem." She spoke in a raspy contralto.

"Do you want to start recording?"

"Shit, you weren't kidding about this being strictly professional. We haven't even ordered yet."

"I know. I'm sorry. Jenny was upset when I told her I was going out again. She thought I'd be able to spend some time with her folks. She just thinks I'm avoiding them."

"Are you?"

Cooper laughed. "That's beside the point."

Natalie took her APD out of her back pocket and placed it on the table. Before directing the device to record, she leaned in close to Cooper. "Listen. We don't need to eat. Don't feel like you owe me anything. I'm a big girl, I can grab a bite on the way home. Now," she said as she directed the APD to begin recording and settled back into the booth, "what can you tell me about the men in the pickup?"

Noah Bridger, a white man in his mid-thirties, sat behind the wheel of his car, waiting. The car, a dark green Mustang, was pulled over to the side of a gravel road. Noah had worked on the car's engine for the past six months and felt that this Mustang rode as well as any of his racing cars. Sitting on the dashboard was a figurine of St. Christopher, the patron saint of travelers. The gravel road was flanked by fields of mustard greens. The leafy plants stood in neat, parallel rows that shot off toward the horizon. In each field rose a few dozen soaring, bright white wind turbines. The turbines' three blades turned in the breeze. The height from field to blade tip at the crest of the rotation reached two-hundred meters. Noah sat and watched the whirling blades of the nearest turbine. The motion was hypnotic.

A hawk screeched and flew high above the road. Its shadow crossed the rocks ahead of the car.

Noah checked his reflection in the rearview mirror. Looking back at him was a youthful man with old-school Aviator sunglasses, a grey U.S. Patriots cap, and a round, clean-shaven face. He was glad that he wore the sunglasses. He did not wish to see the fear in his own eyes.

The Mustang was parked near the border of what Federationists called the White Zone and, though it was only a couple hundred kilometers from his home and family in Hereford, Texas, Noah felt as if he were light-years away. He had never been this close to "Civilization", as he and his neighbors mockingly called The Federation-occupied lands. He did not want to be here any longer than he needed to be. But now, the other car was running late. Not alarmingly late, but late.

Seconds ticked by and Noah's anxiety grew. He began to doubt why he involved himself in such a dangerous plan.

Noah played with the settings on the control panel and expanded the vehicle's alert system to three-hundred meters.

"C'mon," Noah muttered to himself. The escape plan had been detailed down to the minute. He knew that he should have been on the road with the others by now. He thought it was uncharacteristic for Wade to be late, but, then again, he did not know the husband of his wife's sister very well.

Wade had approached Noah two weeks ago. Noah had been in his garage, working underneath his stock car, when the bellow of Wade's voice startled him. He had knocked his head on a box section before he rolled out to meet his brother-in-law. Wade told Noah that he needed him for something and that he was the only man he could trust for the job. Noah had been filled with pride that his venerable relative needed his expertise and agreed to be a part of the operation after only ten minutes of discussion. He was beginning to think that he should have thought and prayed on the proposition a little longer.

The Mustang's computer alerted him: "Vehicle approaching—Three-hundred meters—East."

Noah looked behind him and expected to see the Gendarmes, one of the resistance's names for the French-born Federation Security Officers. Instead, he saw a white utility van tearing down the road. It was Wade.

"Praise Jesus," Noah exhaled aloud. He rubbed the St. Christopher figurine on the dashboard, stepped out of the car, and popped the trunk.

Inside a spacious, sparsely decorated office on the seventy-second floor of The Global Federation of Nations' North American Security Office Headquarters, Juan Carlos Luna gazed out his window. The building sat on the southern edge of Roosevelt Island and his office looked west over the site of the former United Nations Headquarters in Midtown Manhattan. The entirety of Roosevelt Island had been purchased from the United States federal government by the GFN in 2057. Construction of the campus for the North American branch capital began immediately. The SOHQ was the first portion of the campus completed. The building rose like a pyramid with no capstone. It stood eighty stories high and it spanned the width of the island. There were eight square sections of the pyramid ascending from the largest section at the base and the smallest at the apex. On the terraces of each of the sections, massive redwood trees genetically designed for the mid-Atlantic climate had been planted. The effect was startling. Against the steel and glass of Manhattan rose an enormous, forest-covered mass that looked like it belonged in the Catskills. Since its inception, The Global Federation of Nations' North American Security Office Headquarters was known, simply, as, "The Mount."

Luna was alone in his office, waiting for a phone call. It was late, but his responsibilities as the North American Security Office's Lt. Director of Border Integrity required him to keep an unorthodox schedule. He was well beyond fifty and he was an attractive man. He had dark skin, dark hair, and dark eyes. A silver moustache hung from his nose like a crescent moon in the night sky.

The Lt. Director had earned the nickname "La Frontera" due to his legendary escapades heading STAB, or the Special Tactics for Advancing Border force. STAB worked to secure the GFN border in the American West. His actions in the field during the early years of America's adoption of the Basic Human Standard, the principle foundation of the GFN, led to his current position within NASO. He was a man revered by both those working directly for him within NASO, as well as the highest-ranking generals in the United States military.

While he waited for the phone call, Luna pulled up virtual-reality-infused satellite images of the San Luis Valley and Sangre de Cristo mountain range. The 3D topographic imagery was projected above the teak floor. Luna zoomed in on specific areas by moving his hands outward on the portion of the map he wished to see in more detail. The land he studied was currently in the Grey Zone. The Grey Zone was an area outside of the borders of GFN White Zones, but was currently being monitored and actively secured by SO forces. Luna headed all operations in the North American Grey Zones. During his six years as Lt. Director of Border Integrity, his territory had shrunk and fractured. His work had thus far been a success.

Drone footage showed a live-stream of STAB Unit India X-Ray 6 as it advanced south down I-25 toward Colorado City from Pueblo. The STAB units were methodical. This corridor had been transitioned from a Black Zone to a Grey Zone three years ago, but NASO was still working to ensure a successful and complete incorporation. Black Zones were areas where the GFN had no presence at all. During the acquisition of Black Zones, The Federation tried desperately to limit all civilian casualties and this practice took great patience. It had been nearly two decades since the United States government accepted the Basic Human Standard and joined the GFN, but many Americans were still adjusting to the new political landscape. Others were downright hostile to the transition. In the months following the United States' ratification of the treaty with The Global Federation, there was intense fighting from coast to coast. The Resistance and The Federation both suffered tremendous casualties. However, due to American military might and reinforcements from the European and Asian Security Offices, White Zones were established along long stretches of the coasts. Those that opposed The Federation

moved inland and the primary method of warfare shifted from
military to economic.

After intense fighting and massive blood loss on both the
Resistance side and The Federation side during the first four
years of GFN policy, a new tactic was adopted by The Federation
and American leadership. Any populous resistant to the GFN
would stop receiving federal aid and, more devastatingly, would
be placed under an embargo. Economic refugees throughout
the country had fled their homes to the White Zones under the
protection of the GFN while millions remained in the Black
and Grey Zones and struggled financially. Wanting to avoid
more bloodshed, the GFN and D.C. adopted the strategy of
"Generational Manifest Destiny." There would be no more
major military maneuvers that put unwitting civilian lives at
risk. Instead, the reach of the GFN would creep slowly inward
city-by-city, town-by-town, house-by-house.

The live feed showed STAB Unit IX-6. The unit was currently
stationed at a private property on the northeastern outskirts of
Colorado City.

"Report," called Luna and the unit's roster and the latest log
from the squad leader materialized at the base of the projection.
In the middle of the roster list was the name "Andre Cannon."
Next to the name there was a white circle with a red cross inside.
This symbol signified that the SO was still convalescing from an
injury or illness. Luna tapped the circle and a bar graph appeared.
The graph indicated that Andre Cannon was roughly eighty-five
percent healthy. Luna knew that any Security Officer under
ninety-five percent health level would not be participating in
raids. Instead, they would be performing menial tasks for the
unit as well as surveillance work. La Frontera's interest in the
young SO was familial; the boy was his nephew.

Andre Cannon was only 22 years old. He had always looked
up to his well-decorated uncle. He joined NASO the day after
finishing high school. Once he graduated training from Fort

Stevenson near Bloomington, Illinois, he was assigned to the Mobile Observation and Targeting Division (MOAT). MOAT's objective was to surveil and patrol the dynamic twenty-kilometer buffer between the White Zone and Grey Zone. Like his uncle, Andre Cannon was a soldier who was always squared away. He excelled at his position in MOAT and was quickly promoted to his current STAB unit. Six weeks-ago Andre was shot in the thigh by a sniper on a ranch south of Pueblo. The ensuing assault by Unit IX-6 leveled the barn that housed the shooter. Once the property was secured, the team found that the sniper had been a girl no more than twelve years old.

Andre had a short stay in a mobile hospitalization unit, and, once declared medically fit, was sent back to the field. Juan Carlos had told Akna, his sister and the boy's mother, that he would keep a close eye on his nephew. Juan Carlos had been sending her messages reiterating that Andre was safe and performing admirably.

As Luna read young Andre's weekly performance log, the phone rang.

Natalie was flustered as she walked up the stairs of the hotel after her meeting with Cooper. The "dinner" had not gone how she had hoped, professionally or personally.

At The Mantle, Cooper had seemed distracted and was dismissive of Natalie's questions regarding the identities of the terrorists. NASO usually released the names of attackers as soon as possible, typically no more than four hours after the incident. It had been longer than twice that time and Natalie had hoped to get the identities first, but Cooper was uncooperative. Natalie wondered if Mrs. Gates had given her husband a small window for the meeting and that was why he had kept the conversation short. Thinking of the other woman made Natalie's stomach turn.

When she arrived at her hotel room, she sat down on the bed and opened her APD. She had planned to sift through the local news stories regarding the bombing but brought up the recorded conversation with Cooper instead. She broadcasted the recording to the room's quantum dot screen, put aside her APD, and laid back on the bed.

The screen showed the pair sitting at The Mantle. The screen's brightness automatically increased to accommodate for the dim recording. On screen, Natalie leaned over the table, passing her glass of Scotch from one hand to the next. Cooper's back was straight against the booth and his attention flitted away from the booth toward a group of patrons a few tables away.

Natalie's voice was audible over the room's wireless speakers. "What can you tell me about the men in the pickup?"

"NASO has yet to release the names of the individuals suspected in today's attack."

"No shit, Coop. That's why I'm asking you."

"Although NASO has yet to release the identities of any suspects, the list of identities of those killed and injured in the attack are available."

"Okay." A pause. Natalie took a drink on the screen. Cooper spun his wedding ring around his finger. Natalie hadn't seen his subconscious devotion to the jewelry at the restaurant, but as she noticed it on the replay, she felt disgusted. On screen, she spoke again and reached for his hands. He pulled them away and put them under the table.

"What's wrong with you? You're not yourself."

Cooper coughed and leaned forward. "Do you have any other questions for me regarding today's attack?"

"Yeah, I have 'other questions.' I think I've only asked one question so far…"

"Natalie! Please."

Natalie took another drink of Scotch. "Jesus, okay." There was a beat as she prioritized her inquiries. "Does NASO believe that the attack was carried out by individuals working under the banner of the AFG?"

Cooper shook his head.

"NASO hasn't released the identities of those suspected in today's attack, so there is no way to tie them to the AFA or any other organization."

Natalie laughed. "Was that an answer? I was waiting for you to give an answer while you were talking, but then you just stopped."

Cooper scowled on the screen. Natalie thought that he looked good when he was frustrated.

"Okay, I know you want a quote, so here you go. 'An unnamed Federationist close to the investigation of the attack in Oklahoma City says that the target and methods used during the assault on American citizens is not consistent with previous targets and methods used by the terrorist organization known as the American Freedom Group, leading many to suspect that the responsibility belongs to an unknown party.' There's your quote."

Cooper slid out of the booth, stood up, and looked around the restaurant.

"I gotta go. I'm sorry." He bent down and kissed Natalie on the cheek. She turned away from him. "Remember, there are names that have been released."

Cooper walked out of the frame and Natalie downed her drink.

In the hotel room, she backed-up the recording.

Cooper kissed her cheek on the screen. Her face was turned away. Her eyes were closed.

"Remember, there are names that have been released."

At the restaurant, she hadn't been paying attention to him as he left. She backed-up the recording again.

"Remember, there are names that have been released."

He was trying to tell her something. Natalie grabbed her APD and quickly found the names of the casualties from the day's attack.

CHAPTER TWO

3 May 2072

The north Texas service roads were deserted. Noah Bridger had prayed that they would be. The Mustang rocketed southwest, away from the authoritative grip of Civilization. The muscle car kicked up dirt and gravel as it chased the setting sun. Weeds and potatoes lined the gravel road. The fields badly needed tending. A lone Angus bull stood near the road, chewing cud and watching the car zip by.

The Mustang was cramped. The five passengers left no centimeter of seating unoccupied. Noah fidgeted in the driver's seat and concentrated on keeping the speeding auto stable on the slick gravel. He had pushed his cars to higher speeds during races throughout Deaf Smith County and had driven on roads wet with rain, but never had he felt so unsteady commanding a vehicle. Noah wiped the sweat from his brow, then gripped the steering wheel tight with both hands. He wished that he had the assistance of the vehicle's advanced control system, but once activated, the computer would automatically slow the auto to one hundred kilometers per hour. That was not nearly fast enough.

Noah had been ferrying the fugitives on the service roads for a little over an hour. When the utility van had first arrived at the rendezvous point and parked off the road fifty meters from the Mustang, Noah ran to meet Wade and collect two large, black canvas bags. As he removed the bags from the van, he expected Wade to thank him for his assistance again, but he offered no gratitude; he was busy wiping down the van with the other three men. Noah put the canvas bags in the trunk of his car and, soon after, the men piled in and they were ready to depart. As Noah shifted the Mustang from first to second gear, an explosion erupted behind it. He had known that torching the van was part of the plan, but the sudden violence had startled him, and he veered off the gravel onto the sloped grass. The passengers laughed. Noah looked in the rearview mirror and saw that dancing flames had engulfed the van. He put his eyes on the road ahead and shifted to third.

The car ride had been mostly silent. Once out of view of the burning utility van, Noah had asked the group if they had had trouble getting through MOAT. Wade answered in the negative. Noah had wanted to know why they were late, but there was no explanation. Wade sat in the passenger seat next to Noah, his head back and eyes closed in a meditative trance. Noah had not been told the names of the three passengers seated in the back of his Mustang before the mission. Two of the men wore loose-fitting jeans and dark, homemade hemp jackets buttoned to their throats. They appeared to be in their late 30s and would occasionally whisper to each other. The man sitting behind Noah, wearing a Stetson low over his brow, introduced himself and the two others to Noah. Their names were Brickson Newsome and Otis Daggart. That was the last the passengers acknowledged their driver. Newsome wore a black, wool beanie despite the hot weather. His face was flushed red. The fourth man, Daggart, was much younger than the others. Noah guessed that he was no more than 20 years old. Daggart wore grey overalls and a dirty, white-and-blue-striped Oxford. He was restless and squirmed in the back seat until one of the others struck him across the chest and hissed at him to be still.

Up ahead, a silo broke through the flat horizon, shimmering in the light of the setting sun. Noah was relieved to spot the group's destination.

The video call Juan Carlos Luna had been waiting for had not brought good news. The suspects of the Oklahoma City terrorist attack had been identified. One of the men, Otis Daggart, had been in NASO custody within the last six months. He was the grandson of a wealthy robotics CEO. Last winter, Daggart had been apprehended in Charlotte after he was suspected of laundering money to organizations on the GFN terrorist watch-list. Because the arrest occurred within Federation boundaries, it had been outside the Lt. Director's jurisdiction. However, he remembered that Daggart had been released due to financial and political pressure from his grandfather, as well as some crafty accounting that made the charges difficult to stick. Luna thought that it was a shame that the young man had continued to pursue violent activities after his arrest. Luna would make sure his wealthy patriarch would not use his influence to free Otis Daggart again.

Luna sat behind his desk and looked out the window at the moonlit tops of the redwoods planted on the terrace below. Looking at the trees, he realized he shared a kinship with the fauna. Like the redwoods, he was a wild creature that had been domesticated by The Mount. He wanted to be in the field. Diplomacy was too lethargic. In the field, action was taken quickly, instinctively. There was no bureaucracy. The unit moved together as one entity. There were no egos to fuel. The unit's movements were swift and fluid and purposeful. The unit was one. The unit was just.

The Lt. Director pushed the nostalgic thoughts of battle from his mind. The Daggart boy and the others were now most likely on the run somewhere in his territory and, although he was stuck in an office overlooking Manhattan, he could still be just.

After looking over the names of the casualties of the attack at The Bucket Bistro, Natalie called her editor at the *Chicago Tribune*. It was after normal business hours, but Natalie knew she could reach Joseph Kalani whether he was at the office or not.

"Natalie," he answered energetically. "How's Oklahoma? Should we be expecting you back in Chicago *sooner* than you *stated*?"

Natalie rolled her eyes at the man's lame joke but couldn't keep herself from chuckling. Joseph had been skeptical that his correspondent's trip would be fruitful since it did not fit within the pattern of the attacks she focused on.

"Hello, Joseph." Natalie paced the room while the editor's wizened face bobbed on the room's QLED wall screen. "I'll be back in Chicago later than expected actually."

"Oh?" Joseph said incredulously. "Have you met a strapping, young cowpoke? A man with the ranch of your dreams? I never pictured you with a country boy, now that I think of it."

Natalie laughed. "What is *wrong* with you?" she chided.

"A few too many glasses of Moldovan Gamay, I'm afraid." Joseph was sitting in the driver's seat of his two-door Tesla coupe. He leaned out of the screen and said something to the passenger in his car.

"Joseph!" Natalie called the editor back to attention. "I'm not sure when I will be back in the office. There are a few things I would like to clear up here."

"Oh?" Joseph asked again, this time out of curiosity. "Anything your boss should be aware of?"

Natalie shook her head. "It's probably nothing. I got a lead on one of the victims. A man named Daniel Dotson."

Joseph sat up in the car seat. "The Federation employee?"

"Yes." Natalie was initially surprised that Joseph recognized the name but knew she shouldn't doubt his talent for recall. Even when he was loaded. "He worked at NASO. Mid-level guy. I've done some digging on him and there are some," Natalie paused, "inconsistencies. Like I said, it's more than likely nothing, but I would like to check it out."

"That's fine," Joseph said. "Keep me updated. And get some rest. You look haggard."

Natalie's jaw dropped in faux-recoil and she walked to the television screen with her middle finger extended, then ended the call with her boss.

Noah's Mustang pulled off the gravel road onto a long, smooth blacktop driveway. A handsome barn stood against the twilight sky next to a rustic Victorian farmhouse at the end of the drive. About two hundred meters to the left rose the silo the group had seen as they approached the property on the gravel road. Before Noah could put the car in park, the passengers opened the doors and exited the vehicle. The three in the backseat departed without a word. Wade, with his passenger door open, turned to Noah and put a hand on his shoulder.

"Thank you," Wade said.

Noah could only nod at his brother-in-law. All his previous doubt had vanished when he heard the gratitude in this man's voice and Noah felt that he had truly made a difference. Wade had talked about being "patriots" and "Crusaders," and now Noah knew what the man had meant, and the thought made him emotional.

His job was done. He had successfully ferried these four men to Frank Powell's land. Now he was to head home. That was it. Mission accomplished. After grabbing the cargo from the trunk, his passengers walked briskly toward the silo. Noah rubbed the St. Christopher figurine on the dash and thanked God everything had gone so well.

Noah put the car in reverse. His headlights shone on the trotting men. Suddenly, one of the silhouettes dropped from view. Noah slammed the brakes and stared at the crumpled mass laying in the tall grass. In the silence, gnats danced in the lights of the car. They were not alone.

Filled with confusion and fear, Noah sent the Mustang hurtling in reverse down the drive. A cacophony of gunfire broke through the silent night. Bright lights sparked across the property. A swarm of men, guns drawn, converged on Noah's passengers. On the nearest gunman, Noah thought he spotted the dreaded GFN Field Patch on his fatigues. The Field Patch was the hated symbol that gave the Gendarmes their other Americanized pejorative: "Yellow Eyes". The trapped men put their hands in the air. Noah flipped the car around and worked the stick. The road was clear. He stomped on the gas pedal, trying to mash it through the floor mat.

As the car neared the end of the paved drive, Noah heard the glass of the rear windshield crack, then shatter. Shards of glass burst onto the driver's seat. Behind him, two SUVs emerged from behind the barn in pursuit of the Mustang. The nearest portable spotlights swung down the drive. The beams hit the rearview mirror and nearly blinded Noah. He smacked the mirror to the side, then turned off the drive onto the gravel. The Mustang slipped and spun until Noah corrected it. The SUVs followed, slowing at the turn. The Mustang accelerated.

Noah's seat belt was twisted tight against his throat. He reached to unfurl and loosen the strap. The polyester webbing on the front of his shirt was sticky, warm. Noah looked down. A crimson inkblot spread across the shirt. One of the Yellow Eyes' bullets had found its mark and cut through his skin above his collar bone. Noah had driven injured before. Years ago, he had won a race while driving with three broken ribs after a collision. Now, he needed to drive through the pain again. His internal engine released the adrenaline he needed to ignore the injury.

He could not be distracted. The SUVs were gaining on him and he was sure backup would be joining them soon. He wouldn't be able to outrun them long.

Noah went to turn on the Mustang's computer system, but smoke sizzled out of the control panel. It had also been hit. He reached into the backseat, grasping for anything that could help him, but he found it empty. Headlights from the chase cars shone brighter in the rearview mirror. He put the Mustang into fifth gear and the car shot down the road. The lights from the SUVs dimmed, but Noah knew he didn't have much time. With his injured shoulder, he doubted he could keep the Mustang at this speed on the slick gravel. As he tried to steer the car with his knees, Noah took off his shoe and quickly removed the lace, then tied the gas pedal down and connected the lace to the wheel to keep the car steady. He moved the car to the side of the road, keeping the tires centimeters from the drop of the ditch. Then, Noah unfastened his seat belt, cracked open the door, and tumbled out.

The Mustang continued to speed down the road, teetering on the edge of the ditch but keeping on the gravel. Upon jumping, Noah contorted his body to avoid landing on his injured shoulder. He hit the ground and the wispy grass softened his impact. Lying in the ditch, clinging his chest, he watched as the lights from the SUVs grew larger and brighter. Soon, he could not see into the light. Noah burrowed his head into the earth, gnashed his teeth, and prayed. Gravel flew off the road and onto Noah's back.

It worked. The SUVs followed the decoy.

Noah needed to move. The Mustang would lose control any second now. After searching the car, the Feds would realize the driver had escaped. He needed to find a place to hide. Quick.

The lights in Juan Carlos Luna's office continued to gleam while the floors below were cloaked in blackness. The glow looked like a campfire burning on the side of The Mount. It was close to 23:00 and Luna had been watching the apprehension of the terrorists suspected in the Oklahoma City attack for fifteen minutes. One of the suspects had been shot and killed at the onset of apprehension. The deceased was identified as Otis Daggart, the young man the GFN Justice Department had let free. Luna had planned to send Daggart to rot in a cell at the Nunavut Deradicalization Center, but a bullet in the brain would suffice.

The seizure of the suspects had slightly deviated from procedure, but La Frontera remained calm and optimistic because his Chief Deputy Arnie Jones was heading the apprehension. Due to a "quality intelligence source," a STAB unit aided by a few members of the Texas Military Brigade, the TMB, were in position and waiting for terrorists upon their arrival. Besides Daggart, the three other men directly involved in the attack were in custody. Though shots had been fired, there were no casualties to either the STAB unit or to the TMB The intel regarding the driver had been incorrect; the team was not told that there would be a fifth man. The identity of the driver was currently unknown, and he remained at large. The getaway car, a gas-powered Ford Mustang, had been found turned over a klick away from the property. The driver was not in the wreckage. *How had they not been prepared to stop that Goddamn car?* Luna thought. He made a mental note to ask Jones about the intelligence source.

Luna wasn't worried about finding the missing accomplice. He had faith in Jones and knew that there were few places to hide in the surrounding, low-lying potato fields. If the team on the ground couldn't apprehend the driver in the next few minutes, then a V-480 Valor tilt-rotor helicopter would be on the scene equipped with a ten-thousand-watt LED spotlight.

The bird would light up the north Texas sky. The dark wouldn't cloak this fifth man for long.

Luna had watched the entire apprehension unfold before him from the confines of his Roosevelt Island office. Embedded within the body armor of each STAB member was a camera that recorded and streamed the action to the Forward Operating Base, or FOB, fifty klicks away, southwest of Amarillo and to the SOHQ. In addition to body cams, drones hovered high above the property and gave an aerial view of the operation. These recordings gave off-site commanders live look-ins on any NASO operation in the world, but were also used to train the units for future missions. By studying and correcting their own maneuvers, implementing successful tactics pioneered by other squads, and learning the habits of their foes, NASO became the most skilled, intelligent fighting force in the history of the world.

Luna paused the live feed. He backed the recording to the moment the car arrived on scene and watched the car park. With his screen split into quadrants showing four different angles, he watched the men exit the vehicle and grab equipment from the trunk, then start moving toward the silo. A flash appeared from a second story window of the farmhouse. Daggart dropped to the ground. Luna had seen the young man twitch his rifle before being struck. It had not been an overtly aggressive action, but the Lt. Director knew that it could be construed as such. Jones must have had a reason to tell his snipers to take out Daggart at the slightest hint of engagement. *Fine. The boy was filth.*

Next, on-screen, a barrage of bullets rained down upon the other three suspects. These shots were aimed not to kill, but to halt any movement from the suspects. This tactic was called the "ring of fire" by those within The Federation Security Offices. NASO's official priority was to acquire captives, not kills. The Federation aimed to distance itself from the enemy combatants by using law and order as retribution. The official line was to use justice and not brutality. There would be questions regarding why

Otis Daggart had been killed during the operation. NASO would state he had acted aggressively. The public would believe the GFN's statement. If the action had taken place within the White Zone, the GFN would be compelled to release the recordings at the behest of a District Court. However, since the operation took place in the Grey Zone, no such District Court existed.

Luna agreed that the GFN must be held to a higher standard than the scum they fought. At the same time, there needed to be exceptions, or the virtues of The Federation would never win. Luna switched to a full-screen shot from a lead Security Officer's body cam. After the torrent of gunfire, the surviving men had diligently dropped to the grass. Within seconds the officer and his fellow team members were on the fugitives. Quickly, they were bound in PARA plastic hand and ankle restraints and moved to a waiting prisoner vehicle.

Watching these military excursions always drew out Luna's own combat memories. These memories were never the horrifying flashbacks many military veterans experienced, rather, they were more like fond recollections of a time passed. Tonight's operation reminded Luna of a mission he led nearly thirty years ago, when the Basic Human Standard and The Federation were only ideas in the mind of French député Antoine Dubois. On that day, Luna's U.S. Ranger Alpha Company had captured the leader of a fundamentalist Islamic terrorist organization, along with six of his lieutenants and aides outside Erbil.

After decades of military and technological advancement, war remained very much the same. In Kurdistan, his Ranger squad had awaited the arrival of the self-proclaimed kaliph at a spot given to them by an inside source. There had been a brief firefight, but the Second Ranger Battalion had the better position and had quickly disarmed the kaliph. Then as now, superior intel won the battle.

Luna watched on the hologram as the V-480 Valor approached the property. Luna switched to the video cam located on the chopper's skids. The full topography of rugged farmland came into view. The skid cam's heat sensors showed a small herd of pronghorn flee from the helicopter's spotlight. The Valor approached the site of the wrecked Mustang. The heat sensors showed a dozen SOs and Brigadiers walking around the accident but did not pick up the runner. He wasn't within the initial perimeter of the crash site. The unit would need to expand the search perimeter.

The property was large. The Lt. Director knew it could take a little time to locate the fifth man. He sent a message to Arnie Jones's assistant, Odyssey Thacker, to forward the Chief Deputy's report to Luna's own assistant. He would not be present to read the field log as it was submitted.

Juan Carlos Luna shut off the video. He left his office near the top of The Mount and headed home to his husband.

Natalie Kelley ended the video call with her editor, then checked the online forums to read non-accredited takes on the day's attack. After decades of increasingly false stories perpetrated by the media, the line between fact and fiction became nearly indistinguishable. In the 2040s, the American government opened libel laws. Due to the substantial increase in lawsuits, Congress created the Media Accreditation Board to tackle the problem. The Board was modeled after the FDA. News programs and publications were still permitted to freely release content, but only those accredited by the Board would be "MAB approved." To obtain accreditation by MAB, a news organization must score a "truth-rate" above eighty-five percent. At the announcement of the formation of the Media Accreditation Board, groups led by First Amendment advocates were furious. Millions of protestors took to the streets. There were riots. However, after the initial Board was selected that touted respected lawyers and journalists from both sides of the aisle, the anger abetted. Hoaxes in the media nearly disappeared. Polls showed that the average citizen's understanding of current events was significantly more accurate than before. The people acquiesced to this new regulation.

The *Chicago Tribune* had been an accredited news organization since the formation of MAB. Natalie hadn't personally had any issues with the Board during her career, but she still knew there could be value in sources printed without MAB approval. With universal access to the internet, as well as professional grade recording equipment included with every APD, anyone on the planet could be a journalist and none of these amateurs went through the accreditation process. Natalie knew the power of these online forums. She had found the primary source for her most famous publication on one of these unaccredited sites. MAB-approved news organizations often bought unaccredited information from eyewitnesses who uploaded their videos, pictures, and testimonies to social media. There was a vast wealth of untapped information available on the web.

Natalie also knew the dark power such platforms could wield. Early in her career she covered an incident in Detroit where Simon Herschel, a rabbi, was stabbed to death outside of a synagogue. Using unaccredited information, a Muslim man named Ibrahim Nadhim was identified by virtual sleuths as the culprit. A group of Islamophobes, impatient with the local police's inaction in arresting Nadhim, stormed his house, lit it on fire, and hung the man from a flagpole. His young daughter was badly burned in the blaze.

Four days later, the rabbi's cousin was arrested. He confessed to the police that he had been trying to extort the rabbi and, when Herschel did not give in to his demands, he murdered the man. The story had deeply unnerved Natalie. However, she continued to skim the forums looking for anything of substance, trying to ignore the ignorance and fallacies. She knew it was part of the job.

Natalie poured a drink of Scotch from one of the mini-bottles she kept in her overnight bag and absentmindedly glazed over conspiracy theories and hateful rhetoric until she came across a still of a video recording of the event. The image was posted by a user named Lily Lee. She was looking to sell the video. Natalie found it tacky for people to monetize their experiences of tragic events, but this practice had become the norm.

The image displayed on the screen of her APD made Natalie pause. She looked at it closely, then sent Lily Lee a message looking to purchase the video. Natalie looked at the image again. She recognized the NASO employee, Donald Dotson. He sat on the edge of the screen while the other patrons ate their lunch. In the middle of his forehead was a dark circle. Across the length of the image was a telltale vapor trail. His head was frames away from exploding.

The early night air grew cool around Noah. His racing heartbeat began to dip with the dropping mercury. After he evacuated the Mustang and rolled to a stop he waited for the chase cars to pass, then crossed the gravel road and sprinted toward a line of willows visible in the distance. The loss of his left shoe made it awkward to run—he wished he hadn't left it in the car, but he had no other choice. Moving unevenly, his bare foot landed directly on an unharvested tubular and he fell to the ground. He got up and kept running. Less than a minute later, he reached a small, wooded cluster, panting and breathless. He looked over the field. He saw no noticeable tail. He may have bought himself some time, but he could not stay in the shallow wood long; the Yellow Eyes would soon find him. He needed to find a more secure hiding spot. Noah looked around him. The fields extended acres in each direction without any break. There was nowhere to go, nowhere to hide.

He crouched against the trunk of a willow and hit his palms against his temples. *Think! Think!*

He breathed slowly, heavily. His body and mind began to settle. Noah looked around at the terrain again. He knew this place. *Of course, this was Frank Powell's land.* He had forgotten where he was in the haste of his retreat.

Noah inserted his Reader and it connected to his APD.

"Call Frank Powell," he whispered, and the line began to ring.

Noah lay between the willows as he waited for a connection. In the distance, the spotlights near the silo moved and cast a wider net of illumination. The connection went dead in his ear.

"Redial," he muttered, and the line rang again. *Jesus, help me, I don't have much time.*

The phone continued to ring. Noah shook as the realization that he was completely alone began to settle over him. *Please, please, please pick up.*

Finally, a connection!

"Bridger?! What the hell are you calling me for?! I told you not to—"

Noah cut the man off before he could finish. "Frank, listen. I'm in trouble."

"If anything goes wrong, those bastards can trace the call. Why the hell would you think it was a good idea to call?!"

"Jesus, Frank. They're here. They were already here. Waiting for us! I don't think you need to worry about traced calls."

"No."

"Yes, Frank! They're here. Where's—"

"No! They couldn't be! How did they know?"

"Please, Frank!" Noah's voice raised above a whisper and, as he noticed his increased volume, the air sucked out of him. The line was silent. Noah retreated back to his hushed tone, then continued. "Please. Frank. I need your help."

There was a deep inhale on the other end of the connection. "Where are you now?"

"East of the farmhouse. In the fields. By some willows."

"And they are looking for you?"

"Yes. I bought some time by creating a diversion, but not much. They'll be here soon."

"Noah, they'll be there before you know it. They'll pick you up on their heat sensors."

No! He hadn't thought of the Fed's technology. He assumed he just needed to keep out of eyesight, but it wasn't as simple as that.

"What do I do?" His voice quivered.

"You need to cloak yourself somehow. Take off your clothes."

"What? How will that help?"

"Damnit, Bridger. Trust me and take off your clothes."

Noah obeyed and lay in the wood, naked.

"You need to listen to me carefully, Bridger. This is your only shot. When I'm finished talking, you will need to break your APD. Even if it's encrypted, they will trace you. Do you understand?"

Noah sighed and inched through the weeds between the willow trees. He answered, "Yes."

Frank Powell gave Noah the instructions he needed to evade the Feds. Then the ear piece was silent, and all Noah could hear were the sounds of men and machines looking for him.

A small, blue, singular-person cab, called a SinCab, glided off the highway and into a lush student development in Norman, Oklahoma. Within, Natalie Kelley rolled past efficient, compact houses rented to the upperclassmen at the University of Oklahoma six blocks off the campus. The avenue was lined by full-bodied pistaches and OU flags and moving, luminous street art.

The SinCab, controlled by a central computerized dispatch, utilized a thin, designated lane which allowed it to zip past the full-sized autos on the road A sitcom played on the windshield as the meter-wide vehicle ushered Natalie through the student neighborhood. Once the one-seater arrived at the given destination, the door opened, and a voice prompted Natalie to exit the vehicle. Natalie stepped out and the taxi disappeared around the corner, off to pick up its next fare.

Natalie walked quickly up the LED footpath. Halfway to the home, the images on the path below changed from a swamp terrain to a beach scene. Natalie stepped off the diodic sand and knocked on the front door. From inside the house, she heard the pounding of music. The door opened to the back of a young woman's head. She yelled into the heart of the house, her words broken by laughter.

"Oh," she said as she turned around and saw Natalie waiting. She looked confused. "Can I help you?"

"Yeah," Natalie replied, "are you Lily Lee?"

The young gatekeeper craned her neck back and shouted up the stairs, "Lily! Some lady's here for you!"

She left the door open and walked away. Natalie stepped into the house. The strong stank of pot mixed with the aroma of synthetic cinnamon smacked her as she moved inside. Music and joyous cackling bounced down the hallway to the small foyer. Natalie closed the door and leaned her back against it.

Natalie heard movement from the level above. A small, Asian woman wearing earmuffs, bright green lens-less glasses, a black tank top, and leggings bounced down the stairs. As she approached Natalie, she smiled and extended a hand decorated with a constellation of tattoos. As she held out her hand, her tank top sprouted sleeves that rolled to her elbow to adjust to the temperature downstairs.

"Ms. Kelley? I'm Lily."

"Nice to meet ya, Lily." Natalie smiled and let go of the girl's hand.

"We'll go upstairs."

They reached the landing at the top of the stairs and Lily led Natalie into her bedroom. As soon as Lily shut the bedroom door, Natalie was swathed in a dry heat.

"Do you have the cash?" Lily asked, getting straight to the point. Her top's sleeves had slipped back to a tank top.

Natalie's finger ran over the folded cash in her back pocket. She was lucky to have left it in her overnight bag from the last trip. The *Tribune* skirted MAB procedures by labeling the purchase as one of equipment, not services, which would require the paper to bring Lily on as a temporary contractor. This was easier to accomplish with hard currency. When Natalie first introduced the idea to Joseph, he had been uneasy, but, after some money-saving successes, he had warmed to the practice.

"I'd like to see the video first. That's what we usually do." Natalie looked down at Lily as she began to pull the file up on her APD.

"Yeah, sure. Whatever works for you. 'Long as I get paid, I don't give a shit." Lily found the file she wanted, and the scene played before them.

The video showed a graphic design office. In the left corner was a VR pod where designers could play around with any material, color, or texture they could imagine to create designs. Along the back wall was a row of a dozen or so 3D printers. To the right, the room opened to a grid of work pods that filled the remainder of the frame. A woman stood in the center of the shot. She talked to someone off-screen while she tweaked her impending monologue.

"We were just shooting a video update to send to our clients about the firm," Lily offered. Natalie continued to watch the recording. "I like to have the recording going for a minute or so before we actually begin, so we have some wiggle room in the editing process. Plus, I get a kick out of filming people when they're getting ready to speak on camera. There's something about that nervous anticipation that I find just fascinating."

The woman on screen was flattening her skirt and smoothing stray hairs.

"How long have you worked there?" Natalie asked, feeling the same nervous anticipation as the woman on screen.

"I'm just interning. And six months," Lily answered, then scooted up in her chair. "Any second now…"

The camera's angle of view moved from the woman to the street two stories below.

"I heard the gas engine and I love classic cars, so I instinctively turned the camera toward the noise," Lily explained as she grabbed the bong on her desk. "Wanna hit?"

Natalie shook her head and gave a small wave of apathy. Her concentration was devoted to the scene that unfolded before her. The pickup truck came into view. A beat-up red Ford. It slowed to a crawl as it approached the intersection of The Bucket Bistro. It stopped in front of the restaurant, blocking the right lane. There were only a few other cars on the street.

Then, the bloodshed unspooled in a blur. Three figures rose from under a tarp in the bed of the truck. Each figure was armed with an automatic weapon. Natalie thought they looked to be old AK-12s. Gunfire exploded from the bed. The pickup inched forward as waves of bullets tore into the Bistro. Chaos erupted on the patio; bodies hit the cement either in cover or due to carbinic force. One of the men in the bed hurled a projectile deep into the belly of the building and a burst of flames spilled out of the windows and lapped across the patio. The Ford accelerated and sped out of frame. The camera continued to focus on the warzone below while an obscenity-laced voice narrated the wreckage. From the moment the first shot was fired to the climactic explosion, less than a minute had passed. That was more than enough for Natalie to see. The video would get hits. People always watched such carnage. However, Natalie was only interested in the first few frames of the video, the moments before the mayhem.

These frames showed the murder of Donald Dotson.

Lt. Director Luna walked onto the pedestrian bridge over the East River. Behind him was the Mount, its bulk blocking out the moon, and the peaceful grounds of the GFN's North American Headquarters. Ahead of him was his Midtown condo and the hustle and bustle of New York City. "The City That Never Sleeps" had gotten a little rest in the last few years. The prohibition of all personal automobiles on the island of Manhattan had quieted the city down, but even without the swarm of auto traffic, the borough still pulsed with the life of its three million inhabitants and five hundred thousand passenger drones moving across the sky. The drones moved nearly a thousand meters above the city sidewalks, leaving the ground to pedestrians.

The population of Manhattan had plateaued for ninety years until, following the lead of Seoul and Tokyo, New York County became the first car-free zone in America. A land grab unseen since the opening of the American West occurred with the elimination of roads, parking lots, and garages. As the car-centric infrastructure was ripped up, the City and the GFN built a vast new tunnel system of metro rails and SinCab lanes, as well as two-hundred-eighty drone docks throughout the city. Each dock was seven hundred meters high and housed up to fifteen-hundred passenger drones or, as they were lovingly called in New York, "canaries" for their yellow color reminiscent of the famous cabs of yesteryear.

Once this new infrastructure was completed, the "Big Boom" began. The City of New York, American federal government, and the GFN raked in exorbitant amounts of cash from the auctioning of these new plots of real estate in Manhattan. Prices were initially set around $4 billion per acre. This value, however, turned out to be much too conservative. In one instance, a real estate consortium based in Abu Dhabi bought six acres perpendicular to the Holland Tunnel on what used to be Highway 9A. This plot was sold for $622 billion dollars. A one-hundred-thirty-story condominium named the Holland Tower was built on the newly acquired land. The building cost an additional $88 billion dollars to build. Once complete, it housed nine hundred eighty units, as well as six restaurants, forty-five 3D printing kiosks, three gyms, a theatre, and a load of other amenities. For those wishing to live at Holland Tower, the average price per square meter was $140,000. It was the most expensive private building in the world.

Jay, Juan Carlos's husband, had joked about moving into the Holland Tower when the couple first moved to New York. Juan Carlos had told Jay, "someday," but he honestly enjoyed the modest flat they owned in Hell's Kitchen and hoped to never leave.

As Luna neared the end of the bridge to the city he had grown to love, his APD chirped. He opened it. There was a message from Chief Deputy Arnie Jones in north Texas. The fifth man had been identified by facial recognition software. His name was Noah Bridger. He had no criminal record, but the Analytics team at the Mount was working to compile a background. He was still hidden, but now that Luna knew his name, the man had nowhere to go. He would be apprehended soon.

Luna reached the end of the bridge. There was a white guard-house adorned with the GFN Field Patch to his right and, beyond the guardhouse, a fence. Luna walked to the guardhouse.

"Evening, Richard," he said to the tall, black guard with white hair.

"Lt. Director. Working late again?" the guard asked, smiling.

"Oh, just one of those nights," Luna said as he stepped inside the sentry's box and gave Richard his APD. The Federation kept meticulous track of all personnel and material coming into and leaving their extraterritorial complexes. To those passing by this entry point to Roosevelt Island, the security barring entry to the Headquarters appeared minimal. The only visible boundary was the ten-foot, bulletproof, transparent polycarbonate fence. Juan Carlos Luna knew that there was strategy in this feeble display.

New York City was the first American metropolis to petition the United States government to agree to the Basic Human Standard. The New York City Council had already began implementing many of the principles outlined in the initial Montpellier Accord. Mimicking the principles of the Treaty on The Global Federation, New York City implemented the most democratic socialist government in America. Once the "Big Boom" was announced, millions of additional jobs opened across the city. New York City's unemployment rate dropped below three percent. Other cities saw New York's success and followed its lead. Soon a coalition of seventy-eight of the most populous one hundred U.S. cities petitioned Congress to adapt the BHS. The United States signed the Treaty on The Global Federation two years later.

New York had been such an active leader in supporting the GFN and, unlike in cities more reticent to accept the GFN, neither a strong U.S. military presence nor a heavy NASO presence was needed to quell the dissent or control the populous. New Yorkers supported Antoine Dubois and his Federation.

The lack of visible military presence calmed the citizens of New York, but the Lt. Director knew broad security measures were present. Many plots to attack the North American Headquarters had been thwarted by the invisible defense established by NASO across the five boroughs. Agitators were holed up in lofts and offices across the city, but the GFN handled them silently. Totalitarian governments of the past had used their militaries to display strength and dominance, even when they had little of either. The Federation's philosophy opposed these elementary exercises of power, believing the mightiest hand is the hand unseen.

While the chatty gatekeeper told Luna about his new, additively manufactured kidney, the Lt. Director thought about the hidden security procedures designed to monitor access to and from Roosevelt Island. Snipers stationed in the redwoods of The Mount kept their rifles trained on the grounds every second of the day. Land mines were peppered across the complex, programmed to detonate only if an unlicensed weapon was detected. Boats patrolled the East River constantly, circling the island with state-of-the-art motion detection equipment. Every centimeter of the Headquarters was monitored by classified technologies that kept track of every step and breath on the premises. Fixed satellites kept a constant vigil high above. Though it didn't look the part, Roosevelt Island was a twenty-first century fortress.

Richard cleared Luna for departure and wished him a good night before he returned to his stool and steaming cup of coffee. The Lt. Director faded into the urban sprawl of Manhattan, leaving the guns and bombs and secrets of The Mount behind.

Noah Bridger crawled through the willows to the open field as weeds and brush scraped and scratched his naked skin. He looked across the edge of the last potato row. It was hard to see in the darkness. *Frank said it would be here.* He slinked down the line. Overhead, he heard a thumping noise. He looked behind him. There was a helicopter with a bright light shining down on the dry Texas landscape. He needed to hurry. He reached the end of the column of potato plants. The dirt was hard. He started to dig.

The sounds of the men seemed to come from all around him. He was going to be caught. He was going to die. He was going to leave his wife a widow and his children fatherless.

There!

He felt the smooth plastic on his fingertips and yanked the irrigation tube out of the ground. He bent the plastic, but the structure kept. He dug further down the column and took nearly a meter of tubing from the earth. He gripped the tube tightly and bent downward. He felt the plastic arc, then snap. Water spewed from the busted pipe, flowing over the dirt below.

Noah wasted no time. He rubbed the new mud onto his hands and spread it across his bare body. He was covered. Not completely but enough. He didn't have enough time to be completely thorough.

Now what?

Noah closed his eyes and thought of what Frank had told him.

"First, you will need to cloak yourself from the heat sensors. With the heat sensors, they will find you any minute." Noah had done that. *What was the next step?*

He remembered. *The tractor.* He looked back toward the farmhouse. The mobile spotlights continued their march away from the silo into the vastness of the fields.

He ran. His mud covered naked body slid through the night air. The wind was cool against the unpainted swaths of skin. He ran fast, his legs gliding along the edge of the field. He could not see the tractor yet. Frank had said to run for the barn. Noah could see the structure in the distance grow larger, but still did not see the tractor. The presence of the helicopter confirmed that it was the Gendarmes that had been lying in wait. They were getting closer to him. And he was getting closer to them.

Overhead, the chopper turned quickly. It was coming his way. *The call. They must have traced the call.* The chopper was headed straight toward the clump of trees he had been at only minutes before. He hunched down, hoping to burrow into the earth away from the bright light overhead, but he kept his legs pumping. The light moved back and forth below the helicopter, scorching the earth below. If he was caught in the hellish beam, the mud would not be able to hide him. It would be over.

He sprinted and dove in a track of weeds at the edge of the field. He felt the itch of the nettles immediately. He looked toward the barn. *Where is it?* He peered into the night and let his eyes grow accustomed to the darkness.

Finally. There! The tractor! A silhouette of blackness had emerged against the velvet curtain. *The tractor!* It was less than fifty meters away. Noah looked behind him. The guards on foot were headed his way. Their flashlight beams swayed over the potatoes. *Move. I need to move.*

The chopper started flying in concentric circles away from the trees. Noah looked back at the helicopter. The glass reflector of the light shone like the closest full moon Noah had ever seen. It was eerily beautiful. With his hands on the ground, he bear-crawled toward the tractor. He could hear the words of the men clearly, their flashlights bouncing into the cloudy night.

He reached the rusted vehicle, short of breath. *Now what? Something about the clutch.* He crouched behind the far tire. His brain was muddled. All he could hear was the crushing sound of his freedom being gripped tighter and tighter by a foreign vice. He had to think. *Think!* His mind went blank. He crawled into the cab and blocked out the lights and the noise. Frank's words came back to him. He lifted the clutch and turned the wheel ninety degrees to the left. That was it! He looked behind him. A sheet of grass started to roll back. He was so close! Freedom was below him. He looked toward the willows. The guards were still some distance away, but the chopper's circling moved closer to him. He stayed in the cab until the chopper banked, taking its deadly light away. He jumped out of the cab and sprinted, then slid next to hatch at the edge of the grassless strip. There was a keypad. *The code?! What was the code?!* The voices of his pursuers came closer, the beams of their flashlights hit the barn now. He was in their crosshairs. His fingers shook. He pressed the buttons on the keypad and prayed to Jesus that the combination was right. The lights were brighter. The words clearer, crisper. The helicopter was coming back. It arced straight for him. He pressed the final digit. There was a hiss of air against the roar of the chopper. He flung the hatch open and began to climb down the ladder when he stopped. *He had to hide the entrance.* The hatch and bare strip of earth were still visible. *They would know where he was.* He lunged back up to the top rung, closed and secured the hatch. Listening intently, he heard the turf roll back, drumming on the metal roof above.

He stood on the ladder and breathed heavily. The bunker was pitch black. He moved his feet slowly down the ladder. He kept his eyes trained on the darkness above, praying that it would remain. He could not hear the men. He could not hear the chopper. He could not hear anything.

Had they seen me?

Noah reached the cement floor and fell backward. The ground was cold. He curled up and closed his eyes. He knew that if the chopper had seen the entrance that the Feds would be above him any second, working to open the hatch. He was stuck. There was no other way in or out. He wouldn't know if he had been spotted until noise and light poured in from the breached hatch. Noah kept his eyes closed and his knees against his chest and his arms cupped over his head.

The fugitive prayed that there would be no sound and that there would be no light.

CHAPTER THREE

4 May 2072

The morning sun shone through the thin hotel curtain. Natalie Kelley's eyes opened as the muted light washed over her face. She hadn't slept much the night before. After leaving Lily Lee's house in Norman with the video file transferred to her APD, she stayed awake listening to news reports. The reports detailed the arrest of three men in the Grey Zone connected to the Bucket Bistro attack. One suspect had been killed in the apprehension. Once the names of the four suspects were released, Natalie spent the next few hours researching the men and what ties they had to any terrorist groups. The dead man, Otis Daggart, had been arrested for suspicion of laundering money to the Christian Patriots, but had been released before a trial. The other men had no terrorist ties, just a smattering of petty crimes between them. They had no military experience, no link to the American Freedom Army. Natalie suspected that there may be a link between Daggart and the AFA but could not uncover any evidence. In fact, prior to his release from custody, she discovered posts by the man calling the Freedom Group "a bunch of gutless pussies."

The tragedy in Oklahoma City had none of the Freedom Army's trademark characteristics. The AFA claimed ownership of the attacks within hours of the maneuvers, there was no ownership claim yet. Their perpetrators wore fatigues, these men wore civilian clothing. The ranks were pulled from the disgruntled servicemen and women of the armed forces, these were small-time crooks. Her suspicions had been correct: this attack had not been executed by soldiers. It was the act of amateurs.

Without a connection between The Bucket Bistro and the AFA, Natalie's investigative work in Oklahoma City should have been complete. In the warm morning glow, however, Natalie felt a swollen unease within her. Her mind returned to her conversation with Cooper and the video she had purchased from the coed.

She sat up in the hotel bed, stretched, and commanded the room to open the blinds. She then pushed a button on the nightstand next to her and a voice responded, "Good morning, Ms. Kelley. The time is 06:52."

"Shit," Natalie mumbled. She had slept less than she wanted, but her racing mind told her she wouldn't be getting any more rest.

Lee's video would not leave her.

In her line of work, Natalie had watched hundreds of videos of violence spanning the globe. Every corner and every person had a camera. But this one stood out.

Natalie grabbed her APD from the nightstand, found the video file, and pressed play. She yawned and cracked her neck. The screen on the wall remained blank. Natalie groggily pressed play again, then rose from bed and walked across the hotel room to grab a cup of tea. In the kitchenette, she pressed a button on a prefilled cup and the liquid inside began to heat. The television screen remained blank. Puzzled, she sat back on the bed and looked at her APD. A message marked URGENT was blocking any other functions from being performed. Natalie opened the message. It was from Joseph.

"Need you in Philly—bridge explosion early this morning. Casualties few. Timer malfunction suspected. This one seems more in line with the AFA."

Natalie knew her editor was correct in his suspicion that the Freedom Army was behind this incident from the terse summary he provided. The Freedom Group preferred to hit deep inside the White Zone and aimed to shake the confidence of the citizenry. AFG President Hill had implemented this new strategy for the last eighteen months. The AFA had lost countless skirmishes with NASO up and down the Grey Zone before changing tactics. Hill knew that the AFA could not win any battles against The Federation's superior military, but they could destroy the confidence people had in The Global Federation. Hill had often released videos after an attack on a coastal White Zone target that told his audience that no one inside the GFN's borders was safe.

These were the types of strikes Natalie had been following around the country.

She could be in Philadelphia in just a couple of hours. She had begun to form a reputation as an expert on the American Freedom Army and hoped to parlay her expertise into her first book. Natalie dismissed the message and the video began to play.

The video again solidified her suspicion that the AFA was not behind the attack here in Oklahoma. These were pissed-off cowboys in a pickup truck. Knowing all of this, Natalie wrote to Joseph and told him that her instincts compelled her to stay in Oklahoma City, even though the next portion of her book was most likely out east.

The video ended. Natalie's tea was warm now and, as she sipped it, she put Lily Lee's video on loop.

The mud had dried and speckled and fallen off Noah Bridger's naked body. He felt like a Copperhead shedding its skin. His left shoulder throbbed, but the pain from the gunshot was never as intense as he had imagined. The bunker was still without light. He stood and felt along the wall for something, anything. After a couple of seconds, his fingers felt the cold metal of a power generator. He flipped the switch. Two rows of hanging bulbs flickered on and filled the bunker with light.

In the light, Noah tried to visually inspect the wound, but his neck would not crane to get a clear look, so he explored the injury with his fingers. He chipped the mud away from his shoulder with his finger nails. The wound felt insignificant—the bullet had only skimmed the muscle above his left clavicle.

The bunker walls were lined with storage shelves. On the nearest shelf, he found a case of bottled water and washed the cooled blood and flakes of dirt away from the wound. The bleeding appeared to have stopped. Noah located a first aid kit and cleaned the gash with sanitary wipes. On the nearest shelf was a stainless-steel pan. Noah picked it up and used its reflection to inspect his punctured trapezius muscle. The cut was approximately three centimeters long and a centimeter wide. Using the contents of the first aid kit, Noah put antiseptic on his shoulder and taped a large, white bandage over the wound. He rooted through the storage shelves and found new underwear, a crisp pair of khaki pants, and a clean-pressed black shirt. He dressed and felt refreshed.

The bunker was much bigger than Noah had expected. He grabbed another bottle of water from the depleted case and opened a can of beans, then searched through the cubbies for a mechanical clock. After descending the ladder, Noah had curled up on the floor and prayed that the hatch above wouldn't open. At some time while in the dark and on the cold cement floor, he had fallen into a deep, black, dreamless sleep. Now that he was awake, he needed to plan his next move and that move would depend on knowing how long he had been sequestered in the bunker.

Noah was not prepared for this. When he had agreed to help Wade, he never let his mind wander to the possibility of becoming a fugitive. He was not a soldier. He was a farmer. And a gearhead. And a husband. And a father. That was all.

Jesus Christ, please guide me. I do not know what I have gotten myself into.

The bunker was roughly two hundred square meters. It was larger than Noah had expected because he knew it to be Frank

Powell's secondary bunker. Powell had shown off his primary bunker to anyone that visited his property since it was first christened five years ago. It was directly under the farmhouse and was nearly as spacious and well-decorated as the home above. Noah had been in that bunker a half-dozen times. He was always impressed by the comfort, technology, and style it radiated. Powell had designed it for long-term habitation in the event of a global catastrophe, such as a nuclear winter or global epidemic. It was meant to be a safe extension of the house above. Powell had even boasted to Noah that he often slept down there though there was no apocalyptic threat above.

The space Noah now found himself in had none of the glitz of the primary bunker. The primary bunker had heated wood floors. The ground in this bunker was cement throughout. The walls of the primary bunker were wallpapered and lined with taxidermied game, some of which were so endangered that, if discovered by the authorities, would lead to felony poaching charges against Powell. In this bunker, the interior walls were concrete bricks and the ceiling above appeared to be concrete as well, though the roof was not visible because the lightbulbs hung too low. There was no paint. No decorations. No style of any kind. This bunker rejected comfort for pure practicality.

Noah walked the length of the bunker and took inventory. The shelving on the left-hand side of the bunker was filled with stacks of canned and freeze-dried food, bottled water, bedding, clothing, and an assortment of tools and other miscellaneous supplies. At the end of the bunker on the back wall was a small outcrop where a hole in the ground served as a lavatory. On the right-hand side were racks of automatic rifles, standard rifles, shotguns, and handguns. There were boxes of explosives, piles of ammunition, knives, Kevlar, and other types of weaponry.

This second bunker was Frank Powell's armory.

Lt. Director Luna exited the elevator on the seventy-second floor of The Mount. He was immediately greeted by one of his assistants, Deborah Johnson. Luna was well-known for his philosophy regarding strict separation of his work life and his home life. Deborah was accustomed to Luna's morning ignorance and respected the man's desire to obtain balance in a field where a domestic life was nearly impossible. Luna's strict "no work" policy when he left Roosevelt Island often caused him to keep long hours, but when he was away from the HQ he was unreachable. Luna's husband, Jay, was understanding when the Lt. Director put in a marathon day of work, because he knew that their time together would be uninterrupted. Luna understood that few other people had his sort of stamina, so he employed two executive assistants, each working ten-hour shifts. Deborah worked the early shift.

Deborah had been Lt. Director Luna's Co-Executive Assistant for four years. A short, black woman in her mid-forties, Johnson had initially been wary of the awkward hours. She had previously worked in military administration for the U.S. Navy and the promise of a high clearance level led her to an interview. She thought she could make the job work since her two boys were teenagers and did not need her around the house any more. Once Deborah heard what the GFN offered in salary and benefits, she agreed to the job immediately.

Deborah came into the office every weekday morning at 03:00. She sifted through the news of the previous few hours and prepared a briefing for Luna when he arrived at SOHQ, which was usually around 05:30. Today, the Lt. Director was a little behind schedule, but Deborah suspected that he had dined on an early breakfast with Jay after hitting the gym. She wasn't sure if the man ever slept.

It was a quarter past six when the elevator doors opened, and Lt. Director Luna stepped onto his floor. His handsome face showed a hint of surprise as he found his first-shift assistant waiting outside the parting glass doors.

Before Luna could wish Deborah a good morning, she pushed him back into the elevator.

"They need you upstairs," she said to him.

"Good morning to you too, Ms. Johnson," Luna responded as he backpedaled into the elevator. He held the door open and looked down at Deborah's round, pretty face. "Awful early for her, isn't it? Any idea what it's about?"

"Joyce didn't say."

Joyce Erickson was North America Security Office Director Dierdre Farrelly's executive assistant. Luna knew that Deborah wouldn't speculate on the content of the meeting if she didn't hear the information directly from the source conducting the meeting. He liked to joke with her about this.

"Care to wager a guess?" Luna asked as he placed his thumb on the biometric scanner and pressed the button for the penultimate floor.

Deborah smirked, shook her head, and walked away as the glass doors closed and the elevator zoomed skyward.

The elevator car reached the Director's floor quickly. The glass doors opened to a steel wall. On the steel wall was an ocular scan to which Luna submitted. He then spoke his name, which matched the voice pattern in the GFN's database record. The steel wall slid upwards and revealed a small vestibule with five Federationists dressed in grey fatigues and armed with TS-33 assault rifles. Luna didn't bother to offer pleasantries to any of the Security Officers. He knew they wouldn't respond. One of the SOs approached Luna, stuck a cotton swab inside his mouth, and handed it to another SO. That officer ran the sample through a computer while the other officers held their firearms at a forty-five-degree angle from the floor, their fingers teasing the trigger guards. The Director changed methods of DNA collection often, making it nearly impossible for an impostor to predict which procedure they needed to be prepared for. All of this was in addition to the substantial security measures the rest of Roosevelt Island and The Mount provided. The Director was a paranoid woman.

Having confirmed Luna's identity, the SOs lowered their weapons and guided Luna to the bullet proof door on the opposite end of the vestibule. The door opened and exposed a grand hallway with gilded sconces and mosaics covering the walls and crystal chandeliers hanging from the ceiling.

The first time Lt. Director Luna saw the Director's floor, he had scoffed at the extravagance and wastefulness of it all. He knew that The Federation worked tirelessly to minimize waste in government, attempting to maximize revenue for each person to obtain the Basic Human Standard. It was also an effort to acknowledge and attempt to improve the public's poor perception of government. Aware of the GFN's policy toward such government waste, Luna grew more and more irritated with the lavish Director's floor as he made that original walk to Farrelly's office. He felt like he was in Napoleon's Louvre or one of Dubai's island hotels, not a Federation building. When his irritation grew to anger, he expressed his disgust to his escort. The escort guffawed and simply told Luna, "She paid for all this herself."

Luna had taken little time to consider Director Farrelly when he first accepted his current position; he was more concerned with matters in the field, not the office. Upon hearing that his new boss was never in the military, Luna had instinctively dismissed her. Luna adopted an "out of sight" philosophy when dealing with civilians in a military context. He believed that there was nothing he could learn from a superior with no military background because they viewed the world through a very different lens. He would make no glaring mistakes that would require the attention of his superior and would agree to mission objectives, but he would never accept ignorant means of execution.

After their initial meeting, Luna grew curious about his new boss, so he did some basic research. Defense Director Dierdre Farrelly was a sixty-one-year old "Renaissance woman" from

Atlanta. Her father had been an agricultural engineer concentrating on developing a new generation of safe and effective genetically modified crops; her mother had been a professor of Pediatrics at the Emory University School of Medicine.

Farrelly had been an unbelievably gifted child. At six, she composed a symphony that was performed by the renowned Cleveland Orchestra. At nine, she published a paper on the vocalization patterns of humpback whales. The family made a fortune when the fifteen-year-old prodigy created a digital marketing campaign that persuaded an American public leery of GMOs to embrace her father's new, cheap, alternative agricultural option. Within a year, most vendors in the country were selling out of foods with the "Farrelly Foods" stamp, leading serious agriculturists across the country to attempt to duplicate the Farrelly growing process—not because it was the best, but because it was in demand.

When Dierdre's parents died suddenly in a car accident, she inherited the company at the tender age of twenty-three. By this time, in addition to running Farrelly Foods, she had graduated from MIT with a master's degree in Security Studies. She wrote her thesis paper on the correlation between hunger and war and titled it "Edible Kevlar: How Bread Can Stop Bullets." The missive was internationally published and became a bestseller. Not since Norman Borlaug had a person made so many headlines in the name of nutrition. Under the helm of Dierdre, Farrelly Foods acquired food depots and transportation companies around the globe, cornering the food delivery industry on every continent. She was even able to obtain the endorsement of the President of the National Farmers Union.

It was during this process of globalizing cheap, healthy foods that Farrelly met French President Antoine Dubois. They quickly became professional and personal confidants. Dierdre Farrelly was an early, integral advisor to Dubois during his crafting of the Basic Human Standard. Farrelly's professional life took her from

Farrelly Foods to the foundation of C. Darwini's Web Services, which became one of the preeminent cybersecurity firms in the world.

Luna had learned all he needed to from his research and he was impressed. His new boss was a brilliant mind, but she had still never experienced the heat and rush of combat. *So be it.* He would have to operate without help from above, which worked fine for him. He was free to operate according to his own methods.

Luna dreaded being summoned to the Director's floor. He felt as though she viewed him as a relic of the past. She was a philosopher. He was a gladiator. They seldom met face to face.

Walking down the hall, Luna spotted dozens of people who worked diligently in the offices he passed. He knew none of their names or positions. When he reached the Director's door, Luna nodded to Ms. Erickson and moved to enter the office.

"It'll be just a minute, sir," Joyce told Luna without looking up from her work.

Luna shrugged, took a seat outside the Director's door, and waited. He hated idleness. His mind drifted to last night's seizure of the suspected terrorists. He hadn't heard if the team had captured the remaining fugitive yet. He wished Deborah had briefed him.

Lost in thought, he distantly heard Joyce call out to him. He looked up.

"They're ready for you now, Lt. Director."

They? The hairs on Luna's neck bristled as he rose from the chair. Like a lone wolf traversing an unfamiliar canyon, he expected an ambush. It was unlike the Director to bring another member of the Security Office to a spontaneous meeting. She wanted her participants to always be prepared, so they would waste no time. The Lt. Director was not prepared for the meeting, so he thought the other participants must be.

Juan Carlos Luna walked into the Director's enormous office. He did not notice any of the artwork or luxuries inside. His heart beat forcefully against his chest. On the far side of the room, a flame lapped at its obsidian tomb. Next to the fireplace in a tall leather chair, Director Farrelly waved him forward. Across from her with his right arm on the mantle, speaking to the Director, stood Secretary-General Antoine Dubois.

When she left Chicago, Natalie had not expected to stay in Oklahoma City for more than twenty-four hours. After watching and re-watching the recording of The Bucket Bistro attack, she needed answers and answers took time. She put on her stale clothes from the day before and jogged down the stairs to the hotel lobby where she located a 3D printer. She designed three simple outfits, sent them to print, and ran back upstairs to her room to take a shower. As she dried off there was a knock on the door and when she opened it, her freshly printed clothes were lying folded on the floor. Natalie changed quickly, grabbed a condensed high-caloric nutrition bar called a Snack-Stat from the vending machine, and headed out. She decided to walk back to the Riverside District as she organized her thoughts. The day was grey, and a light drizzle danced in the air. Her editor, Joseph Kalani, had been puzzled by her decision not to travel to Philadelphia to investigate the blundered incident there, but he had been supportive. He trusted her instincts.

Natalie couldn't stop replaying the Bucket Bistro recording in her mind. She had watched it a dozen times as she drank her morning tea. Each time, she concentrated on the frames before the mayhem broke. She had slowed it down, zoomed in, and isolated the only scene she cared about.

In the video, Donald Dotson dropped to the ground before any shots were fired from the bed of the pickup truck.

Natalie considered all possible options. Maybe the man had a heart attack causing him to tip back in his chair just before the attack and was then struck by an errant bullet. Maybe there was a glitch in the recording. Maybe the camera angle was playing tricks on her. As she continued to watch the recording, Natalie grew more certain of her lurking suspicion: she believed that the man had been struck by a high-caliber bullet which knocked him directly backward. The impact of the bullet had occurred before a single shot was fired from the pickup.

Natalie hated conspiracy theories. Even with the Media Accreditation Board, a great deal of a journalist's work was in debunking the spew of shit that flooded the cyber-sphere. Conspiracy theories were an assault on truth.

However, Natalie now believed that a true conspiracy played out on a busy street corner on the Great Plains. She was certain that during the attack on The Bucket Bistro, there had been a second shooter.

Inside the bunker, Noah Bridger grew restless. He longed to be home with his wife and children. This entire experience had been like a bad dream. He did not know what he was doing. He wondered how long he had lived in this nightmare; how long ago he had been shot.

Noah had scoured the shelves looking for a working clock but had found none. The bunker was cold. He had wrapped himself in a harsh, wool blanket, but chills still crept down his spine. He had made four attempts at ascending the ladder, but always ended back on the floor of the bunker. On his latest try, he nearly made it to the hatch before turning back, deciding that it was not time. But now, as he sat on the frigid floor and ate freeze-dried venison, his impatience trumped his fear. He was tired of being in limbo. He had prayed to Christ for guidance and felt the Spirit rise within him and summon him home.

Within the first hour after waking in the bunker, Noah had packed a knapsack with the provisions he would need to get home. He figured it would take five days to get back to his ranch and keep out of sight of the Gendarmes, so he grabbed a week's worth of food and water. He would need to move fast, so he packed light. He also grabbed a change of clothes, boots, a blanket, a map to plot a path to circumvent the authorities, and a compass. The boots he found were too large, so he stuffed torn pieces of blanket in the toe to tighten them.

He was afraid the Feds would be staking out his home, but he did not know where else to go. He decided he would deal with that when the time came. He grabbed the knapsack and then removed a 30 ought 6 from the gun rack. He knew there were many other options that would provide more firepower, but he had little experience with those more advanced models. The old rifle would do. He slung the gun over one shoulder and the knapsack over the other and set his left foot on the first rung. He vowed this time he would make it out of the bunker.

Noah reached the top of the ladder and pressed his forehead on the cool metal of the hatch. *Christ, be at my side.* He released the lock and spun the wheel until he heard the air pop. He scrunched in the shaft and pulled the hatch down. He reentered the code on the shaft's keyboard and the turf above unrolled and let light into the manmade hole. Noah took a deep breath of fresh air. The smell of cottonwoods drifted down into the bunker and the sounds of birds chirping bounced above. He climbed out of the shaft and, keeping low to the ground, he reached down and closed the hatch. He then poked the numbers on the outer keypad and watched the turf roll back into place. The turf met the natural grass seamlessly; no one would know the bunker was there. He looked up at the sun shining through a thin veil of clouds. It appeared to be midmorning. *But what day was it?*

He knelt on the ground and removed the compass from his knapsack. The grass rubbed along his legs against the khaki. He needed to head west. He oriented himself then consulted the map. *Soon this nightmare will be over.* He stood and stretched in the open field. *Soon I will be holding Marie. Soon I will be surrounded by my children.* As he took his first step, he felt a hammer slam into his left shin. He dropped back to the ground, holding his leg and screaming. His hands were warm with blood. Figures in black rushed toward him. They were yelling. Their weapons were fixed on him. He could not hear what they said over his own screams of anguish.

Noah remembered he was armed. To the men, he would appear dangerous. He remembered Daggart's fall to the ground. He reached for the rifle slung over his shoulder, hoping to cast it aside to prove that he posed no threat to the quickly closing storm. A shot rang out and a puff of dirt erupted next to his face. He threw both hands in the air. He closed his eyes.

"No! Stop!" was all he could shout. His whole body was wet, covered in blood and sweat and tears. He heard the stomping of boots close in on him and suddenly a force pressed down on his chest. As he felt the restraints on his wrists and ankles, he whispered to himself, "My God, my God, why have you forsaken me?"

There were few incidents in his life that had left Juan Carlos Luna truly stupefied.

The first occurred when he met Jay Greenberg while walking through Hance Park in Phoenix. He was only sixteen years old. The gorgeous young man with curly red hair had run across two games of bocce ball to get his future-husband's attention. Once he had it, he would not stop talking. Juan Carlos couldn't think of a single thing to say to the stranger but knew that he wanted to listen to him for a long time. They married two years later before Luna was deployed to the Baltic by the U.S. Army.

The second incident occurred when Luna was a Captain in the 75th Infantry of the United States. The formation was better known as the Army Rangers. Captain Luna and his unit were clearing a town in rural West Virginia of any unauthorized firearms or dangerous objectors to the American agreement to join the flourishing Global Federation of Nations. The work was laborious and often mundane as the soldiers went door to door and town to town finding few illegalities. Luna had been clearing towns during this Preparation Period for eighteen months and experienced only a few dozen violent episodes. Most of the threatening individuals had consolidated in communities in the country's interior.

There were people everywhere that vocally opposed The Federation. They vowed to deny the Basic Human Standard and to deny the increasing interconnectivity of the globe. In fact, many people seemed to deny the once-unarguable fact that time marched forward, that time couldn't be captured, that each second was inherently different from the next, but these vocal opponents of progressive globalization dared not raise arms against the mightiest military force that the world has known. With an influx of Federation cash and personnel, the United States armed forces teamed with NASO to form a military might which terrified even their loudest critics.

From his experience overseas, Captain Luna knew that most of these protestors who so vilified The Federation and held tightly to ideas that were fluid when written three hundred years ago would eventually embrace this new government due to the rapid increase in quality of life. As a U.S. Army Ranger in the Middle East, the American military had a significant presence in the countries ravaged by decades of war. In Saudi Arabia, he remembered witnessing citizens, barefoot and hungry, hurl rocks at the GFN Security Officers as they swept through the suburbs of Riyadh. Three years later, after flying back to Camp Comanche in Tumair, he saw those same poor dissidents prospering within the confines of the Montpellier Accords that first united France, Spain, and Germany under the same regulations envisioned by Antoine Dubois.

As Luna's squadron approached this tiny hamlet in West Virginia, the atmosphere was different than other Prep Period Ops, or PPOs. It was a cool, fall morning. The trees burst with color: yellows and oranges and reds. There were no citizens waiting to meet the soldiers with signs of protest. There were no families welcoming the soldiers to their town. There were no people walking the streets or peeking out of windows. There was no one. Luna told his unit to proceed cautiously. As they searched the homes and stores, each building came up empty. Off the main street next to the town cemetery, there was a small Baptist church. The fence surrounding the church was broken and the windows were boarded. The white paint was peeled, and tufts of moss grew around the front door. As Captain Luna walked around the church, he kept his weapon ready. There was an opening between two of the boards that were nailed across a window near the back. Luna peeked inside. Within the sanctuary of the First Baptist Church of Deer Haven, Juan Carlos Luna discovered the town's population: they were all dead.

The town had committed suicide.

The stench of death smacked the Captain in the face as he entered the church. The doors had been padlocked from the inside. His unit needed to use a battering ram to gain entry. The bodies sat neatly in the pews and slumped against the stone walls. Parents held the hands of their children. A single bullet hole was found in the forehead of each of the townsfolk. Their faces looked peaceful. Bibles were open on many of their laps, the pages splattered with blood. At the front of the church, near the pulpit, the corpses of three men were splayed out. Next to each of these men's dead bodies was a handgun. The backs of their skulls were blown open—Luna suspected these men had died from a self-inflicted shot through the soft palate. Bloody footprints weaved through the church and stopped in front of babes wrapped in blankets, elders with oxygen tanks, and everyone in between. The footprints ended at the altar. Here lay the executioners.

Luna kept his steely gaze and cool demeanor as his squad noiselessly tallied the dead. The final number of deceased matched the census records for the town: All two hundred and seventeen citizens of Deer Haven, West Virginia, were accounted for. All two hundred and seventeen citizens of Deer Haven, West Virginia, were dead.

Luna led his unit into the hills outside the town and set up camp. It was a little before noon. His unit was scheduled to secure another town, but Luna delayed the PPO. The Rangers in Luna's squad had never retired without completing the daily objectives, but they did not question their leader's decision. They were all shaken. Luna retired to his tent and seriously questioned America's involvement in The Global Federation. *How could an entire town choose death over association with such a noble cause?* During his self-examination, the unit's medic came in with the results of the blood tests that the Captain had ordered on a handful of the townsfolk. High levels of a homebrewed sedative were found in their blood, indicating that those executed were in a state of semi-consciousness when they were shot. *Lambs to the slaughter.*

Luna pictured how the scene had unfolded. Families putting on their Sunday best and walking to the church hand in hand. Mothers comforting their crying children. The distribution of the sedative. The singing of hymns. An entire town looking to enter the Kingdom of Heaven together. An entire town massacred. Luna rushed outside of his tent and vomited on a pile of dead leaves. His First Sergeant, Arnie Jones, ran to his side and asked if he was okay. He wiped the bile from the corners of his mouth, but he could not answer.

Now, for the third time in his life, Juan Carlos Luna was speechless. He had never thought he would meet Secretary-General

Antoine Dubois. From a young age, Luna had been devoted to the principles of equality, compassion, welfare, and progress. Then, Dubois burst onto the global scene when fear and war and famine had spread throughout the world and he preached and enacted those same principles. The man's political innovations and inspiration had helped billions across the globe find a better life. Now, in Director Farrelly's office, Luna walked toward the giant, radiant man. When the Secretary-General extended his hand, it was like touching the flesh of an ideal. Luna thought he introduced himself to the man, but he could not be sure he had actually spoken. Then, Farrelly led both the men to a pair of Chesterfields in the corner of her office.

Luna took a seat next to Farrelly, opposite Dubois. On the sofa, his back and legs felt rigid as he waited for the most famous man in the world to speak. After a moment, the tall, dark man leaned forward.

"Lt. Director Luna, I am here to personally ask for your help."

A little before noon, Natalie found herself in a budding development of the suburban town of Meeker. Many lots in the neighborhood outside of Oklahoma City were still unclaimed. Others were occupied by automated machines that were busy constructing new residences. The morning's rain had turned the red dirt of Oklahoma into crimson slop. Natalie had tried to contact the family of Donald Dotson but had been unsuccessful. She grew frustrated before she looked again at the press release that detailed the identities of those killed in yesterday's attack. Another name caught her eye on the list: Samir Nejem. The press release said that Nejem was an employee of DefCorp Dynamics. She tried to call Nejem's widow, but there was no answer. Annoyed by inaction, she rented the only sportbike-electrocycle on the block and drove to Nejem's listed address. Now, her white sneakers dyed red with earth, she was in front of the property.

On her way to Meeker, Natalie had listened to the *Tribune's* archival entry for DefCorp. DefCorp Dynamics was the newest state-sanctioned weapons manufacturer in the United States. Headquartered in Oklahoma City, it was the closest weapons manufacturer to the Grey Zone in North America. DefCorp had been started by retired NASO Lt. Director Shaleigh Yao. Since its incorporation, the company had been notoriously tight-lipped in regard to the press. There were few quotes in the *Tribune* archives attributed to the corporation, but there were many quotes from NASO expressing their excitement and satisfaction in working with DefCorp. The odds that Dotson, with NASO, and Nejem, with DefCorp, knew each other were slim. The weapon's manufacturer employed thousands of people in the area, but Natalie felt she needed to eliminate any lingering doubt concerned with a possible connection.

Natalie was nervous as she advanced up the walkway to the front door. She abhorred questioning people enduring tragedy. From a purely journalistic standpoint, she thought the answers friends and family members of a recently deceased person provided were often shallow and cliché, providing no depth to a piece, only a heart-wrenching sound bite heard hundreds of times before. On a personal note, she knew how annoying and obtrusive journalists looking for a story could be. Natalie's father had been murdered by anarchists when she was an undergraduate at Northwestern and callous reporters would not leave her to mourn in solitude. From that point on, she vowed to be sympathetic and understanding if she needed to interview a person in grief.

Before Natalie could ring the bell, the front door opened partly. A pretty woman wearing a hijab stood inside, one hand on the knob, her head on the casing.

"Yes?"

"Hi," Natalie said, caught off guard. Her throat jammed, and the words labored to get out. "I'm Natalie Kelley. I'm with the *Chicago Tribune*. A journalist." She caught herself stumbling and breathed deeply as she coiled her hands into tight fists. "First off, I would like to extend my deepest sympathies to you and your family. This must be an unbelievably trying time. Oh wait, you are Faye Nejem, yes?"

"Yes, that's me. How do you do, Ms. Kelley?" the woman inquired as she extended her hand to Natalie. Natalie uncoiled her fists and accepted the woman's offering.

"I'm fine, Mrs. Nejem. Thank you. I'm very sorry for just showing up at your front door like this. I tried to call earlier, but there was no answer." Natalie was regretting her decision to spontaneously appear on this woman's stoop. "If this isn't a good time, then—"

"No, no. There's no need for apologies." Mrs. Nejem smiled, then opened the door the rest of the way. "Please, come in."

Natalie followed Mrs. Nejem into the house. The house was brand new and so too were the furnishings. Advanced Robotics were busy cleaning the living room even though it already looked spotless. As Mrs. Nejem led Natalie to the kitchen, lighting illuminated their way and extinguished behind them. When they arrived in the kitchen, Mrs. Nejem said "tea" and instantly the kettle began to brew.

"Please, Ms. Kelley, have a seat."

"Thank you, Mrs. Nejem," Natalie replied as she sat. She studied her host closer. Though her skin was dark, her features weren't as exotic as Natalie expected.

"Please. Call me Faye," the woman said. And as if she were reading Natalie's mind, she added "my Samir's from Jordan. I was born and raised in Pensacola, Florida. I met Samir in college and there, I fell in love with him. Before we wed, I converted to Islam for Samir. I was faithless at the time and just wanted to be a good spouse, but I soon embraced the teachings of the Quran."

Faye blushed and looked at her shining floor. "I'm sorry. Talking about him makes it feel as if he were still alive, somehow."

Faye looked up at Natalie and smiled.

The tea kettle whistled. Instead of moving to grab it, Faye took a seat next to Natalie while a small AR brought the kettle and two cups on a tray to the table. The AR stopped, poured the tea, and set a cup in front of each woman. Faye stared kindly at Natalie as she blew on the tea and took a sip.

"I would like to ask you a few more questions about your husband, Faye. Are you okay if I record our conversation?"

Faye nodded her approval. Natalie removed her APD from her back pocket and placed it on the table, then directed it to begin recording.

"This is Natalie Kelley with the *Chicago Tribune*. I am interviewing Faye Nejem. Mrs. Nejem. Faye. Can you please spell your name?"

Faye complied.

"You are the spouse of Samir Nejem?"

"Yes."

"And how long were you and Samir Nejem married?"

"Twenty-three wonderful years."

"Your husband was an employee of DefCorp Dynamics. Is that correct?"

"Yes." Natalie noticed the woman acted more restrained following her initial torrent of sentiment.

"And how long was Mr. Nejem an employee of DefCorp Dynamics?"

"Oh, only about 9 months, I believe."

Natalie wasn't surprised by the short duration of employment. DefCorp had only been operational for four years and was growing rapidly; in fact, it doubled personnel in the last year according to filings.

"I know that you can't discuss many details regarding your husband's work, so I will try to stay away from anything that could be considered a breach of contract."

"Thank you."

"Where was Mr. Nejem employed before joining DefCorp?"

"He was a teacher at a high school in Pensacola."

This answer surprised Natalie.

"Really? What did he teach?"

"History and civics."

"Not science or math?"

"No. History and civics. He loved America and loved teaching about America."

This was even more surprising. Though the press release did not say, Natalie had assumed that, due to the expensive new house and his possible connection to Dotson, Samir Nejem was in Research and Development. It would have been unusual, yet not unprecedented, for a science or math teacher to move to weapons R&D, but a history teacher? It didn't fit. She took a sip of tea and regrouped.

"So, Samir was happy with his teaching job?"

"Oh, yes. He loved it. And he loved the kids. He even coached the track team in the spring. They were runners-up at State one year. Samir was an excellent coach. He ran the 1500 at Florida. But he loved teaching even more. Ever since he was a small boy, he read all he could about America and always dreamed of coming here. He—" Faye seemed to catch herself again, "he was definitely happy at his job."

Natalie paused to make sure she worded her next question correctly. She didn't want to offend the widow.

"Did you have many discussions regarding his joining DefCorp?"

"No. Not really. I trusted my husband completely, so when he said that he had been offered the job here in Oklahoma and that he thought he needed to take it, I didn't question that."

Natalie looked at Faye quizzically.

"We had some… troubles in Pensacola. Samir thought it would be nice to have a fresh start."

For the first time during their conversation, Natalie saw true pain in Faye's eyes. The eyes had contained sadness before, but it had been a comfortable sadness. Now the eyes contained great hurt and it made Natalie feel uneasy.

She stood up with her cup of tea and walked to the window. The backyard was perfectly manicured and was punctuated by an enormous stone fountain.

"You have a beautiful home here."

"Thank you," Faye replied, looking around at her surroundings as if she noticed them for the first time. "DefCorp provided everything when we moved. Samir and I never cared much for such lavishness. He made very good money as a teacher once GFN minimum salaries were in place for educators, but we never spent much of it on ourselves. Most of it went to Samir's family in Amman and to zakat."

Natalie returned to her seat.

"Excuse me for saying this, Faye, but I'm taken aback by how calm you are. I was anxious coming here. I expected you to be…"

"Hysterical?"

Natalie laughed. "I guess, yeah. I'm just impressed."

"Yesterday, when I heard the news that Samir was killed, I was a mess. Weeping. Angry. But while working with our imam to prepare Samir for burial, he consoled me. He told me to look at the good we had done in our life together. To think of all the happy times we had. When we buried my husband this morning, Imam Naser reminded me that Samir is with Allah now."

Natalie watched sympathetically as Faye cried for the first time since they first met. The delicate tears flowed softly. Faye wiped them from her eyes with a tissue.

"I am happy now. I am happy to know that Samir is with Allah now," Faye said as she pocketed the tissue.

Natalie placed her hand on the woman's knee and offered her words of comfort. She then removed it, in an attempt to regain her professionalism. She cleared her throat and took a drink of the mint tea.

"Faye, this may be a completely random question, but have you heard of a man named Donald Dotson?" Natalie asked. She didn't want to bother this woman any longer if she didn't need to.

"Of course."

"You have?" Natalie was surprised.

"Well, I'd hope so. He spoke during the Walima at our wedding."

They had injected him with something for the pain. The throbbing in his leg had abated and a calm washed over Noah Bridger as the chopper flew over the Texas plains. Once he had been restrained, the Gendarmes loaded Noah into a helicopter where a medic worked on his leg. He was told that the tibia of his left leg was broken. The medic had treated the break with a low-intensity ultrasound pulse to accelerate the natural healing at the cellular level, then put the leg in a liquid cast.

The Federation SOs inside the helicopter surprised Noah. They spoke to him with civility, not hostility. Noah feared that they would become aggressive any moment, but the drugs soon took care of his anxiety.

After the medic tended to his leg, he asked Noah if he was injured anywhere else. He dreamily pointed to his clavicle. The medic cut away Noah's shirt and peeled back the bandage on his left shoulder. The gash from the first bullet was bright red and showed signs of swelling.

"I'm going to clean this out, so we don't get any infection. Okay?"

Noah nodded, caring little about his surroundings.

"I feel like I'm flying," he said to the medic.

The medic laughed. "You are."

Noah was going to clarify himself, but decided the effort wasn't worth it. He closed his eyes as the medic dabbed the wound with solution, stitched the cut with an automated hand-held suturing device, then re-bandaged his shoulder.

The helicopter continued to glide through the sky as drops of rain splattered on the windshield. The pilot chatted with his copilot as the helicopter flew on auto. The medic placed a blanket over Noah as he fell into a deep sleep.

"We've reached a preliminary deal with the American Freedom Group. Large swaths of the Grey Zone will accept the *Standard humain de base*. This deal will put us on the path to incorporate those communities still isolated in U.S. Black Zones. I am personally going to meet with John Hill in Santa Fe as he signs and adds the name of the AFG to the Treaty of The Global Federation. After the signing, we will conduct a joint press announcement. As I understand it, you oversee Border Security for North America. Is that correct?"

"Yes, sir," Lt. Director Luna answered Secretary-General Dubois.

"As the person in charge of Border Security, the aforementioned Grey Zone, as you Usonians call the territories, is within your jurisdiction, is that correct?" Dubois asked. The man seemed to need to know that he was being understood completely.

"Yes, sir."

"And the city called Santa Fe falls within your jurisdiction?"

"Yes, sir."

"Good." His French accent was thicker in person than it was in his media appearances. Dubois leaned back and folded his hands behind his head as he stretched.

"We are going to need your full concentration on securing the area before the signing. As always, freedom of speech is not

only tolerated, but encouraged. But we cannot have any violence
hampering the signing. We do not want another incident like
St. Petersburg."

La Frontera nodded to signify his understanding.

"Good. The details have been uploaded to your APD. I want
you to get started on clearing any combative communities right
away. Do you have any questions?"

"No, sir."

"*Bien.* Good."

The Secretary-General rose from the sofa.

"That's all, Lt. Director."

Luna stood and shook Dubois's massive paw, then shook
hands with Director Farrelly.

The Director addressed Luna.

"I have full confidence in your ability to complete this task.
If you need any assistance, don't be afraid to reach out to me."

"Thank you, ma'am," he said, then left the Director's office.
She had never been so eager to offer assistance to her lieutenant.
Luna thought she was putting on a show for Dubois. So be it.
He had work to do.

Natalie listened to Faye Nejem detail her husband's friend-
ship with Donald Dotson. She said that the two had met as
teammates on the University of Florida's track team. After college they remained friends, even after Dotson joined the GFN
Security Office and was sent to Sicily. Faye said Dotson had a
sister that was killed in one of the open carry riots in Florida.
He was a true believer in The Federation's policy and vision.
Samir was not as ardent a supporter of the GFN as Donald, but
he understood the politics necessary for an evolving world. As
a student of history, he knew that isolationism and Nationalism were accelerating civilization to destruction. He idealized

America, though, and didn't want to see the ideals written down by the Founding Fathers compromised by a foreign influence.

After he finished his overseas tour, Dotson found a position within the newly established North American Security Office. He often tried to get Samir to come and work with him, but Samir was happy teaching. When "the trouble" happened, Donald called right away and told Samir not to worry. He had a great job for him available in Oklahoma City. Because of Dotson's influence at DefCorp, there was hardly an interview process at all. Samir had looked for other teaching posts, but with "the trouble" still unresolved, there weren't any schools that were interested. Faye never told Natalie what "the trouble" was and, even though her job was to collect facts, she never asked the grieving widow. She figured she could look into it once she got back to her hotel room.

Natalie knew that due to the Nejem's nondisclosure agreement, Faye was unable to discuss what Samir's job at DefCorp had entailed, but she was surprised to hear Faye mention that her husband had been traveling a great deal since he started his new job.

The conversation drew to a close. Faye told Natalie that she had been very isolated after she and her husband left Florida. Natalie felt genuine empathy for the widow, so when Faye asked her to come back to the house in a day or two, she agreed. Faye mentioned that she would do a little poking around the house to see if she could find anything of note to share with the journalist, but Natalie figured the woman was just lonely and looking for someone to talk to. It didn't sound like the couple had made many friends in Oklahoma City and Faye hadn't mentioned either of their families.

Natalie left the Nejem residence feeling confused and saddened. Samir's role at DefCorp appeared ambiguous at best and Faye's quiet sorrow struck a chord with her. The rain had picked up again and pelted the red Oklahoma earth. Rain water eroded the naked construction lots and ran off into the street. Natalie jogged to the electrocycle and put on her helmet. She started the bike, made a U-turn, and started back for the city. As Natalie charged away from the widow, the rain hammered her helmet and she vowed to do something to help Faye Nejem.

The drugs wore off and Noah Bridger's consciousness flickered back. He was still in The Federation helicopter. His leg felt like it was in a vise, the pressure building every second. He grunted and turned his head to the interior of the chopper. The medic was buckled in next to him.

"You're awake," the medic said.

"Where are you taking me?" Noah asked drowsily.

"Forrest City," the medic answered. "We're almost there."

The mention of Forrest City sent a shiver down Noah's spine. Forrest City Processing Facility in Arkansas was one of the main holding facilities for suspected terrorists who awaited trial in a Global Federation Court of Justice, or GFCoJ. As part of the Montpellier Accords, the GFN had international judiciary to try crimes against The Federation or Federationists. Before it was a GFN holding facility, Forrest City had been a federal prison. Those found guilty in the North American branch of the GFCoJ were sent north to the island prisons of Nunavut.

American politicians on both sides of the aisle had been adamant that the GFCoJ not infringe upon the established American judicial system, whether American citizens were tried by The Federation or by federal, state, or local courts of the United States. NASO Director Dierdre Farrelly had been a vocal proponent of trying any terrorist activity aimed at The Federation in a GFCoJ. Noah had heard many stories detailing the GFCoJ's corruptions. He knew members of the resistance were terrified of the GFCoJ and claimed that they were nothing more than kangaroo courts.

"For what? I was just checking on my friend's property while he was vacationing. What's this all about?" Noah pleaded weakly.

The medic laughed. "You don't need to convince me, man. I'm just your doctor."

Christ, help me. Noah thought. He could not go to Forrest City. It was a brutal, medieval place where archaic instruments of torture sat openly in the hallways and the screams of the tormented kept the inmates up all night. Noah had heard that most people who awaited trial in Forrest City died before their court date.

The medic saw the look of consternation on Noah's face.

"I know what you've probably heard about Forrest City, but it's not true. I've treated men before you whose faces also went white at the mention of Forr-C. Those there aren't interested in the horrors you've heard. Trust me. I've been there many times and speak from experience."

After he spoke, the medic checked Noah's vitals. The injured man looked at the doctor.

"You honestly believe that, don't you?"

"Of course, I do."

Noah thought that the medic seemed like a decent man. *How could a good man get behind such a corrupt government?* None of Noah's family were sympathetic to The Federation. Neither were any of his neighbors. In fact, Noah had had little interaction with those who supported the snail-suckers. And that's the way he liked it. This seemingly decent man was but a cog in the global machine. He had been brainwashed. He spewed propaganda. And he was dangerous.

These men were the warped majority. They were not the fanatics that started the revolution to dystopia, but the ordinary citizens that allowed it to happen without even seeing what was happening—or had not wanted to see what was happening. Noah remembered the words Wade had told him when their families got together two Christmases ago: "These men have traded away their values and their rights for a false sense of security. For the illusion of progress without questioning that which was deemed inevitable."

The Yellow-Eyed medic seated next to Noah was the exact type of man who bargained off American values to a foreigner. And Noah hated this man. These people had abandoned God and put their faith in the slippery, stained hands of humanity.

The helicopter began to descend.

"Your vitals are looking good," the medic said. "They'll take that cast off in a day or two."

Noah could not speak to the medic. His civility masked his wickedness and Noah felt weak that he had accepted aid from one of these profane men. He prayed to God that the Lord would keep him strong during his bondage and that, somehow, he would break free from his chains and see his family again. Soon.

CHAPTER FOUR

4 May 2072

Juan Carlos Luna returned to his condominium, packed two suitcases, and said goodbye to his husband. Jay had seen Luna leave for a mission many times before, but each time he experienced the same mix of fear and pride that he did when Juan Carlos left for boot camp when they were teenagers. Luna hated to see the anxiety on Jay's face, but his duty was more important than any one man.

Luna took a canary uptown to Yorkville, then walked through security, and across the bridge to Roosevelt Island. From there, he made his way to the small airstrip at the north end of the island. Parked on the runway was a Jules T-190 supersonic blended wing body aircraft. Twelve of the Lt. Director's top Deputies and three executive assistants stood chatting near the air stair as they awaited La Frontera's arrival.

The Deputies stopped talking and stood at attention when Luna approached. The Lt. Director shook hands with each of his staff and ascended the air stair. The others followed him into the plane.

The interior of the aircraft was furnished as a mobile command post. If needed, any NASO mission on the planet could be coordinated from eight thousand meters above the ground. Luna walked past the military equipment and took a window seat in the last row of the twenty-passenger jet. The seat was spacious and comfortable. The Deputies found their own seats; some pulled out their computers to work while others continued their conversations from the tarmac. The space next to the Lt. Director remained empty.

Once all the passengers were on board, the aircraft began to taxi. Though there was not another aircraft on the Roosevelt Island runway, air traffic control needed to wait for open airspace from nearby LaGuardia Airport, which had become America's busiest airport after an expansion that annexed Riker's Island. After a short delay, the T-190 accelerated and lifted off. Luna looked out the window and watched the ground retreat to the sky. Roosevelt Island looked small compared to the sprawling metropolis of New York surrounding it. The aircraft banked above Brooklyn and headed over the open waters of the New York Bight. Luna watched intently as teams of barges worked to construct the massive floating barriers designed to stop the ever-rising sea level. New York Governor Cora De Souza predicted the seawall would be complete by the end of the following year.

Luna pulled the shade over the window. The Jules T-190 would be touching down in Santa Fe in approximately ninety minutes. The Lt. Director decided he would use that time to get some rest.

The Federation helicopter that carried Noah Bridger landed on the helipad at the Forrest City Processing Facility in eastern Arkansas. Forrest City sat atop a geological feature named Crowley's Ridge and overlooked the cotton fields and deciduous trees of the Arkansas Delta. The processing facility held some four hundred suspects that awaited trial for crimes against The Federation. The average stay of each prisoner was a scant sixty days; the GFCoJ claimed to respect every individual's right to a speedy trial.

From the chopper, Noah was immediately taken to the processing facility's infirmary. At the infirmary, he was examined by the quiet, studious on-site physician. When the medic from the chopper briefed the physician on the prisoner and his injury, Noah thought he saw the physician recognize his name. *I must have been on the news,* he thought. He prayed that Wade's previous assurances regarding his family's safety would remain true. *Please, Marie, be proud of your foolish husband.*

The Forrest City physician used what he called nanotechnology to treat the tibia fracture. Noah could not be sure what the man was doing but had no choice but to let him work on his leg. After the thirty-minute procedure, Noah was taken by wheelchair to a holding cell in the infirmary. He wore a clean, polyester uniform provided by the medic. The cell was sparse and well-lit. The walls and floor were painted white. There was a single bed with a thin sheet and small pillow on one end. Noah's leg still ached, but he found that he could put pressure on it. He paced the cell and tested the leg per the physician's instruction. His movements were unsure, but he found he could walk with some care.

Noah heard a beeping sound come from outside his cell, then, the sound of the locks as they released. A young, black man with a shaved head walked into the cell. His jaw was angular and lined with a thin strip of black stubble speckled by premature dots of white. He wore a sharp blue suit with razor-thin lapels, a handsome, silk charcoal vest, and a light blue bowtie. His outfit stood out against the fatigues that the Gendarmes wore throughout the processing facility. Outside the cell, Noah saw one of those faceless fatigues standing guard. The well-dressed man had a black satchel strapped across his chest and carried a steel chair behind him. The door to the cell shut and locked behind him.

The man extended a hand to Noah.

"My name is Kendrick Rhodes. I will be representing you in your case against The Global Federation."

Noah shook the man's hand. Rhodes sat in the steel chair, then extended his hand toward the bed. Noah sat uneasily on the stiff mattress.

"First, Mr. Bridger, I am required to ask if you have a different attorney that you would like me to contact to represent you. If so, I will reach out to him or her and advise them to get to Forrest City as soon as possible. While waiting for your desired representation to arrive at Forrest City, I advise you to exercise your right to remain silent until your chosen representation arrives. If, at this time, you do not have any other options for representation, then I will continue to serve you." The man looked at Noah sternly, trying to communicate a message he could not express out loud.

Noah only knew one attorney, but she did not have a license to practice in a Global Federation Court. Ms. Emerald Blonski lived some forty kilometers away in Dimmitt, Texas, and had abandoned law once The Federation had overthrown the United States government. Blonski had been called to participate in a few trials at the ad hoc courts established in the Texas Grey Zone, but she spent most of her time farming and ranching like all the other settlers. Noah's only option sat before him.

"Are you a God-fearing man, Mr. Rhodes?"

"I am," Rhodes said as he pulled out a chain from beneath his suit. At the end of the chain was a gold Crucifix.

"Then it looks like you're going to have to be my guy."

The rainfall eased as Natalie Kelley parked her rented electrocycle a block from The Bucket Bistro. The perimeter that was cordoned off had shrunk as parts of the area had been declared secure. Many different terror organizations were known to use the convergence of Federation personnel and spectators as an opportunity to detonate a secondary explosive device or conduct another assault. This diminished perimeter signified that such a second wave would likely not occur. *Amateurs,* Natalie thought again as she walked down the empty street.

Natalie walked down the sidewalk opposite the hollowed bistro. The debris from the attack had been mostly cleared from the street and portico. A section of the exterior of the building was missing, which exposed the empty restaurant inside and the sagging floor from the office space above. Wires and plumbing hung down from the second and third floors, broken and dangling. Natalie recorded the scene until a local uniformed officer requested that she put her APD away. She had often argued with such officers and objected on the ground of freedom of the press, but today Natalie simply acquiesced and turned away from the tidied carnage.

Natalie walked into the building facing The Bucket Bistro. This was the building from which Lily Lee had shot the video that Natalie purchased on behalf of the *Tribune*. The walls of the lobby were painted neon green with pink trim. Stark-white furniture adorned the lobby and pseudo-modernist art was displayed on the walls. One of the pieces displayed was a moving 3D image of a woman taking a photograph of a man sculpting a man painting a woman etching a hunt on a cave wall. Each layer of the image was in the medium of the outer layer. The image was at least five meters high and stretched from floor to ceiling. Natalie strode past it to the reception desk at the back of the lobby.

Seated behind the reception desk was a young, Cherokee girl. Her hair was blown-out and she wore purple lipstick, heavy purple eyeshadow, and a dress with hues that mutated and orbited the color wheel. Her appearance accentuated the hip culture the building forcefully exhibited. Natalie felt slightly ridiculous wearing her plain white scoop neck T-shirt and tan shorts. She shrugged off the feeling and decided it was this lobby that was ridiculous.

"Is the building manager in?" Natalie asked the receptionist as small robotics airbrushed intricate, temporary designs on the girl's forearms.

"No, she's not. Sorry, hon," the girl said without looking up.

Natalie looked around the empty room in a pointless attempt at finding someone else to question. There was only the receptionist.

"Do you have any idea when she'll be back?"

"Probably quarter hour. Maybe half hour."

Natalie could wait. She found a seat on one of the white couches and began dictating notes to her APD.

"You here about the craziness from yesterday?" The receptionist was now looking at Natalie.

"I am."

"Yeah, you look like you're here about the craziness from yesterday."

Natalie wondered how but brushed the observation off.

"Were you here?" Natalie asked the receptionist as she turned to face the desk.

"Uh-huh. Right here."

"You have a decent view of The Bucket from that desk, huh?" Natalie asked as she gazed out the glazed floor-length windows.

"Yeah, I guess so."

"Did you see the attack, then?"

The girl laughed. "Hell, no! Once I heard the shit goin' on outside, I was under the desk with my hands over my head just like they taught us in school. I was like that until the troops came to escort everyone out."

"I see." Natalie was growing impatient with the girl. She didn't seem to be of any help, so Natalie went back to working on her APD.

"Wait, is it Wednesday?" the receptionist asked.

"Yes, it is," Natalie said as she sat back down.

"Mrs. Lawrence won't be back in today if it's Wednesday."

"Great." Natalie said as she rose from the couch, miffed.

Natalie walked across the lobby to the exit. As the doors opened automatically, she turned around.

"Did you notice anyone unusual come in this week?"

"Unusual?"

"Yeah. Maybe someone who doesn't work here?"

"There was a painter working in the building the last couple days. Big, sexy brute. Carried a dick-ton of equipment with him like a pack mule. Not sure why they needed him instead of AR, but honey, I wasn't complaining."

Natalie stopped in the open doorway.

"Where was he painting?" This painter piqued Natalie's curiosity.

"An office on the second floor. What a stud. Didn't come in today though. Sadly. He must be done."

"Can you take me to the office he was painting, please?"

"Go on up. Not sure which office it was, but I'm sure you'll find it."

"Thanks."

Natalie strode back from the open door. She felt reenergized. She hurried past the reception desk to the elevator bank where she pressed the "up" button repeatedly. After a short wait, she grew impatient and darted to the stairwell. Once she reached the second floor, she easily found the vacant office complete with a slapdash paint job. From the window, she had a clear view of three small ARs sweeping the remaining rubbish off The Bucket Bistro's portico.

Kendrick Rhodes reached into his satchel, pulled out his APD, and set it on his knee. He then retrieved a pair of navy, thick-framed eyeglasses, and a handkerchief. He wiped the glasses with the handkerchief, placed them on the bridge of his nose, and put the handkerchief back in the satchel.

"I won't have lasers anywhere near my eyes," the attorney told Noah Bridger in a pre-emptive attempt to answer a question about why he wore glasses.

Rhodes looked at his APD. "Mr. Bridger," he started, though he did not need to capture Noah's attention. "The State of Texas has charged you with four counts of aiding and abetting in the commission of a criminal activity. Each of these charges carries a maximum sentence of six years in state prison. Additionally, the GFCoJ has charged you with one count of conspiracy to commit a terrorist action against The Global Federation of Nations or employee of The Global Federation of Nations. This charge supersedes the four counts of aiding and abetting and will be addressed in court first. If found guilty, you will spend up to thirty years at the Nunavut Deradicalization Center. If found guilty and transferred to Nunavut, the State of Texas will try you for the charges of aiding and abetting via satellite from Nunavut. If found not guilty, you will be moved to Austin and tried by the Texas Department of Justice. Do you understand the charges against you?"

Noah dipped his head in understanding. He was facing fifty-four years. His children may have grandchildren before he got out.

"Mr. Bridger, I need verbal confirmation. Do you understand these charges that have been filed against you?"

"Yes. I do." The words struggled out, leaping from his throat like a frog on flypaper.

"And do you understand the incarceration that awaits you should you be found guilty of said charges?"

"Yes. I do."

"Alright. Good." Rhodes made a mark on his APD. "Now, I need to inform you that you have the right to declare a plea of guilty at any time before the commencement of your trial. Would you like to plead guilty at this point in time?"

Noah thought for a moment. He wasn't sure how The Federation's judicial system worked, but he thought he may face leniency if he pleaded guilty. He didn't expect them to find him innocent, even if he were. But Wade always seemed to have a plan. If he pleaded guilty, there was no going back. Rhodes glared at him from behind his blue spectacles. Noah felt a swell of courage build inside him.

"No, sir. I would not."

"Good." Rhodes made another mark on his APD. "I would like to inform you that the men that you are accused of aiding and abetting, as well as conspiring with, are also incarcerated here at Forrest City. Now, Federation officers are going to take you to an interrogation cell. I will accompany you to the interrogation. As your representation, I advise you to practice your right to remain silent during this interrogation. After the interrogation, you will be led to the general population of Forrest City. Do you understand?"

Noah looked at his lawyer, incredulous at first. His attire and speech were so well-mannered; he was surprised by the attorney's sly recommendation to remain silent. A bond of trust began to form between the men. *This man must have been sent by God to save me.*

Noah smiled at Rhodes, then mimicked an action of zipping his lips.

The beeping of his APD roused Lt. Director Luna from his nap mid-flight. He reached into his pocket and retrieved the device. He had an incoming call.

"Luna," he answered, rubbing the sleep away from his eyes.

"Hello, sir." It was Brandt Bonner, the general of the Texas Military Brigade. Bonner's first military action occurred while in Luna's Ranger unit in Kurdistan. The Texas Military Brigade was a sovereign military unit created in negotiations during the Savannah Conference which enticed the southern United States senators to approve the Treaty of The Global Federation. Bonner was a proud Texan and was honored to head the newly formed armed force. "We've discovered something."

"What is it?" Luna asked as he continued to gaze out the window.

"A tunnel. South of Houston, in Wharton. It's massive."

"How massive?" Luna opened the window shade and looked out on a sea of puffy clouds below.

"The main tunnel is nearly one hundred kilometers. A drone was sent in to map it. It ends in the San Bernard National Wildlife Refuge."

"I'm guessing the wildlife refuge is on the coast?"

"It is, sir."

"How did you find this tunnel?"

"We received a tip from a reliable source and sent a team to scout the residence. No known terrorist links from the occupants, so the team was only two men. When they arrived, they were greeted by gunfire. One of our guys was wounded. His partner called for backup and after a short firefight, we took the house."

"Any additional casualties?"

"No, sir."

"What about on the other side? Any women or children?"

"No children. One woman shot and killed. Three men and another woman arrested. Minor injuries."

"And the tunnel was on the property?"

"Yes, sir. We found the entrance to the tunnel when we discovered a bunker in the cellar. That's when we sent the drone in. The drone detected no signs of booby traps, so our guys just went in."

"Any press yet?"

"No, we want to know what we're dealing with first."

"Good." Luna stretched out in the back row of the plane.

"Sir, the drone we had on hand was just a small bug drone, so the footage was shit. But from what we saw, this is the most sophisticated tunnel we have seen. There were shadows that suggested auxiliary tunnels. Also, it looks like there are pit rails on the ground. We didn't see any carts or anything yet, so they may be in the aux tunnels. I should be on-site in about twenty minutes, so I will know more then. I wanted you to hear from me first in case this got out."

"Okay. Keep me updated, Bonner."

"Yes, sir."

Luna ended the call and looked out the window again. The clouds had become patchy and let rays of sun slip through to light the country below.

This was the second tunnel that the Texas Brigade had discovered this week. The first was east of Houston near Beaumont which also led to the Gulf of Mexico in a National Wildlife Refuge. The Beaumont tunnel had been crude like the tunnel systems they had found in the past. There were alcoves stacked with illegal weapons, but no people and few leads. When he suspected the tunnels were being used by GFN-resistance groups, Bonner had reached out to the Lt. Director for Federation assistance. Two weeks ago, surveillance detected a man with links to the American terrorist groups purchasing massive amounts of excavation machinery and equipment. Drones followed him for two days before he was seen purchasing "melt", the street name for 3D printed amphetamine. He was arrested on the drug charge, but his interrogators had been focusing on the equipment purchase. The man wasn't talking yet, but La Frontera had faith that Bonner and his Brigade would soon make a break in the case.

Luna knew he would not return to his nap, so he went to the small kitchen on the T-190 and grabbed a cup of coffee. The coffee heated as the Lt. Director returned to the seat. Taking the first hot sip, he turned his attention to Santa Fe and the biggest mission of his career.

The office still smelled of fresh paint. Natalie studied the room. The window swung open from the bottom via a remote panel on the wall. The door locked from that same remote panel. The walls had been painted white but faint shadows of a darker shade still lingered beneath. Freckles of white paint dotted the forest green carpet. A wadded ball of blue painter's tape had been left in the corner. There were no overt signs of this office hosting an assassin the previous day. Natalie could not be certain that the man that camped out in this room was a sniper, but the sloppiness displayed convinced her he was no professional painter.

Natalie looked out the window. She curled her forefinger until it made a circle with her thumb. She squinted with her left eye and looked through the tactile scope. She had a clear view of the entire portico across the street. It was possible that a shooter could hit Dotson from this window. She needed to know more about this painter.

She left the room and walked around the second floor. There didn't seem to be anyone working on this floor; most of the employees must have been given the day off to emotionally recover from the incident. The only person to speak with was the flighty receptionist. Natalie headed back down the stairwell. Maybe she could benefit from the girl's ennui.

"There's nobody up there," Natalie said to the receptionist.

"Nah, they all have the day off. Because of the craziness."

"You didn't get the day off?"

"The boss said I didn't need to come in if I was too shook-up. But I wanted the hours. I'm trying to go to Phuket this summer for *Sax Khon the Beach*. It's a Jazz-Piphat Festival."

Natalie walked to the door and ignored the girl. She counted ten paces, then turned around quickly.

"I nearly forgot," she said as she walked back to the reception desk, "is there any way I could see the recordings from yesterday?"

The receptionist shrugged. "Sure. The boss showed some other dudes this morning. Don't know why she'd have a problem with you seeing them."

Other dudes, Natalie thought. *GFN Security Officers! Had they come to the same conclusion?*

The receptionist reached under the desk and grabbed an APD, entered a code, and pulled up the previous day's recording.

"Knock yourself out," she said as she handed the APD to Natalie.

"Thanks." Natalie took the device and sat down in a billowing chair farthest from the reception desk.

The timestamp on the recording said 11:35, just a couple minutes before the attack began. Instead of pushing play she rewound the recording to 07:08, when she saw the office manager unlock the doors to the building. She played the recording at three times the speed but watched carefully as employees walked through the lobby. Her eyes were peeled for a brute in a painter's outfit.

Shortly after Kendrick Rhodes left Noah Bridger in the infirmary holding cell, two armed guards shackled him and led him out into the hall. *We must be going to the interrogation room,* he thought. *Just like Rhodes said.*

The building Noah and his escorts walked through was old. He surmised that this section of the complex was part of the original American federal prison which begot the GFN processing facility and there appeared to be minimal renovations since it was built way back in 1997. With the ankle restraints and newly acquired limp, he struggled down the hallway. Impatient, one of the escorts nudged Noah with the butt of his rifle. Noah lost his balance and stumbled. He was saved from falling to the tile floor by the other escort who grabbed him by the crook of his arm. This escort stabilized Noah before he gave his partner a quick glare.

The officers led their prisoner through a back door and out of the administration building. A sticky heat smacked Noah instantly. In the distance, he thought he heard muffled voices until a low-flying plane droned overhead. Since Noah had been on a stretcher when he arrived, this was the first real look he had at the processing facility. To his right ran a tall chain-link fence and beyond the fence was an open field which slanted upward. The three walked along a paved sidewalk toward a large, square building thirty meters ahead. The building, freshly made of gypsum plaster and fiberglass rovings, was a stark contrast to the weathered administrative building behind. To Noah's left ran a line of cedars whose lowest branches brushed the ground. The full trees obscured Noah's view into the heart of the processing facility.

The group stopped. The officer who had made Noah lose his balance entered a code on a touch pad outside the door and submitted to a retinal scan. The door buzzed and opened automatically.

The cool air-conditioning hit Noah right as he walked into the building. The interior of the building was as modern as the exterior. The white floors of the hall glistened under the solar-powered lighting. Noah's escorts greeted two officers seated behind a large, black security desk, then took a sharp right. They reached a thick, black door with another keypad and retinal scan.

Once through the secure door, the officer who had helped steady Noah took the wrist and ankle restraints off him. This room was more conference room than interrogation cell. *Did they take me to the right place? Had Rhodes been wrong?* Wooden floors and muted yellow walls greeted Noah. Beneath an oak table in the center of the room lay a lush Aubusson rug. Six bonded leather Captain's chairs surrounded the table. In opposing corners, like boxers in a ring, stood two tall ficuses. Noah's escorts led him to one of the Captain's chairs and slid him into it.

"Have a seat," he said, pushing him down into the chair. "Someone will be right with you."

The officers left the room.

Noah felt uneasy. His experience so far did not match his expectations. He felt like he was waiting for a business meeting, not about to be interrogated by Gendarmes.

The air-conditioning blew into the room and the ficus opposite Noah swayed under the vent. He tapped his fingers on the table to the beat of an old church hymn and hummed along nervously.

Noah Bridger, in a foreign state and under arrest, waited for his fate. And he was scared.

The Jules T-190 touched down in Santa Fe a little after 19:00 local time. There were no Federation buses waiting for Luna and his Deputies at the decrepit municipal airport. Three American military trucks had come from Holloman Air Force Base to transport The Federationists. The caravan arrived at The Railyard Inn twenty minutes after landing. The hotel was located a few blocks west of the New Mexico State Capitol where the signing would take place and would serve as a temporary operating base.

Luna told his team to lay low for the night and that they would meet to discuss their agenda the next morning. A few of the Deputies went to the hotel bar, others straight to their rooms. Luna dropped his luggage off, then walked the streets of Santa Fe. The sun dipped toward the horizon and turned the desert sky pink. The mountain air was cool and crisp. Up ahead in a deserted parking lot, a few vendors packed up their makeshift booths. The men were Hispanic. They wore faded denim jeans and frayed straw hats and dried dirt stuck to their brown skin.

"*¿Todavía puedo comprar algunas frutas?*" Luna asked one of the men.

"*Sí,*" the man said, and motioned to the cargo in the back of the truck, then to the few crates left on the ground. "*No es un buen momento para que la fruta. Tenemos muy especias.*"

The man started picking up a crate of thyme.

"*No. Quiero fruta. ¿Tienes alguna?*"

"*Sí, sí!*" the vendor said as he dropped the crate of thyme and walked back to the truck. He lifted a small container from the bed and brought it to Luna. "*El ruibarbo es muy delicioso.*"

"*Bien. Voy a tener un cuarto de kilo.*"

The man packed a bag of rhubarb and handed it to Luna. Luna paid him in cash. He gave the man a small tip.

"*¡Gracias, señor!*" the man called as Luna walked away from the vendors. He broke the stalks clean off the rhubarb and threw the poisonous leaves away in a compost container. He bit into the first stalk, savoring the sour taste. His hands grew red from the juice.

A block later, Luna stood in front of the New Mexico State Capitol.

He walked the entire circumference of the building. Nicknamed "The Roundhouse," the New Mexico state capitol building was the only round capitol building in the United States. After he completed his walk around the structure, Luna wandered through the more than six acres of garden surrounding the building. The grounds were quiet. Clouds of bugs were thick between the plants and the bushes grew wild and the hedges were untrimmed.

Tomorrow he would take a look inside.

It was getting dark. Luna started back for the Railyard Inn, done with work for the day. In two weeks, The Global Federation of Nations would peacefully meet with the American Freedom Group; the same people the Lt. Director had been fighting for years. He had known this day would come and he had tried to prepare for it. His superiors may sign a treaty, but he would never trust these murdering assholes.

After ten minutes of watching sped-up surveillance footage of the lobby, Natalie Kelley spotted the painter. The receptionist was correct: he was a very large man. He wore baggy blue coveralls, but his bulging muscles were still visible as he strode through the lobby. A blue baseball cap sat low on his brow. The cap covered his face from the camera. Natalie scanned the room and saw the twinkle of a small lens in the far corner, opposite the lobby doors. She looked back at the surveillance footage.

In one hand, the man carried a plastic paint can. In the other hand, a long, cylindrical bag made of ballistic nylon which presumably carried a ladder. Natalie pictured the office upstairs. The distance from the floor to the ceiling was only about 3 meters. The painter would only need a small stepladder to reach the top trim, so why did he carry such a long bag? *To transport a hidden rifle and tripod*, the conspiracy theorist in Natalie whispered.

Right now, she had no leads and no evidence; only conjecture. She needed something concrete. She needed more.

She needed to see the man's face.

She looked around the room again and saw another camera behind the reception desk. She called out to the receptionist.

"Is there any way you could change the settings, so I can see the footage from the other camera? The one behind you."

The girl looked annoyed. She hadn't planned on the visitor lingering so long. "Do you want me to just load yesterday's footage to your APD?"

Natalie was surprised by the girl's flippant attitude once again. "Uh, sure. That would be great." Natalie moved toward the reception desk. "Actually, can you load the last three days?"

"Why?" The receptionist asked, showing her first sign of intrigue.

"I'm interested in that painter," Natalie said simply.

"I already asked him out. He's not available."

"Oh," Natalie laughed. "That's too bad. I'm actually interested in some of his equipment."

"So was I," the girl chimed and looked at Natalie who forced a smile.

"Whatever," The receptionist took the building's APD and Natalie's APD and tapped on each a few times. Seconds later, she placed Natalie's APD on the desk. "There."

Natalie grabbed her APD. "Well, thank you!" she said to the girl. "Have a nice day!"

The receptionist didn't respond. She was busy doing whatever the hell she had been so preoccupied with. Natalie didn't mind. She needed to get back to her hotel room. She needed to see this painter's face.

Noah Bridger waited in the interrogation room for what he figured was ten minutes. As he waited, he prayed. The door opened loudly and interrupted his pleas to God. A man and a woman Noah did not know entered the room. They were followed by Kendrick Rhodes, his representation. The man and woman both wore Federation Service Dress uniforms, in contrast to the fatigues of the officers that escorted Noah from the infirmary holding cell. Rhodes took a seat next to Noah; the man and woman sat across the table from him.

The woman spoke. "I'm Specialist Meredith Biagi and this is Specialist Tyler McGraw." She had white, freckled skin and auburn hair. Her hair was pinned back, and her large ears flowed out like sails filled with wind. She situated her APD on the table. "We're here to ask you a few questions, Mr. Bridger. Before we start, can we get you a glass of water or something else to drink?"

Noah stared at the wood table and studied the dark, meandering grain. He didn't answer.

Rhodes addressed the Specialists. "I've informed my client to practice his right to remain silent during this interrogation.

It looks like that's going to apply to whether or not he wants something to drink."

"So be it," the woman said, then turned to her partner. "McGraw, go grab a couple teas. Rhodes, you want something?"

Kendrick Rhodes glared at the woman's familiarity. "I'm fine, thank you, Specialist Biagi."

The man left the table and walked out of the interrogation room.

Specialist Biagi spoke to Noah, "Mr. Bridger, we're concerned that you might be mixed up in something that you didn't mean to get mixed up in and we're here to help. *Mister* Rhodes there just said that you intend on remaining silent. I hope that's not the case."

Noah didn't say a word. He cracked his fingers under the table and hoped to release some of the tension building up in him.

Biagi continued. "We obviously have you on the property of Frank Powell within twenty-four hours of the arrests of the men charged with killing sixteen innocent people. We've recovered your Mustang outside of the Powell property and have lifted fingerprints of all four murder suspects from the interior of the automobile. On top of that, one of the suspects is cooperating with us and has identified you as the driver of the Mustang that fled the scene last night. We've dropped those charges, Noah. We've dropped the evading arrest charges because we know that you didn't know what was happening."

Noah knew they were giving him an out, but he wouldn't take it. They wanted him to give up the others. They had marked him as a fool and were working on tricking him. All his life, people had tried to trick Noah. He wouldn't fall for it any more. *Especially not to these slimy, liberal Feds.* He kept his mouth shut.

"Mr. Bridger, despite what your representation may have told you, it is *not* in your best interest to remain silent." Biagi leaned forward, her elbows propped on the table. "I am here to *help* you."

Specialist McGraw walked into the room carrying two compostable cups filled with tea. He handed one to Biagi and took a seat next to her.

"Has he said anything yet?"

Biagi shook her head.

"Listen, Bridger, you don't want to go freeze your balls off in Nunavet. I don't want you to freeze your balls off in Nunavet. And God knows your wife doesn't want you to freeze your balls off in Nunavet. But you gotta just talk to us, man." McGraw sported a crew cut that needed a fresh trim. His service uniform was slightly ruffled.

"Noah," Biagi said, her face concerned, "you need to think of Marie. You need to think of your children."

Noah's legs shook, despite the aching from his gunshot wound. Anger built up inside him. *I will not be tricked. Do not use my family against me.* He closed his hands into fists and rested them on top of his thighs.

"Your family needs you," Biagi was almost pleading with him. "If you talk to us, we'll be able to set up a video call with them. If you help us, you will see them soon. They need you, Noah."

Rhodes had sat patiently throughout the duration of the interrogation with is arms crossed over his chest but now he leaned forward.

"I think it's quite clear that my client has no desire to talk to you at this time."

Biagi ignored the attorney. "Noah, listen to me. I am a Christian woman. I go to church every Sunday. I know it can be hard to be a believer in these secular times. But, I think—" she paused, "I think God would want you to be with your family. God wants you to protect them. He wants to comfort them. He wants—"

Noah couldn't contain the fury rising inside him anymore. He thought of Wade giving him the opportunity to be what he had called a "true, Christian man." Hearing Wade's words echo inside him, he violently rose from the table and knocked

his chair backward. Noah Bridger looked Biagi in the eyes and
roared, "God wants you dead!"

The gibbous moon hung above the scrubland of the battered
Santa Fe railyard as Lt. Director Juan Carlos Luna returned to
the hotel from the capitol. He walked through the lobby to the
bar and ordered a tall beer, then took a seat on the patio outside.
The desert air had dipped from cool to cold and Luna pulled
the lapels of his jacket tight across his chest. As he packed his
tobacco pipe, Arnie Jones took a seat beside him.

"Best part about being in the Grey Zone, huh?" Jones said to
Luna and took out his own pipe. Here, the smoking of tobacco
outside of a private residence was still permitted.

Chief Deputy Arnie Jones had been Luna's first NASO
appointment. Before he joined the GFN security office, Arnie
had been Luna's right-hand man in the Army Rangers. He had
a round, happy face that had been crinkled by sun and time.
He wore a black pyramid mustache and had wispy white hair
atop his head. His eyes were thin and were the strongest feature
inherited from his Filipino mother.

The two men sat in silence as they looked out over the moonlit railyard. Without federal or Federation money to maintain
infrastructure, freight rail service fell, and passenger travel plum-
meted as the proxy governments of the Grey Zone could not
afford basic upkeep. As part of the Washington Amendment,
select corporations were still allowed to export goods to established hubs outside the White Zone. These freights carried the
necessities. However, with no tax incentive and waning consumer
interest, the corporations had minimal incentive to provide
upkeep to the rail lines beyond the immediate, necessary fixes.
Urban areas of the Grey Zone were the hardest hit after the
American adoption of the BHS. Most people migrated to the

White Zone while others moved to farm in small, rural communities. Those that adopted an agrarian lifestyle had the same difficulties that the early American pioneers had encountered. In the face of such hardship, these right-wingers patched together to form communes in the vision of Marx and Bakunin.

"Looks like it's gonna happen, eh, boss?" Jones said as he puffed on his pipe.

"Yes. It does." Luna answered solemnly.

"And you're in charge of making sure it does."

"One of life's great ironies, I suppose."

"You're not thinking of doing anything *loco*, are you?"

Luna turned to Jones. "No. No, of course not."

"That's good to hear."

"I'm a soldier, Arnie, not a politician. I've always been a soldier. I'll always be a soldier. And I will always follow an order given by that man."

Luna's admiration for Secretary-General Dubois was well known. Though he hid his contempt for others well enough, he was unabashed when speaking of the Frenchman.

They sat quietly in the brisk night and smoked their pipes. Luna gulped his beer, then turned to his Deputy.

"I just don't trust those bastards, Arnie. They're wolves in sheep's clothing."

"Dubois has found himself in these situations many times before. He worked this sort of deal for years in Russia. In Korea. Look at the work he did in my mother's Philippines. Hell, he had to work with French nationalists long before the GFN existed. The man's a genius. He knows what he's doing."

"It's the combination of such nationalism and such fanatic devotion to faith that scares me with these American groups."

"The Americans will be easy compared to some of the other religious groups. Look at the Israelites. They have been fighting for their small strip of land for thousands of years. Their mandate comes directly from God. These people," Jones waved his hand, "these people's grandfathers stole this land, remember. It isn't even theirs to begin with. And the values they hold so dear come from money-hungry evangelists and John fucking Wayne movies."

Luna finished his beer. "That may be the case, my friend, but they all have guns. And they all want to use those guns. And Arnie, I just don't trust them. They want total bloodshed."

Arnie Jones patted his boss and friend on the hand. His face was sad.

"We won't let that happen, boss. We won't let it happen."

On her way back to the hotel, Natalie Kelley stopped and bought a pint of Scotch. Once in her room, she poured herself a glass and pulled out her APD. The uploaded files were there.

"God bless that little goldfish," Natalie said to herself.

Natalie pulled up the footage from the camera behind the reception desk. She opened the file marked 3 May. *What time had the painter walked in? Around 08:30?* She played the recording from 08:20. People laughed and talked as they walked in. Others moved through the lobby sleepily, but none of them had had any idea that slaughter would take place across the street in just a few hours. Natalie looked for the painter and hoped this camera would give a better angle of his face than the other.

There.

She stopped the footage and brought it back slightly.

The painter walked in. This camera really stressed his tremendous size. He appeared over six and a half feet tall and must have had well over one hundred and ten kilos of muscle. He was an Adonis. The ball cap was low on his brow, the bill shaded his face, and he carried his head against his chest. Natalie slowed the recording to play frame-by-frame, yet she still couldn't get a good look at his face. The receptionist walked up to him. He stopped although he clearly had not wanted to. He kept his head down. She kept talking. *He lifted his head!* Quickly, before he walked away.

She slowly rolled the recording back and froze it on the best still of his face.

"Gotcha."

He had sharp cheeks, a hooked nose, and a protruding chin. His face was jagged and dark with tan. He had bright emeralds of eyes. *Weren't assassins supposed to blend in?* Everything about this man made him noticeable. She studied the face, zoomed in on the features, looked it up-and-down, over-and-over again. He didn't look real.

He didn't look real!

This man wasn't real. Everything from head-to-toe was prosthetic. It had to be. She took the still and sent it to an old college classmate who was a plastic surgeon in Los Angeles and asked if he would be able to deconstruct the face to a more natural state.

Natalie downed her Scotch and crawled into bed as the painter's malleable visage flickered behind her lids. The conspiracy grew. A second shooter. A phony painter. If she read the story, she would dismiss it as paranoid bullshit. She needed more. She needed hard, definitive evidence.

Still, she felt optimistic and as she drifted to sleep, a smile spread across her lips.

CHAPTER FIVE

5 May 2072

Juan Carlos Luna jogged west through Santa Fe to the foothills of the Sangre de Cristo Mountains. As he reached the outskirts of the city, a coyote darted in front of him. Thin, mangy, and skittish, the animal paid no attention to Luna as it crossed the pockmarked road. The stars shimmered in the inky night sky and the waning moon slid toward the distant black peaks. It was a little after 04:00. The more time he spent at home with Jay, the harder it was for him to sleep on the road. As a soldier in the field, he had slept when he needed to and woke when he needed to. He had been like a machine, powering "off" when it was calm and "on" when danger arose. *I've grown soft in my advancing age.*

The hotel was still asleep when he returned from his run. He peeled off his sweaty clothes and hopped in the shower. As he dried off, he checked his APD. He had four messages from Brandt Bonner of the Texas Military Brigade. Each message requested that the Lt. Director call him immediately. Luna put on his black, pleated trousers, then called Bonner as he heated a cup of coffee. Bonner answered on the first ring: "Sir."

"A little early, isn't it, Mr. Bonner?" Luna teased as he buttoned his light blue shirt.

"I'm sorry, sir," Bonner sounded frazzled.

"What is it?" Luna asked.

"The tunnel we found yesterday—we placed surveillance equipment at the entrance in the wildlife refuge. There was—there was some activity just off the shore in the Gulf. There was a sub, sir. It certainly wasn't manufactured in any GFN sanctioned plants. But it's very well-built. It was unloading cargo."

"Jesus, what kind of cargo?"

"Well, when the surveillance picked up the sub, we already had men in the tunnel and in the refuge, so we were able to get the jump on them. We waited for one of our boats to get in position at the mouth of the bay before we made our move. They weren't prepared to have any company and by the time we moved in on them, they were surrounded by thirty brigadiers."

"What kind of cargo was it, Brandt?" Luna placed his frayed, green cotton tie on his collar.

"It was mostly small arms and ammunition. Some artillery. But it wasn't the munitions that most concerned us, sir. One of the men we arrested was a Texan who was wanted for questioning. The rest, the other nineteen men—we suspect are *resistência brasileira*."

"Fuck," Luna stopped knotting his tie. "Where are they now?"

"We took them all to a makeshift compound on Galveston Island."

"Are they talking?"

"Silent. Just like the group outside Austin last month."

"At least we can definitively link them to the tunnels now. You need to find the connection, Brandt. The collusion with the Brazilians can no longer be considered an anomaly. There is a deliberate effort to bring Brazilian resistance fighters to Texas. If the compound on Galveston Island is secure, I want you to keep them there. I don't want them transferred to Forrest City. I want this to be handled by you Texans, is that understood? I don't want the Fed dealing with this right now. Not yet, at least. Not until we know what they're doing and how many are already here. We need answers, Brandt."

"Yes, sir. Galveston is secure. We'll keep them here and we'll find out all that we can."

"Alright," Luna exhaled loudly, then twisted his tie into a slipshod knot. "I'm counting on you, son. Make them talk. We can't have every jerkoff rebel in the Western hemisphere parading through Texas. It needs to stop. These men need to be the last." Luna was about to hang up but went back to the line. "Also, good work, Brandt. Thank you."

Luna still had two hours before he was to meet with his Deputies at the capitol. He sat down at the room's desk and started combing through The Federation's files on the Brazilian Resistance.

The *resistência brasileira* was led by a man named Hugo Schmitz. Schmitz was a banker; cruel, aggressive and successful in his dealings. He made a fortune by implementing predatory lending policies that left more than a million Brazilians homeless and penniless. He was also the chief architect in expanding the Free Trade Zone of Manaus to other cities in the State of Amazonas. He referred to himself as an Überkapitalistischen and believed it was man's duty to enrich oneself to the fullest.

In addition to his Darwinian business position, Schmitz conducted a radical, survivalist private life. He used his ten-thousand-acre compound outside Borba to house a cache of weapons and train young men into a faux-paramilitary group. To Schmitz, combat was sport. He hosted complex war games on the compound and offered millions of dollars to the winners.

Hugo Schmitz helped make many people very wealthy. One of those people was real estate developer Karen Moretti. In 2056, Moretti became President of Brazil and named Hugo Schmitz her Finance Minister. The Moretti administration attempted to bring a contingent of Latin American countries together in an agreement to rival the GFN. The contingent was to be called BoLAS, or Band of Latin American States. But as GFN countries prospered, those that would form BoLAS squabbled over the power structure of their agreement as recession hit these GFN holdouts. The deal fell apart. Under Moretti's leadership, the favelas swelled and the GFN offered nearly $300 billion to replace the slums with adequate housing. When Moretti's term ended, Schmitz ran on the party ticket but was blown out by the pro-GFN candidate. The Überkapitalistischen, humiliated in the political realm, retreated to his hometown of Borba and his compound. There, he gathered his mock militia and told them the time for simulation was over. It was time for real battle. It was time to kill. The paramilitary used their experience and knowledge of the local rivers and jungle to wage a devastating guerrilla war.

Within a year, many of Schmitz's BoLAS allies, themselves in political disgrace, brought their own militias and joined Schmitz deep in the rainforest. Schmitz offered huge cash incentives to officers of Latin American armies to join the *resistência*. With a stockpile of cash, Schmitz recruited some of the most talented *coronels* in South America. His militia swelled to over five hundred thousand men. The fighting in the Amazon became the bloodiest in GFN history.

The chamber was much more comfortable than Noah Bridger had pictured. It was more of a dormitory than a prison cell. He had imagined a damp, cold, bleak dungeon. That is not what he encountered after his outburst during the interrogation. As he yelled at the Specialist, the two uniformed officers burst through the door and roughly removed Noah from his seat. Noah started to resist, but as the officers grasped his underarms, he caught a glimpse of those still at the oak table. His attorney, Rhodes, looked only mildly disappointed, and made a listless protest against the rough treatment of his client. The attorney's words had no impact on either the officers nor the flailing Noah.

What stopped Noah from fighting the officers was the sheer horror plastered on Specialist Biagi's face. The thought of his words being able to so personally affect a member of the emotionless machine that was The Federation flattened him. The terror displayed by the woman was not in response to any immediate danger she thought she may be in, it was something much deeper. It froze Noah. The officers carried him to the cell with no further resistance.

A few moments after the officers deposited Noah in the infirmary's cell, the physician who had performed the nano-surgery on his broken leg entered on the pretense of following up on the operation. After a very brief examination of the tibia, the infirmary doctor gave Noah a sedative. He was frightened at the prospect of having any more drugs administered to him by The Fed. They could inject him with anything. They could be trying to kill him. To experiment on him. To make him sick or incapacitate him. Worse yet, they could be brainwashing him. But as the doctor slipped the needle into his arm, Noah embraced whatever solution was being pumped into him. The previous forty-eight hours had emotionally and physically depleted him. As the drugs coursed through his veins, Noah Bridger closed his eyes and welcomed his slip from consciousness.

When Noah awoke, he was once again unaware of the time. It was an irksome trend. The electric lights in the room were dimmed low and his eyes needed a few seconds to adjust. He had been moved from the infirmary. Noah sat up and took note of the new cell. He could not believe that this was a prison cell.

Having lived his entire life in Hereford, Texas, Noah had heard horror stories about the men and women in the so-called "White Zone." He had heard that The Federation used drugs and hypnotherapy to control dissidents' minds. That, when The Federation moved into a previously unoccupied town, the Gendarmes made the Vikings look like choir boys. That The Federation sterilized Christian women who refused to have abortions to keep the population in check. Noah had heard that The Federation was a vacuum: it sucked the individuality and freedom from men. It was the Greatest Industrial Revolution. It turned men into machines.

But in this cell, there were plants and art and colors. There were freshly washed sheets and recently scrubbed floors. Across the bunk was a small screen which showed a distorted, dim reflection of the cell. Against the wall opposite the metal door, there was a small, wooden desk and a matching wooden chair. Above the desk was a small window, which let the early morning moonlight in. These things had no function for a machine. *Why were they put here?* Noah thought. *Why were they trying to provide comfort to their enemies?* This thought challenged all he had heard and believed about The Federation. He then realized that it wasn't this room that was challenging his beliefs. *Mind games. That's what this cell is. It must be part of some mind games orchestrated by the Fed.* Even with this realization, Noah remained uneasy. The thing that kept him uneasy and that gnawed at his core was an image. Specialist Biagi. *That woman. Her face.* He kept seeing her face in every corner of the cell. He couldn't shake a feeling that he tried to bury. *She hadn't been afraid for herself.* Her fear was more abstract. She felt fear *for* Noah. Not only that, she felt sympathy for him. *Could she be afraid that she wouldn't be able to help me?* The fear was interlocked with a deep despair. It nearly destroyed Noah to think that a Fed would want to help him in some way. It shook all truths Noah held close. Doubt stirred in him kinetically, the atoms of uncertainty heated to a frenzy.

He needed to rid himself of the idea—it was making him weak.

To rid himself of this cancerous idea, Noah thought of the herd of men and iron which swarmed upon the men at the silo. *They killed that boy.* He thought of the bullet striking his leg.

What have they done since I've been locked up? He thought of faceless Yellow-Eyed monsters burning down his ranch. He thought of vile criminals in their globalist rags shackling and gagging his wife and children. He thought of the tears running down Marie's face as she was violated by those that had ignored the Voice of God. He thought of his family's lifeless bodies left in the smoldering ashes of his home. This violence, this terror is what those in Hereford knew that the comfortable zombies on the coasts had not heard. Or refused to hear. He could not afford to let his thoughts weaken him again.

Noah Bridger vowed to never second guess his beliefs again.

Natalie Kelley woke up hungry. She had been busy in Oklahoma City the last couple of days and realized she hadn't eaten anything but Snack-Stats since she left Chicago. She dressed and walked down to the hotel kitchen. Natalie ordered farm-fresh eggs, bacon, and rye toast. She left her APD in the room and enjoyed the meal without distraction. Once all the liquid yolk had been mopped up by the toast and her plate was clean, Natalie returned to her room replenished and checked her APD. She had a message from Xavier Lau, the craniofacial surgeon and fellow Northwestern alumnus.

"Hey Nat! Hope you're well! Took a brief peek at the image you sent and there are definitely some alterations to that face. It will take me a little time, but I think I can deconstruct it for you by the end of the week. Stay safe! Let me know when you're in LA next, good-looking! I'll take you out on the town."

Natalie rolled her eyes at Xavier's decade-long pursuit of her and concentrated on the rest of his message. She was relieved to find out that her instinct was right—the face had been cosmetically altered. She wished that Xavier would get back to her with his deconstruction sooner but knew she could not push him. She would need to be patient. She thought about reaching out to Cooper again to see what they had on the painter but decided she could wait as she didn't wish to talk to him unless it was necessary. Since there was not a whisper of the second shooter in the media, Natalie figured NASO must be keeping their cards close to the vest.

Natalie thought about what she had uncovered yesterday. She was building a solid foundation for a breathtaking exclusive. She was optimistic that she would excavate the rest of this conspiracy theory. As she thought of what she had learned and what she needed to do next, her thoughts turned to Faye Nejem and Natalie's confidence warped to sadness.

Natalie feared that although Faye Nejem presented a strong façade yesterday, she may be drowning in despair on the inside, screaming in the empty space of her mind, unable to even hear her own cries. Natalie had built such a sturdy exterior wall before, only to have her soul crumble like a dried sand castle in a salty gale.

In her grief, Natalie had isolated herself, but Mrs. Nejem did not have a choice in her loneliness. She remembered Faye's invitation to come back to her home. She did not think the woman would yield the information she needed, but something pulled her to that suburban home. Natalie realized that she wished to comfort her. She had not gotten the widow's phone number but knew that Faye would be home since she was still observing Iddah. Not having a clear next step in her investigation, Natalie walked outside the hotel, hopped on her sportbike, and headed east to Meeker.

The bike wove through the thicket of pedestrians and electro-cycles and autos of Midtown, Automobile Alley, and Culbertson. Natalie passed over the light-rail tracks of metropolitan Oklahoma City, then hopped on the elevated cycle freeway that took her over the crowded commercial district. Below, the city bustled with people as they commuted to work. Stuck in traffic, Natalie watched the pedestrians and SinCab passengers and electrocyclists. Only two days after a deadly terrorist attack a few miles away, the desire for normalcy lay heavy on the city streets like a thick fog. Natalie wondered how many of the commuters were worried that there may be another attack. How many worried that this time they would be caught in the crosshairs?

The traffic lightened once Natalie reached Nicoma Park. She turned off the computer guidance and manually took control of the bike. She shifted up a gear, moved to the open, outside lane, and twisted the throttle. It was good to be on a bike again. Natalie had owned an electrocycle when she lived in Evanston, but since she bought her condo a block from the river, she sold the Suzuki. That was three years ago and every time she drove a bike since, she had the same thought: *I need to get a new sport-bike. Once I finish the book, I'll have the money to get a souped-up new Raitoningu. If I ever finish that damn thing.*

Twenty minutes later, Natalie spotted her exit. She drifted to the right lane and decelerated as she curved down the off-ramp. Meeker was an embryonic community, one which developed more every day. As she neared Faye's neighborhood, she passed pristine commercial buildings and department stores and warehouses. Drones scurried out of the warehouses carrying crates and boxes as they fluttered in and out like bees at a hive. She noticed the streets were recently paved and the traffic lines were crisp and bright. This suburb was the quintessential example of a privately-planned community. All this land was owned by Def-Corp. They started building the infrastructure and commodities before they moved their employees in.

Natalie turned the sportbike onto Faye's street. The empty lots crawled with different construction-programmed Advanced Robotics. Foremen moved from lot to lot, overseeing the ARs and trying to make up for any time lost due to yesterday's rain. Natalie parked the electrocycle in Faye's driveway and, as she removed her helmet, hoped she could be of some consolation to the woman.

Juan Carlos Luna sat on a hard, wooden bench in the rotunda of the New Mexico State Capitol Building. From the travertine marble floor to the stained-glass skylight was a height of twenty meters. The rotunda was decorated by the flags of New Mexico's thirty-three counties, as well as a large American flag. Luna noticed that the green, blue, and yellow flag of The Federation, which showcased the Moi-Leakey cylindrical projection world map and winding arrows, was missing.

The Lt. Director's Deputies stood around the turquoise-and-pink eagle statue at the center of the room, joined by a few Security Officers who wore black fatigues and TS-33s. STAB Units Juliet Echo 3 and Echo 5 had been recommissioned from the Grey Zone town of Taos to provide Luna's team with intel and protection.

When the clock struck 09:00:00, Luna rose from the bench and walked to the center of the rotunda. The Deputies and SOs stood at attention.

Luna spent forty minutes briefing the team on the specifics of their mission. He assigned each Deputy a task to complete over the course of the next week. They would meet every morning to discuss progress. Luna stressed that the team's main objective was to be the protection of Secretary-General Dubois. Their secondary objective was to make sure that the treaty with the American Freedom Group was signed. Over the course of the next week, they would work to identify any persons or groups in the area that might pose a threat to the Secretary-General or the signing.

After he dismissed his team, Luna walked through the entire capitol building, stepped on every tile, and eyed every square inch. The signing would be public, so this made the capitol the most vulnerable stop for the Secretary-General. On his initial walk-through, Luna identified the weaknesses he was trained to recognize from his time both as a Ranger and a Security Officer. He noted the standard security defects described in the military manual he helped write. Then the Lt. Director made a second walk-through. This time, he forgot the manual and cased the building as if he were going to personally assassinate Dubois. With years of experience securing locales, Luna had put himself in some extremely dark places while he mimicked the terrorists he was charged with stopping, but found that the practice worked.

After he completed his second walk-through of the capitol building, Luna went back to his hotel room. Given the manpower provided him, Luna was confident that the signing would be successful. Though Santa Fe was his primary task, there were other important issues the Lt. Director needed to address. He called General Brandt Bonner of the Texas Military Brigade.

The slot on the cell door opened. An envelope slipped through and dropped to the floor. Noah rose from the bunk and plucked the envelope off the floor. He sat down on the desk chair beneath the window and tore the envelope open. The room's lights brightened and the screen on the wall powered on.

A woman's face appeared on the television screen. She was young and gorgeous with milky skin and long, black hair. Inside the ripped envelope, Noah found a metal key on a plastic key ring. The woman on the screen began speaking:

"Hello, this message is to inform you of the rules and regulations pertaining to all residents of Forrest City Processing Facility. You may review these rules and regulations at any time. To do so, just turn your video monitor to station 00. If you have any additional questions after viewing this video message, ask any of the processing facility employees.

"Now, I will read the rules and regulations outlined during the Hanoi Convention for residents of any GFCoJ processing facility. These rules and regulations have been ratified by every sovereign nation that adheres to the Basic Human Standard.

"Chapter One—Designation of Residents of Global Federation Court of Justice Processing Facilities.

"The Montpellier Accords, signed by France, Germany, and Spain on 10 April 2045, designate that any individual…"

Noah slowly lowered himself onto the bed. *Hanoi Convention? Montpellier Accords?* Noah didn't know what this woman was talking about. The language she used was dense and the terms foreign. However, he did pick up that she addressed him as a "resident." *Cowards don't even have the decency to call me a prisoner.* The woman droned on. Noah tried to follow but found that he retained very little information. What he did understand was that he was being held in this place against his will by people that carried guns. That's all he needed to know.

The woman spoke for over an hour. He was relieved when it ended, though it did not answer any of his questions. The screen turned black. Noah stood and stretched. Shadow-streaked sunlight spilled through the window and illuminated the wooden desk below. He walked over to the chair and stood on it to look out the window. The cell was partially submerged underground—the window, although toward the top of the cell wall, was only a few centimeters off the ground outside. He saw dirt and the base of a shrub. An earthworm crawled across the dirt into the plant.

A voice startled Noah. He jumped at the sound, almost tipping over the chair. Once he regained his balance, he saw the woman's face on the television again. She started her spiel from the top. Noah stepped off the chair and marched to the metal door at the opposite end of his cell. He pulled down on the handle. The door was unlocked.

Natalie Kelley walked to the front door of the Nejem residence. She expected the door to open and Mrs. Nejem to greet
her like last time, but it remained closed as she reached the
stoop. She waited a few seconds for the state-of-the-art security system to alert Faye of her arrival, but the door stayed still.
Natalie rang the exterior bell and rapped the brass knocker.
There was no answer.

Natalie knew that while she practiced Iddah, Faye would
not leave her home; she would only be able to receive visitors at
home and would not go out in public. The Quran called for an
Iddah period of four months and ten days, which ensured that
any offspring that the widow might bear would surely be the
product of the deceased. Faye mentioned yesterday that, due to
ever-changing professional and social demands, her Imam told
her that the over-a-third-of-a-year period of sequester could
most certainly be shortened. As of yesterday, she was waiting
to hear from Imam Naser regarding the duration of her Iddah.

Natalie tried the bell again. There were no cars parked in
the drive or on the street, only her electrocycle. There did not
appear to be any other visitors to the Nejem residence. Natalie
tried to look through the transom windows, but they were wavy,
and she only saw distorted shapes and colors. She walked off the
front porch and around the house on the dark green, well-kept
grass. She passed the windows on the side of the house and
tried to look inside, but they too were glass block. Natalie knew
the isolation that Faye must be feeling. She knew how it felt to
want to be left alone to wallow in your own sorrow. Sorrow and
loneliness could be like mud; dirty and reeking but protecting
you from any other hurt. Natalie was glad that she had come to
visit the widow to show her someone cared about her anguish.
Now if only I could reach her.

Natalie reached the sliding glass back door. There was a deep
purple drape that blocked any view inside and the door was
locked and unmovable. After she knocked on the back door

and pulled hard at the handle, she noticed that the kitchen's sin-gle-hung window was cracked slightly. She walked to the window and found it too high to peer into. She stretched and stood on her tiptoes, and felt her shoes sink into the muddy mulch that edged the siding, but she still could not see inside. She looked around the backyard and spotted a ring of concrete wall blocks that encircled a young, pink dogwood tree. She picked up one of the heavy blocks, carried it the mulch, and dropped it below the window between two budding flowers. As the weighty block slipped from her hands, it scratched her ankle. Natalie hissed and cursed to herself, then gingerly stepped up onto the block. She placed her fingers on the stool of the window frame and pulled herself up, conscious of the scrape down her leg. Look-ing through the open slit between the glass and the stool, she could see most of the kitchen. It appeared as pristine as it had been yesterday; one of the small cleaning ARs was polishing the granite counters. Natalie craned her head to the left to get a better view of the hallway leading out of the kitchen. She squinted and saw something on the floor of the hallway. It was a strewn navy-blue kitten heel. She tried to look further down the hall, but the tinted window obstructed her view.

Natalie tried to push the window up further with the palms of her hands, but it wouldn't budge. She trotted to the dogwood, grabbed another block, and placed it on top of the base block. Again, she pushed up on the lower rail. This time, with better leverage, the window creaked, then groaned. Suddenly there was a snap and the window launched upward, crashing into the head jamb. An alarm immediately started screeching from inside the house. Natalie had lost her footing on the stacked blocks but saved a fall by grabbing the side of the house. Bent against the siding, she moved the uneven top block flush with the base block and, after she tested the sturdiness of her two-unit tower, she stood up and looked through the open window into the kitchen. The high-pitched scream of the alarm pinged out into the yard and strobe lights flashed inside and outside the home. A calm, commanding voice announced there was a break-in at a rear-facing first-level window. Natalie, with her head craned into the kitchen and her hands over her ears, yelled into the suffocating noise to Faye. She expected to see the woman either flee the home or investigate the incursion, but there was no movement inside—even the AR had stopped as the alarm wailed. Natalie again spotted the blue shoe laying alone on the floor. Using her arms to steady herself on the window sill, she leaned into the kitchen while her feet hovered over the concrete blocks. She could see the rest of the kitchen and into the dining room. Beyond the abandoned shoe lay a bare, tanned foot. The foot was motionless. At first, Natalie thought the prone body was enveloped in a long, dark, flowing dress. A moment later, her mind registered the dress was two different colors. Raised above the carpet were the outlines of two legs in a tight, violet pair of pants. A calm, glacial lake of black liquid had flowed out from the legs, its shores blended into the light carpet. Blood.

Natalie Kelley's arms buckled, and her chest hit the window sill. Her dangling feet searched for her tower, but, in her panic, she knocked the top block loose from the bottom. She followed the slipped block and fell from the sill. When she hit the earth, her hands and knees buried into the loose mulch. She tried to catch her breath. As she inhaled deeply, there was a catch in her throat. Tears swelled in Natalie's eyes and before she could stop herself, she retched over the blooming begonias in the Nejems' backyard.

There were few new developments for Juan Carlos Luna from Texas regarding the recently detained Brazilian submariners. None of the prisoners were talking. General Bonner said he still had men exploring the vast tunnel system. They had mapped

over one hundred and thirty kilometers of tunnels thus far. They
had found entrances to the tunnel at an additional six residences,
but each property was vacant by the time the brigadiers arrived.
The submarine bore no markings nor forfeited any additional
information apart from the men and the arms. The boat was
shipped to Galveston Island so Bonner's team could conduct a
series of identifying tests on it.

As he disconnected with Bonner, Luna looked at the clock.
There is still time. The Lt. Director rushed down to the parking
lot where a black, electric SUV sat idling along the porte-cochère.
He jogged toward the vehicle. A man with an assault rifle exited
the passenger seat and crawled into the back. Arnie Jones sat
behind the steering wheel, wearing SO fatigues. He yelled out
the open car door:

"Glad you could make it, boss!"

Luna responded with a smile. He had told Jones to leave for
the expedition at exactly 12:45, whether the Lt. Director was
present or not. He did not like to keep people waiting. Luna
slid into the passenger seat and a safety harness rolled across his
chest. Jones put the car into drive and started out of the parking
lot. Due to the risk of attack and the ever-present need for eva-
sive maneuvers during an official security operation, Federation
vehicles in the Grey Zone were never computer-operated and
always had a trained, focused driver at the wheel. This was an
official security operation.

"Get me a handle, will ya, Owens?"

Luna turned to face Deputy Amir Owens. Owens was a
young black man with a buzz cut and bright-white teeth, and
fatigues that matched Jones's. He had scars that ran down his
right cheek and neck, courtesy of a dirty bomb in the Black
Hills campaign: on patrol between Deadwood and Rapid City,
the then-nineteen-year-old tripped a wire and was sprayed by
broken glass and nails. In the years after the injury, as he worked
his way to capture Lt. Director Luna's attention, he opined that

the scars were a blessing, a constant reminder for him to be more cautious in the field. Owens reached into the bed of the SUV and unlocked a titanium briefcase. He picked up the receiver and connected it to the stock, then installed the bolt carrier and trigger module before he finally slipped in a loaded cartridge. In total, it took Owens less than ten seconds to transform five pieces of aluminum alloy into the most efficient killing machine in human history.

He handed the weapon to Luna. Since the manufacture of the first TS-33 assault rifle fifteen years before, it had been the primary weapon for Federation Security Officers around the world. Running solely on electrical energy instead of gunpowder, the TS-33 emitted no sound and no heat which made it impossible for the gun to be picked up by geothermal glasses. The TS-33 had biometric palm scans, so the weapon was only able to be fired by pre-authorized SOs. The software within the weapon corrected shots based on environmental factors such as wind speed and direction, barometric pressure, humidity, and altitude. The weapon used smart-bullets as ammunition which homed in on body heat and could be set to release a toxin into the blood if the shooter needed a definitive kill.

Luna placed his hand on the biometric scanner and logged in to the weapon. The weapon's software kept track of each bullet fired from the weapon and each smart-bullet had an individual SKU number. The computer used laser geometrics from the rifle and the smart-bullet to score each "hit" by measuring the density and composition of the material the bullet struck. Based on the measure, the bullet could determine what kind of fat, tissue, bone, or other material the smart-bullet passed through and could calculate what part of the combatant's body or advanced robotic or vehicle the shooter hit. This preliminary data was followed up by the Security Officer himself, who needed to visually confirm each hit when possible. For misses, the smart-bullet measured the distance that the bullet passed by a significant source of body heat. The smart-bullets were also connected to sensors in all field drones which increased the amount of data collected from each shot. While the TS-33 was the primary weapon used by The Federation, other weapons used by the Security Offices utilized the same software. This adherence to cutting-edge technology for all SOs, as well as a devotion to data collection and analysis, made The Federation Security Offices the most efficient, intelligent military force ever.

The GFN preached a stiff trigger to its SOs and disciplined any man or woman who fired at a rate consistently above the average of the unit after a review of the unit's recordings. With this policy, The Federation's goal wasn't to conserve ammunition—it was to make sure that every SO that discharged their weapon was shooting only at a target deemed currently threatening. The events that inflamed dissidents of The Federation the most were situations when unarmed people, especially women and children, were killed during a GFNSO mission. Three riots in the last twenty years had occurred in response to a civilian death by the Security Offices that ended with over five hundred casualties and one trillion dollars in damage.

These incidents reinstated the Security Office's policy that any collateral damage was unacceptable. In the short-term, a civilian casualty drastically stalled the establishment of the Basic Human Standard in transitioning communities. It was also a PR nightmare for the GFN because there was often public footage of the incident. The long-term prospects were even more detrimental. The killing of a civilian non-combatant during a SO mission could potentially convert dozens of apolitical, ordinary citizens into blood-thirsty, revenge-seeking terrorists.

Luna remembered the GFN policy as the SUV rolled west out of Santa Fe on a dusty, pockmarked highway. He disagreed with the view. He believed that there were no non-combatants in the Grey Zone, but he was a devoted soldier and respected the regulations of the Office. During his Federation service he had only two civilian deaths under his command.

None of those missions were as important as this one. The Lt. Director tightened his grip on the TS-33 and hoped he wouldn't have to use the weapon during the next two weeks.

The cafeteria of the Forrest City Processing Facility was filled with a couple hundred chatting, munching inmates. Noah Bridger saw only a couple armed officers who stood around the perimeter. He walked around the outside of the tables, looking for his brother-in-law. All the inmates at Forrest City were men. Most of the men were white. Like Noah, each inmate wore black polyester pants. However, not all the men wore the same bright-yellow, short-sleeved shirt as Noah. He looked around the cafeteria and saw red and blue and green and orange shirts. Though there were different colors, on the front and back of each shirt the inmate's first initial and last name was etched in large, black block letters. Noah scanned the faces and read the names, hoped to find "W. Barrineau"—he needed the man's guidance to make sense of the situation. He had made half a lap around the cafeteria and had not seen a familiar face. The colors and sounds and smells were overwhelming. He couldn't concentrate to find Wade or any of the others, so he walked faster and looked harder.

There. The flowing, brown mane was unmistakable, even from behind. The unfinished-looking Cajun name spread across his vast shoulders. Noah moved past the serving counter without grabbing a plate and toward the table in the center of the room. He pivoted and picked his way to the table. A smile grew across his face as he neared his relative. Wade Barrineau sat on the bench at the end of the table. Across from him were two men Noah recognized from the rear seat of his Mustang. He could not see the names on their royal blue shirts. It didn't matter if he did not remember their names—he knew their faces.

In front of each inmate was a near-full plate of food which included a hoagie, pasta salad, canned peaches, and baby carrots. Wade drank a glass of milk and the two other men had iced tea. None of those seated noticed Noah as he approached. They were surprised when he tapped Wade on the shoulder. Before Wade could lower a quarter of a peach punctured by his white, plastic fork, Noah had embraced him. Noah was shocked by his own burst of intimacy but continued to grip Wade tightly around the shoulders.

Wade patted Noah's hand as the limbo-ed peach dripped sweet juice on the table.

"Noah," He shook his head back and forth. "Noah, we thought you had made a clean getaway."

Noah released his grip and took a step away from the table. He cleared his throat.

"I'm very glad to see you here," he announced as Wade scooted down the bench to clear a space for him.

"I won't say the same, considering the circumstances," replied Wade and the two men sitting across from him laughed. "But," he put the peach in his mouth and sucked the fruit down his throat, "if we must be here, it is good to be here together."

As Noah sat down he recalled the names of the other two men: Aiden Stevens and Brickson Newsome.

Wade looked at Noah, concerned.

"Have they treated you alright?"

Stevens and Newsome ate their sandwiches. Newsome had a purple ring around his left eye.

Noah nodded his head. "Fine, I guess. I think the medic fixed my leg up alright."

Wade's eyes widened and turned to the other side of the table. He then gave his attention back to Noah.

"What happened to your leg?"

"It was—" Noah stammered. He never thought he would utter this sentence. "I was shot."

Wade rocked his head back. "They *shot* you?!" His tone and actions were dramatic.

Noah nodded his head and a chuckle escaped him. "Twice, actually."

Wade laughed heartily, and the two other men followed suit. He clasped a thick hand on Noah's triceps. His soft, brown eyes centered on him. The gaze made Noah feel uncomfortable.

"You have spilled blood for the Lord, Noah. He will remember that. We will all remember that."

Wade Barrineau was three years Noah's senior. He was married to Marie's sister. The men had been family for five years, but never developed a close relationship. Noah was a man who melted into the shadows of a room; Wade was a man whose charisma was so great it pulled the walls in. At family events, there was always a crowd around him that orbited under the force of his gravitational charm. Noah would listen to the man speak and laugh from a distance, but they never had a serious one-on-one conversation. At least not until Wade approached Noah in the garage to ask for his help.

Wade was one hundred and eighty-five centimeters tall and had a solid build under a wide frame. His skin was permanently pink from the sun. His hairline had retreated to the middle of his scalp, but his long, brown curls cascaded down his neck until they rested softly on his shoulders. His milk-chocolate eyes sat back in his face and his thin lips were surrounded by a salt and pepper beard. He had been born and raised in New Orleans. He owned a hardware store in Lubbock. He met Marie's sister six years ago at a church bake sale. They had three children, twin four-year-old daughters and a baby boy.

In all regards, Wade Barrineau and Noah Bridger were not family but mere acquaintances. Noah had heard many delightful anecdotes but very few personal details about Wade. *Still, it is better to be here with Wade than by myself. In fact, besides Marie, I don't know who I'd rather see.*

"Here, eat." Barrineau ripped his hoagie in two and placed it in Noah's hand.

Noah took a bite, chewed hungrily, then took another.

"This place—" he started as he chewed his food, then swallowed, "this place is not what I expected."

"Did you expect rats and shackles? Damp stone floors? Torches lining the walls?" Stevens said. He had a slim face and high, gaunt cheekbones. His crystal-blue eyes peered at Noah as he snickered.

"No," Noah said as he looked around the cafeteria. "I guess I don't know what I expected."

"The stories circulating about this place's barbarism obviously aren't all true," Newsome chimed in, pointing around the room with his plastic utensil. "But this place is no less dangerous. Instead of hammering you into submission, they lull you into it. They give you a little now, so that they can take everything later."

Noah hung his head. He felt embarrassed at his lack of knowledge.

"Yeah," he said meekly. "I just didn't know what to expect."

Wade placed his hand on Noah's forearm and broke the tension.

"Have you said anything to them, Noah? During interrogation?"

"No. My attorney or whatever told me not to say anything. Until I spoke with you."

"Rhodes?" Newsome inquired.

"Yeah."

"He's a good man," Newsome responded as he drank the juice from his bowl of peaches. In his late twenties, he was the youngest of the four. He was tall and muscular and wore long sideburns and a short haircut. His heterochromatic eyes gave an exotic flare to a traditionally handsome face.

"He's your representation, too?" said Noah.

"Daggart had said to contact him if anything happened. He's a friend of the cause. Worked cases at Toledo Processing before coming here. Has a solid record, apparently? That's what Otis said, at least."

"Where is that other man—Daggart?"

"They killed him," Stevens said harshly. Newsome made a small cross over his lips in memory of the fallen.

The table was silent for a moment. Noah noticed the chattering of the other prisoners for the first time since he sat down. The casualness of the lunch made Noah uneasy.

Noah shook his head in disbelief. "I never thought I'd be in prison."

"I never wanted to be back," Wade said. Noah was stunned. He stared at his brother-in-law who speared his fusilli and tomatoes. He looked across the table at Newsome and Stevens. Neither man looked surprised. Noah had previously wondered what Wade's past life had entailed, but he never thought that his biography would include a rap sheet.

"You—" he started. "You were in—"

"Are you still hungry, Noah?" Wade interrupted. Noah managed a shallow nod.

"Then go and get some food. When you're done, I'll tell you how we're going to get out of here."

It took five minutes for the police to respond to the alarm at the Nejem residence. Three minutes later, they found Natalie sitting under the opened window, her head on her pulled-in knees next to a pool of vomit. Natalie's foot was on the shore of the pool and sick dribbled onto her shin from the flower petals above. She was crying. When the first police officer, a young woman, approached her and put her hand on Natalie's shoulder, she jumped.

"Are you alright, ma'am?"

Natalie looked up, her wide eyes wet with tears. She could not speak.

"Come with me," the officer said. She grabbed beneath Natalie's armpit and pulled her up to her feet.

The officer led Natalie to the front of the house. There were two police cruisers parked in the street. An ambulance screamed down the road. The officer sat Natalie down, then fetched a blanket from the trunk of the lead cruiser and wrapped it around her shoulders.

An older, male officer sat down next to Natalie. He removed his police cap and placed it against his side, revealing his matted, grey hair. He reached into his pants' cargo pocket, removed a hydration pack, and handed it to Natalie.

She took the pack and drank it while the fog slowly receded from over the bay of her mind.

"How are you feeling? Are you okay?" the older officer asked.

"Yes," Natalie said softly.

She looked at the officer seated next to her.

"Is Faye—is she dead?"

The officer nodded. "Yes."

"What happened?"

The officer ran a hand through his hair and massaged his scalp. "She slit her throat."

"No. She couldn't. She wouldn't."

The man stood up and placed the cap back on his head.

"Were you a friend of Mrs. Nejem's?"

"No. I...no."

"No?" He asked. "May I ask what you are doing here?" The officer was suddenly suspicious.

"She wouldn't do that. She seemed..." Natalie stopped and shook her head, trying to clear the cobwebs. "I'm a reporter for the *Chicago Tribune*. I met Faye, er, Mrs. Nejem yesterday. I'm writing about the shooting downtown. We just met yesterday. I, I came today to follow up."

The officer nodded, his suspicions appeased for the moment. He extended a hand to Natalie. She grasped the hand and pulled herself up.

"I'm Deputy Rodney Greene with the Lincoln County Police Department. The young woman who found you is Deputy Sara Morales. Do you have identification?"

"Identification? Yeah. Shit. Of course," Natalie said as she became more cognizant. She extended her arm and Detective Greene scanned her Implanted Wrist Chip with his APD. He read the information from the IWC and seemed satisfied.

"Ms. Kelley, we are going to have to take you to the station to ask you a few questions. Is that alright?"

"Yes, of course."

"Okay, follow me," Greene said as he walked toward the lead vehicle. "Morales! Let's go!"

Deputy Greene opened the back door of the cruiser and Natalie sat inside. She looked out the window and saw Morales jog toward the car. She felt the bile rise in her again, and she covered her mouth. The image that kept projecting on the screen of Natalie's memory was not Faye Nejem's lifeless legs and the blood-stained floor; it was the ghost-white face of her father. His eyes rolled back, his mouth opened wide, and a gurgling hole in his throat.

The black SUV that carried Luna, Jones, and Owens rolled up the drive of a large country estate. The Deputies had taken off their Federation insignia-marked fatigues and donned black sports jackets. At the end of the drive, a large, white house perched on the edge of Grasshopper Canyon. The house, which overlooked a dried streambed, was three stories high. On the front was a large, open sitting area with several Doric columns. The house belonged to Raul Ramirez, a wealthy man who had made his fortune mining the New Mexican land for uranium. He was a vocal opponent of The Federation but privately that opposition slacked when his bank account was threatened.

To maintain his lifestyle, Raul Ramirez secretly provided The Federation with information while the GFN provided him with medical supplies and equipment to distribute to the people living outside of the White Zone. He told the local merchants that he smuggled in the medicine from a contact in the unincorporated state of Java. During the first year of complete economics sanctions that were implemented by the GFN, an estimated two hundred thousand Chinese died from hunger, exposure, or lack of medicine Secretary-General Antoine Dubois had been devastated by the report and confidentially vowed to his regional Directors that no person on the planet would lack "living necessities." Xi Fang, the Vice Secretary-General, argued that this "mushy approach" would weaken the sanctions. A compromise was met and the plan for bribing informants with saleable living necessities was hatched. There were hundreds of informants selling GFN-manufactured goods like bread and water and antibiotics to people that hated The Federation.

This informant program had considerable drawbacks. Lt. Director Luna thought about Ramirez's situation. Locally, "Ramirez the Rat" had a very loyal workforce that was known to be violent and well-armed. If it was revealed that the uranium-miner-turned-medical-supplier was a Federation informant, there would be outrage. Ramirez, his family and employees, and many innocent, sick people would die. Many within the GFN disagreed with these deals as well. They believed the intel received from informants was not valuable enough to make such amoral men rich. Also, looking through a less-humane lens, they despised the idea of providing living necessities to those they viewed as enemies of the GFN. Lt. Director Juan Carlos Luna was one of these staunch opponents of such deals.

Jones parked the SUV in front of the sprawling porch and the men stepped out with their TS-33s tight against their ribs inside their jackets. A young Mexican girl sat in a rocking chair as her small bare feet dangled high above the wooden porch.

Luna smiled and waved at the girl.

"*¿Tú papá aquí?*" He called, and she ran into the house.

The men stood on the porch by the open door while the small girl fetched Ramirez.

A few minutes later, a fat man in a light, polyester jumpsuit walked outside.

"*Joder!* Luna! Thee fuck you doing here?"

"Raul!" Luna responded as he walked past the fat man into the house. He pointed to the girl that had been sitting on the porch. She was hiding behind one of Ramirez's thick legs. "She one of yours? *Que linda.*"

Ramirez chuckled. "Ah Christ, who knows? *Venemos*, come in, come in."

He led the men to his study.

"I can't have you *pendejos* storming in here, man. I got face to keep. I got neighbors. I got kids, yeah?"

Luna sat down in a deep leather chair and took out his pipe. "You don't have to act all hard in front of us, *Graso.*"

Ramirez lunged at Luna, his eyes burning with hate and his index finger inches from the pipe. Owens restrained him, and Jones leveled his rifle at his chest. Luna tsk'ed and waved the hand that clutched the pipe.

"No, no, *Graso*, not here. You don't want that faucet to turn off, do you? Where else would you get money for your little tribe here? Even worse, you don't want those neighbors knowing your *La Federación's soplón*, huh? To be honest, I would love to put the word out and watch those animals rip you apart. But it's not that time. Not yet, so sit the fuck down."

Ramirez lowered himself back into a chair while Amir Owens shut the thick office doors.

Luna puffed his pipe and blew a cloud of smoke high into the air where it flattened as it hit the mirrored ceiling.

"You calm?"

Ramirez nodded.

"Good. Fifteen million dollars in vaccinations will be at your disposal when you give me what I want."

Ramirez eyed Luna, then looked at the other two men in the room.

"Okay," he said and took out a thick cigar. "What do you need from me?"

Noah ate a full tray of food. Once he was finished, he followed Wade to the exit of the cafeteria. The cafeteria was less crowded than it had been when he had first entered. After he deposited his tray at the cleaning station, Noah turned quickly and crashed into another inmate. The man's half-eaten tray flipped and splattered food on Noah and Wade's bright colored shirts.

"Watch it, asshole!" the man snarled at Noah.

Noah was frozen. Stevens and Newsome crowded around the collision. Wade stepped in the middle.

"Easy, brother," he said to the man. Wade pointed at Noah; dressing stuck to his neck and fusilli clung to his shirt. "This man is not your enemy."

The man glared at Wade, then looked Noah up and down. He stepped through the men and muttered, "Asshole needs to learn to walk."

Noah let out a deep breath. He hadn't realized he'd been holding the air in. *How am I ever going to make it here?*

"Come," Wade brushed the pasta off Noah's chest. "We'll get you cleaned up."

Noah looked at the mess of food on himself. The yellow was darkened by a splatter of peach juice from above his navel to the waistband of his pants. He then looked at Wade as a piece of salad fell from his beard onto his blue shirt. A group of men in green tops walked by.

"Why the different colors?" Noah asked, but Wade had already started out of the cafeteria. As Aiden Stevens bumped past Noah, he answered out the side of his mouth. "Threat assessment."

Noah followed Wade and Stevens out the exit and into a long hallway. Inmates loitered against the wall. There were no guards in sight.

"They just let you go wherever you want?"

Newsome made a wide circle with his finger. "They know where we are."

Noah saw several small cameras mounted on the walls.

"With so few guards, can't we just overpower them? We must outnumber them at least ten-to-one. There must be some blind spots here. Wade, you said there was a plan to get out of here. Is that the plan?" Noah grew excited at the prospect of freedom.

Stevens turned around and spoke to Noah, backpedaling down the hallway.

"A few months back, some of the guys in here thought the same thing. They were well organized, too. Sixty-odd bulls spent a week making weapons out of shit laying around here. They thought they had found the blind spots where they could make and hide the weapons. No one stopped them as they amassed an arsenal of spears and clubs. They even manufactured a cache of bombs out of hydrochloric acid from toilet bowl cleaner and tin foil from the kitchen. Still no one was questioned. No one was caught.

"Early one morning, before sunrise, the men converged on the yard. There were no guards outside. They targeted the interrogation building. They had heard that would lead them to the armory. It took them less than a minute to place and arm their homemade bombs. There were no alarms. After the blast, the men rushed the smoking gap in the wall. The guards were inside.

Waiting. Fully armed. Twenty men went down in the first wave.
A few seconds. The rest scattered into the yard. Turrets, hidden
in the building and ground mowed down the rest. Fifty-six men
were killed in forty-five seconds. The others died of their wounds
later that day. Next time you're out in the yard, look at the wall
of the interrogation building. There won't be a scratch on it."

"Jesus," Noah said softly.

Wade stopped and hit Noah in the chest with the back of
his hand.

"Hey!" he said while his hand still pushed on Noah.

The impact hadn't hurt Noah, but it certainly surprised him.
Wade's face was red. For the first time since he had learned
of their mission, Noah saw his brother-in-law angry. He then
remembered how he had heard Wade declare his disgust at blasphemy. Before Noah could apologize, Wade had waved his hand
in front of his face.

"Take off your shirt."

Noah was confused. "What?"

"I'm going to get you cleaned up." Wade opened a door leading into a restroom.

The car ride from the Nejems' to the Lincoln County Police
Headquarters in Chandler was quiet; the silence was only broken
by the coded messages on the police scanner. Upon arrival, Officer Morales led Natalie to a small room off the garage. The room
was furnished with a metal table and four metal chairs, nothing
else. Officer Greene went to the vending machines and fetched
three cups of tea.

Morales pulled out a chair for Natalie to sit in, then took a
seat opposite her. A few seconds later, Greene appeared, placed
two cups on the table, and sat next to Natalie. He blew on the
hot tea and took a sip.

"Now, Ms. Kelley, before we get started, I'd like to inform you that our conversation in this room is being recorded. Is that okay?"

"Yeah, of course."

"Okay, good. Now," Greene looked at Natalie's identification screen on his APD, "would you pronounce and spell your last name please?"

Natalie pronounced and spelled her last name for the two officers. Then she told them her occupation and employer and told them what she was doing in Oklahoma City. She told them about her initial meeting with Faye Nejem yesterday and she told them how she ended up at the house again today. The officers listened patiently and didn't press Natalie on any points. They let her dictate the flow of the conversation. After ten minutes, the officers stopped asking questions and Natalie was told that she could leave.

Recounting her experience of the previous two days cleared Natalie's mind and her journalistic instincts returned. Before she rose from the chair, she had some questions of her own.

"You're sure that Mrs. Nejem committed suicide?"

Officer Morales took the lead.

"Right now, suicide is the leading candidate for cause of Mrs. Nejem's death. There will be an autopsy performed today to see if there are any signs of trauma apart from the cause of death."

"So, any signs besides the injury to her throat?"

"Yes."

"Like, what? Bruises on her arms or wrists? Would it show any sedatives?"

Morales seemed slightly annoyed. Before she could answer, Greene spoke.

"It will be a complete autopsy."

"Did you see any signs of an intruder when searching the house?"

Morales growled to herself. "Just you."

Greene cast a glare at his partner and spoke to Natalie. His voice was tired. "Look, Ms. Kelley. I've been a cop for twenty-five years. Suicide is a major problem. You said it yourself that the woman was mourning and lonely. We'll do our due diligence, but I'm sure that our final report will say that Mrs. Nejem killed herself."

Natalie stood up to leave but stopped as a thought struck her. "What did the security footage show?"

Morales tucked her hair behind her ear and looked at Greene. "Unfortunately, during construction in a neighboring lot, the power was cut to all the homes in the neighborhood. So, we don't have any recordings of the incident."

Natalie placed her hands on the back of the chair, leaned forward, and breathed deeply.

"That doesn't strike you as suspicious? Or at the very least odd?"

Greene shook his head and finished his tea. He drummed his fingers against the side of the cup.

"No. It doesn't strike me as suspicious. Orwell's Blazer, right? Easiest answer's the best one?"

"Occam's Razor," Natalie corrected, softly and mostly to herself.

"What's that?" Greene asked.

"I just don't think she would kill herself."

"I'm sorry to say it, Ms. Kelley, but you hardly knew this woman. You have no idea what she would or wouldn't do."

"I just didn't get that feeling from her." Natalie was becoming stubborn to the point of annoyance. She knew that the officer's assessment of their relationship was accurate, but she *felt* that Faye wouldn't kill herself. She shook her head. "I just don't think she'd do that."

Officer Morales was silent. Officer Greene sat forward and folded his hands on the table.

"We found a suicide video on her APD, Ms. Kelley."

"Fuck." Natalie pulled her hair back, so it was taut against her head. "Jesus Christ." She let her hair fall back down, laying softly on her shoulders.

"Can I see it?"

Officer Morales shook her head. "No. I'm sorry."

Natalie walked to that door and it opened automatically. "Will you let me know what the autopsy finds?"

The black Suburban left the canyon estate, its cargo consisting of Lt. Director Luna, Chief Deputy Lt. Director Jones, Deputy Lt. Director Owens, and a newly acquired list of names gifted by Raul Ramirez. Luna recognized about half of the twenty-some names on the list of individuals that were most likely to attempt to disrupt the signing between the AFG and the GFN. He would put Jones and Owens in charge of tracking down, questioning, and keeping tabs on most of the names over the next two weeks. Today however, there was one name that Luna wished to pay a personal visit.

Peter Whetstone was known as "the Atom Bomb" for his explosive temperament and was a well-known and vocal opponent of The Federation. Before the American Congress approved the Treaty on The Global Federation in 2057, Whetstone served as the congressional representative for New Mexico's second district. In Congress, he was best known for authoring a pair of anti-immigration bills. The first was known as the American Castle Bill. In the American Castle Bill, Whetstone proposed that the United States build a series of moats and battlements along the nearly thirty-two-hundred-kilometer border between the United States and Mexico. The second bill that he was notorious for authoring was officially called the Illegal Alien Criminal Solutions Act but was dubbed the "Slavery Re-Institution Act" by the left. Whetstone proposed that, instead of deportation or even imprisonment, illegal immigrants convicted of a crime would enter forced labor camps to work on government projects for an undetermined amount of time. States could also sell illegal immigrants' work rights to private corporations, with no wages going to the workers. Whetstone's home state of New Mexico, being on the southern border, was set to gain a tremendous profit from this act. Neither the American Castle Bill nor the Slavery Re-Institution Act sniffed a vote on the Senate floor, but Whetstone made a name for himself among jingoists and xenophobes. In a last-ditch effort, on 14 December 2056, the fiery congressman made an impassioned speech on the House floor on behalf of the opponents of what he called "the surrender." Whetstone's fiery speech was not enough to overcome the concessions gained in the Savannah Conference and Congress passed the resolution to adapt the Basic Human Standard and join the GFN with a vote 323 "FOR" and 112 "AGAINST".

Mexico had joined The Federation in 2054, three years before the United States. Once the Mexican government adopted the BHS, illegal immigration to America dropped to nearly zero. Whetstone, his career objective accomplished without any personal contribution, turned his full attention toward distancing the American government from The Federation and returning to a period of isolation. On 10 February 2057, as President Madison Harris affirmed the ratification of the constitutional act to join the GFN, Whetstone, two of the other three New Mexico congressional representatives, six of eleven Arizona congressional representatives, and the congresswoman from Colorado's third district moved from Washington to Santa Fe to establish what they called the New American Desert State. Whetstone, in a special election among a group of "appointed representatives" was unanimously voted the first Governor of this new state. He appointed close political allies to key positions within the new state.

The Desert State existed with little interference from the NASO and had been declared a Black Zone. As such, it experienced economic embargo but little military intervention. After ten years of governorship, Whetstone announced that he was stepping down. Rumor had it that he suffered from a progressing yet undisclosed neurological disease. His lieutenant-governor and long-time Chief of Staff, Curtis Sheets, succeeded him in the top position without a vote, but Whetstone remained a looming figure in the governing of the NADS. After thirteen years of sovereign and dictatorial rule and drastic economic decline, many NADS communities pledged allegiance to the democratic AFG or declared themselves to be outside any large, governing body. The NADS could barely function. Hundreds of schools had closed. Infrastructure was crumbling. Inflation was soaring, and crime was rampant. In 2070, seeing no other options, Sheets announced that the NADS would consider working with The Federation due to the disastrous state of the region's economy. Whetstone was beyond furious.

In a series of tirades, Whetstone compared Sheets to Judas, Brutus, and Satan himself.

He accused the Governor of personally receiving hundreds of millions of dollars in kickbacks for joining The Federation. He called for "any loyal American to eliminate that sonuvabitch." Because he knew of Whetstone's fanatical public following, Sheets called upon him to meet and discuss the best path forward for the people of the NADS. Without even taking his seat, Whetstone physically assaulted Sheets with a walking stick. He was detained by the Governor's staff and exiled to Los Alamos, home of the Manhattan Project. Sheets said of the exile that, "the atom bomb was born there and now the Atom Bomb will die there."

After Whetstone's exile, he called for a citizen's mutiny against a government that no longer had their interests at heart. There were violent protests in the streets of Santa Fe, Albuquerque, Durango, and Tucson. At least two hundred people were killed.

As the riot in Santa Fe climaxed, a Molotov cocktail flew onto the roof of Governor Sheets's house. From inside the besieged residence, he made a plea to the rioters to stop. He conceded to their demands, reversed course, and stated that the people of the NADS would never work with The Federation. This had been Whetstone's last public political action and it had been a victory. Though statements were released from Los Alamos that were attributed to the former congressman, he was never seen in public again. Many speculated that his neurological disorder had finally gotten the best of the old warrior, but others believed he bided his time to make a final effort toward restoring American sovereignty.

Lt. Director Juan Carlos Luna knew what the man could be capable of, so he had never dismissed the rumors of his continued defiance. Rumors that his exiled home of Los Alamos was now a militarized compound. Rumors that he was building an army.

Luna had experience with militias and terrorists that pledged their loyalty to the ravings of Peter Whetstone, so he knew how powerful the man could be. It was now time to test the rumors, to see just what the old bastard had been doing the past few years. There was no concrete intelligence confirming that Whetstone was even still alive, let alone controlling a militarized force. Still, the Atom Bomb mythos made his heart beat a little faster.

As the SUV bounced along the potted highway, he asked Owens for another clip from the supply case.

"Many people say they found God, Noah, and that could be. But the truth in my case is that God found me."

The faucet in the bathroom was running full-blast. The water pounded against the porcelain basin. Wade stuck Noah's yellow shirt under the water and scrubbed the stained area with a worn, wool pad.

"God found me at my lowest point. As a teenager, I used and dealt pot and melt in New Orleans. I was peddling unregistered 3D guns to gang bangers. I beat a man within an inch of his life when he tried to short me. I was sentenced to ten years at the Louisiana State Penitentiary in Angelo. I fought and got high for two of those years. Then, one night, I heard the voice of God."

Wade removed his own stained shirt and placed it under the water. His chest and stomach and ribs were covered with scars. Noah stared at the gnarled skin.

"The Lord said that I was to be his vessel and that I needed to purify myself physically and spiritually. That night, in my bunk, I sharpened my fingernails and clawed away all the sinful ink I had desecrated my body with. Then I began to read the Words of God. All of them. The Old and New Testaments. The Quran. The Gnostic Gospels. The Book of Mormon. And after reading these texts and following the Voice of God, I knew what I needed to do. These scars," Wade ran his hands over the torn ridges of his torso, "are a reminder of my wicked past."

Noah couldn't believe what he was hearing. He couldn't believe what he was seeing. He had always considered his relationship with God as a personal one, but he had never had an experience like the one his brother-in-law was describing.

Wade wrung the shirts out in the sink, then placed them under the hand dryer.

Over the roar of the dryer, Wade yelled to Noah.

"This," Wade pointed around the bathroom, at the walls of the processing facility, "this is but a road block. We will not be here long. God will guide us. He will guide you, Noah. You, too, are His vessel. There is a reason you are in this place. What is to be done, will be done."

Wade handed Noah his shirt back. The stain was gone, but the shirt was still damp. He put it on. The wet fabric clung to him.

"What do you need me to do, Wade?"
"Tell them the truth. Tell them everything."

Natalie was lost in thought until the police cruiser stopped in front of the Nejem residence. Yellow police tape wrapped around the yard. She left the cruiser quickly and walked to her electrocycle. Parked behind her bike was a forensic van; Natalie didn't look to see if there was anyone in the van, nor did she look at the orphaned house. She mounted the bike, backed out of the drive, and sped away from the Nejems' and out of the nascent neighborhood. She turned off the vehicle's computer. The bike tore down the highway back into the bustling city. Natalie weaved through traffic and flew down the road aggressively.

Natalie concentrated solely on guiding the sportbike. She blocked out any thoughts of Faye's dead body. She blocked out any thoughts of her father, lifeless on the cement sidewalk of Millennium Park. She pulled the throttle toward her and the bike accelerated. A red light blinked on the dash which signified that the electrocycle was traveling at dangerous speeds. Natalie ignored the warnings.

When she reached her hotel, she did not stop. Without destination, she drove the electrocycle and whizzed through the shade of the buildings above. She tried to drive away from the ghosts of her past, but they stalked her, stuck to her no matter where she turned or how fast she drove.

Her father. Her father. His face. The memories flashed before her eyes. His face. Alive one moment. Dead the next. The blood spilling from his body like a pierce in a dam, staining the ground, flowing, flowing, never ebbing back.

Natalie did not notice that she had closed her eyes. The electrocycle's computer system screamed at her and the emergency brakes tightened quickly. There was a screech as the bike skidded, which caused her to jostle forward. Her stomach rammed against the handlebars. The air left her body. A stationary truck was parked twenty meters ahead. From the back of the truck, drones were busy unloading boxes and flying them into the nearby buildings. The passersby on the street stood still and waited for a collision. The bike finally stopped a few meters short of the truck. A long, black tire mark snaked down the street behind the now-resting vehicle. Embarrassed, Natalie paddled her toes against the cement, eased the bike past the truck, and disappeared around the nearest corner. Her abs ached. Her heart pounded against her chest cavity. As she held her stomach, she parked the electrocycle and dismounted.

She removed her helmet and dropped it onto the pavement. Natalie sat on the curb and wept.

Out the passenger window of the black Suburban, Lt. Director Luna watched as the abandoned homes and businesses of the town formerly known as White Rock appeared and vanished out of view. Each edifice had been stripped of any useful materials and the mountain vegetation had advanced quickly in the hollowed shells of buildings. The Suburban bounced and dipped on the cracked and scarred road, its suspension straining at each crater. The road worsened and forced Jones to slow to a crawl. After half a klick of devastated pavement, he left the road and drove through the sage. A pack of stray dogs emerged from a beaten barn and chased the car. The mass of mangled fur sprinted through the brush, yipping and barking, for a few hundred meters before they finally retreated to their den.

Luna and his Deputies approached Los Alamos. The group had put their fatigues back on and had been silent for much of the ride. Ahead of them, the road was blocked by a series of three K-rails that were covered in graffiti. The message "TRESPASSERS

WILL BE SHOT ON SIGHT!" spanned the length of the K-rails. Surrounding this warning were the stars and bars of the ancient American Confederacy, fascist European insignia from the twentieth century, and the Blue Ox symbol of twenty-first century American fascism. Jones steered the SUV back onto the ragged road and stopped fifty meters before the barrier.

"Not a very high-tech perimeter," Jones remarked, and Luna nodded.

"Be alert," he commanded his men.

The trio stepped out of the Suburban, their fingers on the triggers of their weapons. There was no one in sight. Luna called out to the desolation to announce that he was a Federation Security Officer. He wanted whoever might be listening to know that if there was an incident, there would be hell to pay. There was no answer.

He checked his body-cam to make sure it was working and led Jones and Owens forward until they stood directly in front of the K-rails. Luna called out again.

"I am Lt. Director Juan Carlos Luna! I am here on behalf of the North American Security Office of The Global Federation of Nations! I am here to speak to Peter Whetstone!"

The men waited, their rifles ready. The only reply came from a nearby meadowlark which sang and bounced on the ground.

Luna shouted again.

"I am Lt. Director Juan Carlos—"

There was a great smash against the K-rail and concrete dust exploded into the sky, where it briefly floated before it was ushered off by the wind. The men ducked behind the K-rail.

Luna used the wireless microphone on the lapel of his jacket.

"You are shooting at Security Officers of The Global Federation of Nations, goddamnit. I urge you *not* to fire another shot. We are here to speak with Peter Whetstone."

There was another whish and collision against the K-rail. After the echo of the crash subsided, a man yelled from somewhere inside the isolated town.

"Listen, you dirty fuckin' beaner! You're not gonna step foot here! This land is independent! You got no authority here! Only Euro-Americans can walk on this ground. If you want to talk to Mister Whetstone, you and your nigger boy are gonna have to go home."

There was another pop and another slam against the K-rail.

"Only one-hundred percent bona fide Caucasians are gonna be talkin' with Mister Whetstone!"

Luna looked at Owens; his smile stretched the scar on his face. "Shall we waste him?" he asked as he raised an eyebrow. He spoke only mostly in jest.

"Fuck it. Let's get out of here," Owens replied.

"Goddamn trash," Luna muttered. Then he turned to his top Deputy, still crouched behind the K-rail. "Arnie, designate two STAB units to come back here. We don't have time for this shit. Surveillance, no breach. Confirm they aren't a threat to the treaty. I'd wager they don't even know what the hell's going on outside these walls." Luna peeked over the concrete edge. "Once the treaty's signed, we'll make sure to come back and take care of these racist shit-birds."

Luna then spoke into the lapel microphone again.

"We are going to stand up and move back to our vehicle. If you fire one more shot, we are going to have to respond. Do you understand?"

There was no answer.

"Do you understand?"

"Just get the fuck outta here, you monkeys!" came the reply.

The three SOs rose and walked backward toward the Suburban, their weapons alert. They could not see the man who had been shooting and shouting at them.

Once they stepped back into the vehicle, they relaxed the TS-33s.

Jones drove the vehicle over the curb, turned it around, and drove south away from Los Alamos.

"Where the hell was everyone?" Owens asked from the backseat. "I thought he was supposed to have a following of thousands. It was a fucking ghost town there. Where the hell *was* everyone?"

Luna looked back at the abandoned town. Though they had just been shot at, he felt relief.

"I think the old congressman may have finally lost his grip."

As the Suburban rocked over the rough landscape, the three men began to laugh at the ghost town. At the lone sentinel. At Whetstone. At the absurdity of hate.

The prison yard at Forrest City was occupied by all two hundred eighty-two "residents" of the processing facility. A few minutes before they were gathered, the lights throughout the complex had turned light blue and a woman's voice commanded the men to move to the yard in an orderly fashion.

Noah was tense. He had been in the chapel with Wade when they were told to move to the yard. Noah had risen immediately, but Wade continued to pray. Barrineau didn't budge from the pew until two guards entered with TS-33s. Now, joined by Stevens and Newsome, the men stood in the middle of the nervous inmates. The air was cool as the slipping sun hid behind cinder clouds. The murmurs of the prisoners bounced along the walls of the grey yard.

The number of visible armed and uniformed guards increased ten-fold as the men waited in the yard. Whatever was happening, they wanted to make sure they had the detainees under control. Per the chatter in the yard, most of the men seemed to think that there was going to be a mass announcement made, the implementation of a new, major policy. Noah heard one man, his voice shaky, loudly express his fear that they were about to be exterminated, gunned down by the guards above. Noah's gut tightened, and he turned to Newsome as the man's apocalyptic fervor grew. Newsome furrowed his brow, shook his head, and dismissed the man.

They kept waiting in the yard. The predictions and speculation grew louder and more exaggerated. The competing voices swelled until a man standing near Noah yelled.

"Shut up! Shut up! Everybody just shut up!"

The inmates obeyed, and the yard grew silent.

Noah could hear a distant hum. It grew louder and nearer. It was a helicopter. The guards on the rail overlooking the yard stiffened. Three guards left the catwalk. The others adjusted their positions to cover the newly vacant ground.

Noah spoke, to no one and everyone. "Are they taking one of us away?"

"No," Newsome answered, "they're bringing someone in."

The inmates all turned toward the helipad. Noah could not see over the heads and buildings and fences and trees. He grabbed the shoulders in front of him and hoisted himself up, but still could not see the source of the noise. A few moments later, the noise from the chopper flatlined.

Noah leaned over close to Wade. "Who do you think it is?"

Wade shrugged his shoulders. He looked bored. The crowd grew louder. They yelled at the guards above, searching for answers.

"Who? WHO?!" they screamed. They feared it was someone they knew or, worse, someone they idolized.

The men standing in front of Noah were furious. They suspected that the high-profile detainee was a man named Augie Rook. Rook was wanted for the bombing of the Ellie Caulkins Opera House in Denver during a performance of William Tell three years ago. One hundred seventy-eight men and women were killed. Another three hundred ninety-six were injured. Rook was presumed to have retreated to a network of caves in the Sawatch Range. He was the leader of a fringe terrorist organization known as the Liberation Grizzlies of the West. In addition to fighting STAB units in the Grey Zone and orchestrating a few small bombings on the West Coast, for the past six months the LGW had engaged in skirmishes with the American Freedom Army. In videos Noah had watched online, Grizzly lieutenants claimed that the Freedom Army was just a front for NASO. Noah wondered if he had seen any of these men in the videos.

Noah leaned close to Wade again.

"Who do you think it is?"

Wade looked at the dirt of the yard, then at Noah. "It doesn't matter."

"What do you mean, 'it doesn't matter'?"

"I mean, it doesn't matter. It could be anyone. It could be Rook. It could be John Hill. It could be George Washington, risen from the ground of Mount Vernon. It does not matter. They want us to guess. They want us to believe it is the person closest to us. They want us to think it is the man we admire the most." Barrineau summoned a glob of mucus from the back of his throat and fired it at the dirt. "It's all a game, Noah. Pretty smart, really. Misinformation is the most powerful information. The truth is never shocking. It may be surprising for a second, but it is soon accepted by the conscience. There soon comes a point where that shocking bit of earth-shattering information seems like it always was. Incomplete information, well, that festers. That can drive a person mad. I'd bet they're in there processing a specter. I'd bet there is no high-profile detainee."

With that, Wade walked through the crowd and to the far end of the yard where he sat on the cool earth. Noah followed.

Once Natalie ran out of tears, she wiped the remaining wet-ness from her cheeks and rose from the curb. She looked around.

She had parked the electrocycle in the shadow of a large brick church. The bulk of the church rose to a ridge, like a barn. A tall bell tower sat on the vaulted roof at the front of the church. The bell tower was flanked by two stubby, crenellated towers, one on each side. Natalie admired the church as she walked around it. Back at the front steps, there was a sign that announced that the church was St. Joseph's Old Cathedral.

Natalie climbed the stairs, opened the dark wood doors, and walked into the Cathedral. She had not been inside a church since her father's murder. After fourteen years, she felt that now was a good time to have a word with God.

She walked to the front of the cathedral and sat in the first pew. She stared at the small gold crucifix against the pink backdrop. *Why,* she thought, *why the fuck have You done this to me? You gave Your Son, but You took my father from me. In front of me. You shoved this ugly world right down my throat when I was still just a kid. He was the only man I have ever loved. And You took him from me.*

She waited for the tears to come again, but they did not. Her face was red with anger.

Natalie felt a large hand rest upon her shoulder.

Lost in thought, she jumped at the touch.

"I didn't mean to startle you, dear."

The hand belonged to the cathedral's priest. He was a tall, lean, black man with short, cropped white hair, and a white goatee. He had long ears that hung from the sides of his long face.

"Are you here to give confession?" he asked, his tongue thick with a West African accent.

Natalie shook her head. "No. No. Thank you, though."

"Do you mind if I sit down and pray with you, child?"

Natalie slid to her right and the old man eased himself into the pew.

The journalist and the priest sat in silence. Natalie bounced her leg, anxiously. The priest's cologne was strong. He was still next to her, his head bowed slightly, his eyes closed, and his hands intertwined in his lap.

"You're not comfortable next to me?" he asked, after some time. "The pew moves as if there is an earthquake."

Natalie laughed, then quickly covered her mouth.

"It's not that. I—" she trailed off, "it's been some time since I was here. In a church, I mean."

The priest nodded as if that was exactly what he expected.

"You are a Catholic?"

"Yes. Well, I was."

"You will always be a Catholic, my dear. Even if you don't want to be."

Natalie thought for a moment. "That's an unsettling thought."

"It is not meant to be. You have been washed in the waters of the Church," the priest rubbed the back of his hand on the whiskers of his chin. "I only mean that you will always be one of God's children. Even when you are angry at God."

"I'm not angry at God," Natalie quickly retorted. She sunk her shoulders at the weight of the lie.

"Child, I do not know what ails you. And even if I did, I doubt I could help. I am a stranger in a collar to you."

Natalie was surprised by the man's frankness.

"I will only tell you this: your being here, in this church, it is a good thing. You are searching for answers and that is always a good thing."

The priest's chocolate eyes were soft as they looked at Natalie.

"Now, will you make an old man's day and say a prayer with him?"

The priest's hand was extended toward Natalie, his palm up. Natalie gave him her hand; the priest's giant mitt wrapped around her whole palm and the two bowed their heads.

"Our Father, who art in Heaven…"

CHAPTER SIX

12 May 2072

Lt. Director Juan Carlos Luna and his Deputies had been working in Santa Fe for a week and the town had noticed their presence. Over the past seven days, the number of Federationists temporarily residing in the city had risen to nearly two hundred. The Railyard Inn continued to function as the Fed's HQ and had turned on their "No Vacancy" sign for the first time in fifteen years. Since the motel was at capacity, RVs were parked in the lot for the overflow of Federationists and visitors.

Luna and his team had started the false rumor that The Federationists were in Santa Fe searching for a fugitive serial killer. The Lt. Director had even assigned a team of Security Officers to conduct a faux investigation and question people in the area regarding the whereabouts of the fugitive. The man the team sought was a real serial killer named Grayson Gills, who was suspected of murdering five women along the eastern seaboard, but Luna knew that they would not find the killer in Santa Fe. Intelligence indicated that he was decomposing in the basement of an illegal casino in Baltimore's Koreatown.

The people of Santa Fe were beginning to question the GFN's presence, but tonight the charade would come to an end. At 19:00 EST, Secretary-General Antoine Dubois would announce that the American Freedom Group would soon ratify the Treaty on Global Nations. Although the last week had been busy for Juan Carlos Luna, he knew that it would be nothing compared to the chaos he would face after the announcement. A flood of protesters, agitators, supporters, and media would descend upon Santa Fe. He expected the town to nearly double in size.

However, it was not the mobs that worried Luna. He knew that his team could control the crowds and that they could never disrupt the signing. What concerned the Lt. Director were the men named on Raul Ramirez's list. His team had only been able to locate eight of the twenty-three names. NASO databases listed each of the located individuals as "Green" or "Yellow" threat levels which meant that the SOs agreed that none posed a serious threat. Of the missing fifteen people, seven were deemed highest-level, or "Blue" threat levels. It concerned Luna that these six men and one woman were apparently phantoms. Locals claimed that each of the "Blues" had died, but gossip that regarded terrorists' state-of-life was always popular. *After the announcement*, Luna thought, *we'll have more terriers to hunt these* fantasmas de ratas.

In addition to securing Santa Fe for the treaty signing, Luna attempted to continue his normal duties as Lt. Director of Border Integrity. Although he had relegated much of the work to his Deputies that remained at The Mount, he continued to monitor their progress. Second only to the treaty signing was the situation in Texas regarding the detained Brazilians. He had been in communication with General Brandt Bonner of the Texas Military Brigade over the last week but had learned little. Still none of the detainees had talked. The tunnels had been completely mapped and the submarine tested, but those investigations yielded little information. Luna ordered Bonner to keep the men in Texas for the time being. He did not want the GFCoJ's strict human-rights guidelines to harness the interrogation of the men. A member of the South American Security Office was traveling to the holding facility in Galveston to work as an advisor to the Brigade. Outside of Luna and the Deputy from SASO, there would be no other Federation interference for the time being.

Luckily, besides the detention of the Brazilians and the constant skirmishes of the Grey Zone, it had been a relatively slow week for NASO. Although outside of his Border Integrity jurisdiction, Luna continued to read memos regarding incidents that occurred within the White Zone. The most severe included a fifteen-year-old boy in Harrisburg, Pennsylvania. The teen stabbed six other teenagers with a steak knife at a local swim club. He killed one of the victims. His mother had told the teen that his father had died in a construction accident when the boy was an infant. In truth, the mother had left the boy's abusive father. The teen then conducted research on his father and discovered that he was alive in Nunavet for terroristic actions against The Federation. Angry and full of new levels of testosterone, he lashed out "in the name of America and his father." In order to stop the attack, one of the other swimmers present at the club tackled the young perpetrator into the pool and drowned him. Other reports included a woman in Santiago, Cuba, who tried to drive her car into a Federation supply convoy and a group of bandits in Monterrey that attempted to breach a Federation ammunition depot. In both cases, the suspects were detained before they could complete their crimes.

Luna had been getting up at 05:00 every morning. Last night, he had enjoyed his first substantial talk with Jay since he left, so he did not get to sleep until after midnight. Today, he didn't wake until 06:30. The first thing he did was go for a run across town. During the run, he replayed the conversation he had with Jay the night before. He missed his husband; Jay was apolitical, and Luna loved that about him. He would offer Juan Carlos unwavering support and assurance regarding the success of the signing, without being bogged down by the ethics and principles of the act—that was all the business they would discuss. As he jogged to the old municipal airport, Luna pictured Jay doing the mundane daily activities that he missed. After a week of eighteen-hour days, Luna had felt worn down, but last night, awash in the voice of his love, he felt refreshed.

After he got ready, he had his daily Deputy huddle at the capitol. Luna liked to have these meetings in the building to familiarize his team with the surroundings and to remind them of the weight of their mission. After the huddle, Luna went back to the Railyard Inn to conduct general Border Security business. He spoke with Bonner and was glad to hear that his friend from the Rio HQ, Javi Glas, was helping the TMB. He also spoke to a STAB unit commander in El Salvador who lost an SO during a raid on a drug compound north of San Miguel.

Finally, he and Chief Deputy Jones met to appraise the status of the nearest STAB unit's current missions. It had been determined that ten full STAB units would be brought out of PPOs to offer additional security to the signing. Which units would be deployed to Santa Fe would be determined by which were in the best position to leave their Prep Period Ops. It looked like Andre Cannon and STAB Unit IX-6 would be one of the special forces teams assisting in the protection of the signing. Lt. Director Luna was excited to see his nephew. By the time Dubois arrived in Santa Fe, Cannon would be just one of two thousand Federationists in the city. Although there would be too much work and too many people, Luna would try to make some time to visit the boy's unit. Luna and Jones had finished their appraisal and had selected the ten STAB units that would be moved to protection detail. Barring any major developments, the commanders of those ten units would be alerted tomorrow.

Luna and Arnie left the Railyard Inn to pick up lunch from a street vendor. They ate and smoked and talked. During their meal, Lt. Director Luna kept looking at his watch. The Secretary-General would make his announcement in five hours. There would be a massive amount of pressure on the city and the man, but Luna could not wait.

It had only taken a day for Xavier Lau to deconstruct the image of the painter. The portrait provided was unrecognizable to Natalie, but Xavier was an expert in additive facial construction. In addition to being a craniofacial surgeon at Cedars-Sinai Medical Center, Lau was employed by studios to construct facial alterations for Hollywood's theatre district. Over the past week, Natalie had run Xavier's portrait through every database that she had access. She found zero results—the man did not exist. Natalie sent Xavier another message hoping for a second deconstruction, but he was in New York working on the facial designs for a Broadway musical called *George W. Bush: Space Cowboy*.

After she had found Faye Nejem's body, Natalie took the earliest flight back to Chicago. She spent a few days looking for more evidence to sustain her "second shooter" theory, but there was little she could find. She reached out to the Dotson family, but they offered no comment. She contacted the building manager, but she said that they had no record of hiring a painter for the second-floor office. Natalie could not reach anyone at the company that the painted office was rented to. She talked to local law enforcement and witnesses, but no one hinted at the idea of a conspiracy. After four days of dead ends regarding The Bucket Bistro attack, a swell of rumors rushed through the *Tribune* offices. Speculation was that the American Freedom Group would soon be signing the Treaty on Global Federation. Natalie had anticipated this development.

While she had concentrated her work on the activities of the American Freedom Army and she dove deeper into the AFG's activities and member's private online statements, Natalie grew to believe that the AFG's envelopment by the GFN was inevitable. She often alluded to this inevitability in her articles. As a governing body, the AFG was a failure and as their government fractured and weakened, the attacks by the AFA became less common and less gruesome. Natalie had believed that John Hill and the American Freedom Group leadership were secretly preparing for negotiations with Secretary-General Dubois and American President Alton Wilson. With the recent increase of speculation of the same, it appeared that Natalie had been correct.

Natalie was apathetic regarding the treaty. She knew that an agreement between the two parties would not mean instant peace. On the contrary, she feared that an official partnership between the GFN and the AFG would create a vacuum of power for dissidents and, until the Grey Zones were completely secured by NASO, that void would most likely be filled by a more militant organization, such as the Liberation Grizzlies of the West or the Uberti Cattlemen. After fifteen years of living in a libertarian haven, there were plenty of pissed off people that would revolt against paying any liberal taxes, especially those to The Global Federation.

However, politics did not much interest Natalie; it was the people that interested her.

Most of the journalists that worked for the *Chicago Tribune* did so remotely, but Natalie liked working from Tribune Tower. She liked the office. She liked the view. She liked the sanctity of her desk and, most of all, she liked the thin, liver-spotted editor, Joseph Kalani.

Natalie sat in his corner office now and he asked her what she had uncovered in Oklahoma City. She admitted that she was at an impasse. She did not tell her editor about the second-shooter theory. She realized that she needed more before she could vocalize it.

Natalie laid out a preliminary outline that detailed the history of the AFG. If, or when, the treaty was announced, she wanted to put together a series of profiles on the key players of the signing. As they talked, Joseph received a message from the

Press Secretary of the North American Branch of The Global Federation of Nations: Secretary-General Antoine Dubois and President Alton Wilson would be making a joint-statement this evening from New York. Joseph read the message to Natalie, then smiled.

"This time, the gossip appears to be true."

Inside the walls of Forrest City, time marched on the same as it had in the wide-open spaces of North Texas. Noah had not expected this. He thought that life as a captive would be fundamentally different than his life before, but he was surprised to find that it was not so different. Soon after being brought to the processing facility, between the anxiety and boredom that festered in the prison, Noah had established a routine in waiting. He prayed in waiting. He ate and exercised and conversed in waiting. Always waiting. Waiting to be summoned back to the interrogation room to confess his crimes and, somehow, put the escape plan in action. Wade told him he needed to be patient.

A week passed, and Noah continued to wait. The sun rose and set, and Noah waited. The moon appeared and disappeared, and Noah still waited. He was tired of waiting. He wished to unburden himself. He wished to be free.

During his routine in waiting, Noah seldom left Wade's side. Like he was at an Easter barbeque, Noah's brother-in-law seemed entirely at ease inside the prison's walls. He told Noah that there was no need for fear, or anxiety, or desperation because whatever was to happen would happen with the guiding hand of God. Noah wanted to believe that this was true. It was the only momentary comfort he could find in this place. But still he doubted.

Noah spent hours listening to Wade's philosophical musings. The man was an intellectual powerhouse, espousing ideas that

Noah could seldom grasp. In the heat of his orations, Wade seldom asked Noah for his opinion on the matters on hand. This pleased Noah, for he did not know what he would have to say should his view be required.

Noah gave no mind to the other detainees at Forrest City. None of the inmates had been residents of the processing facility for longer than ninety days and this lack of permanence led to a less territorial and more passive population. There were the occasional brush-ups, but none of the organized crime that had plagued penitentiaries for centuries before. None of the inmates had the time to grow scalding rivalries with one another; their hate was directed solely toward The Federation.

On his ninth day in captivity, a guard approached Noah in the mess. The group was finishing their lunch. Seeing the guard approaching, Wade spoke to Noah.

"It's time."

Though he had been hoping for this moment, now that the act of confession approached, Noah was frightened. When the guard reached the table, he told Noah that the doctor wanted to examine his broken leg. With the daily administration of painkillers, he had forgotten the injury, but, at the mention of the doctor, an ache pulsed through his shin. Noah was relieved to find that he was only wanted for a medical examination, but as the guard took him away, Wade grabbed his wrist. His eyes sensed something more. He looked at Noah deeply and said to him,

"Remember, my brother: 'You will know the truth, and the truth shall set you free.'"

The lobby of the Railyard Inn was filled with every Federationist in Santa Fe. The men and women watched the temporary projection screens that had been set up along the walls. They

waited to watch the announcement from their boss, Secretary-General Antoine Dubois. Though each Federationist knew what the speech would declare, they were excited to witness this historic event. Many of the men and women present had spent years working toward this very act. They had dedicated their careers to incorporating the Grey Zones of the frontier and bringing the Basic Human Standard to their fellow Americans. Though the lobby of the Railyard Inn was one of the few gathered groups of people to definitively know what was going to be broadcasted, they were not alone in anxiously awaiting the announcement. When the reclusive Secretary-General spoke, the entire world listened.

Since his inauguration as President of France, Antoine Dubois had had a complicated relationship with the public. He knew that to be a good leader he must be a man of the people, to be always accessible. And this was not a problem because he liked the people. Being with them and hearing their problems and giving them hope. However, he had witnessed too many leaders get caught up in their own image. Too many leaders purposely blended the line between politician and rock star. Or even politician and idol. Before he was an elected official, Dubois had spent half his life in the spotlight. As an Olympian and young activist, he had entranced legions not just in France, but across the planet with his athleticism, charisma, and intelligence. After years in the public eye, he shied away from the recognition and admiration. As President, he let those in his cabinet take credit for many of the civil and economic advances made under his leadership. But as he tried to recede from the headlines, the public only wanted more. During his presidency, this desire to be open to the people, but to redirect their reverence, was a spiritual struggle.

In 2043, Antoine Dubois resigned after only a year and a half as the final head of the Fifth Republic. His resignation shocked the world. He announced that he could no longer lead such a great country when there were others in the world that suffered so terribly. He triumphantly declared that he would establish the *fédération mondiale des nations* and bring prosperity to the planet. Once he resigned as President, he embraced his reclusive nature. He did not need the people to follow him; he needed them to follow the ideals outlined in the Montpellier Accords, to follow the ideal of the Basic Human Standard.

Antoine Dubois worked behind the scenes to make his vision a reality. His successor, Nicole Hidalgo, announced the establishment of the Sixth Republic and the new constitution was written with the BHS as its focal point. When Hidalgo, German Chancellor Werner Ude, and Spanish Prime Minister Ahmed Alvarez officially signed the Montpellier Accords and officially formed The Global Federation of Nations, Antoine Dubois only spoke for ten minutes. However, his ten-minute speech was the most watched event in human history.

In the decades that followed, Dubois established the same routine. He seldom delivered a solo statement and tonight was no different. Luna expected the Secretary-General to make the announcement of the signing, then turn the microphones to President Wilson and Director Farrelly. He would answer only two or three questions from the press himself.

As he sat alone in the lobby, the Lt. Director watched as the screens played archival footage of Dubois shaking hands with American leaders; giving his "One World, One People" speech in front of the Eiffel Tower after the synchronized nuclear blasts in Tel-Aviv, Tehran, and Mashhad; and the teenaged Dubois playing rugby in the 2028 Olympics. Over the speakers, a broadcaster vaguely speculated on the nature of the upcoming announcement.

Arnie Jones pulled out the vacant chair next to Luna. The noise from the crowd swelled as the people anticipated the announcement. The Lt. Director was seated in the back of the lobby, near the doors leading out to the portico. He nervously tapped on his APD. In a few minutes, the dusty town of Santa Fe would become the epicenter of a political earthquake and the thoughts of eleven billion people would turn to the southwestern American town.

Though he knew what the Secretary-General was about to say, Juan Carlos Luna was still filled with anxiety. He worried that he was protecting a mistake.

When Chief Deputy Jones spoke to Juan Carlos, the Lt. Director jumped.

"Didn't see me sit down, huh?" Jones said.

Luna regained his composure. "No, I did," he lied, then cleared his throat and continued. "I couldn't hear you over all the damn noise. What did you say?"

Jones laughed and patted his friend on the back. Having known the man for years, Arnie knew that his superior was self-conscious about being lost in thought. Luna the soldier was ever-present, focused, and observed every small detail. He was this man nearly all the time, but on some occasions, occasions which were becoming more and more frequent, he became Luna the philosopher. At these times, his sharply tuned senses and instincts lay dormant, they—

There was a shattering of glass at the front door. Then, there was an explosion. Luna and Jones, in the back of the lobby, immediately rushed toward the blast, their pistols drawn. A torrent of gunfire pounded the building and grew louder as Luna inched through the panicked crowd. His boots crunched shards of broken glass. He moved past those crying for help. Terror-stricken administration workers ran for help as the SOs in the lobby advanced on the assault. Lt. Director Juan Carlos Luna focused on the smoldering opening to the parking lot only a few meters before him. He needed to get outside of the chaos to find where the shots were coming from. He needed to silence them.

"What do you think?" the *Chicago Tribune* editor-in-chief Joseph Kalani asked Natalie. They sat in his office and watched the broadcast coverage before the Secretary-General's statement.

Natalie was following the boats on the Chicago River from the floor-length window while she peeled an orange when her mentor changed gears. They had been sitting in his office for an hour, waiting for the announcement to begin, but up until this point they had only been bullshitting. Now it appeared her boss wanted to get serious. Natalie finished peeling the orange and threw the rind into the compost bin.

"I think he might be overreaching."

"Is that what you're going to write?"

"Hell, no. I still want readers."

She bit into an orange wedge as Kalani laughed the throaty, high-pitched laugh he was famous for.

"You've criticized Dubois before and your readers didn't go anywhere."

"I've criticized The Federation before. I've been critical of President Wilson and the Senate before. But I haven't besmirched the Immaculate Antoine Dubois in a column yet," Natalie shifted her response. "I haven't had an opportunity to. Up until this point, he's stayed out of dealing with the AFG."

"But you think he's making a mistake now?"

Natalie shrugged. "We all knew this day would come. It was inevitable for a group like American Freedom to agree to the BHS eventually. There are just too many wealthy men that backed the AFG that have watched as their fortunes evaporated. Those rich men must have realized that the only way to get back in the game was to play by Dubois's rules. But I thought this would happen later. I thought the militants would have more influence in the decision. I'm interested to see what kind of provisions the

AFG will amend to Montpellier. Immunity for the commanders? Shortened sentences for those already in Nunavut? The AFA may be retreating, but they're still strong. They—" she stopped and thought, "I just think it may be hasty is all."

She took another bite of the orange. The juice dripped onto her chin and she wiped it off with the back of her hand. "Then again, I don't have access to the AFG. John Hill hasn't granted me an interview for eight months. And his lieutenants won't give me more than two sentences since he rages every time I quote someone from the Group."

Kalani laughed again. "You did imply that he used Ronald Reagan's cryogenically frozen head as a sex toy."

"Not in my *article!*" Natalie said defensively, then laughed. "That little prick needs to discover a sense of humor."

She finished the orange and wiped her pulpy hands on her khaki pants. Kalani had a 3D holographic puzzle in front of him that he was working on.

"When was the last time you went out on assignment?" Natalie asked her editor.

"Oh, Jesus," Kalani mused and leaned back in his chair while he stared at the ceiling, "I've been editor here for sixteen years. And before that, I was editor of *Renaissance Weekly*, so—" he closed one eye and thought, "shit. Twenty years or so." He leaned back toward his desk and puzzle. "Why?"

"You should come with me for the treaty signing," Natalie said. She was weary of another road trip after Oklahoma City. She hadn't confided in Kalani about how shaken she was after finding Faye. She had told him the police had found the woman dead.

"I couldn't," Joseph said, but Natalie saw that he contemplated the idea.

"C'mon," she urged him. "It's not like they need you here, Joe." Natalie gave him a sly smile.

A beeping sound came from Joseph's desk. He pressed a button; the floating puzzle was replaced by the image of a face. It was the *Tribune's* receptionist.

"Mr. Kalani?"

"Yes, Jeremiah?"

"There is a package here for Ms. Kelley."

Kalani looked at Natalie with raised eyebrows.

"Thank you, Jeremiah."

The floating face disappeared and was replaced by the puzzle. Joseph went back to moving the puzzle pieces through the air.

"Expecting something?"

Natalie stood up. "Yeah. I preordered your coffin years ago. Figured you'd be dead by now."

Joseph laughed. "Jesus, Nat, that was unnecessary."

"How's the leg holding up?" the physician asked. It was the same doctor that treated Noah's leg the week before when he first arrived at Forrest City.

Noah was sitting on the examination table. He flexed the leg, then stood up to put weight on the healing bone.

"Yeah, it's fine," he walked a few paces like he was trying on a new pair of shoes. "It was sore for a day or two, but it's been fine since." He felt uneasy, but that feeling had nothing to do with his injury. He felt uneasy because he had expected to be escorted to the interrogation room, yet he was back at the physician's office just like the guard said. *Had Wade been wrong?*

"Good," the doctor responded as he pulled out a handheld x-ray wand. Noah sat back on the examination table. "And no difficulty walking?"

"No," Noah answered. The physician passed the wand over his left shin and looked at the screen on the wall to Noah's left.

"It looks like the bone is healing nicely. There's still a slight fracture though, so I am going to inject a solution of nanos that should finish mending the fracture in a day or two."

"Nanos?" Noah asked.

"Synthetic chondroblasts."

The physician's answer did not enlighten Noah, but he did not follow up.

The physician walked across the examination room and opened a cupboard. From the back of the cupboard he grabbed a large syringe. The syringe was already filled with liquid. He walked back to the examination table and sat on the stool. He wiped Noah's leg with an antiseptic pad. The needle sparkled in the LED lighting. The physician injected the solution into Noah's leg. The solution burned and as the nanos spread through Noah's leg, the burn spread.

Noah balled his fists around the crepe paper and let out a small whimper. He scowled at the doctor.

"Sorry, I know that hurts," the physician said. He tossed the syringe into the waste depository. "Hopefully this'll be the last time I see you here."

The physician walked to the door and opened it. A guard came in and Noah jumped off the examination table. The leg still burned, but he could walk on it.

As he walked out of the exam room, Noah's hands became clammy. His heart pumped faster. *Is it time to confess? Or would there be more waiting?* He did not know if he wished to be taken back to the detainee's quarters or to the interrogation room.

The guard led Noah out the back of the administration building.

It was time.

They headed for the Officer's Quarters and the interrogation room. They went to the same door Noah had been led to for his first interrogation. Like that first day, he had instructions on how to conduct himself, only this time they came from Wade. Mr. Rhodes, Specialist Biagi, and Specialist McGraw sat at the oak table. The guard led Noah to the seat next to his attorney. The two Specialists conversed with each other.

"The leg alright?" Rhodes asked his client. Noah nodded. As the attorney looked under the table at Noah's leg, he followed-up with another question. "The doctor needed to give you an injection?"

Noah was caught slightly off guard by his attorney's understanding of a medical exam completed only a few minutes ago. He shifted in the chair, trying to find comfort. "Yes," he rubbed the leg, "he said it should be fine in a day or two."

"Good," Rhodes said and turned to the interrogators. "Specialists, I understand you have some questions for my client?"

Lt. Director Luna reached the blown-out entrance of the Railyard Inn less than a minute after the explosion tore into the building. There were at least a dozen Security Officers firing through the smoke into the parking lot. The parking lot returned fire. Luna tried to look through the fog of terror to identify the source of the attack. He stealthily moved out of the building into the open air. He expected a deluge of bullets, but the barrage never came. There were only sporadic pops from between the cars. He took cover behind a brick column on the edge of the *porte-cochère* and assessed the situation.

Two small groups of SOs advanced in the parking lot. They wore jackets, and t-shirts, and ball caps, and were covered in soot. A few were armed with TS-33s, others with SIG Sauer P840s. The sirens of local emergency vehicles wailed in the distance. On his second day in Santa Fe, Luna personally met with the local police chief and fire chief under the guise of searching for the fugitive Gills. The Lt. Director had been unimpressed with the dilapidated state of the civil service departments. He asked the volunteers to stay on alert while his team was in town, then paid them to ensure that they would. As the first antiquated ambulance turned off Guadalupe Street and down a frontage road to the Inn, he was thankful that the fire chief had kept his word that his volunteers would be available to The Federation. A rusted fire truck chased a pair of ambulances.

In the parking lot, the advancing soldiers fired their weapons and closed in on the targets. Luna thought there must be only six or eight combatants assaulting the Inn, but they were well-hidden. The team of SOs would neutralize the threat shortly. Luna needed to focus on taking control of the rescue situation. Though he was well-versed in crisis, his experience lay in creating destruction, not cleaning up its wake. The Lt. Director turned on his lapel microphone and began walking back into the hotel lobby.

"Everyone please stay calm. Emergency vehicles are on the way. Bring all injured individuals to the front of the lobby so—"

Thunderous, rapid gunfire erupted from the parking lot. Luna dove to the ground. He lay on his elbows and turned his head toward the wounded hotel. The Federationists moved to the front of the lobby and retreated into the hidden recesses of the Railyard Inn. The ground exploded around them as bullets rained down through the two-story-high breach created by the explosion. Pieces of tile splattered into the air and chunks of plaster and brick and glass pelted down, swirling around the men and women with cyclonic fury. Luna lifted himself to his hands and knees and moved forward through the parking lot back to the hotel, his pistol in hand. As he crawled, bits of broken glass ripped his pants and dug into his skin. After a few seconds, he joined two SOs behind a concrete column near the entrance. The column was gouged and tattered.

Luna looked to the sky. A drone with a rotary canon hovered and launched 40mm shells at the building. At the street entrance to the parking lot, a second drone riddled the emergency response vehicles. The remaining SOs hid behind a line of RVs at the edge of the lot and fired at the drone. Twenty meters away, Luna spotted the black Suburban that he had utilized earlier in the week. It was parked between a pair of white sedans. The Lt. Director closed his eyes, took in a deep breath, then burst toward the car.

His old legs didn't move as fast as they once had, but they were still powerful. He kept low to the pavement and used the parked cars as cover. Overhead, the drone continued its assault on the hotel and it either did not see or ignored Luna. *It's got to be running low on ammunition,* Luna thought. As he reached the Suburban he held his wrist next to the IWC reader on the driver-side handle. The vehicle unlocked, and Luna quickly crawled inside and climbed over the seats to the back of the vehicle. Once in the trunk, Luna shuffled through gleaming Haliburton cases until he found the one marked "XM70." Before he could open the case, an explosion rocked the parking lot. Luna instinctively covered his head as the vehicle rocked.

Outside, the drone continued to assault the hotel. Luna turned to the second drone but did not see it in the air. Smoke billowed into the air at the edge of the lot. On a small, grassy hill near the frontage road, Luna saw the drone. It had been knocked out of the sky but remained lethal. Luna saw that the drone had taken out the first and fourth emergency vehicles on the frontage road and created a shooting gallery at the choke point. The vehicles' frames were riddled with bullets. Smoke and fire leapt from the engine blocks. On the ground, the crippled drone spun and fired rounds sporadically into the dirt and air as it tried to lift-off.

A pair of SOs advanced on the drone and emptied their clips on the injured aircraft. The machine's gun sputtered and whined until there was an electric short and the murderous pest faded into dormancy.

One left.

Luna unlocked the stainless-steel case. Inside, cradled gently by foam, were the components of an air-burst grenade launcher. Luna, his hands steady, assembled the weapon, then inserted a 30-mm grenade and latched the barrel. He used the butt of the weapon to break the glass out of the window of the gate, then aimed the XM70 at the drone and, as he did so, the aircraft lowered and changed angles for a better shot into the lobby, dropping empty shells like hail onto the parking lot. Luna adjusted his position in the trunk and scooted back on his knees to find a better angle. The drone became stationary about twelve meters above the ground. Its assault swelled. *My God, how was that little bastard equipped with so many bullets?* Luna fixed onto the drone with the grenade launcher and fired. The shell arced toward the drone. Luna watched as it appeared to move in slow motion. A meter from the flying machine gun, the shell detonated. The concussion slammed the drone into the side of the building. The craft spiraled to the ground like a hornet missing a wing. A burst of small fire came from inside the hotel to finish off the machine.

Luna loaded another 30-mm canister into the XM70. He slid out of the backseat of the Suburban and moved toward the remaining combatants. The major threat was contained, but Juan Carlos Luna had questions. And he was going to get answers.

Natalie walked from the Executive Editor's office through the near-empty press room to the reception desk by the elevators on the twenty-eighth floor of the Tribune Tower. Jeremiah, the newspaper's receptionist, sat behind the desk. Young, tall, and with a face pocked with acne scars, he smiled at Natalie as she walked toward him. When she reached the reception desk, Jeremiah stood up and handed the journalist a large, aluminum box. There was a padlock on the latch of the box. It was heavy and awkward. Natalie needed to rest the box on her knee to secure a better grip. There was a tag taped to the lid of the box. On the tag was feminine handwriting that read simply: "To Whom It May Concern."

"Who's it from?" Natalie asked Jeremiah. He spun the small, silver ball at the end of the bar-piercing in the top of his ear.

He looked at the receipt on his APD.

"I just have a routing number. No name."

"Where did it come from?"

Jeremiah looked at the receipt again. "Oklahoma."

Natalie thanked Jeremiah and walked toward her desk in the press room. She rotated the box as best she could to find any other hints at the identification of the sender but found none. The box was forest green with silver stainless steel latches. There was a black scuff along the side of the box. Natalie shook the box and heard a dull thump against the side.

Receiving a physical parcel was rare for Natalie; most people sent her follow-up information electronically. She was puzzled by the package's sudden arrival. She thought back to her trip and about the conversations she had in Oklahoma City, but could not recall requesting anything that needed to be shipped. As she reached her desk, Natalie placed the box on the surface. *Who could have sent this?* The faces of those she met with turned through her mind, like slides on a projector. Cooper. Lily Lee. The airheaded receptionist. Then, Faye Nejem's dark, stoic face flashed before her and she tried to think of something else, but it was too late. The next image came, and Natalie shuddered. She saw the blood-stained carpet pooled around the woman's legs. Then, another image, from a different time. She saw the blood-stained cement beneath her father's head. She shook her head rapidly to dislodge the image from her mind.

"Natalie!"

A shout from across the office.

"Natalie!"

Across the press room, Joseph Kalani stood in his open door frame. His slight body trembled. The few other *Tribune* employees working late in the office stopped what they were doing and looked at their boss. Natalie left the box on her desk and jogged to Joseph. Her APD, along with all the other electronics in the office, began to chirp relentlessly.

As she reached Joseph's office, the man grabbed her arm and pulled her inside. He didn't say a word; he only pointed to the television screen on the wall. The screen showed an aerial view of a wall of smoke. Overhead the PA system crackled and the bells which signified an incoming emergency message chimed. The television screen turned black. Then, a red screen with white text appeared. The text read, "Emergency Alert System. Notification to Follow." A voice began to speak over the PA system and the text changed on the screen.

"Emergency! This is an official message from the White House. Emergency! Coordinated terrorist attacks began at 18:58 Eastern Standard Time in New York, San Francisco, and Santa Fe, New Mexico. These terrorist attacks targeted employees and territories of The Global Federation of Nations. For those in Manhattan, San Francisco, and Santa Fe, stay indoors! To ensure the safety of all American citizens, anyone in a Federation building who is not designated E-3 must evacuate immediately. Please follow stated and practiced evacuation procedures to ensure safety. Listen for instructions from local authorities and follow them quickly and carefully. Repeat: coordinated terrorist attacks are underway against GFN territories. Stay away! The press conference of Federation Secretary-General Dubois has been postponed. Please stay tuned to your local news affiliate or go to EmergencyUpdate.gfn for more information. Thank you."

Throughout the announcement, Natalie craned her head upward to hear more clearly. The text on the screen lagged a second behind the PA announcement. With her head still bent back, she slid onto the cool couch in Joseph's office. It had been nearly a year since the Emergency Alert System had issued a nationwide alert. Joseph stood next to Natalie, rested his hand on her shoulder, and muttered under his breath, "This is gonna be bad."

Noah Bridger had been in the interrogation room for a little over an hour. He had answered the Specialists' questions truthfully when he could and told them that he did not know when he did not know. His attorney, Kendrick Rhodes, sat silently as Noah spewed his story. When he had finished talking, when the Specialists had no more questions, and he had confessed to his part in the attack, he did not feel the freedom of a clean conscience. He felt only exhaustion.

Noah had never spoken at such length and with such intensity before. His throat ached. He looked down at the untouched cooler glass of water in front of him. A wide ring of water surrounded the cooler on the table and the condensation fogged the glass. He picked up the glass and drank and when there was no more water left, he said, "I guess that's it."

The Specialists thanked him and left. Noah asked Rhodes what would happen next. Rhodes explained to his client that they would interview the three other conspirators and once those interviews were complete, they would take the four men to The Global Federation Court of Justice in Memphis for a trial. Noah wanted to ask his attorney why he had been told to relay his crime. *Shouldn't I have confessed only after a deal had been offered? Had they found some new evidence that would free us?* He wanted the attorney to tell him his fate, but he knew that the room was being recorded and that Rhodes could not give him answers. There were ears everywhere. He would be left to wonder why he had thrown himself to the mercy of jackals. He wondered if his attorney even knew why he had been told to confess.

Instead of asking his attorney the questions on his mind, he sat quietly and stared at the table. A minute later, a guard entered the room. Noah was led to a holding cell in the Officer's

Quarters, away from the main cell block. A revelation of fear shocked Noah as he reached the cramped solitary holding cell. A question shook him. *Am I a patsy? Can I trust Wade? Do I even know him?* Noah didn't know the answers to the questions that swirled in his head and that frightened him. As he sat in the cell, he did know that he had been the first one to talk and, right now, the only one. He was alone, and he felt that loneliness. Panic rushed over Noah. He paced in the cell and prayed.

Lord, would Wade betray me like this? Could he? Would You let him?

Wade could be pushy. He could be stubborn. Noah had even seen glimpses of rage within his brother-in-law and he had admitted to having a criminal past. But, could the man be treacherous? Could the same man Noah had spent the last week following, listening to, believing in, betray him? *Could he?*

No. Noah stopped pacing and sat down. *No.* He would not be betrayed. He needed to have faith in his allies. He needed to have faith in Wade. He needed to have faith in God. *It is God's plan. What is to be done, will be done.*

But still, the creeping feeling of betrayal had snuck out of the pit of Noah's gut and snaked toward his brain like a poisonous vine. He needed to eradicate these toxic thoughts. *There is a reason I am in this place,* he told himself, repeating Wade's words. *I am a vessel of the Lord. What is to be done will be done.*

The Security Officers had apprehended three male combatants in the parking lot. The prisoners were lying face-down on the cement when Lt. Director Luna reached the group. Some SOs restrained the men on the ground, while others fixed their guns on the men. A few ambulances not immobilized by the drone attack had jumped the curb. They drove over scrubland to circumvent the wreckage of the smoldering vehicles that blocked their path to the Railyard Inn. Luna holstered his pistol and spoke to the nearest Federationist on the scene.

"Just three attackers?"

"Five," the SO pointed behind a row of parked cars. "Two were killed."

"None got away?" Luna said as he scanned the horizon. "No runners?"

"I didn't see any."

"Send some drones and officers out to search the vicinity. Just a couple. We're going to need all the help we can get here."

"Yes, sir."

The SO ran to the hotel in search of any able Officers to accomplish the Lt. Director's task.

Luna watched as the last combatant's ankles were restrained. The man squirmed and kicked at The Federationist that shackled him. The Fed struck the man in the spine. Between the wailing sirens before him and the screams and cries behind, Luna heard a voice call out to him. He turned and saw Jade Carson, one of his Deputies, running toward him. Black soot streaked across her caramel face; her black pants and blue t-shirt were ripped which exposed bloody and burned skin beneath. Her green eyes watered as Luna looked at her and, now that she had his attention, she struggled to speak.

"Yes? What is it?" Luna barked. He was impatient. There was work to be done. "Jade!" he yelled. "What is it?" He shook his head at her lack of response and tried to move past her. The Deputy grabbed his arm and stopped him. Her voice was a whisper, buried by the surrounding sounds of chaos.

"You need to come with me."

Luna removed her hand. "What? What do you need? Speak!" Luna shook her. He was consumed by the still pumping adrenaline from the attack.

Carson opened her mouth, her voice cracked as she spoke. He could barely hear her. "You need to come with me," she repeated.

"Goddamnit, I can't hear you, Jade."

Carson's eyes focused and she looked at Luna. "Lieutenant, you need to follow me," Carson commanded, this time with some force. "It's Arnie."

Luna was concerned. "What's Arnie?" he asked.

One of the ambulances stopped next to the gathered group of Security Officers. Luna had not noticed, but one of the SOs had been injured during the counter-assault. Two other SOs carried the injured officer to the ambulance. She appeared to be bleeding from her torso. The other emergency vehicles drove as close to the front entrance as they could. EMTs ran inside, carrying duffel bags of medical equipment. Luna could not hear his Deputy.

"What's Arnie?" he repeated.

Carson shook her head, then answered by leading the Lt. Director to the ravaged lobby. Luna began to understand the situation. He sprinted past Carson and pushed his way into the hotel. He feared for his friend. The lobby revealed the extent of the carnage.

Bricks.

Glass.

Debris.

Blood.

Limbs.

Bodies laid still in the rubble. Breathless. Lifeless. The stinging smell of sulfur filled the room. A small fire still burned near the beverage station and Federationists used thick curtains to snuff it out. Soon a hotel employee arrived with a fire extinguisher and sprayed the blaze.

Bricks.

Glass.

Debris.

Blood.

Limbs.

Everywhere Luna turned he was met by chaos, but he could not find Arnie Jones. *Was that good? Was he among the bodies? Was he up and walking?* Carson caught up to her superior and placed a hand on his back. She guided him through the wreckage.

Bricks.

Glass.

Debris.

Blood.

Limbs.

The Deputy led Luna over the flesh and detritus to the back of the lobby where he saw the round, pale face of Arnie Jones limp on the lap of his assistant. Blood cascaded from his mouth, stained his mustache, and spilled onto the woman's white skirt. His head trembled, cradled in the woman's hands. Her tears dripped onto his face, plopping gently onto the smeared blood. The Deputy Lt. Director's eyes were closed tight, and his hands were folded over his gushing stomach. His shirt had turned crimson and was sopping wet. His chest heaved as his lungs searched for the next breath.

Luna fell to the floor by his Deputy's side and kneeled in the blood and dirt. He grabbed Jones's hand and held it in his own. It was hot and sticky and slick, like it had been dipped in a burgundy tar pit. He lifted Jones's shirt above his stomach, looking for the injury. The skin was covered with a thick layer of blood. He tried to wipe the blood away, but it just sloshed around and never seemed to dissipate. He spotted a half-drank bottle of water on the ground and crawled over to it. He unscrewed the top of the bottle and poured it on his friend's stomach. The water thinned the heavy blood and unveiled the skin underneath. The wounds were revealed. Luna saw four coin-sized holes, each gurgling blood. They formed a line starting above the right hip, slanting upward across the stomach, and ending below the sternum.

"Arnie! Arnie!" Luna yelled. "Goddamnit, Arnie!" he screamed as he slapped his Deputy's face. Arnie's eyes fluttered and showed glimpses of white but struggled to open.

Jones's grip tightened in Luna's hand. He looked like he was trying to speak but, as his mouth moved, no words came forth—only blood as his grip went soft.

There were no final words before Arnie Jones died on a grubby hotel floor. Juan Carlos Luna dropped his head onto the still chest of his dead friend and cried.

Natalie Kelley and Joseph Kalani watched silently as the news coverage of the carnage played out on the screen in the editor's office. Natalie was surprised that she could still be horrified by what she saw on television. Having watched broadcasted war and calamity since she was a child, she sometimes feared that she had grown immune to the showcase of human destruction. In this moment, she realized that fear was unfounded.

The screen showed a reporter in front of the GFN-NA West Coast Division Center. The building usually shined above the bay in Fisherman's Wharf but now spewed smoke which shrouded the landmark Golden Gate Bridge. People walked by the reporter, dazed, their faces and clothing covered in ash and dirt. The local reporter on scene had little information to share. She only repeated a string of despairing adjectives. Previously, the television had broadcasted an aerial shot of Roosevelt Island. The drone footage, careful to stay out of The Federation no-fly zone, showed a beached submarine on the eastern shore of the island. The shot was dark, and the in-studio voice-over brought little illumination. The program switched scenes to shaky, shocking footage streamed live from a hotel employee in Santa Fe. The man walked through a dismantled lobby while he provided shaky, nervous commentary. Someone yelled at the amateur

videographer to "shut that fucking thing off and help someone!"
The broadcast showed the floor, then went to black. The screen
returned to the reporter in San Francisco.

The messages on Natalie's APD were piling up, but she did
not read them. She was glued to the images playing out in front
of her.

Joseph broke the uneasy silence which germinated in the
room. "What do you think? Dubois still gonna deal?"

Natalie just shook her head. The man was always thinking
ahead.

"It looks bad," she mustered. "Really bad. Hopefully he's not
dead."

Joseph shrugged off the last statement. "Rubbish. He's not
dead."

Natalie continued watching the TV. Joseph voiced the course
he believed the Secretary-General would take.

"They need to at least put out a press release regarding the
contents of Dubois's announcement. They will need to quiet any
conspiracies that are sure to be swirling around. So—"

Natalie shushed him. Cooper Gates, Assistant Press Secretary for the NASO, appeared on screen to present information
regarding the attacks. Natalie did not flinch at her ex-lover's
appearance. She began to record what the man said on her APD.

The briefing began: In New York, a submarine, undetected
by GFN security measures in the East River, landed on Roosevelt Island at 18:56 EST. There, an estimated twenty assailants
disembarked and charged The Federation Communications
Office Building. When they reached the Comm Building, a bomb
detonated, ripping open the southeast corner of the building.
It is believed that the terrorists targeted the Communications
Office Building because the perpetrators suspected that the
Secretary-General was present. Fortunately, the Secretary-General was not on Roosevelt Island at the time of the attack and
the building was sparsely occupied. The Secretary-General is

currently safe. His location is classified. A firefight took place between the assailants and GFN Security Officers. Casualties in New York appear to be low. The Federation could not confirm whether any of the assailants had been detained alive.

In San Francisco, the GFN-NA West Coast Division Center had been attacked at 15:58 Pacific Standard Time. Many Federationists were present at the Division Center at the time of the attack. There was an explosion which is believed to have originated beneath the building. Evacuation is an ongoing process due to the extensive damage. There have been reports of gunfire following the initial blast, but these reports have not been confirmed. Casualties in San Francisco are unknown, but they are believed to be high.

The third attack took place in Santa Fe, New Mexico. Cooper only confirmed that there was an "incident" there. He could not verify anything further, but rumors circulated. After Cooper finished his public briefing, the news anchor tried to piece together what had taken place in the forgotten Grey Zone city. Currently, the only confirmed information directly from the site was the APD footage from the hotel employee and widely putative posts and reports from uninformed Santa Feans. The news said they believed the attack took place at a local hotel called the "Railroad Inn". The anchor repeated speculation that there were several Federationists in the amateur APD footage. That is as far as the anchor was willing to speculate, but Joseph went further.

"Obviously, the treaty was going to be signed there. But why Santa Fe?" he mused.

"Does it matter?" Natalie asked, annoyed. Joseph was a warm, caring man most of the time, but, when discussing coverage, he sometimes became callous. This foible made him a successful editor, but Natalie hated to see the trait in her friend.

She had seen enough. She had heard enough. She kissed Joseph on the cheek and walked out of his office without saying a word. She had a big day tomorrow. She would be on the road again. She just didn't know where she was headed yet.

For the last week, sleep had eluded Noah Bridger. No matter how tired he felt, when he lay in his bed, he could not sleep. Anxiety kept him awake. Fear kept him awake. Being away from his family kept him awake. He would feel tired and close his eyes, but when his body's energy was depleted, his mind would race.

When he did find sleep, it was sudden and unexpected. It crept up on him in the cafeteria or in the yard or in the chapel. He would nod off and wake soon after with a jolt. Now, while he sat in an unfamiliar cell and fought off the thought that he may have been betrayed by a man he had grown to trust, all he wanted to do was sleep.

He lay on the bed and closed his eyes and tried to shut off his mind. He could not.

After some time, he heard the door lock release.

"Get up," a guard commanded.

Noah opened his eyes. The bright lights of the room sent spots across his vision.

The guard pulled Noah from the bed and led him to the back of the Officer's Quarters and to a part of the processing facility Noah had not been to. The thoughts of betrayal circled and closed in Noah's mind.

"Where are we going?" he asked.

"Transport," the guard replied, tersely.

Noah expected that answer. He had even hoped for it, but when he heard the guard vocalize his hope, a wave of terror passed through him. At Forrest City, he was a detainee. A suspect-in-waiting. After trial, he would be a convicted terrorist. He had already confessed. What he needed to know now was that he wasn't alone. That he had not been betrayed. He needed to know there was a plan.

The guard led him outside the building and into the muggy Arkansas air. The sky was dark, and the stars twinkled above. The ground was wet and the strong smell of petrichor hung heavy. With his hand on Noah's back, the guard pushed Noah toward the chain-link fence. A gate opened. Beyond the fence, Noah saw a large van idling. Its bumper faced Noah. The lights were off, and the electric engine emitted a soft hum that was only broken by the songs of crickets. On either side of the van stood two men with TS-33s. Noah thought he heard a drone overhead but couldn't see it against the inky sky.

The back of the van opened, and a light shone from the interior. Two titanium benches were erected on each side of the van's interior. Aiden Stevens, Brickson Newsome, and Wade Barrineau sat inside. There was an empty spot on the bench next to Wade. It was reserved for Noah.

The shooting had stopped. Emergency response vehicles had parked outside the Railyard Inn. The injured were moved to the opening where the lobby met the outdoors. A chisel of order began to chip away at the slab of chaos. Juan Carlos Luna's head still lay on top of Arnie Jones's stiff chest. The spew of blood from his gut had slowed to a leak. Luna's face was painted red. His hair stuck to the deputy's torso as the pool of blood cooled and dried.

Luna remembered the last time his head had rested on his old friend. Thirty years ago, the two were in the Orontes Valley and conducted a raid on the compound of a Wings of al-Buraq leader in Syria. Luna was at the front of his unit. It was early morning, but the heat had risen with the sun and baked the unit. The troops stalked through the chest-high grove of olive trees.

The Rangers had executed a dozen of these missions across the region.

He was on the ground bleeding heavily before he even knew what hit him. Somehow the preliminary recon sent to scout ahead of the raid had missed a mine from the compound and the little bastard had ripped into Luna, cut up his legs, and nicked his femoral artery. Thank Christ it had missed his manhood. Jones, who had been trailing his captain, pulled Luna behind a dusty embankment before the smoke from the Italian-made land mine had cleared. He nearly suffocated as his heavy breath piled against the respirator of his combat mask. He took the mask off his wet skin. The smell, like a barn full of rotten eggs. Weaponized malodorant from Alpha Company. The vomit. The stench. The pain.

Gunfire spewed from the compound. Jones held Luna's head in his lap and placed a damp cloth over his mouth and noise. He told his captain that it was only a scratch, while the medic rushed over to tourniquet Luna's leg. Luna urged the men to move forward and complete the mission; he had not feared death as the sounds and smells of war enveloped the olive grove. He was afraid he would become a cripple. He told Jones over and over again that he would rather die than lose his leg. Arnie Jones stayed with his friend as bullets rained down around them. He stayed even when his ranking officer ordered him to advance on the compound. He stayed with the bleeding man until a medivac chopper landed at the edge of the olive grove and carried him to safety.

Juan Carlos Luna stood over the body of Arnie Jones. He had been too late to comfort him. Too late to carry him to safety. Fury grew inside him. He needed to do something. He needed to make things right. Luna checked the clip on his sidearm. It was full. He took off his jacket and placed it under Arnie's head, then marched to find those bastards in the parking lot.

The bottle of Scotch that sat on Natalie Kelley's desk was nearly empty. Natalie had feared attacks like this when the American Freedom Group had joined the GFN. AFG President John Hill had his faults, but he had always seemed to keep his militants under a semblance of control. They were rabid dogs on a long leash before and now that leash was off.

On the "L"-ride home to her apartment in McKinley Park, Natalie had hammered out a preliminary outline that summarized the little that was known about the coast-to-coast attack. She pored over her vast collection of notes and reports on the AFA and researched the group's most militant lieutenants. In a press world which coveted being first above all else, Natalie was an outlier. She had not built a reputation as a promising journalist by breaking news, but on the extensive, in-depth coverage that took time to write. She was working to parlay that investigative journalism into her first book, but it seemed that the more she wrote, the more there was to uncover. The torrent of news never ceased.

As a journalist, Natalie was at her best when she was building relationships with people mired in the muck of the struggle. Although she had built relationships with Security Officers, STAB units, and attack survivors, her true knack lay in obtaining the stories of those who fought against the GFN. Natalie had been criticized for giving such people a platform, but she felt that it was necessary for The Federation to understand their opposition. Her articles often filtered through the propaganda of such groups and illuminated the true, human motives of those who considered themselves "freedom fighters". Her critics said she aided criminals and terrorists, but she tried to ignore those claims. She deeply believed that her work helped NASO by providing insight into the opposition. Only a fool would fight an opponent they did not understand.

Her most widely-recognized published piece covered the Order of Bedlam, an international anarchist group started by students at Cal-Berkeley. The Order of Bedlam had targeted both Federation and American Independence groups. During its infancy, The Order used nonviolent means to disrupt governmental practices. These nonviolent means included the hacking of transportation systems, publishing confidential and personal material of GFN and American government employees, and disabling energy sectors. Over time, The Order's tactics became radical and violent.

Eighteen months ago, an earthquake struck the Pacific Northwest and disabled the reactor cooling systems at the Columbia Generating System in southern Washington. Those injured by the earthquake or exposed to radiation at the nuclear power plant were taken to Kadlec Regional Medical Center for treatment. The hospital overflowed with patients when an explosion tore through the emergency wing. The Order claimed responsibility for the bombing. They released a statement which simply said: "Mother Nature started it. You made it worse. The Order will finish it." Days after the attack, Natalie met with the founders of The Order of Bedlam for two days in the Black Zone. The young men and women discussed their anarchist origins, the attack at Kadlec, and the future of The Order. All six founders were killed by a STAB unit a week after Natalie's lengthy interview. Her piece on The Order of Bedlam gained her worldwide acclaim and she had been named a finalist for the Pulitzer Prize.

With a belly full of Scotch, Natalie mused on her work covering the anarchists. Though she was very proud of her work on The Order of Bedlam, she wished it did not have to come at the expense of her relationship with her fiancé. Time and time again, Natalie put her work in front of her fiancé until one day she came home to their apartment; he and his things were gone.

She and Dwyane had dated for seven years after meeting in a university support group for students who had lost a parent. She had loved him, but found she wasn't devastated when he left. Life moved on.

However, the pangs of loneliness still stabbed her on occasion. Natalie, being the obstinate woman she was, had never reached out to Dwyane, although she had often wanted to. Coincidentally, the marquee on a children's theatre at the end of the block urged pedestrians to "Buy tickets / Call Dwyane", but she never took the sign's advice. When her brain floated in alcohol, she yearned to call him. Just to catch up. Just to know he was okay. Just to hear his voice.

She poured herself another drink and looked at the box that had been delivered to the *Tribune* office. She felt trapped like the contents of that aluminum container. She thought that if she liberated what rattled inside that old box, she would liberate herself from her personal and professional confinements. Her relationship with Dwyane would never be fixed and she would not gain the access to the Freedom Army that she craved tonight, but she could open the box.

Natalie pulled on the deadlock, but it was tight around the latch. She wanted to open the box. She needed to open the box.

The prisoner transportation van left Forrest City and travelled east toward Memphis and the GFCoJ District Court. Noah's legs and hands shook with nervousness. Chained next to him, his brother-in-law Wade kept his head down and his eyes closed. He concentrated on something Noah could not see and his lips mouthed words Noah could not hear. Newsome and Stevens sat on the opposite side of the cargo hold. Noah was elated when he saw the others in the van, but now the silence eroded his delight.

"Wade," he whispered, "you said there was a plan, right? What's the plan?"

Wade kept his eyes on the metal floor and shook his head. There was a pounding on the partition. A voice came over the speaker in the cargo hold.

"Shut the fuck up back there!"

At the processing facility, Wade had told Noah to trust him and follow his instructions. Noah had obeyed. Now he wished that the trust would be returned—their situation appeared dire and a morsel of knowledge could bring him hope.

"Wade," he started again, "what are we doing? Where are we going?"

The speaker crackled. "If you don't shut your Goddamn mouth, I will zap the shit out of you!"

Noah stopped talking. He shook and stewed nervously as the van sped forward. The tranquility of the others bothered him. They knew something that he did not and that made him angry.

Wade lifted his head and nodded across the hold, giving Newsome and Stevens some sort of signal. Then, he reached into the waistband of his blue prison scrubs. He removed a pair of hidden spectacles from inside his pants. The spectacles belonged to Kendrick Rhodes. Wade kept the glasses between his knees and fiddled with them. There was a snap and he turned to Noah.

"Noah, I'm sorry, my brother, but this is likely to hurt quite a bit."

In the parking lot outside of the Railyard Inn, two bodies lay on the concrete, each punctured by bullet holes. A portion of one of the bodies' skull was blown away. The other's chest had been pierced by three shots. The bodies were uncovered, ignored. On the curb at the far end of the lot, the dead men's compatriots sat with their wrists and ankles bound. One of the detained received medical attention for a gunshot wound to the shoulder. Another of the men already had an arm bandaged from an injury sustained in the battle. They were silent. A ring of SOs surrounded the men and awaited instructions on what to do with their captives. Luna marched toward the group and pushed through the Officers on-guard.

"Sir," one of the Officers said to Luna, but the Lt. Director ignored him. Luna un-holstered his sidearm and marched to the nearest detainee, the one with the bandaged arm. Towering above, he slammed the butt of the gun into the man's nose. He heard the cartilage crunch. The man doubled-over. Luna grabbed his shaggy black hair with his free hand and brought the captive to his feet. The SOs tentatively approached their superior but made no direct action to intervene.

The detainee was wobbly. His head tried to dip down to his chest, but Luna kept his hand in the man's hair. He pulled the wet hair back to keep the man's eyes locked on his own. The captive was shocked, frightened. He tried to look at the Officers that had restrained him for some relief. Luna had not seen combat for years and the raw, potential energy of inaction became a surge of blinding, kinetic violence.

The detainee tried to drop his head again to escape Luna's rabid gaze, but the Lt. Director's grip was tight. Luna launched his forehead at the detainee's face. There was a loud thud. The detainee struggled and tried to find a way to counter, but his wrists and ankles were bound. He could not reciprocate the strike and he lost his balance and fell to the ground. He stayed on the ground. His head and knees were heavy on the concrete. He gasped for air. Luna reached down and grabbed him by the throat.

"Get up! Get up you fucking coward!"

The group of Security Officers around the Lt. Director grew. There were now non-combat Federationists and hotel employees and local Santa Feans. Some of the SOs worked to move the civilians away from the scene, while others stood around anxiously, not sure what to do.

Luna tightened his grip around the man's throat and thrust him upwards. The detainee flew up through the air before he was on his feet.

Luna muttered to himself. "You fucking coward. Fucking coward."

The captive struggled for breath and Luna relaxed his grip.

"Did you hear me? I said, 'You're a fucking coward.' I'll take those restraints off and we'll see what kind of a man you are."

Luna let go of the man's throat. He put his pistol in his holster and reached to unlock the restraints. As he bent down, the bound man swung his body and struck Luna's temple with his elbow. Luna, crouched and slightly stunned, sprung at the man and tackled him onto the concrete. On top of the man, Luna pounded his face with closed fists. He felt a force pulling him off the man. He swung his arms wildly to break free. The detainee coughed and spit and spewed blood and teeth and phlegm. Luna broke free from his subordinates and dove back on top of the man. He pressed his hand against the man's face and dug his thumb into the man's eyeball. The man began to scream, the yell stifled by the pool of blood in the back of his throat, his words muffled by the debris in his mouth. Luna's thumb pressed harder until there was a pop. The man's scream turned primal. He gurgled blood and began to choke on himself, his face white and red and mashed. The hands were back on Juan Carlos Luna and a pair of EMTs rushed to the injured man. The two other detainees stared at the scene in horror.

The fury continued to ooze out of Luna like pus from a breached abscess. He looked at the faces of the people who pulled him back. Security Officers started to move the gathered crowd out of the parking lot, using their weapons to emphasize their commands. Within the newly established perimeter, Luna saw Jade Carson. The Deputy was shouting at him.

"Sir! Sir! There were others, sir!"

Luna was confused. He looked around the property but saw no other combatants.

"Sir, New York and San Francisco were hit. San Francisco is bad," she paused and waited for a response. When none came, she yelled again. "Sir!"

He looked at Carson.

"New York and San Francisco?" he asked.

Relief washed over Carson when he acknowledged her.

"Yes. The Director needs you to contact her right away."

Luna's mind began to clear. He was needed. Carson started to lead him back to the hotel away from the detained. The lot had been cleared of nonessential civilians.

"Dubois?" he asked.

"He's fine."

"How many dead?"

"Only a few in New York."

"In San Francisco?"

Carson paused again. "We don't know."

Luna stopped walking and looked at his Deputy.

"How many, Jade?"

Carson breathed in heavily. "At least a hundred. Almost certainly more."

Luna looked at the GFN Field Patch on his uniform. Staring into the Ring of Light, he knew these bastards had struck a blow to the Heart of the Illuminated World. He heard stifled laughter slip from the uninjured detainee. Luna, with one fluid motion, removed the SIG from its holster, aimed it at the smirking captive, and fired. The man's head jolted back, and he fell to the ground.

Luna re-holstered the pistol as Carson stared in disbelief. He started to walk back toward the hotel, and Carson followed.

"Get the Director on the line for me, please, Jade."

Natalie Kelley had tried to pick the old padlock on the box with a stripped and stretched hairpin, but it didn't work. She had seen this maneuver in the movies but couldn't duplicate the success of the caper films. After she had tried for fifteen minutes and opened another bottle of Scotch, she took a hammer to the padlock. On her first swing, she missed and dented the box. She lined the hammer up again and, this time, scored a clean strike on the padlock. However, when she surveyed the damage, the lock remained intact. She tried again. And again. And again. The lock remained secure.

She stopped and stared at the box. It looked like she felt: beat to hell and no closer to enlightenment. Natalie blew her brown hair away from her face and smoothed it back along her head. She left her hands on the back of her neck and rubbed her trapezius muscles. She walked to her kitchen and commanded her fridge to pour a glass of water. She drank the glass greedily, wiped her mouth, and placed the glass in the sink. *Why the fuck would someone send me a locked box without a key?*

Natalie went back to her desk and sat in her chair. The speakers in her ceiling played music from *El Jardín de las Hadas*, a samba-fused opera that debuted in Buenos Aires and became a global phenomenon the year previous. Natalie looked forward to seeing the show when it came to Chicago's AllStateFarm Randolf Theatre. She bobbed her head to the music and shook the box. Again, she could hear soft thumping against the metal sides, but the movement gave little insight to what lay inside. She asked her APD the best way to open a padlock and the results included using a paperclip or a hammer, two avenues that had already led her to a dead end. Her APD also suggested that she use a bolt cutter. She didn't have one, so she went to the closet to activate her 3D printer. She found that she was out of the aluminum-oxide cartridge she would need to make the tool. She told her APD to order another cartridge. It would arrive in two days.

Natalie took the last drink of Scotch from her highball and looked at the box again. She shook her head in confusion. She was glad the lock had given her a reprieve, but the same disgust she felt when she left the office returned. She had not checked the news wires regarding the attacks. She did not want to know the extent of the carnage. Not now—that could wait until tomorrow morning. Now she just needed another drink.

"What's going to hurt quite a bit?" Noah Bridger asked his brother-in-law. He was alarmed. Aiden Stevens and Brickson Newsome looked on in interest. Noah repeated his query, louder this time. "Wade, what's going to hurt quite a bit?"

The hold's speaker crackled. "I told you to shut the fuck up back there!" Noah felt a jolt through his lats. The electric shock lasted a few seconds. Noah clenched his jaw and dug his fingernails into the palms of his hands. When the shock ended, it had drained the energy out of him.

Wade held the glasses discreetly between his thighs. He broke a temple from the glasses and dropped the rest of the frames to the floor with a metallic "tink." He held the thin temple steady and started to screw the silicon temple tip. As he screwed, a needle emerged from the opposite end of the temple.

Noah lazily watched Wade. He tried to speak but couldn't find the words. He tried to move, but his body disobeyed. The jolt had paralyzed him.

Wade finished screwing the temple tip. The previously hidden needle had expanded to a length of roughly five centimeters. He turned toward Noah. The restraints kept him upright, but he was able to wiggle close. The needle crawled between Wade's index and middle fingers until the tip touched the skin of Noah's forearm. Noah sat and watched, paralyzed; fear drained the color from his face. He tried to speak, but still found his vocal cords torpified from the electric shock.

A voice bellowed from overhead. "What the hell are you doing back there?"

Wade rammed the makeshift needle into the extensors of Noah's left arm. The metal pierced through his skin and ripped past his nerves. The stabbing pain was soon overtaken by a rush of hot energy that originated in his shin. The devastating energy consumed Noah. His vision became blurred, then filled with spots.

Next to Noah, an electrical discharge seized Wade. His hands dropped onto the bench and his head hit the wall of the van. The vehicle slowed. The spots in Noah's vision devoured his sight until they were all he could see. The pain and energy continued to flow through his body. Noah closed his eyes and lost consciousness.

CHAPTER SEVEN

13 May 2072

Natalie Kelley's head felt like an axe had been driven through her skull. She woke up on her couch shivering, wearing the same jeans and button-up she had been wearing the day before. The taste of stale Scotch stuck in her mouth explained her morning discomfort. She looked at her well-made bed through the open door with envy.

Natalie rose from the couch, kicked an empty fifth on her way to the kitchen, and drained a tall glass of water. She opened the cabinet next to the refrigerator, took out a plastic bottle, and popped a hangover remedy pill. She shook the bottle and only a few pills rattled inside. She commanded her kitchen to order a refill of the drug.

Natalie looked at the clock and was relieved to find that it was only a little after 07:00. The world had kept marching forward while she drank alone in her apartment and now she needed to get back to work to catch up. Her chest was tight and her hands quaked. She cursed herself, although she did not know exactly why. She stripped off her day-old clothes and made her way to the shower to wash away the whiskey that still filtered through her pores.

She hoped the rush of cold water on her skin would help calm her nerves. Natalie could not shake the feeling of guilt that rose within her as she tried to reconcile the previous night's actions. Possibly the biggest story that concerned the AFA in years and she figured it was a good time to get loaded. She realized she did not even know how big of a story it was; she had been off the grid for the past ten hours. *Stupid!* She put her palms against the tile of the shower and let the current flow over her. She shook her head at her immaturity. She knew that she had been wound too tightly the previous few weeks, but still she chided herself for dealing with that stress poorly. She held her hand out and the shower box on the wall dispensed a pool of shampoo onto her palm. She closed her eyes tight and vigorously scrubbed the shampoo into her hair, clawing all the way to her scalp to try to dig away the negative thoughts. Once her hair and conscience were as clean as they would be, she commanded the water to turn off, then stepped out of the shower.

As she dried herself, Natalie heard a pounding on her apartment door. She wrapped herself in her bath towel and grabbed her toothbrush. She pressed a button on the brush and a cool, blue paste flowed over the bristles. When she got to the door, she looked at the security screen and saw her editor rocking impatiently in the hall. She opened the door and tried to give Joseph Kalani an inviting smile, but the bubbling toothpaste started to seep from her mouth. She started to laugh and sent minty spittle into the air. Covering her mouth, she motioned for Joseph to take a seat in her living room as she walked back to the bathroom.

Natalie emerged from her bedroom a few minutes later wearing navy canvas pants and a light-blue, basket-weave top. Her hair was still wet, and she had yet to apply makeup, but Joseph was still struck by just how good looking of a woman she had become. Natalie had met Joseph when she was still in high school at a regional journalism seminar. Joseph took an instant liking to the young woman when she had approached him after the lecture and told him that his shirt tail had been untucked during his presentation to the room. Joseph was a three-time Pulitzer Prize winner and had a reputation as a Rottweiler that was willing to do anything to get a story, but this girl showed no fear in pointing out a flaw. He liked having the reputation of a cutthroat, but never felt that it was warranted; he was just a man that did not conform to the diplomacy of his profession.

When the two first met, Joseph had just recently been hired as the editor-in-chief of the *Chicago Tribune*. He had quickly grown tired of the sycophants and politicians in his newsroom. This girl was a breath of fresh air. Joseph invited fifteen-year-old Natalie to visit the *Tribune* and a mentorship blossomed. He encouraged her throughout high school and college and hired her the day she received her diploma from the Medill School of Journalism. In the less-competitive role of editor, he had enjoyed the opportunity to pass his journalistic knowledge on to a member of the younger generation. Joseph and his wife never had any children of their own and, when Natalie's father was killed, he eagerly jumped into the role of father figure. Sometimes, he wondered if his patriarchal eagerness had been too aggressive.

As Natalie walked to join Joseph on the couch, he picked up the empty Scotch bottle and held it accusingly.

"Is this why you couldn't get back to me last night?"

Natalie shrugged, grabbed the bottle, and tossed it into the recycling bin. She sat down on the couch next to her boss. Towel-drying her hair with one hand, she laid the other on the old man's arm and asked, "What brings you so far away from the Magnificent Mile this early in the morning, Joseph?"

"I didn't hear from you all night, Natalie! I was trying to get ahold of you for hours! That's what brings me here so early."

Natalie closed her eyes, slunk her shoulders, and leaned her head back on the couch. "I was just catching up on some sleep, Joe."

Joseph ignored her attempt at provocation. Natalie only called him "Joe" when she wanted to get a rise from him. "Well, I hope you're well-rested, because we're going to San Francisco in an hour."

Natalie opened her eyes. "We?"

"Yes, we. I'm going out there with you. The rumor is that Dubois is going to be in town meeting with the families of those Federation employees that were killed." The editor checked his watch. "I'm taking your advice. Now, go pack and I'll meet you at Obama Station. I'll let you get ready."

Joseph let himself out of the apartment. Natalie sat on the couch for a few moments before she got up to pack. Twenty minutes later, she was on her way out of the door, her bag strapped across her chest, when she saw the beaten, metal box where it sat on her desk. Without thinking, she grabbed the box and left the apartment.

When Noah Bridger came to, he was wrapped in a heavy blanket. He could not think deeply. Only instinctive realizations came to him. He was alone in a tent. His exposed cheeks and ears were cold. He could hear a fire crackling outside. There was a great pain rooted in his leg which branched all through his body. He let out a loud moan. He saw his breath in the pillowy light. The pain was even more intense than it had been when the bullet crashed into the bone. Noah lifted the blanket off him and examined the source of the pain. He was naked. A thick bandage was wrapped around his leg from above his ankle to below his knee. The bandage was stained red with blood. Noah reached down to unravel the bandage but found that it was still wet. He left the bandage intact. His confusion began to recede. He scanned the tent for some water or something for the pain in his leg but did not find either. There was only a small knapsack with his yellow prison scrubs and a change of clothes in a corner of the space. His body grew cold in the open air of the tent and the wet blood on the bandage made the skin around the wound grow even colder. He put on a pair of jeans and a flannel shirt.

Suddenly, the realization that Noah was not bound or impris-
oned struck him: *I'm free? I'm free! How?*

Noah wrapped the blanket over his shoulders and tried to
stand. As he put pressure on the injured leg, blinding white pain
shot through his body and he crumpled back to the ground. He
heard a stirring outside; someone poked at the fire. Careful to
keep pressure off the leg, he crawled to the opening of the tent
and zipped open half the slit. He peeked outside, like a ground
squirrel out of its burrow. The sky was grey, and clouds hung low
and heavy over the tree line. A faint streak of sunburst peeked
through an opening of the gunmetal clouds.

The air outside the tent was cool and crisp and smelled strongly
of burning wood. He saw a fire dancing to heights of nearly two
meters. In front of the glow, Noah saw an unfamiliar silhouette
prodding at the flames. A group of small, brownish-green tents
were arranged in a semi-circle around the fire. The color of
the tents matched the color of the clearing in which they were
erected. Each tent had a series of geodesic tubes running along
its exterior. The wind blew the smoke from the fire away from
the tents across the vacant plots and into the trees beyond. Noah,
his head poking out of the tent, called to the fire keeper.

"Hello?" His voice was scratchy and soft. The figure turned
its head from one side to the other, straining to identify the
sound. Noah cleared his throat and called out again, louder
now. "Hello!"

The fire keeper made an about-face and walked toward Noah's
tent. The figure was tall and strong, but as it walked toward Noah,
he could see breasts rising from beneath her jacket. Her hair was
pulled up and buried beneath a ball cap. She crouched down in
front of Noah when she reached his tent. Her face was dirty, but
underneath the dirt, Noah made out handsome features. Shining
through the grime were a pair of dazzling blue eyes.

"How are you feeling?" the woman asked Noah.

Noah looked at her, studying her, and asked "Who are you?"

"My name is Sonya," the woman answered. She looked past Noah's face and into the tent. "I'm going to clean your leg."

She stood up and walked to a different tent at the end of the arc. A few moments later, she came back to Noah with a small plastic first aid kit and sat on the cool grass.

"Spin around," she said to Noah as she made tiny circles with her index finger.

Noah was confused by the woman's presence. "Who are you? Where are—"

Sonya interrupted him. "I need to clean that leg. Now, spin around." Her tone was authoritative, yet compassionate. Noah obeyed.

He used his elbows to scoot back into the tent, then rolled over onto his back. As he moved his body, the pain flashed from his leg to his skull. Carefully, he kept the leg elevated and finished twirling. Once the flashing pain subsided, he bent forward, opened the tent's flap completely, and stuck his legs out. Sonya put his left foot on her thigh. She took out a pair of scissors from the first aid kit and cut the bandages on the leg. She doused the leg with hydrogen peroxide. The antiseptic mixed with the wet blood from the bandages and stained her hands. She wiped them on the grass. She wadded the red-and-white dressing into a ball and placed it into a plastic bag.

The hairs on Noah's leg were sticky with blood. A smaller, flesh-colored bandage remained covering the wound. Sonya took a wet wipe from the first aid kit and cleaned the remaining blood stuck to Noah's leg. The white wipes quickly turned red and a neat pile of crumpled, stained wipes formed between Noah's shins.

"Does it hurt?" Sonya asked.

"Yes," Noah answered. He leaned back and put his head on the inflated ground of the tent. He grimaced and admitted to the woman, "It hurts a lot."

The woman nodded in understanding and dropped the final wipe on the pile. Sonya removed the plastic bag with the bandage and added the wipes to its contents. She placed Noah's leg on the ground, stood up, and brushed her hands off on her black pants. On the way to her tent, she tossed the refuse bag into the fire.

Noah closed his eyes and felt the breeze blow on his freshly cleaned skin. The pain he felt was unlike anything he had ever felt before. A constant, deep throbbing was centralized on his left shin, but every half minute, a burning rush of fire shuddered throughout his whole body. After a few minutes, he heard Sonya approach. She was carrying a small, circular tin. She knelt on the ground outside of Noah's tent and peeled the final, flesh-colored bandage from his leg. The hairs were uprooted from his shank, but he did not feel ripping action; he only felt the same white-hot pain that he felt since he woke. A long, deep gash stretched down Noah's shinbone. This was not the same wound he received from the gunshot. This gash was fresh, and Noah felt the full impact of his blackout.

"What happened?" he asked Sonya again, showing more alarm than before.

She shook her head without looking at him. A series of stitches clumsily crisscrossed over the gash. The blood around the gash was heavy and, as it sat on Noah's leg under the tight bandage, it had mixed with dirt and dust to become a sort of paste. Sonya worked at cleaning this bloody paste diligently and, once she completed the task, she unscrewed the lid to the tin can and removed a glob of mint-green gel. The gel was cool on Noah's skin.

"This will help with the pain in your leg. It will also help prevent an infection."

"The leg doesn't hurt." Noah started. "Everything hurts. My blood feels like it's boiling." The statement made little sense to Noah as it drifted to his ears, but it was how he felt. Sonya nodded as if she somehow understood and finished applying the gel. She rummaged through her bag and pulled out a large syringe. Seeing the surgical instrument brought a rush of memory back to Noah. He remembered Wade creating a syringe from Kendrick Rhodes's glasses in the back of the transport van. Fearful of the object, he tried to move back into the tent, but Sonya held his leg.

"You're not sticking me with that," he forcefully told the woman.

"This will help with the pain, Noah," she said reassuringly, as she loaded the syringe with a clear liquid. "It will make that boiling feeling go away."

"You're not sticking me with that." Noah repeated, this time with less conviction.

Sonya looked at Noah and smiled. "You need to trust me. I'm your friend." Noah felt the syringe pierce his skin. A chill instantly fought the molten pain in his body. He laid back and let the chill consume him.

Lt. Director Juan Carlos Luna had not yet slept. Once his rage had subsided, he had moved into measured action. His team had been attacked and they needed their leader. He and his able-bodied Deputies established a makeshift triage with the EMTs in an abandoned shopping mall to the north of the hotel.

The Lt. Director, with a dozen Federationists, took a cadre of SUVs to search Santa Fe for any citizens that had a medical background. Using a combination of incentives and threats, Luna wrangled a few dozen New Mexicans to work the temporary triage. They ferried in sleepy doctors and nurses until the first wave of medical assistance arrived from Window Rock in the Navajo Nation.

By sunrise in Santa Fe, outside emergency crews had moved all the injured from the Railyard Inn south to Christus St. Vincent Hospital. Luna saw the money funneled to Raul Ramirez in action and he was not impressed with the health care The Federation had purchased from the New Mexican smuggler. The building had been looted and there were hardly any employees staffed as The Federationists tried to put the hospital in working order. There was not enough medical fare in Santa Fe to treat all those injured in the attack. Those with life-threatening injuries were flown nearly five hundred kilometers to Evans Army Community Hospital outside of Colorado Springs. Colorado Springs, though still surrounded by Grey Zone territory, had been firmly guarded since the American signing of the Treaty on Global Nations because it was home to the Air Force Academy. There were dozens of pocketed, fortified, military communities like Colorado Springs in the American West.

These Militarized Zones, unlike GFNSO Forward Operating Bases, were protected and operated solely by the American Armed Services and were not used during any offensive maneuvers. Due to a lack of success in attacking the MZs, as well as loud disapproval from Grey Zone inhabitants critical of attacking the American military, opposition forces left the bases alone. The existence of such a base was a godsend to Juan Carlos Luna. The Commander of the Colorado Springs MZ offered to help with the injured as soon as she heard of the attack and sent a wave of aircrafts to evacuate more than two dozen Feds from Santa Fe.

Those minor injuries who were not airlifted had to wait a few hours at the triage or Christus St. Vincent for medical assistance, but as time passed and additional personnel and equipment reached the city, the wounded were tended to. At least twenty people had died and more than a hundred were injured, but in the chaos it was difficult to determine the exact numbers. As the mountains' long shadows spread over Santa Fe from the glare of the rising sun, Luna felt that the situation was beginning to be controlled.

Luna returned to the Railyard Inn to take a quick nap. He had not stopped moving for the past twelve hours. On the third floor, he had nearly reached his room when he saw the fuming visage of Amir Owens at the exit to the stairwell. The Deputy moved toward the Lt. Director.

Luna stopped in the hall and waited patiently for Owens to speak to him, but the man kept his mouth closed. From a few meters away, Owens lunged at his superior. His bloody, ashen hands were clenched tight on Luna's jacket and shirt. He pushed the Lt. Director hard against the drywall, shaking a cheap painting off its hook. His aggressive action tore the top button lose from Luna's white shirt.

"Did you kill one of those motherfuckers?"

Luna looked Owens straight in the eyes, then tried to move past him, his anger bubbling. Owens tightened his grip and pushed Luna against the wall again. His boot stepped on the painting and the glass crunched.

A snarl came across Luna's face. "Let go of me, Deputy." Luna grabbed the wrist of his restrainer. "That is a direct order."

Owens swallowed hard and gripped harder. "Listen, I'm not going to let you run around here like some bloodthirsty asshole," he slowed his speech, "you need to calm the fuck down." Then, he moved his face close to Luna's ear and finished. "Sir."

Luna struggled against his Deputy, but the young man's grip was strong. He held onto the Lt. Director. Owens saw the fury in the old warrior's eyes. He had seen that fury before and wanted to bring the man back to sanity.

"This isn't Mindanao, sir. People need you."

The mention of the lawless, failed American military campaign slapped Luna with the efficiency of an open hand. The United States' last overseas campaign was a military failure in addition to a compilation of human rights violations that still haunted Luna. He looked at Owens and once he saw the concern in the man's face, began to understand the severity of his grievous action in the parking lot. He hung his head.

"I'm sorry, Amir," he admitted. "It's just—"

Owens cut him off. "I understand, sir. There's no time for that, though. People are dying. They need their leader to be clearheaded. They need you to be the rock, not the spear."

Luna knew this was true. He was ashamed by his rage. He wished Jay were here to tell him everything was alright, but there was no time for self-pity. He collected himself and walked with Deputy Owens to the lobby of the Railyard Inn. The conversation had recharged him; he no longer needed sleep. People had died on his watch and Lt. Director Juan Carlos Luna would do everything in his power to make sure that no more lives would be lost.

Chicago's Barack Obama High-Speed Rail Station, constructed in the late 2020s, was an ode to the former President by Vice President Joe Biden. The high-speed rail system in which the Obama Station was a hub had a rocky history: the first route of the system was completed ahead of schedule and traveled from Philadelphia to Chicago, but the rest of the thousands of kilometers of track remained unfinished for nearly two decades due to a new administration's budget re-allocation. The Obama Rail Station was a monument to the optimistic ambitions of the early thrust to surpass East Asia in hi-tech infrastructure, ambitions which never completely materialized.

Natalie Kelley made it to the station with only fifteen minutes to spare. Joseph Kalani was waiting for her outside.

"Why the hell did you bring that?" Joseph asked as he pointed to the locked metal box.

Natalie shrugged, and Joseph took the box from her and strapped it to his own suitcase. As they entered the station, the suitcase followed a meter behind Joseph and zigged through the crowd and other luggage after him.

The main terminal of the station was huge and airy and had a high, glass ceiling lightly stained with iconography of Chicago history. Separating the station's north and south gates was a water feature, three meters wide and filled with lights and fountains and waterfalls. The terminal was crowded with people, most of whom seemed to be discussing the terror attacks from the night before. Natalie sensed that the crowd was on edge. There were several Federation Security Officers visible walking through the terminal. A few were even armed with TS-33s.

Despite having taken her hangover pill, Natalie felt slightly queasy and claustrophobic immersed in the mass of travelers. She hurried to the platform, following the pastel sunbeams from the ceiling above. She was trying to focus on the job ahead. On the way to the rail station, she had contacted a Federationist in San Francisco to set up a meeting. Luckily the woman had not been injured in the attack, but Natalie could hear that she was rattled. Natalie reached the assigned gate, but Joseph was not behind her. She stopped and waited a few moments for him. The herd of men and women passed by, but she did not see her editor. The PA system announced that their train would be closed to boarding in ten minutes.

Natalie stood on her tiptoes but could not see into the crowd. She became anxious. She jumped into the rush of humanity and began to nervously look for her boss. She had visions of the man on the ground, his hand over his heart, gasping for air. She worried for him. *Why did I pressure him to come?* Sweat began to bead on her brow. Finally, next to the waterway's rusted steel hog statue, she saw Joseph speaking with an SO. The Officer wore a black uniform and stood aggressively close to Joseph. Natalie rushed to his side.

"There you are," Joseph said. "She wants me to open the box, but I told her I couldn't open it because it isn't mine."

The Security Officer turned to Natalie. "Ma'am, is this your luggage?"

A man who was walking by nudged Natalie, knocking her against the polished ledge of the waterway. The crowd seemed to constrict around them.

Natalie was irritated at the delay. She just wanted to get on the train, away from the crowd. "I wouldn't call it luggage," she started, but changed course. "Yes, that is my luggage."

"What do you have inside?" The SO asked.

"Well, to be honest, I don't know. I couldn't get the damn thing open."

"Okay. I'm going to have to take a look." The SO said as she placed the box on the ground. "Do you mind if I break the lock?"

Natalie laughed. "I'd be ecstatic if you broke the lock, miss. But please hurry. We have a train to catch."

The SO produced a small wand from her utility belt. The wand emitted a narrow laser beam which cut through the padlock easily. The padlock fell to the floor and the SO brushed it aside. Natalie watched as the padlock was kicked by one traveler, then another. It skated along the slick floor until it disappeared under the marching feet.

As Natalie watched the padlock vanish, the SO opened the lid of the box. She held the lid open at an acute angle. Natalie looked as the SO searched the box, but the green lid blocked her view. The SO rummaged, uninterested and, as Natalie moved to her side, she closed the lid and told Natalie and Joseph they were cleared to go. The Officer placed the box on Joseph's automated suitcase and disappeared into the crowd.

"We need to go," Joseph said to Natalie and headed for the platform. The suitcase followed him, led by his Implanted Wrist Chip.

Natalie readjusted the strap of her bag and caught up to the trailing suitcase. She opened the lid to the box and looked inside. There was a thick stack of papers. She thumbed through the stack. The papers were of different sizes and different shades. Some had clean, straight edges and others had torn edges. *Who would want me to have all this shit?* She shook her head and looked at the first few sheets. On each page she found succinct, handwritten notes but the notes were gibberish. They appeared to be coded. *If someone wanted to keep these secret, why not encrypt a file?* Page after page had terse, unintelligible messages. The suitcase stopped, and the PA announced there were only two minutes left to board the train.

Noah Bridger felt like a winter stream flowed under his skin. When the icy current reached his heart, he gasped and clutched his chest, then tried to sit up. The frozen brook branched back through his veins and scratched every nerve as it traveled to the tips of his fingers and toes.

"What did you do to me?" he angrily asked Sonya, still struggling to breathe.

Sonya put her finger on his lips and moved her hands over his eyelids.

"Shush, now," she whispered and moved away from the tent to sit by the fire. The chill returned to Noah's heart, lessened in severity this rotation. As Noah tried to calm his breathing, he watched Sonya sit and the fire dance as the sun rose above the tops of the oaks.

After a few minutes, the blood bubbling inside Noah warmed and his body began to return to normal. All but his leg. He could not feel the area around the wound. The gel Sonya had slathered his leg with shined on his shin like a newly waxed floor. He moved out of the tent and scooted on his backside as he used the palms of his hands to creep forward. Birds called to each other in the trees that surrounded the camp. Sonya nodded at Noah as he stopped next to her, then looked back at the fire. Shadows from the sun and the fire Pliéd and Fouettéd across her face. Her cheeks were rosy and smeared with dirt; her black brows grew thick and trickled across the bridge of her nose. The muscles in her neck and shoulders were taut. Noah thought she looked tired. He rubbed his injured leg but could not feel his fingers on the skin.

"When will the feeling come back?"

Sonya continued to look at the fire, then turned to Noah.

"You would rather have the pain?"

"No," Noah looked down and rested his chin on his chest. "No. I just want it back to normal."

Sonya did not say anything. After a few seconds, she moved to stand but Noah halted her by grabbing her ankle. She turned to him.

"What happened to my leg?" Noah asked again, almost pleading now.

"I believe you were shot." Sonya stated. "At least, that's what they told me." She broke the weak grip he had on her ankle and started to walk away.

"No!" Noah erupted, not realizing how loud he yelled. He looked around the sleeping camp and lowered his voice. "No. It was not like this."

Sonya looked down at the leg and eyed the long gash. Drops of blood seeped through the crude stitches.

"We'll get that leg back to normal, Noah. Once we get you to a physician. Once we're out of the forest. Once we're safe."

Noah was not satisfied with her answer. Her vagueness made him afraid.

"Please. What happened to my leg?"

He brought to the center of his mind images from the night before. Wade breaking the glasses. The needle stuck in his leg. The pain. The darkness. "Please. They did something to my leg."

Tears welled up in Noah's eyes. With the pain gone and his leg numb, fear filled him.

"Please. Tell me."

Sonya looked into Noah's eyes and he saw a great depth of sympathy in her gaze. She stepped to him and rested a hand on his shoulder.

"I'm not the one to tell you, because I was not there. But, trust me, I hear that it was for your own good." She moved her hand off his shoulder. "It was for everyone's good."

Sonya walked away from Noah and went back to her tent. He was left alone in the early morning quiet. He was confused. He was afraid. The weight of his situation settled over him. The fear brought no clarity, only questions. *Where am I? How did we get out of the prison transport van? What happened to my leg? How did we get to this spot in the woods? What about my family? Do they know where I am? Do they know I'm safe? Am I safe? Are they safe?*

Noah had no answers. He had not had any answers for days now. Weeks, probably. He felt defeated and lost. He had been lost since Wade dragged him into this mess. *Wade.* Wade would have answers. Noah still felt nothing in his leg. He did not dare stand on it. He looked at the tents nestled around the fire. *Wade has to be here. Somewhere.* He did not know which tent his brother-in-law was in. It did not matter. The questions remained unanswered, but he was determined to discover the answers.

Startling the chirping birds and shattering the stillness of the morning, Noah shouted Wade's name as loud as he could.

Lt. Director Juan Carlos Luna assembled a team of six of his best Deputies—at least his six best Deputies alive and uninjured. The group assessed the security mission's current state over breakfast at a local Tex-Mex restaurant on the southern border of De Vargas Park. The team had been working hard for more than twelve hours straight and the situation had finally stabilized.

The casualty numbers from the attack the night previous were dire. Deputy D.P. McGregor told Luna that twenty-six Federationists had been killed during the attack. Four Railyard Inn employees had died. Thirty-six critically-injured Feds had been evacuated to Colorado Springs and Window Rock. Information that regarded those who had been evacuated was slowly trickling in.

Deputy Nguyễn Thị Vân addressed the table and said that the medical center at Christus St. Vincent Hospital was functioning well for those facing non-life-threatening injuries. Most of those receiving medical care in Santa Fe would be evacuated to White Zone medical centers before nightfall. As Deputy Thị Vân spoke, Luna's APD alerted him that Director Farrelly wished to speak with him. After he finished his huevos rancheros, he thanked McGregor and Thị Vân for their reports and thanked the Deputies for their hard work. Then, he instructed them to start packing. He expected them all to be back on Roosevelt Island by the next morning.

After the breakfast meeting, one Federation SUV had driven back to the Railyard Inn while one waited for the Lt. Director's phone call with Director Farrelly to end. Once Luna put his APD in his pocket, Amir Owens pulled up to the curb. The two had put their tense exchange behind them. Owens felt sorry for the Lt. Director. He knew how deeply devastated the man was by the death of Arnie Jones. The fury that sprung from Luna last night, as well as earlier this morning, spouted from the same well in which he stored his legendary bravery. Within Juan Carlos Luna was a vast reserve of passion.

Lt. Director Luna told Owens that they would not be back in New York by the next morning. He relayed his conversation with Farrelly to his Deputy. Secretary-General Dubois still planned to come to Santa Fe to sign the treaty with John Hill. In fact, Farrelly told Luna that Dubois wanted to move the signing up to the following day: Farrelly had asked Luna if it was possible to host the signing on 14 May without incident. Luna, hoping to redeem what he saw as his own personal shortcomings from the attack the night before and inspired by Dubois's bold action, told Farrelly that if the signing were to be held tomorrow, it would be unimpeded. As Luna finished detailing the new mission, Owens thought he detected a kink in the Lt. Director's optimism.

When they reached the Railyard Inn, Luna told Owens to gather all available Federationists in the lobby for an announcement. He walked to the back porch and, with his pipe packed, struck a match and held it on top of the tobacco leaves. The leaves glowed and burned as Luna puffed at the stem. Once the pipe was adequately lit, Luna inhaled deeply and held the smoke in his lungs. He exhaled and blew the smoke out into the early mountain air. Luna realized he was in the same seat he had been utilizing all week. He looked to his side and saw the empty chair next to him: it was the same chair that Arnie Jones had been sitting in for the past week. *Arnie should still be sitting in that* fakakta *chair.*

Luna drew on the pipe again and remembered his old friend-in-arms. He had a mighty mission ahead of him in securing the treaty signing and wished he had his Chief Deputy by his side to help coordinate the monumental preparations. Ever since they were in boot camp, the man had always had Juan Carlos's back. They had gone through some of the most hellish battles imaginable and now a Goddamn flying robot mowed him down in the hotel lobby of some rundown shithole. It was bullshit, complete and utter bullshit. Luna longed for the days when his enemy was lined up opposite him, when he could see the fear in their eyes and smell the sweat as it poured down their spines. He wished he lived in a time when he could just wrap his hands around the other bastard's throat and squeeze until the life leaked out of him like a punctured tire. Not in a world where some sonuvabitch could cower a world away and murder one of the best men alive from some chicken-shit basement. He had taken his wrath out on one of the goatfuckers in the parking lot, but he knew that man had little to do with the attack. That man had been a pawn, needed only to plant the initial explosion. He was as expendable as the drone; both were mechanical and easily cast aside.

Luna's jaw clenched hard on his tobacco pipe as the anger boiled within him. There was a sudden snap as the stem broke under the pressure of his teeth. The bowl fell onto his lap and the simmering leaves spilled out, singeing his pants. Luna spit the remainder of the stem out and quickly brushed the ash and charred leaves away from his lap and onto the ground. He stomped out the glistening tobacco and smeared the dottle into a black stain across the cement.

He needed to settle down. Arnie would have told him to "Calm the fuck down, *pare,* and keep your head." There was an important mission at hand. A mission, though it may be ill-advised, that must be completed. Lt. Director Luna walked back into the Railyard Inn lobby and spoke to his troops.

Natalie Kelley did not notice the Illinois countryside whizzing by outside her window; she was too busy leafing through the documents strewn across her seat-back tray. Next to her, Joseph Kalani dozed in and out of sleep. The man had an uncanny ability to sleep anywhere, anytime. Years ago, he had told Natalie that sleep was a luxury that only a fool would pass over when it was available. She joked that he had narcolepsy.

The pair had been on the train for nearly thirty minutes and Natalie had not yet looked through a tenth of the papers. She was unable to put together a cohesive pattern of the scribbles, unable to break the cipher. Her first objective was not to answer the "what" of the mystery box, but the "who". There were no identifiable names within the code, no personal markers on the parchment. *Who the hell sent me this package of nonsense?*

Natalie studied the penmanship on each of the scraps of paper. She decided there were at least three different, primary handwritings. The art of graphology had become a rarity in recent decades due to the near-absolute use of electronic communication, but Natalie had an interest in the study because she had taken up calligraphy as a little girl. In his free time, Natalie's father enjoyed creating beautiful, illuminated manuscripts of classic literature. Faulkner. Hemingway. Steinbeck. He introduced her to the twentieth century American greats. As a child, Natalie sat in her father's office, which he jokingly called the "scriptorium," and made her own manuscripts, complete with messy text, crooked marginalia, and simple illustration.

As Natalie grew older, she abandoned the practice, but the lessons she learned came back to her now. As she studied the pages before her, she noted that none of the authors took great care in their writing or had received extensive lessons in penmanship. The writing was often sloppy and at points illegible. Even if she had known the code, she might not be certain of a letter's intent. There was one handwriting that was slightly better than the others. She decided to focus solely on text from that pen.

As the train continued down the track, Natalie poured over the notes. She reached the end of the stack but no definitive conclusions. Her instinct told her that the papers were important, but she still did not know *why* they were important. Or who sent them to her. Or how she was supposed to know what the fuck they meant.

Frustrated, she threw the papers back into the box, shut the lid, and leaned back in her chair. Joseph rustled beside her. If she knew who sent her this box she may know what they were trying to tell her. She thought back to the trip and the only person she thought might have sent the box was Faye. *But why would she keep that a secret? Especially if she was going to...* Natalie did not want to finish that thought. She had called the Lincoln County Police Department to inquire if there had been a mention of the papers in the note they recovered, but they offered no comment. She needed to answer the question of *who*. The sender was her Rosetta Stone; it would unlock the secrets within.

Joseph opened his eyes and looked down at the box. Corners of paper stuck through the crease between the lid and the base.

"What was in your treasure box?" he asked dreamily.

Natalie just shook her head and looked out the window.

"Can I look?" Joseph followed up, reaching for the box.

"By all means." Natalie answered. The old editor opened the lid and pulled out a stack of papers. He glanced at one, then thumbed to the next.

"Huh," he said to himself. He was awake now.

Natalie did not answer. She closed her eyes hoping to get some rest.

"It looks like a Caesar Shift Cipher."

Wade Barrineau thundered out of his tent. He wore only a pair of briefs and his long hair flowed wildly. His stocky, scarred chest puffed out and his bare legs moved quickly through the wispy grass. His cheeks were crimson with fury. Even though Noah saw he had his brother-in-law's attention, he continued to scream his name. He did not know what else to do. Around the camp, others began to emerge from their tents to discover the origin of the racket.

When Wade reached Noah, he greeted him with a quick backhand to the face, grabbed him by the hair with one hand, and put his other hand tight over Noah's mouth. Noah's stifled scream died against the thick skin of the stubby mitt. Wade's eyes bulged and showed his bloodshot sclera. He leaned close to Noah.

"Shut the fuck up, man!" he hissed, then removed his grip and delivered another lightning quick backhand.

Breathless and small, Noah stared at Wade. The violence had not shocked him, but the swearing had. He was silent.

Wade took a step away from Noah, toward the fire and tried to regain his composure. The other members of the camp started to circle around the pair. Noah saw there were about ten people total. Wade spoke to them.

"It's okay. It's okay. Go back to your tents and let's start packing up."

The others moved away slowly, seemingly disappointed with the uneventful conclusion. Noah thought they looked like a pack of hyenas in wait around a lion's kill. As they turned their back on him, he felt like a lifeless carcass.

Wade looked down at Noah again.

"Get in your tent. Before you make an even bigger fool of yourself."

Wordlessly, Wade walked into the tent and stood at the back, large and proud and nearly naked. Noah crawled in behind him and shut the flap to block the wind. The cool morning air seemed to have no effect on Wade, but Noah needed to wrap himself tighter in the blanket.

"Now why were you screaming like a madman? You do realize we are wanted men, don't you?"

Noah, pale and weak, looked up at Wade. He summoned all his courage and voice trembling, he spoke.

"I want answers, Wade," he said. He shifted the weight off his elbows and swung his legs in front of him. He sat stiffly, his back straight against the plastic of the tent. "No. No. I *need* answers. I'm *entitled* to them."

Wade snickered.

"Ha. Entitled," he brushed his hand at the air. "You're a weak man, Noah Bridger. You've always been a small, weak man."

Noah grew angry. He had expected a response to his command, not an insult. "What the hell did you do to me?" he screamed. Then, he picked up the still numb leg and dropped to the ground. "What did you do to my leg?"

"When you were shot in the leg, it gave us a perfect opportunity. You've helped our cause greatly." Wade continued, smugly. "I've done more to make you a productive person than you ever have."

"Just give me a Goddamn straight answer!" Noah winced at his blasphemy and expected another blow from his pious brethren.

Wade picked at the plastic roof of the tent, then flicked a spot where the inflated tube lay on the outside, making an empty, popping noise. He stepped close to Noah and crouched in front of him; Noah could smell the man's hot morning breath before he spoke.

"We needed a way to escape, brother, so we implanted a bomb in your leg."

Lt. Director Juan Carlos Luna's assembled Federationists were professionals, but when he told them that the signing would occur the next day, he knew their confidence in the mission was shaken. Most had lost friends the night before and all had close colleagues convalescing. After breakfast, word had spread that they would be home soon, and relief had circulated throughout the hotel. Now, they had thirty-six hours to complete the biggest assignment of their lives.

Luna told the men and women to get some sleep and that they would reconvene in a couple hours. Reinforcements were already arriving in Santa Fe and, within the next few hours, the security team would be two thousand strong. However, Luna's most trusted and experienced Officers were in desperate need of rest and they had very little time to spare. He hoped that the mission would help them focus and start to move past the atrocity of the night before, but he also knew that they would need time to deal with the trauma from the attack. Coping would need to wait.

With the wounded moved to Christus St. Vincent and the bulk of the debris cleared, the hotel had regained some semblance of a functioning business, barring the massive hole in the lobby entrance. Newly arrived Federation crews sprayed the hole with foam to create a temporary façade. Through the hole, a pair of mourning doves had flown into the lobby and were perched on a ledge overlooking the concierge desk. They cooed and watched the crew work.

Luna's first task was to find a new, larger temporary headquarters. The Railyard Inn was not originally intended to be the final main headquarters, but Luna's timetable had been drastically altered. The location of the headquarters was paramount; it needed to be easy to defend. The Lt. Director cursed himself for the cavalier attitude he had taken in choosing and defending the Railyard Inn. He vowed not to make that mistake again.

Federationists were en route from New York, Toronto, Chicago, and Monterrey. San Francisco, the fifth and final GFN North American Hub, could not send any officers due to the attack on the office the night before. In fact, many of the west coast sub-Hubs were sending their SOs to San Francisco instead of Santa Fe. To round out the security forces, Farrelly doubled the STAB units assigned to the Treaty from ten to twenty. This worried Luna. He could not help but think of the military operations that would be delayed by the signing and feared that, with the attention elsewhere, his forces in the Grey Zone would be compromised. After all, that was his main duty. He wished that he could orchestrate and oversee field operations instead of ensuring the safety of a truce he did not agree with. Instead of making sure no one blew up John Hill and his cronies, he wished he were planning an assault of Salmon, Idaho, the AFG capitol.

True peace with these people will not come from the ink of a pen, but from the blood of their throats.

Luna had tracked the numbers of militants in the Black and Grey Zones for years. Those numbers had been steadily dropping. Obviously, it was favorable to have less enemies instead of more, however, the quantity of foes did not tell the whole story. Luna knew that a cornered enemy was often the most dangerous. A desperate mind bred desperate actions and actions made in desperation could be the most devastating. Desperation had crept over the world as the tenets expressed in the Basic Human Standard first expanded. Change will always scare people, even when that change is for the best. Luna had spent years battling the resistors of change. Now he was charged with overseeing the security of a deal that would not only bring many of those resistors amnesty, but prosperity. At times like this, he would discuss this void of justice with Arnie Jones, but with Arnie gone, he did not want to burden any of his Deputies with his doubts. The men and women were under enough stress already without having to worry about the ethics of their operation.

The signing would take place, and he would make sure of it.

In the lobby, Luna looked at a holographic topo-map of Santa Fe. He found two viable options for a temporary NASO HQ and needed to look at them in person. As the map's projection retreated into his APD, Brandt Bonner of the Texas Military Brigade rushed into the hotel lobby. Behind him, escorted by two uniformed men, was a tall, dark, exhausted man wearing restraints.

"You can read that?" Natalie asked Joseph in amazement.

"No," he answered, still studying the text. "Not yet."

"But you know the coding technique?"

"Yes, I think so. It looks to be one of the oldest techniques there is. A Caesar Shift Cipher is a simple substitution cipher. Say "G" is "G", right? And "H" is "H". Your standard alphabet. With this coding technique, you just slide the base one way or another. If you slide two to the right, then "G" is "E" and "H" is "F", yeah? Easy."

"It is easy, but it's gonna take forever to read it."

Joseph leaned back again and closed his eyes. "Just plug it into your Device. I'm sure that thing can figure it out."

Natalie was upset with herself that she had not thought of that originally. She realized that she had enjoyed the puzzle in front of her, even if it had been driving her mad. That had been one of the reasons she enjoyed journalism so much; she found that the best puzzle of all was trying to piece together people's stories.

She grabbed her APD and quickly found an app to decode the scribblings before her. She plugged in the text from the top page. There was not much there. A moment later, the app translated the text and read, "John. City KS. Talk to casher at petrol shope. One crate."

Natalie read the translation out loud to Joseph.

"It sounds like a drop point," he answered. He sat placidly next to her, his eyes closed and his arms crossed in front of his chest. His fingers played with the white hairs swirling by his elbow.

Natalie translated a half-dozen more notes. The contents of each followed the same formula as the first. Natalie made a list of each of the locations revealed: each location was a border town in the Grey Zone.

Natalie turned to Joseph who still sat twisting his arm hair. "Why would someone encrypt messages with a code that's so easy to break?"

Joseph thought for a moment. "With our computers, I guess any easily read code is going to be easy to break. They must have thought it was a good idea to code their correspondence, but when the time came to actually implement a code, they got lazy. Probably watched too many old spy movies."

Natalie thought to herself. *How would a box full of notes from wannabe spies get in my hands?*

"What do you mean you implanted a bomb in my leg, Wade? My leg's right here! I'm right here!" Noah Bridger yelled at his brother-in-law. He could not believe what he had been told.

Wade took a deep breath. "It was no normal bomb, brother. It was an EMP."

"A what?"

"An electromagnetic pulse."

"An electromagnetic pulse? In my leg?" Noah was still incredulous. "How?" he mumbled. "How?"

"The doctor at Forrest City." Wade answered simply, as if that explained everything.

"The doctor." Noah repeated, dumbfounded.

"Yes, the doctor. He's sympathetic. And he was treated fairly. We were planning on staging a fight or accident in the yard to get one of us to the infirmary, so he could implant the EMP, but then you showed up. And the doctor decided that it was best to use your leg wound as the implantation."

Noah lay in silence and rubbed his leg. He studied the scar. The gel no longer shone around the gash and the new, crude stitches, but the leg remained dull from the ointment Sonya had applied. Noah imagined the intense pain returning and winced.

"My leg," is all he could manage to say. Noah breathed heavily and closed his eyes, trying to organize his scattered thoughts. "If the doctor implanted the bomb, what did you stick me with in the van?"

Wade sighed. "A solution of nanos which activated the EMP." He looked at Noah's leg. "Looks like someone cleaned it. They must have also injected the microbial solution to accelerate the biodegradation of the nanos in your bloodstream. You'll be fine." Wade looked at his plastic analog watch. "We need to get moving. We took care of you last night, but you will need to keep up with us today. We're still in danger."

Noah remained laying between his brother-in-law and the slip of the tent.

"Wade. My leg. What did you do to my leg? Will it be okay?"

He could not process the information he had been given. *Nanos. EMPs. Microbial solution.* The terms were outside his understanding.

Wade stepped over Noah and looked down at him as he spoke. "I did nothing to your leg, man. They did." He pointed, indicting an invisible crowd. "You need to get moving. What has happened, has happened. You must get ready to leave. Get dressed. Take the tent down and put it in the bag. I'll try to find you a crutch."

Wade walked out of the tent. Noah lay on the ground inside and covered his face with his hands. *I just want to be home.* As Noah wished to be elsewhere, Wade's frowning face reappeared in the tent flap.

"Noah, I would very much like to see you on the other side of this. But, my brother, I do not need you anymore," his tone was acrid. "Do you understand?"

Noah was struck by his brother-in-law's harsh words, but with his hands still cupped over his eyes, he managed to nod in compliance. Outside, the rain began to patter on the shell of the tent.

This can't be good. The unannounced appearance of General Bonner of the Texas Military Brigade and the dirty prisoner did not bode well for Lt. Director Juan Carlos Luna. He did not need any distraction from the next day's treaty signing. Luna quickly looked at the clock on his APD. *This better be quick.*

Luna led General Brandt Bonner, the General's subordinates, and the captive to the third floor. The General's subordinates waited in the hall as Luna and Bonner pushed the captive inside the Lt. Director's hotel room. The room, with a neatly-made single bed and a clean, faux-wood desk, had been spared by the explosion at the front of the hotel. Bonner pressed the captive down into a chair near the window while Luna shut the drapes and sat on the bed across from the captive. Bonner moved across the room and stood against the wall by the door. He took his enormous Colt Peacemaker out of its holster and held it in his hand, tapping the muzzle against his thigh.

"Who are you?" Luna asked the captive, his eyes leveled at the man. His hands were held in plastic restraints in his lap. The captive was younger than Luna had originally supposed. Filth and fear and fatigue had aged him.

The captive answered in a hoarse voice, but he was confident in his English. "I am Gabriel Schmitz. You are 'La Frontera'?"

Luna was surprised by the question. He looked back at Bonner and the man raised his hands in incredulity.

"He kept requesting a meeting with you. Wouldn't shut up about it for two days. We ignored the requests at first, but then we found one of the others trying to strangle him." Luna noticed the bruises on the young man's neck. Bonner finished. "We figured if they wanted to shut him up so badly, we ought to give him a meeting."

Luna turned to the captive and answered. "I have been called 'La Frontera.'"

Schmitz appeared relieved, his tense shoulders relaxed a little and the tightness in his face eased.

"Good," the young captive breathed out. "Then you will help me."

Luna snorted, stood up, and walked forward to Schmitz. He leaned down and spoke in the man's ear. "Just why the fuck would I help you?"

The captive was unfazed by Luna's proximity. "Because you are La Frontera."

Luna crouched before the captive and snarled, centimeters away. "I think you've got some bad intel about La Frontera, *cabrito*."

Hope still shone in the captive's eyes. "My brother told me, before he died, that you would help me. That I must find you. I have found you. Now, you must help me."

The train was gliding through the green Iowa cornfields as Joseph Kalani napped and Natalie Kelley decoded the stack of papers on her tray table with her APD. Bright white wind turbines covered the skyscape out the window of the jetting train. Dark clouds formed overhead, and a firm wind pushed the turbines round and round.

In the editor's bag, Joseph's APD began to buzz. Then, Natalie's beeped, and a message popped up on the screen alerting her of an incoming GFN message. Soon APDs in every aisle of the car came to life. Overhead, The Federation's announcement jingle chimed on the train's PA system. Joseph opened his eyes slightly, but kept his head laying on the seat rest. Natalie dropped her APD on the stack of papers and readied herself for the announcement. The familiar voice of the GFN-NA Press Secretary began to speak. The message was brief, but shocking: Secretary-General Dubois had rescheduled the treaty-signing with American Freedom Group President John Hill. It would take place the following evening. The signing would occur at the New Mexico Capitol Building in Santa Fe. The conclusion of the announcement was muffled by chatter among the train passengers.

Joseph Kalani was now fully awake and sitting upright next to Natalie. She looked at her boss and waited for him to speak. A swell of admiration for Dubois filled her as she thought about his persistence, but she also feared that the man was walking into the lion's den.

Joseph grabbed Natalie's hand and turned to her. A broad smile spread across his face.

"Natalie, I believe we need to find our way to Santa Fe."

The numbness in Noah Bridger's leg made it tricky to walk at first, but after some time, and the aid of a broken branch as a crutch, he was able to trudge forward. The rain came down hard, pelting the foliage above the traveling fugitives. The rain funneled down the tree's trunks, careened off the branches, and turned the forest floor into a soft, sloppy mess.

Noah walked alone; Wade and the other men had forged ahead through the woods without him as soon as they left camp. Only Sonya lagged. She walked a dozen meters or so ahead of Noah. Once he caught her sneaking a look back at him as he struggled forward. Wade's warning of not needing Noah anymore was evident in the group's actions. From this point forward, it was survival of the fittest.

Still, despite Wade's apathy toward Noah's plight and his status as a wanted man, trekking through the forest brought a surprising calm to Noah. He always felt a sense of peace in the simplicity of the outdoors. He concentrated on moving forward one step at a time. He did not think of what would happen to him if he were suddenly ambushed, only about keeping his footing on the slick ground. He did not think of his family in Texas, only about moving forward. Noah just needed to be in the moment. He just needed to survive.

Time passed. The rainfall slowed. Birds scampered from branch to branch and Noah marched on. Sonya was always within sight and a few times he spied the others moving ahead. The group reached the crest of a creek and changed course, following the water. The creek flowed strong with the new precipitation and Noah kept his distance from the edge, wary of the precariously muddy bank. His crutch sunk into the spongy soil. His pace slowed, but he persisted; winded, yet undeterred, he quickened his pace. The pain in his leg returned, but the outlines of those in front of him slowly grew larger.

Finally, as the creek grew narrower and the terrain inclined, the group stopped to rest. When he approached, the group was speaking intently. Noah did not care to join the conversation. Instead, he sat on the wet grass and stretched out his leg. Inside his pack, which contained his decompressed tent, he found a hydration pack. He sucked the pack dry as he massaged his aching calf.

He felt a tap on his shoulder and when he turned his head, Sonya was standing above him.

"How's the leg?"

Noah shrugged and continued to rub.

"It's fine," he answered tersely. He tried to remain present and within himself, neither thinking of the group that would leave him behind or the invisible forces chasing him.

Sonya either did not notice his withdrawal or did not care to acknowledge it as she sat down next to him.

He kept his eyes cast downward, but he could hear her breathing next to him and felt her gaze drilling into him.

"Wade can sure be a prick sometimes," she said after a few moments of silence.

Noah laughed and looked over at Sonya. He could not have agreed with her more.

Juan Carlos Luna looked at the man. Through the grime, he saw that he was no more than sixteen or seventeen years of age. He was intrigued by the boy's optimistic command for help but knew a great deal of work lay before him. He could not afford a lengthy distraction.

"You have a limited number of words," he told the captive sitting before him. "Use them wisely."

The young man spoke fast with adrenaline and nerves, but his English was strong and clear.

"My name is Gabriel Schmitz. My father is Hugo Schmitz. I—"

Luna interrupted. "Your father is *the* Hugo Schmitz? Of the *resistência brasileira?*"

The captive continued. "Yes, the same. I am the youngest of fourteen children. I have twelve brothers. When my father was in Brasilia, I was born in the Heart of the Amazon. Instead of a rattle, I played with a rifle and I was deadly from a distance by the age of five. There was peace, but my family was trained like we were at war. When that war started, we were ready.

"When I killed my first Fed, my father threw me a celebration welcoming me to manhood. Hugo Schmitz is a man that has no sympathy for the weak. I grew up in a place of hate. I knew nothing else. I killed many, but I felt no remorse. I lost brothers but was told that they had not been strong enough to survive. When I was eleven, my closest friend was killed by a GFN bomb. I cried, and my father beat me. I did not dare cry again.

"For my entire life, everyone I knew told me that The Federation was pure evil. I had no choice but to believe. This was the life I lived. One filled with hatred. I stalked through the jungle like a jaguar and cut down the evil. I became very good at killing. When you find a roach on your kitchen floor, you do not think before you squash it. It is just done.

"This is what I believed, until my brother told me about a man he called 'La Frontera.'"

As soon as the announcement finished, Joseph Kalani was on his APD, sending a message to a contact in the GFN to get a pair of rail tickets to enter the Grey Zone. Transportation to New Mexico was now the hottest commodity in America. Over the course of his illustrious career, Joseph had saved a great deal of professional clout and seldom cashed in the favors he was owed. The contact came through and the pair were booked for passage to Santa Fe. They would change trains in Denver and head south from there.

Natalie had put away the pages of code and focused on preparing for the signing tomorrow. As Joseph worked on transportation, she looked into lodging for the two of them. After the attack at the Railyard Inn and Secretary-General Dubois's announcement regarding the treaty-signing, Santa Fe was about to find itself under the world's largest microscope. A flood of journalists, supporters, and protesters always showed up for Dubois's public announcements, no matter the occasion. The timing of the signing after one of the deadliest terror attacks in years would only magnify the public attention. Santa Fe, a town ravaged by years of economic sanctions, did not have the infrastructure to accommodate such an influx. The Federation often used such depleted communities as welcoming areas into the Basic Human Standard. It was a tactic originated by GFNs Vice Secretary-General Xi Fang and had been recently utilized in Perth and Chennai. The publicity would show those in the White Zone how bad it could be if they abandoned The Federation. It also gave the GFN an opportunity to later go back to the restored city and showcase the progress that had been made. Natalie found the tactic seemed to be working as she searched for lodging. Santa Fe had little to offer when it came to hotels and inns;

most of the rooms had already been booked and the others were listed at astronomical prices.

Half-jokingly, she informed her editor that they would just need to purchase a tent and camp in a field or alley, but Joseph was not amused. Natalie searched through lodging offered by Santa Fe homeowners, but those prices were even more exorbitant. She was beginning to think that there may not be anything available when Joseph told her to stop looking. He had paid an unspecified amount of money from his personal funds for a suite at the run-down Hotel Santa Fe, Hacienda and Spa. The Hotel Santa Fe was a block away from the Railyard Inn.

Natalie was excited to get to Santa Fe. This was the biggest story of the year and she was going to be on the frontlines with her mentor. She pulled up her research and continued to flesh out the biographical details she had been working on. None of the leadership of the AFG had yet commented on the attacks from the night before. Natalie decided to make the reaction to the carnage the central point of her piece.

In order to fully cover the signing, Natalie would need to speak with representatives from both sides. She sent a message to Sarah Kinsey, a member of the GFN-NA's Communication Department, looking to set up a meeting. She then reached out to a member of the American Freedom Group and scheduled a sit-down with her for tomorrow afternoon. She had not yet met Amy Huong but had corresponded with her in the past and it had been cordial. Two months ago, Amy rose in the ranks of the AFG from spokeswoman to key advisor to the President, John Hill. Natalie suspected that Amy had played a crucial role in orchestrating the treaty.

As the box of scribbled notes sat in the recess under the chair in front of her, its contents slipped into a recess in Natalie's mind and she did not think about them again until the train had stopped.

During the break, Sonya had applied more of the numbing gel to Noah's leg. Once they started moving again, she walked with him. As the rain stopped and the sun pierced the clouds, the pace of the group ahead picked up. Though the two marched almost side by side, they spoke very little.

Noah had asked Sonya where they were headed. She had just responded, "We're getting you home." After that, silence reclaimed the duo.

Even if Sonya had provided a specific destination, it would not have meant much to Noah at all. His geographical knowledge outside Deaf Smith County was poor. Any town name or landmark given could be just down the road from his ranch or in another country and Noah would not know. When he heard that they were headed home, he was satisfied.

They moved forward in silence. Noah was unable to find the monotonous peace he had enjoyed during the morning hike. Now, he became lost in thoughts of home and family. He longed to see them. Noah could tell that Sonya wished to speak to him, but each time she had tried he was short with her. He had not meant to be abrupt, but he could not drag his mind away from his thoughts of Marie and the kids.

After some time, Noah's mind drifted from his family to his traveling companion. Every so often, he would hear her breath or feel her brush up against him as they navigated a tight corridor in the woods. His thoughts turned from Marie to Sonya. He realized he knew next to nothing about his walking partner. As they made their way down an incline, he spoke to her.

Sonya was obviously startled when she heard Noah's voice break the silence and, for a moment, he could tell that she needed to make sure that he had addressed her.

"What was that, Noah?"

Noah cleared his throat and spoke again, louder this time.

"Thanks again for helping with my leg. Are you a nurse or something?"

Sonya smiled at him.

"You're welcome. And, no, I'm not a nurse." Noah thought she had finished and tried to think of something else to say, when she continued. "I was in medical school, but I never finished."

Noah detected a hint of sadness in her answer, but he did not ask Sonya to extrapolate. However, the sound of her voice comforted him: she sounded like Marie, or at least Noah imagined that she did. He wanted to ask her more, to learn more, to hear more of that voice.

"How long have you known Wade, then?"

"A couple of years."

Noah pictured himself at a BBQ, making small-talk with Sonya over burgers and potato salad. Maybe celebrating the Fourth of July with a cold beer and the smell of fireworks, kids running across the yard carrying sparklers and yelling with glee. He continued with the fantasy of familiarity and tradition.

"How did you and Wade meet?"

"We used to fuck."

Lt. Director Luna listened to the young captive's story intently. He thought that Gabriel Schmitz spoke with pure truth: that he had no hidden agenda and that he only wanted Juan Carlos to listen to him. Luna was touched by his belief and leaned forward on the bed, listening to the story. Schmitz spoke with his glistening brown eyes fixed on Lt. Director Luna.

"My oldest brother, Tancredo, first went to the United States five years ago. Our battle had abated, and we had defeated The Federation and they left the jungle. The militias dispersed throughout the jungle in victory. My father, never resting, sensed an opportunity. With the Globals retreating, the Überkapitalistischen had a surplus of arms that he could sell. He sent Tancredo north to sell his arms to the American fighters.

"When Tancredo returned to the camp outside Manaus, he brought no contracts of sale. Instead, he brought Jesus Christ. My father is not a religious man. Hugo had baptized his children as Catholics and took them to Mass every Sunday, but this was only to advance his business interests. None of we Schmitz's had had true faith until Tancredo learned it from the Americans.

"When Tancredo returned, he confronted our father. He said to father, 'Father, though the oppressors may have left, you will not be free until you accept Jesus Christ as your savior.' Father laughed. He told Tancredo 'Son, if you want to live free, you better accept yourself as your only savior.'

"The tension between my father and my brother grew. My father would not listen to Tancredo's sermons on the saving power of the Lord, so 'Credo preached the Gospel to us, his brothers. Tancredo, more than my father, had always been my hero and the words he spoke reached the most tender spots of my heart.

"One day, my father had enough. Drunk, he interrupted 'Credo's sermon. He mocked Tancredo and he mocked Jesus Christ. The two fought savagely, raining blows on each other. After being separated from each other, Tancredo packed his things and moved away from the camp. He took with him a quarter of my father's most loyal soldiers, men who had accepted 'Credo's message of Salvation. I, too, left. That day, Tancredo formed a group he called the *Soldados de Christo*. We began kidnapping Global soldiers and trying to convert them to accept Jesus Christ and refute their allegiance to the secular Federation. We converted some, but most we killed.

"After a few months, as the GFN re-engaged the *resistência* in the jungle, 'Credo told us that we would be moving to the States, so the true believers could start to come together and fight under the Banner of Heaven. There was no discussion. We left.

"After a long journey away from the only home I had ever known, I found myself in a submarine headed for the fabled land of Texas."

"Do you think the signing will change anything?" Natalie asked Joseph.

She knew the question was weak, but she was looking for some insight. Her mentor rarely liked to talk politics. He was successful as a journalist and then an editor because his only agenda was reporting truth. Throughout their journalistic relationship, Natalie had learned to stay away from editorialization and partisan politics. Now, though, she was not looking for professional insight, but personal reassurance. While researching the coast-to-coast attacks from the night before, the anxiety Natalie felt in Oklahoma City began to resurface.

Joseph flashed Natalie a smile. "It will certainly change some things."

Semantics, Natalie thought. A very predictable answer from Joseph.

She turned in her seat and leaned her shoulder and cheek against the leather of the backrest. Her eyes looked at the editor pleadingly.

"Do you think it will be good, Joseph? Do you think it will stop all this killing? Or do you think it will only cause more?"

Joseph thought intently for a minute and then answered honestly.

"I don't know. The Federation and complete globalization is our reality now. There is no going back. It has progressed too far. However, that does not mean that there will be no more resistance. Forward movement will always encounter friction.

To what degree that friction will be, I don't know. I hope that we have seen the worst of it, but I fear that we have not.

"In society, hindsight has shown progressive thought to be, most the time, the moral right. Whether it be abolishing slavery, or giving equal rights to women, or providing shelter for the homeless. Now, we finally have a societal and governmental policy that appears to promote the interests of all people, no matter their race, creed, nationality, or net worth. I think it's inspiring, but progress without some sense of pace can be absolutely devastating. And we are seeing that now. Progress is a force and the resistance is a counterforce. When you increase the force of progress, the counterforce will increase as well."

"What's there to do then?"

"If I knew that, then I would have gone into politics. Not journalism."

Natalie enjoyed hearing Joseph discuss his deep personal views. It was a privilege very few people enjoyed, like diving to the last vibrant coral reef before it bleached.

"Were you ever involved in politics?" Natalie asked. In the fifteen years she had known Joseph, she never thought to ask him that question. It had always just seemed natural that he was in journalism. It had seemed inevitable that he would be editor-in-chief of the *Chicago Tribune*.

"No," Joseph answered, almost sadly. "No. My father was a journalist in Honolulu. When I was a child, there was a congressman there who many thought could be president one day. My father uncovered the corruption scandal that ruined the congressman. I knew from an early age that I would always be better at uncovering things than burying them." Natalie had read about the incident he described in college but had never heard Joseph mention it.

Natalie wished to continue the conversation, but Joseph abruptly excused himself and walked out of the train car. She remained in her seat and thought about why she became a reporter. The job was not in her genes like it was for Joseph. Although she had been successful in her young career, she still doubted whether she had chosen the right path in her life. For the last few weeks, her work had grown stagnant. Her drive had slowed. The AFG, her focus the last year, was moving to join The Global Federation of Nations and she had a front row seat.

If she could not rise to this occasion, she thought she may need to seriously consider a career change.

Sonya's blunt declaration of Wade's infidelity stunned Noah.

"You used to—" he paused, "sleep together?"

She laughed. "Why are you so surprised?"

"Because Wade's so pious. He wouldn't do that."

"Would. Did. Has. Will. The man has needs."

"I don't believe it." Noah replied, without conviction.

"You don't need to believe it," Sonya said. "We met when I was in the AFA. We used Wade's prison connections to recruit low-paid mercenaries. We fucked for a couple of months. Not a big deal, *Sister* Bridger."

As they walked, Noah tried to process this information. Not only was Wade an adulterer, but he had worked with the American Freedom Army. Noah realized he knew so little about his brother-in-law.

The pair reached the summit of a bluff and below, the world opened up. A wide river glistened below them, curving lazily into the horizon. *The Mississippi. It had to be.* Noah felt like they had been walking to the ends of the earth, that they must have already been halfway through Texas, but here was the Mississippi River. His heart sank as he realized how far he had left to go to get home.

On the far side of the river, Noah spotted a flat, thin line through the density of the forest. He stared at the break in the foliage, thinking it may be a creek that led to the mighty river. Suddenly, an object flashed across the line. *God's saved us. A road.* Without considering the consequences, he wished to find the road, stop a car, and offer his yearly wage for a ride to his wife and children. The reality of the past ten days hit him like a sledgehammer: he could not go to the road and find a ride. He needed to stay hidden. He was a fugitive.

He looked down. Near the bottom of the bluff, Noah spotted the rest of the group inch toward the river bank. He figured that he and Sonya stood some thirty meters or so above the river and it appeared that they would work their way straight down.

Sonya began the descent immediately. She was already a few meters ahead of Noah. She used the trunks of the oaks to steady herself and moved down the slope gingerly. She turned back to him, stuck to the hilltop.

"C'mon!" she said, waving her hand forward. "We must hurry!"

Noah stepped down. The dirt was loose under his front foot and rolled down ahead of him. The earth had dried quickly from the morning's rainstorm and was eager to crumble. The others had reached the bank and sat behind some shrubbery, hidden from the road. Sonya moved quickly, effortlessly ahead of Noah. He piddled forward awkwardly, making little headway.

As he moved between the trees, he felt the ground move beneath him. The loose soil flowed, and he searched hopelessly for firm footing. He found none. He felt like he was walking on a sheet of ice.

He fell.

His body skated down the steep hill. He clung at the dirt and grass as it moved past him, but it was fluid and he could find no hold.

As his grasping body accelerated, he looked down at his feet. A large rock lay in his path. It grew as he slid. Suddenly, he felt a jerk on his jacket and the neckline caught tight against his throat: his body stopped a few meters short of the rock.

Noah looked over his left shoulder, his collar choking him. There was a matted path of earth behind him that showed the trajectory of his fall. He bent his knees and dug his heels into the ground, then pushed himself up slightly, loosening the garment's hold and letting himself breathe.

"Grab my hand, Noah!" He heard the voice, sharp and commanding. He craned his neck to look behind him. In his twisted vision, he saw Sonya grasping his jacket tight, her knuckles white and her teeth mashed. She held onto the trunk of a sapling—the tree bowed downhill. He reached behind him and found her forearm, gripped onto it, and felt his nails bore into her bare skin. He began to rotate onto his side so he could climb up, when he heard the loud crack of the sapling.

The beeping of his APD brought Lt. Director Luna out of the hypnotic state created by the Schmitz boy's story. He had listened to it for too long. He had to prepare for the Secretary-General's arrival. There was a depth to the boy that he hardly encountered in his enemies that he wished to explore, but the day dictated he move forward.

"Hurry now, boy. Get to the point." Luna said, breaking the captive's monologue. "Why did you come to find me? Even I know that my reputation is more crushing than coddling."

Gabriel Schmitz fumbled with a response. Luna could tell that he had been practicing his story since he was detained in Galveston, that he had rehearsed every line, and that having Luna break the script smashed his inner thoughts.

"Crushing? La Frontera is not crushing. You are the white knight that rode out of the bowels of The Federation. You are a man of compassion."

Luna dismissed the boy's statement. His compassion for the captive diminished.

"Do not tell me what I am," he warned Gabriel.

The boy was confused. "Why would you deny that? It is true."

Luna grew angry. "What makes it true?"

Gabriel shook and stammered. "My brother, 'Credo, is a man of God. He told me to find La Frontera. He said that La Frontera would help me. He said that La Frontera was the white knight that rode—"

"Why?!" Luna screamed and leapt from the bed. General Bonner fidgeted behind him and looked at the closed door. Luna pulled out his Sig and placed it against the captive's forehead. "You have thirty fucking seconds to tell me why you're wasting my time, or I'll pepper this grubby room with bits of your skull. Yeah?"

For the first time, Schmitz took his eyes off Luna and looked to Bonner. The General gave the captive no relief. He only bolted the lock of the door.

"You saved my brother's life," Schmitz muttered. His lips quivered, and the color drained from his face.

"I never met your brother and I sure as shit didn't save his life."

"You let him live. In the Delta. You let him live."

Luna lowered the sidearm. A faint remembrance twinkled in the darkness of his mind. Of a defiant prisoner, preaching to Luna and Luna letting the man go with a promise. But the memory recessed behind a black curtain of his mind. The Lt. Director had work to do. He re-holstered the pistol and turned to Bonner.

"General," Luna spoke, and the Texan stood at attention, "this boy is mad. Take him back to Texas and find a broom closet to keep him in until I know how best to use him. I have work to do today."

Natalie Kelley had finished eating a small can of mangoes and was slurping the leftover juice when Joseph Kalani came back down the aisle of the train and took his seat next to her. He was smiling.

He looked at the nearly empty can in Natalie's hand and then around at the other passengers. Some enjoyed a snack, while others napped.

"Did you get an extra one?"

Natalie wiped at the sweet juice dripping down her chin.

"An extra what?" she kidded as the liquid sloshed around her tongue.

The smile on Joseph's face grew wider.

"An extra snack," he said and pointed at the can.

Natalie reached into the seat-pouch in front of her and rooted around. She pulled out a packet of oven-toasted, chocolate-covered crickets and handed them to Joseph. His face lit up. The man had been a vegetarian for decades, like over a quarter of Americans, but had always allowed himself to eat insects on occasion. He grabbed the bag, opened the slit at the top, and shook it so a few of the bugs tumbled into his hand.

Natalie watched him savor his guilty pleasure.

"Why were you smiling when you came back to your seat? What were you doing when you were gone?"

It was Joseph's turn to act innocent. He gave a "who, me?" look to Natalie.

He swallowed the first handful and said, "I was thinking about some chocolate-covered crickets," he held up the packet, "and here they are!"

He shook the packet into his open palm and a few more crickets rained down. He put the bugs into his mouth and Natalie could hear the crunch as he masticated. She drained the rest of the mango juice and put the can in the pouch of the chairback in front of her.

Natalie placed her hand on Joseph's wrist. "C'mon, Joe. You were beaming like a Goddamn bride as you were walking down the aisle. What is it?"

Still chewing, Joseph answered her with a wide smile that showed the dark, mushed food on his tongue and teeth.

"Oh, it's nothing," he continued to chew. "You just have an interview with the Secretary-General tomorrow morning."

Noah Bridger could feel Sonya squirming on top of him. He had closed his eyes tight as soon as the pair began sliding down the hill and even though it felt as if they had stopped, he was afraid to open them again. Pain rushed from his hip and spread across his side. He was disoriented. Next to his right ear, he could hear Sonya pant. He could feel her heartbeat on his chest, racing his own.

"Noah," Sonya said. She was shaking him. "Noah."

He opened his eyes. She was laying on top of him, facing him, her nose nearly touching the tip of his nose. He could smell her breath enveloping him; it was heavy and sweet. The earth had stopped moving beneath them and he felt rooted to the ground.

A voice called up from below.

"Are you alright up there?"

It was Wade. Sonya answered him, still lying on top of Noah.

"We're fine!" she answered.

"Then hurry up, will you?"

Sonya made no move; she only studied Noah's face. Noah grabbed her shoulders and she closed her eyes and leaned forward, her lips parted. Noah moved her frame off his body and perched himself on his elbows. Sonya's face reddened, and she slithered down Noah's torso, then legs. She stood up and brushed the debris from her clothes, then extended her hand to Noah and hoisted the man up.

Noah stood on the rock that the pair had crashed into. Without it, they may still be tumbling. He looked back toward the top of the bluff, then down to the river bank below, and surveyed the hillside: they were nearly halfway down.

They forged ahead. Sonya moved quickly. She no longer waited for Noah. There was a ripple in the water and the men moved from their leafy cover to stand on the bank.

The brown water of the Mississippi began to swirl and turn in a space the size of a tennis court. A metallic shine broke through the surface. An object rose from out the river. Once in the air, water drained and flowed like rapids from the object. Noah stared in awe as a massive vehicle hovered a few meters above the water that had hidden it only moments before. He had never seen anything like it before.

Lt. Director Luna rode to the New Mexico State Capitol building alone. He had put the bizarre encounter with Gabriel Schmitz out of his mind. He was focused solely on the job at hand: securing the signing.

When the automated coupe stopped in front of the State House, Luna stepped out and the car turned quickly, zipping away to pick up another Federationist. Luna scanned the Capitol Gardens. Already there were teams of Federationists surveying the grounds. Some SOs walked with leashed black, yellow, and chocolate Labrador retrievers. Luna had witnessed genetically-enhanced canines smell explosives that the most expensive ARs could not locate in the field. A tall, blonde woman walked past Luna with a young yellow lab. The lab stopped to sniff at Luna's legs and, instinctively, the Lt. Director leaned down to pat the dog. The lab snarled, and her handler pulled it away quickly.

"I'm sorry, sir," the woman said and quickly moved the dog away.

In addition to the dogs and their handlers, the Gardens contained groups of SOs trailing behind three-foot robots. These ARs used seismic waves to detect any vibrations from the waves in the rock and dirt to search for any tunnels or chambers underground. When such a vibration was detected, the men that trailed the robot drilled a small hole into the ground, then dropped an insect-drone down the hole to see if the void in the earth was man-made. Because of the tunneling tactics used during the attack on the San Francisco GFN-NA Hub, Luna had double the number of Subterranean Detection Units, or "rodent-hunters." So far, the STDU had discovered no signs of "rodents."

Across the street, the press had already started to gather in anticipation for Secretary-General Dubois's arrival. Currently, there were only a few dozen members of the press at the capitol due to the late announcement. Half of these journalists were based in Window Rock and the others were already on assignment in the Grey Zone. By the following evening, Luna anticipated over eight hundred accredited journalists to descend upon Santa Fe. Originally, when Luna expected a week between the announcement of the treaty and the date of the signing, Luna planned for three thousand journalists; he was glad that the press would be a quarter of the previous estimation.

The area surrounding the Capitol Grounds had been lasered off and only individuals with properly-permitted IWCs were allowed to enter the perimeter. Usually, dozens of media drones would hover overhead, but due to the use of weaponized drones during the previous day's attack, the machines had been prohibited. Luna saw Deputy Thị Vân outside the perimeter among the press with a few armed SOs, interviewing the journalists to make sure they were cleared by NASO.

With nearly thirty hours until the signing, the GFN had already moved seven hundred Federationists to Santa Fe. Five hundred and fifty were with the NASO. The others were spread out among the Communications Department, the Office of Native Lands, the Office of Population Integration, and the Office of Government Liaison. In addition to the seven hundred Federationists, the United States government began to move in federal employees and members of the military. The proxy legislative representatives of New Mexico were due to arrive this evening. The security of the signing was a massive undertaking and Lt. Director Luna had very little time.

Luna thought that meeting with a delegate from any of these organizations would be more beneficial than his next consultation. The Lt. Director brushed down his moustache, checked to make sure his Sig was strapped in its holster, and walked inside the Roundhouse. He was due to meet the American Freedom Group's head of security in the rotunda in ten minutes.

"Wow."

That was the only word Natalie could muster after Joseph told her that she was going to interview the Secretary-General. It was like hearing that she was going to interview Jesus Christ on the banks of the Sea of Galilee—it was rare for Dubois to grant one-on-one interviews. When he did, it was historically with either Jermaine Cliff of the BBC or Pauline Kanté of Le Monde. Natalie would be the first American journalist to have a solo interview with Antoine Dubois since he became the Secretary-General. Joseph must have called in some serious favors to set this opportunity up. Natalie wondered just how much of that long-saved professional capital he had left.

"Wow," Natalie said again. "Well, thank you." She touched Joseph's hand. "I don't know what else to say."

Joseph sandwiched her hand between his. They were thin and wrinkled and brown. "You deserve it," he said tenderly.

After a moment of sentiment, he switched gears, becoming Natalie's boss again. "Now, you'll only have thirty minutes with him. A car will be at the hotel at 09:30 tomorrow morning to take us to the interview location. Do you have enough time to prepare?"

"Yes. Of course," Natalie nodded enthusiastically. "If I didn't, would you try to push it to a later day?"

Joseph laughed. "I just needed to ask. I wouldn't want to put you on the spot."

"Well, I'm on the spot, alright, Joseph, but this is the spot I've wanted to be on for years." She grabbed his bicep above the armrest separating them. "Thank you for this."

"Do you want me to be there with you?"

Natalie thought for a second. "Why, yes. I guess I just assumed you would."

"Okay."

"Why wouldn't you be there?"

Joseph fidgeted a bit in his seat. "I guess I just want you to be comfortable. I didn't want to seem overbearing. I want to let you conduct the interview you wish to conduct."

Natalie looked at the old man's face. In it, she did not see the cutthroat that those in the journalism sphere saw when confronted with the visage of Joseph Kalani. She saw a need for approval. A quiet pleading. A desperation for her to have the same confidence in herself as he did.

Natalie thought that she was one of only a couple people on the planet to see that look from him and she did not like it. The vulnerability exhibited by the man scared her, but the totality of the faith he offered her was even more frightening.

"Joseph, if it was any other journalist, you wouldn't even ask. You'd just be there."

"But it isn't any other journalist. It's you."

"Don't worry about being overbearing, Joseph," she said and gave a weak smile. She could not continue to look at the expression of confidence any longer and lowered her eyes, then looked out the window.

"Jesus, I probably won't even remember you're there when he walks into the room. I'll be lucky to remember I'm there."

Noah clumsily hurried down the slope. He tried to keep his eyes on the ground right in front of his feet, but he kept looking up at the massive machine that had emerged from the river. The machine was still, hovering five meters above the water. It was huge and silver and gleamed pure above the brown Mississippi. A rope ladder had descended from the belly of the machine. Noah continued down the hill, slipping often. Below, Sonya and Wade stood together on the bank and impatiently watched his progress.

Covered in dirt and out of breath, Noah finally reached the flatland of the riverside. His body ached. Sonya rushed to him and grabbed his arm. Dumbstruck, he studied the sub-plane as she pulled him forward. As a mechanic, he was fascinated to see how this machine worked; Noah had worked on muscle cars and tractors but never anything as complex as this versatile vehicle. He tried to apply what he knew about the simple internal combustion engines he worked on to the *thing* floating before him. The mechanics were simply beyond him.

The machine was twenty-five meters long and twenty meters wide. On each side of the hull were two stubby, staggered wings. One wing, positioned closer to the bow of the craft, pointed skyward. The second wing, positioned near the stern, angled downward. This downward-pointing wing hovered close to the water's surface and its tip occasionally dipped into the river as the machine bounced and swayed. On each wing were two turbofan engines. On the back wings, the engines had been rotated so that they faced the water. The power of the engines displaced the water and waves beat against the muddy beach. Noah surmised that the vehicle could use these same engines underwater.

How the hell does this thing work?

He did not have time to fully scrutinize the mechanical logistics. Sonya was pulling his arm. "We need to go. Now." Sonya
led him into the water.

Noah was stunned.

"Who the hell pays for this?" he asked, as they waded through
the river. The water was getting deeper, creeping up his thighs
to his belly.

Sonya yelled over the engine noise and held her arms high
above the artificial surf. "Wade has collected some very wealthy…
disciples."

Disciples? Noah thought, but he could no longer hear Sonya
over the vehicle's rumble.

The water around Noah and Sonya began to recede. They
were under the hull. The pair could feel the air from the turbofan engines blowing against their bodies. The machine had
moved closer to the bank from where it emerged and, as the
engines blew the water away, the water level barely touched
Noah's knees. They reached the twirling rope ladder. The rest
of the group was already inside. *It should be two meters deep
here,* Noah thought as Sonya disappeared into the dark opening above.

Noah put his feet on the first rung and started to climb. The
ladder swung in the wind, then, suddenly, it jerked upward. He
looked down and the opaque water below began to glide away
from him. *My God, they're taking off without me!* Noah grabbed
the ladder tight and pressed his head against the rung in front
of him. The blowing air from the engines continued to rush by
him and his body wagged to and fro. Hugging the ladder, he
moved up one rung, then another, careful not to look down.
With his face still pressed against the rope, he felt a hand tap his
head. He looked up and saw Sonya's face. Her hand guided him
forward. When his head entered the hole, he pushed himself up
and flopped his chest on the rough, metal ground. Screws dug
into his ribs.

Sonya pulled him across the bumpy floor. Behind him, a series of pulleys brought the ladder into the hull. The cargo door shut and locked. Once the door locked, the plane started to aggressively gain altitude. Noah, still laying on the ground, was surrounded by blackness. A voice echoed through the hull and told the passengers to fasten their seatbelts.

Noah rose and tried to feel his way to an empty seat. Twice his prodding hands found the legs of seated occupants and twice, Noah issued soft apologies. The plane was gaining speed and Noah needed to crouch low to avoid falling over. Finally, he found an empty seat. He fumbled for the belt and, with his feet planted firmly to keep him stationary, connected the four-point restraint. A few seconds later, the machine roared and the g-force stapled Noah to the side of the craft.

Lt. Director Juan Carlos Luna walked slowly around the Great Seal of the State of New Mexico in the rotunda of the "Roundhouse." His head was cast downward toward the tiled floor and his hands were clasped behind his lower back. All along the rotunda, from the ground level up the three stories to the blue-and-pink skylight above, Luna could hear Federationists as they worked diligently. Without removing the device from his pocket, Luna asked his APD what the time was, and his earpiece told him. He frowned. Raleigh Barrish, the head of security for the American Freedom Group, was ten minutes late. Luna's annoyance spoiled into anger.

Since his call with Director Farrelly, the full magnitude of the signing had settled upon Luna's shoulders. What would normally be an historic moment now had even more gravity in the wake of the coordinated attacks the night before. He had often worked in the shadows of the GFN, but not today. Pundits were personally blaming him for the failings in security at the Railyard Inn. He needed to shut his critics up. The success of his previous military campaigns in the Grey Zone would mean little to the public if he failed here. In Santa Fe, if something were to go wrong, every aspect of Luna's career would be picked apart until only the stark white bones of failure remained.

Luna continued to make his slow revolutions around the floor's centerpiece undisturbed. The seconds ticked by and he grew more and more irritated. He stopped on one of the brass sunbeams that extended away from the Seal and scanned the room. Still no sight of those bastards from the Freedom Group. He pulled his APD from his jacket pocket and checked the messages. There was nothing from Barrish excusing his tardiness. He put his APD back in his pocket and walked across the Seal.

He had waited long enough.

Luna walked out of the Rotunda. He did not have faith in rogues like Raleigh Barrish and he did not need their help. He knew that the meeting was all for the sake of appearances, anyway. If the shit-stain had shown, he would have just gotten in Luna's way. It was time to move on to the next task.

Luna stepped out of the Roundhouse and into the New Mexican sunlight. The crowd had thickened. There was a commotion in the distance. A group of a dozen men strode past the journalists and spectators. They were dressed in fatigues, each outfit differed slightly from the next. A loud wail broke out over the grounds as they crossed the perimeter. Security Officers on the grounds of the capitol stopped working and aimed their weapons at the intruders. The men continued to march toward the Lt. Director—Raleigh Barrish had arrived.

"Why aren't *you* interviewing Dubois?" Natalie asked her editor. She had been preparing for her interview with the Secretary-General. The train car started to crowd around her. Across the car, a man laughed loudly. A baby near the rear began to cry. The baby's mother placed the child on her hip. She bounced and twirled and whispered into the infant's ear. In the seat directly ahead of Natalie, a woman snored. An AR came down the aisle and collected rubbish from the passengers.

"Because you are," Joseph answered plainly.

Natalie smiled in an attempt to alleviate the pressure she was feeling. "No. Seriously. An interview like this, no, *this* interview would be the perfect ending to such an illustrious career."

A look of mock horror appeared on Joseph's face. "I wasn't aware my illustrious career was ending."

Natalie shook her head. "You know what I mean."

"This is what's best for the paper," Joseph looked at Natalie, but she did not seem satisfied with that answer. "It has taken a lifetime, but I am content, my dear. I truly need nothing else. When I wake each day, I make the choices and perform the actions I want to, not that I need to."

"And this is how you want to live your life?" Natalie asked sardonically, pointing around the railcar and letting her finger linger upon the still-wailing baby, the embarrassed mother trying desperately to quiet the cry.

Joseph followed her finger and answered solemnly. "Yes, I suppose it is. You don't believe me? What do you think I need, young Natalie?"

Natalie thought for a beat, then looked out the window before answering.

"I think you always thought you needed to be revered and respected in this world." Natalie continued to speak without thinking, revealing deeply buried thoughts she was not aware she had. Her resentment for her father's death and Joseph trying to fill the role spilled out into the railcar. "But now, at the pinnacle of your career, you've found that's not what you needed at all. You're searching for love. I think that's what you've probably needed your whole life, but I know that is what you need now. You've isolated yourself from everyone but Chandra, and now, you wish that you had spent your life harvesting love, not respect."

"Oh, really?" Joseph appeared saddened by her harsh, clinical insight. "You have such insight on all others and the whole world, Ms. Kelley, but, you really know nothing yet of the deepest machinations on this Earth. Especially those that function within your own soul."

The train passed the outskirts of a nameless Iowa town. In that town, babies were born, and children were taught. Men and women worked, slept, and played. Love was made, and love was lost. And, when those townsfolk grew old, they died. Every single one of them, some without the luxury of aging. And Natalie, she would know nothing about any of them. She would never even know the name of the town. As she looked out the window, she felt Joseph leave and, even though the chair next to her was now empty, she felt the train car compact tighter around her.

After a few minutes in the air, the force of the liftoff eased, and Noah Bridger could move in his seat. The cabin of the craft was void of all light. Noah leaned forward and tried to look around the room but could see nothing. He heard chatter in the cabin but found it difficult to pinpoint from which direction it came. He spoke into the void.

"Hello? Why is it so dark?"

He heard laughter. The cabin was hot and stuffy and sweat began to pour down Noah's back.

"Can't you turn on a light or open a damn window?"

"This vehicle is without electricity and windows. You'll need to bear the darkness." The voice was Wade's.

"What?" Noah said, incredulously. "Why? What's the point in that?"

"For stealth, Noah. This ATC was built to minimize any chance of detection. The shell of this vehicle can appear as a mirage to an outside viewer. To do this we need to heat the shell to nearly four thousand degrees Fahrenheit. We cannot spare any energy on lights, or air, or even navigational tools."

Noah was nervous and disoriented. He spoke fast. "No navigation? That doesn't seem safe. And what did you call it—an ATC? What the hell's an ATC?"

A voice he did not recognize interrupted him. "An Aero-Thallis Craft. Now shut the fuck up."

Noah closed his mouth and tried to keep calm. Sweat poured down his neck and back and pooled down around his coccyx. Noah lifted the sticky shirt from off his back and tried to draw in some cool air. There was none. His legs bounced with anxiety. His breathing was deep and labored.

"Where is this tin can headed?" Noah asked, unable to keep silent. The blackness squeezed the words out of him.

A voice he recognized as Aiden Stevens snorted and replied. "Tin can. Jesus. This vehicle costs over two hundred million bucks."

Noah spoke without thinking, under his breath. "You think for that much, it'd come fully loaded. You know, with some extra features, like lights and air."

"The fuck you just say?" the unfamiliar voice said angrily. "Listen, you little piece of shit—"

The voice was verbally restrained by Wade.

"Finch, quiet," he said, and the cabin grew silent. Then, Wade spoke to Noah. "We're taking you home. Don't worry. We're taking you home. Try to get some sleep."

Home. Noah's body relaxed in the sweltering heat and he closed his eyes. *That's the best news I've ever heard.*

Raleigh Barrish was a stocky man with bright red hair and a thick beard that stopped at the corners of his mouth. His fatigues were dark green and brown and grey, and the jacket was unbuttoned at the top, revealing a puff of red chest hair and a white tank top. The service name on the jacket had been peeled off leaving a blank spot in the center of the stitching. His heavy black boots had dried mud clinging to them. He wore blue-lensed Taurus sunglasses and his AR-15 hung from a sling and bounced on his pudge. Luna was glad that he had cautioned his team that the AFG security crew may arrive armed.

The Lt. Director extended his hand to the fiery man as they walked toward each other. With the acknowledgement of their superior, the SOs around the group lowered their weapons. "Mr. Barrish, I presume?"

"Colonel. Colonel Barrish," the stocky man said, as he held out his own thick hand. Luna looked over the jacket but saw no insignia for a colonel.

"This must be 'La Frontera,'" Barrish said. He directed his speech not at the Lt. Director, but to his men behind him. He then looked Luna in the eyes. "You, you crazy sumbitch, you're a real legend," he let go of Luna's hand. A few from the pack laughed at Barrish's remark.

Barrish put his hand on Luna's shoulder in an attempt to turn him around to face the capitol. "Now, don't mind us being a little late. We were just out taking care of some business."

Luna stood his ground, avoiding the attempt to get him to spin. He was now eyeing the other members of Barrish's entourage.

"I'd like to start on the grounds outside the capitol here, Mr. Barrish," said Luna.

Barrish dropped his hand from Luna's arm. They stood shoulder-to-shoulder, each facing the opposite way. "Colonel, La Frontera. It's Colonel."

Barrish turned around. "Now, I don't know what you wanted to even discuss here, but it was my idea that we would stand in front of those cameras, smiling for a few minutes. Maybe point at some random shit, make it look like we're working hard together. Then, we'll go inside for about an hour, do whatever we want, and emerge looking strong and confident. But, the truth is, I'm gonna do what I need to do to protect my guy and I expect that's what you're gonna do, too." Barrish wiped his tongue along his bottom teeth, rearranging a tobacco pouch, and swallowed hard with a smacking sound.

Luna shook his head and was about to respond when a shout came from beyond the perimeter. Barrish's entourage turned toward the noise, like a group of prairie dogs alerted to an approaching predator.

Luna heard the screaming voice.

"You fucking traitors! You're all fucking traitors! All of you!"

A short, red-headed man stopped at the perimeter, sensing where the boundary was. The journalists quickly started recording the man. He continued to yell, angrily, playing to the crowd of reporters.

Barrish leaned over to Luna and said with a chuckle. "Don't you worry about little Winston. Brothers can be a real pain in the ass, am I right?" Laughing, the "colonel" prodded Luna's ribs with his elbow.

Luna looked from the man that hurled vile accusations in front of rolling cameras to Raleigh Barrish. He watched as Barrish smiled and waved at his brother.

Natalie sat for a few minutes and stared out the window. Her mind whipped along with the scenery outside. She regretted upsetting Joseph. She knew he was more vulnerable than he let on. He cared deeply for her and that care meant he was easily wounded by her words. Stubbornly, she told herself that she had done nothing wrong, that it was Joseph's fault for having such thin skin, but as the shame rose inside, Natalie knew she needed to find him and apologize. She got out of her seat and walked to the front of the car. At the corridor connection, she scanned her wrist and, once the computer identified her as a first-class ticket holder, the door opened.

The next car was another filled with first-class passengers. Toward the rear of the car, a group of three children were cuddled together under a blanket and watched a 3D recording of a family of Bengal tigers. Many of the recently extinct animals were very popular and featured prominently in media, fashion, and elsewhere. Natalie walked quickly through the aisle and out of the passenger car. The next car she entered was the theatre, where a dozen people watched a movie. The lights were dimmed and, though she strained to identify each of the viewers, she did not see Joseph.

She found her editor in the next car, a lounge with a bar that ran down one end and a series of tables that lined the other. Joseph sat at the back table alone and stared out the window while he nursed a drink. Natalie sat down on the bench next to him, but he kept looking at the cornfields outside. She rested her chin on his shoulder and looked at the landscape with him.

"I'm sorry, Joseph," she said. "I didn't mean it."

Joseph turned away from the window and put his arm around Natalie.

"Yes, you did. But that's okay. It was true. I've just grown sensitive in my old age."

Natalie, with her head on Joseph's chest, picked up his glass and took a drink. She winced as she swallowed. "I hate gin."

Joseph laughed. "You and everyone else these days. No respect for the classic taste. I was surprised to see the bottle of Tanqueray behind the bar."

Natalie reached into the glass and plucked out the lime wedge. She put it between her teeth and sucked out the juice, then sat up. She had been crying and wiped the tears from under her eyes.

Joseph picked the glass up with both hands, took a deep slug, and finished the drink. He kept the highball in his hands, rolling it back and forth between his palms, deep in thought.

"Sometimes, my dear, I truly forget that I am not your father. I feel I too often encroach upon one of your life's sacred relationships. I'll do better."

Natalie looked at his sad eyes. "Joseph, don't. You don't need to."

"I know," he said. "But I want to," echoing his earlier statement and smiling at Natalie.

CHAPTER EIGHT

13 May 2072

Noah Bridger thought that after time, he would grow acclimated to the blackness. He did not. He kept his eyes opened and moving, but it did not matter. He was disoriented. He listened intently for the sounds of the other passengers over the noise of the craft's engines. When he detected a noise, he moved his head to the source of the coughing or snoring. His fingertips explored the metal around him, reaffirming that he remained in a concrete world.

The darkness made every small bump even more exaggerated. After some turbulence, Noah could no longer tell if his feet were pointed to the earth or the sky. His thoughts bounced from his brain through the abyss of the cabin. He found it difficult to concentrate. There was a jolt and Noah was pushed forward. He was unsure whether the ATC had stopped or if it was the halt of time itself. His stomach was in knots. He heard the rustling and clinking of seatbelts, the chatting and shuffling of his co-travelers. Noah released the tongue from the buckle and the restraint rolled off his chest.

A door opened at the front of the hull and light flooded into the cabin. The shocking brightness hurt Noah's eyes. He closed them tight, but the intense whiteness pierced through his lids. He opened his eyes and blinked rapidly. He saw silhouettes moving against the bright backdrop. Floating orbs of purple and maroon and green danced around the silhouettes and he blinked his eyes again and again until the globes were gone. He was the last person seated and when he stood up, a searing pain shot through his leg. He had almost forgotten the trauma his leg had endured while he was in the hot womb of the ATC and the pain surprised him. He fell forward but caught himself against the sleek wall.

He limped out of the hull, the hollow metal echoing underfoot, and stepped into the cockpit. There was an open door to his right. At the nose of the craft was a captain's seat. Directly in front of the captain's seat was a center stick. On the dash behind the center stick there was a series of dials and gauges. Above the dash was a series of small wheels and a mosaic of screens. The screens showed different exterior views of the Aero-Thallis Craft. Noah turned one of the wheels and the image on the screen panned the same direction as the wheel. *Periscopes,* Noah thought. Just as Noah was about to sit in the captain's seat to inspect the vehicle's gadgets, he heard a voice from outside the cockpit.

"I gotta shut that door, so either get out or sleep in there." Noah hurried to the open door, not wanting to see how hot the interior became on the ground.

The ATC had landed in a shortgrass prairie. There was a line of tall dogwoods in the distance. Noah stepped gingerly onto the stairs and descended the steps into the prairie. He nodded at the waiting pilot and hurried around the ATC. When he turned around the nose of the craft, he saw the plain extend, only this time it was not broken up by dogwoods, but by rows of rudimentary shacks. Noah was disappointed that the ATC had not brought him straight to his ranch like he had hoped. He knew it had been a fantasy, but he had clung to that fantasy tightly.

He was not home. He did not know where he was. And, looking over the knee-high grass dancing in the breeze, standing tall above the unfamiliar dirt, he felt exposed.

Lt. Director Luna did not have time to put on a show with Raleigh Barrish. He left the AFG security team standing outside the Roundhouse and walked briskly to a waiting car. From the car, he messaged his team to keep an eye on the brother and detain him if necessary. *Let Raleigh Barrish stand there with his thumb up his ass,* he thought. *Let his pipsqueak brother yell until he's hoarse. I have shit to do.*

He knew his rude actions would not "play well" and that Farrelly would give him an earful regarding "optics," but he did not care. He was not going to appease these anarchists and thugs by taking part in some security theatre. His job was to make sure that tomorrow's treaty signing was secure and that was what he was going to do.

Once back at his hotel room, Juan Carlos phoned Jay back in New York. There was no answer. He left a brief message and returned downstairs. The lobby teemed with maintenance workers and ARs that cleaned up the last of the wreckage from the attack. The familiar, acrid smell of smoke still hung in the air and Luna breathed it in deeply.

The debris and glass and grime had been cleared from the faux wood flooring, but the crews were finding the blood stains more difficult to remove. Luna watched as the cleaning ARs mixed and tried a new solution on the blood stains, but he knew from experience that the floors would need to be replaced. With so much human fuel spilled and pooled on the floor, the blood would have already seeped down beneath the tiles and onto the cement. If, by some miracle, the cleaning crews could get the blood stains out of the faux wood, then the staff of the Railyard Inn would still spot mirages of gore in the lobby. Luna watched the ARs scrub and scrub, knowing their actions were futile.

The blood would be part of the building forever. They could clean and reconstruct, but the Railyard Inn would not last. The blood would seep into the foundation of the hotel and would crack the foundation, bringing everything above tumbling down to lie with the ghosts of the murdered.

Ghosts that included Arnie Jones. He looked at the spot where he had held his friend's head in his lap as the man took in his last breath. The Deputy's blood was still on the wood floor. Like the rest of the dead, his blood had spilled between the cracks of the lobby and burrowed into the heart of the building. It would now and forever be a part of the Railyard Inn.

With his eyes closed, the former Ranger pictured some of the beautiful vistas and rugged mountains where his men had lost their lives. They were good places to die. Honorable places to die. But this run-down hotel was a cheap, unworthy place to die. It could never stand as a monument to the brave men and women who lost their lives here. It, like the entire town around it, was too broken. It needed to be torn down and started anew. Luna thought of a forest fire, clearing the undergrowth, giving space to the seedlings to sprout. *Why do these motherfuckers hold on to such junk so tightly?* He knew that a cleansing fire needed to spread through the Grey Zone to give way to the seeds of progress. He'd let the men of politics plant the seeds of prosperity and equality and hope. He would always be the man with the flamethrower.

Once the Chicago-Rocky Line crossed the Missouri River, a sheet of highly-tinted graphene rolled down over the exterior of the windows. The bullet-proof shell was a new addition to the high-speed cars that passed through the area. Before the graphene shells were installed over the course of three months, forty-seven railcars had been struck by high-caliber rifle shots between the Omaha suburbs and Kearney, Nebraska. Six people had been injured by the rifle blasts and a Michigan octogenarian who had been struck in the neck was killed. Since the armor had been installed, GFN inspectors found bullet strikes on the cars, but there had been no further injuries and minimal damage.

As the covers dropped, overhead lights sparked on and an announcement over the train's PA system alerted the passengers that, "due to safety concerns, an extra security measure has been enacted for this short duration of your journey." By this time, nearly everyone traveling on the Chicago-Rocky Line knew what those safety concerns were and had been expecting to have the "blinds drawn" as they entered Nebraska.

Natalie had left Joseph in the dining car and went back to her seat to prep for her interview with Dubois. She already had a preliminary outline drawn. She decided that she would stick to her expertise and only ask the Secretary-General about the AFG and the signing. Currently, she was debating whether to include a question about how the signing would affect other fringe terror groups in America, but she had not been able to narrow the focus of inquiry. Natalie was a journalist well-known for her laboring, intensive work. With the Dubois interview, she would only have a few days to prepare questions, conduct the interview, and submit an article. This expediency rattled her.

As she debated whether it was wise to give less-established terror groups a global mention, her APD beeped. She had a message. She vocally commanded her Reader to play the message and there was the voice of Cooper Gates in her ear. She had not heard from him since he abruptly left her at The Mantle in Oklahoma City. She had tried not to think about him.

"Will I see you in Santa Fe?"

Natalie was annoyed. She responded simply, "I'll be there."

She expected Cooper to use a line and proceed to try to charm her. It's how their relationship went. They would fight, then not speak, then reunite and have great sex. It was unhealthy, but Natalie enjoyed the drama. When he responded with only "Good," she was surprised and a little disappointed.

She found she wanted the charm. She wanted the drama. "Good" was boring. She thought of responding back, trying to start an argument or draw out the charm, but she knew she had work to do. She needed to put Cooper Gates out of her mind.

She deleted the messages, played Mozart's newly discovered "Piano Concerto No. 28", and went back to work.

Noah walked across the prairie, the pain in his leg more intense with each step. When he reached the shantytown, the others had already scattered into the various buildings. Only Sonya had waited for Noah. It was a troubling theme for him. It seemed this woman, a woman he barely knew, had taken it upon herself to be his guardian. He did not need a strange woman to be his guardian. She crouched next to the closest building and rummaged through her bag. He kept his eyes straight ahead and went to move straight past Sonya, but she grabbed his wrist as he limped by.

"It looks like that legs givin' you trouble again," she said, one hand digging through the bag, the other tight on Noah's wrist.

Noah did not want to admit that he needed more help. He had felt helpless and infantile since he first picked up Wade and the others on that dirt road.

"Ah, here it is," Sonya said, and she pulled out the can of gel. She stood up and threw the bag over her shoulder but kept holding on to Noah's wrist.

Noah stood still. He wanted to be independent and self-sufficient. But his leg did hurt.

"Come on," Sonya said, and she began to lead Noah into the development. "This will make that feel all better." She smiled back at him as they walked.

Noah walked behind the woman. Her legs were fit and strong and they were brown from the sun. She wore small shorts, tight around her waist, that showcased her backside. Noah found himself watching her tanned thighs and the swaying khaki that hid the twin hills of her rump. He felt lust creep from his groin up through his chest and into his throat. He recognized the taste of sin on his palette and looked down at the ground in shame. But he left her hand holding his wrist.

They walked through a few lanes between wooden buildings with tin roofs. Most had only a single room and none had more than two. Noah, not wanting to fall under the hypnotism of Sonya's derriere, studied the buildings. He judged that there were somewhere around sixty structures. Each was constructed out of lumber. The lumber was new—it not yet been weathered. The scent of sawdust wafted through the heart of the shantytown. The buildings were not run-down or decrepit, just sloppy and cheap.

The pair reached a shack in the last row of the village. Beyond this final row, the prairie grass extended into a sloping mound which, though not tall, eclipsed the horizon. Sonya opened a white vinyl door. At the base of the door there were speckles of mud, but the rest of the door was unmarked.

Noah stepped inside the shack and the door closed behind him. The room was no more than one hundred square meters. There were small windows on each side of the room that let a small amount of sunlight in. There was a stove to Noah's right, a toilet to the left, and a single bed at the back.

Sonya pointed to the back of the room.

"Sit down, sweetie, and I'll take care of that leg."

Noah sat down on the bed.

As Lt. Director Luna watched the cleaning crew work in the lobby, his APD vibrated in his jacket pocket. He put his Reader in his ear to hear the message, but before the message played, the device warned him that the information was "Classified and

Urgent." Luna walked outside, through the back door of the lobby, then off the patio and into the old Santa Fe railyard that gave the inn its name. He followed the nearest tracks and, after about half a klick, reached a deserted campus. The campus was surrounded by a waist-high black steel gate. The gate was well rusted, but still stood straight. A sign on the gate read, "New Mexico School for the Deaf".

Amid the adobe buildings of the campus, Luna found a stone bench. He pulled out his APD and looked at the classified and urgent intel he had received from The Mount. The intelligence was a preliminary report on the attacks in New York and San Francisco.

In New York, the security procedures worked adequately. All twenty-one combatants were killed within four minutes of detection. A preliminary response team met the combatants at the insertion point. This response team of six men engaged the combatants in a firefight. They killed three. Sixteen combatants were killed by the sniper team. It took the sniper team three minutes to get in position and eliminate the targets. The final two combatants had slipped by the preliminary response team. Both were killed by an AR machine gun perched on the corner of the Communications Office Building. One of the men had carried a backpack of C-4 plastic explosives. The detonator for the C-4 was shot and the explosives detonated ten meters from the Communications Office Building. The explosion blew out the windows on the west side of the building. A member of the janitorial team was killed, and three others were injured. During the initial firefight, a member of the preliminary team suffered a bullet wound to the leg and was recovering at the Roosevelt Island Medical Center.

The report from San Francisco was much more grim. The death toll was currently at one hundred and five, but was expected to rise due to the fifty individuals still in critical condition. Another three hundred and twelve people were injured in the bombing. Like the attack in Santa Fe, there were at least two men on the ground who followed the bombing with a barrage of gunfire directed at emergency response workers and vehicles. An IED blast leveled the first ambulance on scene, killing the three EMTs on board.

Over ninety-five percent of the casualties occurred when the initial explosive was detonated beneath the basement of the GFN-NA West Coast Division Center. A tunnel—similar to the one found in eastern Texas—had been constructed under the WCDC to deliver the explosive. The explosive tore through the first five floors of the building. Many of The Federationists present had gathered on the lower levels to watch Dubois's announcement. It was determined that the origin of the tunnel was a residence in Glen Park. Both terrorists on the ground were killed by Federation forces. The piece of intel that drew the blood from Juan Carlos Luna's face was the weapons recovered on the suppressed insurgents: a pair of TS-33s.

Natalie was watching the rare interview footage of Antoine Dubois from the past five years. Dubois as an interview subject had become extremely unpredictable in his performances. More recently, he had been terse in his answers; serious and stern. Other times, he would be friendly, warm, and anecdotal. Natalie hoped for the latter. She hoped for the engaging, charismatic leader that captured the world's attention decades before. She wanted to get his vision for the part of America that had been left behind on 10 February 2057, when the federal government adopted the Basic Human Standard after forty out of fifty-two state legislatures had ratified the treaty. She wanted him to explain why those that opposed him then and now should trust him in the future. There had been glimpses of this shining leader in recent interviews and Natalie found and studied these moments.

Her first impression in watching the interviews was that Secretary-General Antoine Dubois did not like to talk about himself. This was a rarity among politicians. The man would rather extrapolate on the ideals of the BHS and his dream of an eventual pivot from the centralized GFN to a sweeping array of progressive, local governments that would continue to administer the principles of the Montpellier Accords in their own fashion. Natalie thought that he was modest, almost to a fault. During the early part of his career, many of his adversaries tried to translate his modesty into a lack of confidence. He was famous for saying that he was "not an innovator." This line was repeated hundreds of times by those who opposed him. In context, the point that Dubois had made was that he did not originate the ideas that became the foundation of his presidency and The Federation, but that he took the ideas of history's greatest thinkers and applied them to modern civilization. Some said that this approach was dangerous, but Dubois was able to assure the world that it was the only necessary way for humanity to progress.

Natalie was currently watching an interview with the Secretary-General conducted by Jermaine Cliff of the BBC. The interview, from 10 April 2070, was in commemoration of the twenty-fifth anniversary of the signing of the Montpellier Accords. Natalie admired Dubois's unrivaled enthusiasm for the power of ideas. His passion and delivery were electric. However, Natalie would need to balance the man's penchant to dive into the abstract with some concrete policy statements. Natalie thought that her job tomorrow was like that of a falconer: she needed to let the man feel comfortable enough to fly outside his natural confines, but also have the ability to bring him back to the ground.

Natalie rewound the recording. Antoine Dubois was musing about health care and quoting Dr. Paul Farmer, but Natalie kept her focus on Jermaine Cliff. She watched his posture as he listened. She studied his eyes as he asked a question. She listened to the tone he used. She thought to herself, *Dubois may be unpredictable, but I can make sure I can account for every single breath I take.*

The anesthetic gel was cool on Noah's shin, but Sonya, kneeling before him, breathed warm onto the flesh above his knee. She did not talk as she worked to soothe the pain in his leg. He watched her hands massage the gel over his tibia. Her blouse was unbuttoned at the collar and Noah could see the shaded skin rise until the fabric of her bra covered her breasts. Lust coiled around Noah like a snake and he felt his lungs constrict.

He turned his head to the side and let the air gush out of him. Sonya stopped applying the gel and looked at Noah. He met her gaze and she smiled at him. Then, her hands moved from his shin, up his leg and onto his thigh. Her outside hand made its way around his hip and grasped his seated rear. Her inside hand meandered up his thigh and under his shorts. When she found the hot crease of his groin, she dropped her head and kissed the wound on his shin. She worked her tongue up and down the gash.

Sonya pulled her legs away from Noah's base and stood up. She inched toward him, then lowered herself onto his lap. Noah's heart was beating fast and his manhood swelled. His mouth was dry—so dry that he could not speak. The snake wrapped itself around him tighter.

He looked at her and she looked back. She glowed with the soft sunlight that came in from the rudimentary windows. Her youthful face was countered by the deep experience of her eyes. She moved sensually, confidently.

As she leaned in to kiss Noah, he held a finger to her puckered mouth. She wrapped her lips around the finger and rolled her tongue back and forth, like the ocean's tide. He pulled the finger away quickly. Persistent, she moved her tongue to the slope of his neck. He grabbed her by the shoulders, but instead of drawing her closer, he pushed her away. He slid out from underneath her straddle, pivoted her to the bed, and stood at the edge.

Sonya looked at him with anticipation, pulled her shirt above her ribs, and rubbed herself.

Noah tucked himself under his waistband and looked at the floor.

"I can't," he muttered, his eyes burrowing into the floor. "I just can't." Without looking at Sonya, he walked quickly out of the shack and the vinyl door shut hard behind him.

A woodpecker flew through the campus and landed on the trunk of a large birch tree. Its chest was white, its wings were black, and its head was a blood-red color. The crimson head had caught Juan Carlos Luna's attention. The bird released a few shrill calls, then proceeded to peck at the base of the tree, creating a rapid series of drums. Luna watched the bird with interest.

He tried not to think about the intel he had just read. The TS-33 was a weapon exclusively used by The Global Federation of Nation's Security Offices. Now, it had been used to cut down those same people that the instrument was produced to protect. It could have been used to cut down Arnie Jones. A great warrior and an even better friend. The software of the TS-33 was designed so that only trained, authorized Security Officers could use the weapon.

The Lt. Director could conjure two possibilities for how the weapons ended up in the hands of insurgents. The first was that the insurgents had hacked the TS-33s software's firewall. If the insurgents could hack TS-33 software, then there were even greater catastrophic consequences for the GFN.

Though the first option was apocalyptic for The Federation's Security Offices, it was the second possibility that made Luna nauseous. The second possibility was that someone within NASO, one of Lt. Director Juan Carlos Luna's colleagues, had overridden the TS-33 software for the insurgents. There had been fear and rumors that someone within The Federation could look to turn a profit and betray their brothers and sisters, but now Luna had the first substantial evidence that this fear had become a reality.

The drumming from the woodpecker continued on the tree, like the *rat-a-tat-tat* of an assault rifle.

Five minutes after the graphene shades opened, Joseph Kalani came back from the dining car.

"I just met the most interesting couple," he said as he sat down next to Natalie.

"Yeah?" Natalie said as she took notes of the video playing on her APD.

"Yeah," Kalani answered. His jacket was balled up in his lap and his sleeves were rolled up just below his elbows. Natalie could smell the sweet gin on his breath and saw his eyes begin to droop. "Going to Estes Park from Naperville."

Natalie looked at Joseph and smiled. "That is interesting, Joe."

"Said they were gonna go paraskiing!"

"Wow," she answered dully.

Joseph shook his head.

"Nearly fifty years old and they're going skiing with a parachute strapped to their backs." He laughed. "Crazy SOBs."

They sat silent for a few seconds.

"You won't find me paraskiing, I'll tell you that, right now."

"Really?" Natalie responded, keeping her head down. "Seems right up your alley."

"No, no, no. That, young lady, is not up my alley."

A minute passed.

"You should ask that Mr. Dubois if he would go paraskiing. I know I'd sure like to see that."

Natalie laughed. "I'm afraid that question just missed the cut."

"That's too bad."

Joseph crossed his arms across his chest and looked around the railcar.

"Make sure you don't forget that box, dearie," he said to her, as he tapped it with his toe under the seat. "I know you have a big day tomorrow, but don't forget that box."

"The box? Why?" Natalie asked Joseph, but when he didn't answer, she saw that he was fast asleep.

Noah walked quickly away from Sonya's shack. He did not look back. His face was so flushed he felt like he would burn his fingertips if he touched his own cheek. He kept his head down until there were no more buildings in his periphery. Out of the village and away from his moral failing, Noah's legs buckled. He crouched in the prairie grass with his hands on his head. He pounded his palms against his temples. *Why did I let that go so far?* For the first time since he had been a child, he felt deeply, truly ashamed.

He wished he could call his wife, to tell her of his mistake. Would she applaud his strength in turning down the seductress? Or would she curse him for being alone with another woman and sitting on her bed? She had kissed him. Licked him. Straddled and groped him before Noah stopped her. He dug his chin to his chest and rocked on the balls of his feet, the tall grass swaying with him.

I've let you down, Marie. Poor Marie.

Does she know I'm here? Does she know I'm okay? Does she know I'm alive?

My God. Poor, poor Marie.

Noah ached for his family. Since he first met Marie, he had never been away from her for more than a night. Now it had been over a week. He needed to find Wade to see when he would be reunited with his family. Wade had told him that they were "going home" but they were not home, and Noah wanted to hold his brother-in-law to his word.

But where was *Wade?*

Noah hadn't seen where he went after they had deplaned. He had been preoccupied by Sonya. *Sonya.* Her name brought his shame back and he started pounding his temples again. He shook his head. *Wade. I need to find Wade. To get back to Marie.* He removed his hands from his head and stood up. He looked down the shanty row and counted fifteen shacks. He could see no movement inside through the square windows, so he walked up to the next row. There was life. Two people. He did not recognize them, but he figured they might know where Wade was. He walked toward them.

They were a middle-aged white couple and they were watching some projection from an APD as Noah approached. The man was muscular and wore a tight, short-sleeved shirt which showed off a tattoo on his bicep. The tattoo was of four ivy leaves aligned in a cross, which Noah recalled was associated with the 4th Infantry Division of the U.S. Army. His hair was cut close and he sported a well-trimmed beard. His face was puny and, even under the beard, Noah saw that his chin slipped into his throat with little distinction. The woman was thick from her ankles to her neck. She wore baggy, long pants, a camouflage jacket tucked behind her, and a bucket hat to shield her face from the sun. Her hair was short, blonde, and cut straight above her shoulders. They each wore a holster that cradled Desert Eagles that glimmered in the sunlight.

As Noah came closer, he saw what they were watching. Projected before them was a man tied to a chair in a dank, concrete room. Behind him were four men, each wearing a mask. One appeared to be speaking to the camera. He pulled out a hunting knife with a fifteen-centimeter serrated blade. He held the blade to the tied man's throat. As Noah moved closer, he saw a GFN patch on the tied man's shirt. Blood sprayed over the patch as the masked man rocked the blade back and forth.

Noah was mesmerized by the brutal footage. The woman's voice brought him back to reality.

"Have you seen this one yet?" she asked Noah. "It's kinda old, but it's a good one."

Noah shook his head. "No. I haven't seen it."

"Oh, my! Well, you're in for a treat!"

The masked man continued to saw the GFN agent's throat. He moved the blade slowly. Blood poured down The Federationist's chest and bubbled out of his mouth and nose. His eyes were still opened. They moved.

Noah looked away, nauseous. He heard the man and woman cheer. He looked back at the video. There was still a body in the chair, but now it was drenched in blood and ended at the shoulders. The masked man held the severed head high and the three others in the video cheered.

"Hot damn!" the man at the shack shouted. "I love it when those cucks in Europe grow a pair and start taking these Yellow-Eyed bastards down."

Noah spotted a date and location on the bottom of the footage: "9 November 2071. Llorà, Spain."

Noah stepped toward the man and the woman. "Do you know where I can find Wade Barrineau?"

The man looked at Noah for the first time. His face grew suspicious and he turned off the video. The woman moved her hand nearer to the handgun on the table.

"Yeah," he answered. "Just who the hell wants to know?"

"I do."

"And who the fuck are you?"

"Oh, I'm Noah Bridger."

The man chuckled and looked at Noah's leg. "*You're* Noah Bridger? The human bomb?"

Noah was surprised to learn that he had a reputation. "Yes, I'm Noah Bridger."

"Well, Mr. Human Bomb," the man said, "your brother-in-law went for a look around the grounds. He should be back shortly." He pointed into the shack. "Grab a chair and take a seat."

The intelligence Lt. Director Luna received from The Mount had disturbed him. The number of casualties did not disturb him. Saddened, yes, but not disturbed. He had seen death at an extreme scale before. He would see death at an extreme scale again. What disturbed Luna was a single line from the report. "Two unlicensed TS-33s were found at the scene." This revelation sent chills down his spine. His initial instinct was to fly to California and investigate how the GFN weapons were used against his fellow Federationists, but he knew he could not. He knew he was stuck in Santa Fe for at least twenty-four more hours and he had a big job ahead of him. He could not dwell on how some pussies used tools of peace to slaughter good men and women.

He also knew that if he followed his instinct to California, he may not like what he found there. And that was a thought he could not let fester.

Luna left the campus and summoned an auto. He needed to survey the two potential locales for the temporary GFN HQ. The car drove him to the New Mexico Public Regulation Commission Building first and he, without looking at the second site, declared the building would work fine as the new headquarters.

The Commission Building was less than one hundred meters away from the Roundhouse. The building, like much of the property in Santa Fe, was in shambles due to the lack of maintenance funds and police protection. Looters had taken most of the furniture, plumbing, electronics, robotics, and anything else they could grab. The copper wiring had been stripped. Mold spread over the floors and walls. Water damage marked the ceiling on the top two floors. It was so bad in some places that holes opened to the outside air. Luna had noticed this level of decay throughout the city, but he had seen worse in the Grey Zone—much worse. Santa Fe still had a local, ad-hoc governmental system that attempted to maintain the town. This ad-hoc government, in partnership with the American Freedom Group, provided roving militia to thwart looters. The AFG charged local governments and citizens a small fee for their services to fund their militaristic endeavors.

Some towns in the Grey Zone refused to pay the Freedom Group. Those towns looked like bulldozers had razed whole city blocks.

Luna sent Farrelly a message informing her that he had established a new headquarters. The Director had made that a priority for her Lieutenant. Now that the HQ was selected, a legion of Federationists and ARs would spring into action to clean and repair the building. The headquarters would be functional by suppertime.

The Railyard Inn had closed to give the staff time off to recover from the attack. Modular structures had been erected with rows of bunks to accommodate the traveling Federationists, but Luna's assistant Deborah had found him a room at a bed and breakfast called Pueblo Bonito. It was near the Georgia O'Keefe Museum, about a kilometer north of the Capitol. He left the car and made his way to his new room.

The Lt. Director took his time walking to Pueblo Bonito. The sun warmed the earth around him and the nice weather seemed to bring people out into the town. Or he just noticed them for the first time. So often he thought of these places as being strictly battlegrounds and the citizens of the Grey Zone to all be combatants, but these people appeared to be just trying to live their lives.

A group of young boys and girls kicked a worn soccer ball on a dirt patch across the street. Their clothes were dirty and ragged. A few were barefoot. They laughed and yelled and chased the ball gleefully.

A cement truck rumbled down the road, spewing a thick cloud of white smoke. A man and a woman sat in the cab and the mixing drum was streaked with graffiti. Luna looked at the roads. They were scarred with cracks and holes. There was so much work to be done here—one truck could hardly make a difference. Still, it lugged on until it turned a corner and was out of the Lt. Director's sight. Luna marveled at people's proclivity to try to maintain even the worst shitholes.

His soldier's eye had long viewed everyone in this environment as a potential threat, but he now thought about who these people were. They were people that walked to work, to meet friends, or to pick up their children. Some were hostile to the GFN and actively worked against The Federation, but others just did not know what was going on in the world outside their town. And most did not care. They had problems at home. The same problems people across the world had. Bad house. Bad job. Bad marriage. Bad kids. And they blamed whomever they read or heard was to blame. And in the Grey Zone, that culprit was often the puppet-president and some Frenchman with his hand on the wooden control. Globalization was a scary, abstract thought for these people. They were isolated. And they tried to make their lives better in isolation.

Luna felt sympathy for them, but then he remembered what that fear and isolation could create. And what it could take away. He stopped looking for humanity among these people and went back to searching for weapons and ambush. He may not be able to enlighten these people or pave their roads or teach their children, but he could rip their weapons away and make sure they did not fuck this signing up.

By the time the conductor announced that the train was approaching Denver, Natalie had settled upon five or six questions she would ask the Secretary-General. Beside her, Joseph slept.

The brand new Colorado Rail Station was southeast of Denver in the suburb of Centennial. The station mimicked the old Denver International Airport and was designed to look like the mountains that rose behind. The chromogenic systems on the outside of the station changed color depending on the season and weather to match the Rockies. This earned the multi-billion-dollar structure the nickname "The Choo-choo Ridge."

The train stopped, and Natalie shook Joseph awake. They gathered their luggage and departed the train. Joseph grabbed a cart for the baggage and Natalie purchased a couple of kale salads from a refrigerator in the terminal. The two headed for the next platform. The station was not nearly as busy as Chicago and Natalie only saw a few local police officers walking among the travelers. A robotic truck slid down the concourse and filled the vending machines. As Natalie and Joseph stood on the moving walkway to the next terminal, images of last night's attacks were shown overhead on massive screens that bent with the curved ceiling.

A massive fireball rising above the San Francisco fog. A parade of portraits of the perished. A stream of Federationists at the New Mexico Capitol Building. Visibly increased security from Hunters Point to the Upper East Side. Footage from a Santa Fe ambulette of a flying drone hammering a blown-out building and a smoldering shell of a first-responder vehicle. Chalky, bloody, crying faces wandering down Columbus Ave.

Every second of news was focused on the terroristic events of the past twenty-four hours.

Natalie had never grown used to the cavalier way violence was displayed in public. When her father was killed, it had been broadcasted nationally. She had watched that clip over and over until she knew every detail of every frame. It had made her physically ill each time she watched it. She would stay up for hours in the middle of the night, watching her father's head explode. Her therapist said Natalie watched the footage because she felt survivor's guilt. She called the act "self-flagellation of the mind". Natalie did this for months until one night, at four in the morning, she vomited on her desk and lap after having watched the clip until her eyes were bloodshot. She ran to the bathroom, sickness dripping off her clothes, and vomited again and again until there were only a few drops of bile left inside of her. The stale, sour smell settled over her apartment for days. To escape the stink and video, Natalie had gone north to Chequamegon-Nicolet National Forest to camp for a long weekend alone. She brought with her nothing that could play the news clip. When Natalie returned, the smell had cleared, and she never watched the video again.

She thought about the recording she had obtained from Lily Lee of the Oklahoma City attack. She had watched it over and over, studying it. She looked at the moment Dotson was killed before the flash of a muzzles from the bed of the pickup. The *Tribune* had published the college kid's video and it was talked about for an afternoon.

Then, the violence and gore had faded into the information abyss. There was something else tragic caught on video. With over nine billion people on the planet and something like forty billion acknowledged recording devices filming at any one second, the odds were awfully high that something horrific was going to wind up under a public lens. And it did. And people watched. And then people forgot and moved on to the next disturbing video.

But Natalie thought that there might be a daughter out there of one of the people killed at the Bucket Bistro. A shocked, grief-stricken girl who was watching that video over and over even though the world no longer seemed interested. The video to her was not news but was the capturing of the last moments of a loved one.

How long would the public watch these images streaming constantly at the train station? How many people would use these images to torture themselves?

The moving sidewalk ended, and Joseph and Natalie found their platform. Their train was boarding; Joseph had purchased first-class seating again. Natalie followed Joseph to their seats, sat down, and started eating her salad. It had been ten years since she last viewed the footage of her father's death but now, as she sat in an antiquated train car, the scene played in the theatre of her mind, frame by frame, not missing a single detail.

As Noah sat with the militant couple, he grew uncomfortable. He had the feeling that he was on the outside of some community joke and he suspected that he was the punch line. His name was Harlan and hers was Shelley and they came from Dodge City, Kansas. Harlan completed a tour of duty in Saudi Arabia as a young man, then managed a genetically-modified tree farm. Shelley had taught fifth grade. Now they were part of "the resistance."

"Which resistance, exactly, would that be? Freedom Army?" Noah asked.

Harlan laughed. He looked at his wife and pointed a thumb at Noah. "This motherfucker here." Then, he slapped Noah on the knee and said, "Boy, you crack me up."

He did not answer the question, so Noah tried another.

"How long have you two been here?"

Harlan unfolded a buck knife and began to pick his nails with it. "'Bout a week. That's when camp went up."

Noah looked around. "Where are we, exactly?"

Harlan looked at his wife again and they both laughed. When he finished his grooming, he threw the knife down and it landed blade first in the grass.

"Boy, they really don't tell you nothin', do they?"

Noah let out a stream of disappointed air. "No, I guess they don't."

"Well, then you must not have clearance then," Shelley said, her voice squeaked, her eyes locked on Noah suspiciously.

"And if you don't have clearance, we can't tell ya. Me and Shelley ain't gonna go around divulging classified secrets to someone who ain't a Man of God. That's a good way for me and Shelley to find a couple bullets in our heads."

Shelley nodded enthusiastically. "We ain't gonna risk gettin' shot just because your dumbass doesn't know where he is."

Noah was offended. "I am a Man of God," he answered honestly.

"If you were a Man of God," Shelley responded, "then you'd have clearance."

"Now, wait a minute, I've been a Christian my whole life." Noah was defensive.

"Being a Christian don't make you no Man of God." Shelley said, and Harlan agreed.

"If you ain't read *The Last Book*, then you ain't no Man of God and if you ain't no Man of God, I sure as hell won't tell you a thing."

Noah grew confused. "*The Last Book?* You mean *Revelations*? Because I've read that."

"Nah, boy," Harlan stopped him. "*The Last Book*. The Prophet's Book. Barrineau's Book."

As soon as Juan Carlos Luna settled into his room at the Pueblo Bonito Bed and Breakfast, he called Jay. He was happy to see his husband's face. Luna had sent his husband a quick message stating that he was okay after the attack, but they had not yet talked. At the beginning of the video call, Luna kept the focus on Jay. He enjoyed hearing about the mundanities of his husband's days in New York. He heard about the walk Jay took with the couple's genetically-modified teacup deer, he heard about the lunch he enjoyed at the café below their apartment, and he heard about the painting Jay ordered from Korea. Then, Luna talked about the attack and Jay listened. Juan Carlos cried for his friend, Arnie, and the others lost, and his husband consoled him. Jay told Juan Carlos that he did all he could and that there was no better man to make things right. Luna hoped that was true. They said goodbye and Lt. Director Luna sat on the unfamiliar bed, wiped the tears from his eyes, and pulled himself together.

He left the B&B for the new headquarters. The group of journalists, observers, and protesters had grown. Any public appearance by the Secretary-General was bound to be a spectacle. The atmosphere was charged as the crowd grew more diverse. The largest contingent present was a group of Anti-Federation protesters. They were not quite matched by those present who supported the GFN. The massing of cameras gave everyone with a special interest a reason to show up.

A group of Native Americans had been staging a sit-in since the initial announcement. They were there to raise awareness of the genocidal takeover of their homeland first by the European settlers and later the American government. The Federation had done a great deal of work to cooperate with indigenous groups across the globe to counteract the results of imperialism, including the expansion and funding of the Navajo Nation around the four corners of the Southwest. The Navajo Nation, as well as Osage Nation, Yakama Nation, Leech Lake Reservation, Qualla Boundary, Pine Ridge Reservation, and other native communities began receiving BHS subsidies from the GFN six years before the federal government ratified the Treaty of The Global Federation in 2051 under the Indigenous Peoples Restitution Act. The communities, especially the metropolis of Window Rock, had flourished under the IPRA, but some prominent Navajos had made a recent push to gain back the entirety of their ancestral territory. They were present and vocal at the signing.

In addition to the Native activists, there was a smattering of other protest groups.

The "Space Colonizers" were present. Thirty years ago, a second-space race had occurred that involved multiple nations as well as many private corporations. With the discovery of liquid water on Mars and the advancement of terraforming technology, a colony on the Red Planet seemed to be decades, maybe even mere years away. With the origin of The Federation, all space exploration was put on hold. The Federation stated that all of humanity's resources needed to be directed toward the people of Earth. Once poverty was eradicated and the excess resources were no longer needed to aid those that needed them, then local governments could set their sights on the stars if they chose to. The "Space Colonizers" were mostly a collection of academics and scientists that thought that, *because* the Earth was in a perilous position, it was a perfect time to hit the reset button and start anew further into the solar system. Dubois argued that he was not willing to give up on humanity's home planet and GFN member states agreed in one of the organization's closest votes ever.

The Matriarchy was also among the crowd. The group had little political platform except the desire to see all government positions occupied by women. The organization's mission statement claimed that, after centuries of masculine rule leading to war, corruption, and inequality, it was time for females to govern. They were well-known among members of the Security Offices for their practice of releasing rodents and insects in Federation buildings, claiming that the pests were a step above the male's occupying leadership roles.

Members of the Church of Wicca called for pagan theological practices to be adapted as the official religion of the United States. Groups of Evangelicals, Wahhabis, Mormons, and the leadership of the Society of St. Pius X gathered for the same constitutional purpose.

There were dozens of other allegiances. Luna expected there to be some minor bickering and some squabbling with these protest groups, but none of them were labeled as a direct, violent threat to the signing. He knew that his threats would not be marching in the streets with signs but would be lurking in the shadows with guns and bombs.

Outside of Castle Rock, Colorado, the diesel-powered train traveling from Denver reached a checkpoint. Natalie and Joseph were traveling in a Victorian-era style passenger carriage, complete with velvet seating, gilded adornments, and antler chandeliers. Joseph had called the accommodations campy, but Natalie found them charming. The passenger carriage was connected to a long line of grain cars. The grain was eventually to be delivered to a Grey Zone informant as part of the GFN "living necessities" program.

Natalie looked out the window. Two American Humvees flanked the tracks. A GFN Security Officer boarded the passenger carriage, followed by three U.S. Army soldiers. Natalie had entered the Grey Zone dozens of times since it was established and had never seen such tight security. Due to the ever-fluctuating Federation borders and the massive amount of land, roads, and tracks to cover, most people traveling from one Zone to the next were often only greeted by an announcement from their

Reader. In truth, physical checks were deemed obsolete by the Mobile Observation and Targeting Division. MOAT used IWC tracking systems, satellites, drones, laser boundaries, and other technologies to monitor the mass migration between Grey and White Zones.

Joseph appeared nervous as the security traveled down the aisle. Natalie thought he had been out of the field and in his lush office for too long. She thought the physical security presence was classic Farrelly—a show of power as an over-reaction to the previous night's attacks. As Joseph attempted to make small-talk with the SO, Natalie silently acquiesced to the IWC scan. She was busy reading Antoine Dubois's past statements on the American Freedom Group.

Joseph patted her arm, gaining her attention. "Natalie? This man asked you a question."

"Hmm?" Natalie muttered and looked up from her APD. The SO was staring at her. He was young, with a smooth face and pudgy cheeks.

"And what do you plan on doing in the Grey Zone, ma'am?"

"Oh, sorry. I didn't hear you. I'm going to be interviewing Antoine Dubois."

Joseph choked on this answer and coughed in surprise.

"Excuse me?" the SO asked.

Natalie looked at Joseph. His eyes were wide, pleading with her.

"I mean, I'm a journalist. I *hope* to get an interview with Dubois. Fingers crossed!" She held up both hands showing the signal.

The SO looked at her and furrowed his brow.

"Right," he answered. "Good luck with that." He then turned to the passengers across the aisle from Natalie and Joseph.

Joseph leaned in and whispered to Natalie. "Are you *insane?!* You can't go around blabbing that you're meeting with the Secretary-General! What the hell is the matter with you?"

Natalie waved him off. "Oh, please. That zygote wasn't going to buy that."

Joseph looked around the car. "Well, someone else might buy it. Who the hell do you think is on this thing?"

Natalie hadn't thought about that. She looked around and recognized a few faces as fellow journalists. The people she did not recognize had the tired, frantic visages of people working to beat a deadline.

"I don't think anyone heard me," she responded, feeling guilty.

"Well, just keep your mouth shut," Joseph replied, with his hand on his head. "Please."

Natalie laughed. "You really are rusty, old man."

Joseph glared at her, then smiled. "You truly are the worst."

"Thank you," Natalie replied before getting back to work.

A few minutes later, Natalie felt the car jerk, then lunge forward. She looked out the window again. The two Humvees escorted the train into the Grey Zone before turning back to the checkpoint.

Noah Bridger asked Harlan and Shelley from Dodge City about *The Last Book*, but the pair remained cryptic. He was not "in the know" and they weren't going to let him in. Shelley found another GFN execution video and played it. This one was from the Republic of Chad. The Federationist on-screen identified herself as a Special Representative for Women's Rights. Her left hand had just been cut off when Noah excused himself.

"Keep to the camp, boy," Harlan said. "You don't want to get lost out there."

"Or run into somebody thinkin' you don't belong," Shelley added, polishing her already gleaming gun. Noah sensed a threat but was unable to respond. He walked away from the couple quickly. When he reached the edge of the camp, he ignored Harlan's warning and wandered up the incline.

When he reached the crest of the hill, Noah was surprised at what he saw. There were about forty men and women diligently working the land. They had created a boundary with wooden stakes and mesh wire. Inside the boundary, the grass had been removed and light brown dirt sat unevenly atop the ground. The men and women were separated into groups and had taped off subsets of the original boundary. The whole garden was a few acres. Noah was unimpressed by what he saw. A quarter of the garden lay in the shade of the hill. The rows of crops appeared to be too close together. Noah looked for the irrigation system but didn't see one. He didn't care.

Surrounding the acres of garden, a thin wood bowed across the landscape. A splinter of six people emerged from the trees and walked around the large, shoddy garden. He spotted Sonya among the six right away. She carried an AK strapped across her back, like the others in the group. Noah could see Wade in the middle, speaking, all eyes fixed on him. He looked larger than he ever did before. Noah sat on top of the hill and waited. He practiced the staunch declaration he would make again and again under his breath.

"Wade. I've done what I said I would. Now you need to send me home."

Lt. Director Luna made his way through the crowd gathered around De Vargas Park to the New Mexico Public Regulation Commission Building. The building had been transformed from an abandoned shell to the hub of GFN activity. Luna looked at the new HQ and was impressed: the sand-colored structure stood three stories high. Drones zipped around the brick track that ran along the top; some were providing security and surveillance while others flew in and out of the fresh-ly-painted white shuttered windows, delivering equipment to The Federationists. Outside the building, on the commons between the Capitol and the parking lot, tall white tents had been erected to expand the headquarters. Luna walked through a light-beam that signified restricted grounds and into the swarm of activity.

As Luna walked up the steps to enter the building, he heard a voice calling his title behind him. He held the door open and surveyed the crowd to see who had been yelling for him. He spotted the source. A young, muscular man jogged toward him. He wore a blue, Hampton-cut suit and his open jacket flapped behind him as he ran. The man's short brown hair matched his tailored Italian shoes in color and polish and Luna guessed his sunglasses cost at least $1,000. The man had once worked at NASO but was now in the employ of the Communications Office. His name was Cooper Gates and the Lt. Director did not have time for him. He walked inside and let the door close behind him.

As he started up the stairs, he heard the summons again, louder now, echoing through the lobby. A few steps later, there was a large, tanned hand on his shoulder.

"Lt. Director. Sir," Gates uttered. Luna looked back at Gates quickly and did not respond until he reached the second level of the building. Once there, he stopped and looked at the man.

"What is it, Gates?"

"I've been trying to get ahold of you for weeks."

"It's been busy," Luna rejoined, curtly.

"I need to speak with you, sir."

"Then schedule an appointment."

"I've tried. I've been waitlisted. This is urgent."

People squeezed by the pair blocking the stairs. Luna grabbed Gates's arm and moved him out of the way. Three years ago, Gates had gone on television and called one of Luna's missions "below the standards set by the GFN." Luna had lost four men on the mission and had never forgotten the young man's assessment.

Now, he leveled Gates with a fiery glare before digging his finger into his chest.

"Listen, you fucking prima donna, this signing is tomorrow, and I don't have time for any of your shit. Why don't you shoo off and try to do some real work for once in your life?"

Luna left Gates standing alone in the hall as people brushed by. The Assistant Press Secretary shook his head and walked back down the stairs.

"When will you be here?"

Natalie Kelley read the message from Cooper Gates on her APD.

She didn't have time for a liaison. Even if she did, she didn't want it to be with Cooper. She responded tersely. "Don't know."

The next message came almost immediately: "Well, let me know when you are in town. I need to see you."

Their entire relationship was predicated on his needs and wants, and Natalie was done with it.

"Listen Coop—it was fun while it lasted, but we aren't going to see each other anymore."

Natalie had never developed deep feelings for Cooper Gates. He was fun, handsome, and good in bed. But he was also demanding, aloof, and married. Their relationship had been messy. Natalie had liked it for a while but was relieved to be moving on.

Another message came through quickly: "Natalie. I need to talk to you. In person. Stop being a child. Let me know when you're here."

Natalie shook her head. Her face flushed with anger. She deleted the message and blocked Cooper Gates from getting through to her. She threw down her APD in disgust.

"You okay?" Joseph asked next to her.

She put her hands over her cheeks to cover the heat. She hadn't told Joseph about her affair with Cooper. She didn't need a professional chiding and personal rebuking from the old man. She nodded, smiled, and lied to him.

"Yeah, I'm fine. Just a little stressed right now."

Joseph looked at her intently. "Yeah. I can imagine. Why don't you take a break?"

Natalie nodded again and dropped her hands to the armrests. She let out a long, deep breath.

She closed her eyes and forgot Cooper Gates. She forgot Antoine Dubois. She forgot Santa Fe and she forgot the train. She was little again. And her father was smiling at her. Natalie knew that she was asleep, but she made herself forget that, too. There was truth and comfort in the dream and she wrapped herself in it.

Noah stretched his leg out on the top of the hill and waited for Wade. Sonya had stopped at the boundary of the garden and talked with one of the workers. When Wade spotted Noah sitting on the crest, he dismissed his entourage and ascended the hill alone. He sat down next to his brother-in-law and looked out over the garden.

"How's the leg feeling?"

"It's fine," Noah answered. He felt small in the shadow of the man. He closed his eyes, clenched his fists on the grass, and turned to Wade. "What the hell's going on, Wade? You said I was going home. We sure as shit aren't home. Where the fuck are we? When am I going home? When, Goddamnit, when?" The words exploded out of Noah like a volcano. He hadn't expected such an eruption. He braced for Wade's equally violent response, but none came. He looked over at his brother-in-law, expecting anger, but was shocked by his expression.

Tears welled in Wade's eyes. He put his hand on Noah's shoulder.

"Noah," he started, "I'm afraid I have some bad news to deliver to you."

"No more games, Wade!" Noah interrupted. He was confused. Scared. "Where *are* we?!"

Wade reached into his pocket and pulled out his APD.

"There's no easy way to tell you this. You must have faith in the Lord during the most trying times," he paused, then stated, "Your family is dead."

Noah sat silent, unable to process the words.

"They were all killed. I only just found out."

Noah couldn't breathe. A lump of terror rested in his throat.

"I'm sorry. I cannot imagine the pain you are feeling. But, Jesus Christ can. You must turn to Him to get strength in this trying—"

"No!" Noah said, choking on the words. "No. Fuck you, Wade. No. You can't keep..." He couldn't finish. Only sobs came forward.

He tried to stand, but Wade's grip kept him grounded.

Wade shoved the APD in front of Noah. Through bleary eyes he saw a picture displayed on the screen. He blinked to focus. He saw his living room. His mantle. His couch. His windows and his rug. His family portrait. Six bodies. Tears blurred his vision again. He stared at the bodies. He counted the bodies, hoping one had been spared. One, two, three, four, five, six. The faces were buried in the blood-soaked carpet. But he knew. He knew the instant he saw them. His family.

Noah pushed away the APD. As his world collapsed on him, he fell backward and wept.

CHAPTER NINE

14 May 2072

Natalie Kelley couldn't sleep.

She had been out for the last few hours of the train ride and was stiff and groggy when Joseph woke her. As they left the railyard and entered the cool, rank mountain air, Joseph covered his mouth and nose with a silk handkerchief to block the stank of sewage. They walked a few blocks to the Morning Cactus Hotel past the site of the recent attack. The battered hotel was concealed by a high, opaque plastic drape. The path from the railyard to the hotel was lit by spotlights and teemed with people. Although the sun had set hours ago, the town seemed to be just now waking up.

In the lobby of the hotel, Joseph found an old rival and invited Natalie to join them for a drink. She declined and went to her room where she undressed and lay in bed. Sleep eluded her. She laid in bed for hours. Adrenaline coursed through her veins. Instinctively, she began to say the rosary to numb her brain. It did not work; her mind raced. She left her bed and tried Tai chi to settle herself down. It did not work, either.

She looked over her outline for the interview but found she didn't need the notes. She knew it by heart. Frustrated, she threw on some sweats and wandered the hotel. It was late, and the bar had closed. The Morning Cactus was deserted, aside from a dozing teen behind the check-in desk. After waking the receptionist, he pointed her down the hall to what he called the "gym". It consisted of some free weights, jump ropes, and an old mechanical bike. Natalie thanked him and started jumping rope. She worked out for nearly an hour. It was almost 04:00. Sweaty and loose, she walked to the kitchen. It would not open for another two hours. Natalie looked outside and saw a row of pickup trucks parked across the street. Men were unloading boxes from the trucks. Under one of the spotlights, there was a white sheet with painted, black text which read "FRESH FOOD".

Natalie walked out of the hotel. The beads of sweat chilled her skin as they crept down her face. She shivered, used the tail of her shirt to wipe away the sweat, and sauntered toward the trucks.

In the distance, past the vendors unloading their wooden crates of food, there was a bright flash. The men stopped what they were doing. There was a booming noise and Natalie felt the ground shake.

Lt. Director Luna was on his morning jog when he heard the explosion. He had started up Glorieta Baldy Road en route to Thompson Peak when the smoke appeared to his west, rising over the pine trees. He had left his APD in the car and hurried back to his point of origin. He sprinted back to the trailhead and was breathing heavily when he reached the sedan.

His APD was filled with urgent messages. It appeared there had been an explosion north of Santa Fe on Highway 285. Luna plugged the coordinates into the sedan's navigation system. In the Grey Zone, he did not have the luxury of giving the vehicle "Emergency Response Right-of-Way." ERROW was designed to speed response times during crises by automatically pulling cars to the side of the road and turning all approaching street lights green. Now, Luna found himself stuck behind a lorry in the New Mexican canyons. He pounded the steering wheel and cursed, then switched the car to manual, and sped past the laboring truck.

Luna's APD read the initial reports through the car's speaker. They were vague and sometimes contradicting, but it appeared that there had been no GFN casualties. Luna was relieved: he had seen too much loss in the last thirty-six hours, experienced too much failure.

Luna whipped the sedan through the streets of Santa Fe. The roads were dark and filled with holes. The car advised Luna to slow, but he ignored the computer. He followed the coordinates north and reached the perimeter on Highway 285 in fifteen minutes. There was already a large crowd gathered. Journalists were reporting in front of a background of GFN vehicles and smoke wisping high into the starlit sky. SOs pushed them back away from the road and onlookers lurked in the sage, whispering to one another, addled and scared. Luna parked the sedan on the shoulder and walked through the perimeter. Three hundred meters away a fire gurgled and burped flames into the navy canvas above.

Wade did not let Noah weep for long. The man was broken after finding out his family had been murdered. Wade cut through the sadness and harvested the anger. Noah had no strength to resist. Before Noah left the camp, Wade had given him a mission. And, he had also given him his Book.

Noah's mind was blank with sorrow. He left the camp under cover of darkness. After some time alone in the black, he turned on the small penlight he had been given and opened Wade's book. After the first reading, he found the words ridiculous. He put the book away, but as his mind raced in the lightless vacuum, the pain came back. He turned the light back on, picked up the book again, and found a random page. He began to read, speaking each word aloud, letting the sounds push away the pain.

The asp that strikes at mankind's heel has revealed Himself. And God said, I will crush his head.

The Beast has risen from the Sea. He has but one head and no horns and he wears no crown. But upon that one head is the name of blasphemy.

The Beast shall harness the power of man and deny the power which is God's.

The Lord our God has spoken to us all, but we have not listened.

The Beast has risen because we opened up the Earth to him.

The Lord our God has not abandoned us; it is us who has abandoned Him.

We have spat on the Tablets Moses carried from the Mount, but God still loves us.

We have crucified His Son time and time again with our sins and He has forgiven us, though each time we know exactly what we have done.

The Lord our God showed us what would come to pass, and we stuck our heads in the sand.

There is no more Revelation; it has been Revealed.

The time has come.

The Lord our God has given us a new Commandment in this time of fire:

"Let Justice be served to those who have shunned the Lord."

The time to repent has gone. The Lord our God calls for action from those that wish to enter into the Kingdom of Heaven.

He that killeth with the sword must be killed with the sword.

We are the Angels of the Lord that slay the Beast.

"Let Justice be served to those who have shunned the Lord."

Noah closed the book and shut off his penlight. He was crammed in the trunk of an old Toyota Camry.

He was a fugitive. He had been sent on a mission and he hoped to die.

In the blackness, the pain returned. Noah turned on his light, aimed it at the book, and read the words out loud again.

Natalie ran back into the hotel and found Joseph's room. She pounded on the door, but there was no answer. She tried calling him, but he did not pick up. People were stepping out of their rooms, looking at each other, awakened by the blast. Natalie continued to pound on the door and call Joseph's name until the door opened. Joseph stood in the frame wearing his baby blue pajamas and rubbing his eyes. His hair was wild and ruffled. Before he said anything, Natalie grabbed his arm and started to pull him out of the room.

"Didn't you hear that?" she shouted at him.

Joseph tried to comb his hair down with his hands and stretched in the doorway.

"Jesus Christ, Natalie, what is it?" he asked, his voice scratching his throat.

"You didn't hear that?" Natalie asked again, incredulously.

"Hear *what*, Natalie?" Joseph saw the people in the hall for the first time. "What's going on? What time is it?"

"We need to get going." Natalie started pulling his arm again. "I was outside. There was an explosion. To the north, I think."

"Natalie," Joseph said, waking up and removing her grip from his arm, "I'm in my Goddamn pajamas."

"Well, change quick and then—"

"Natalie, we aren't going anywhere. You're interviewing the most important man on the planet today. You aren't going to go chase an explosion."

"If we go now, we can file a breaking story, capture some solid footage, and be back in time for Dubois. Just change real quick and we can get on the road."

"Have you slept at all?"

Natalie scoffed. "I'm fine, Joseph. We'll be back in plenty of time for the interview."

"No."

"For fuck's sake!" Natalie snapped. "I've been chasing these fucking attacks for months now and I finally have the opportunity to get on the scene within an hour of these cocksuckers blowing something up and you're saying we aren't going? To hell with that. There is no fucking way—"

"Natalie," Joseph yawned, "if you interviewed the Secretary-General in this state, he would think you're on melt. As your friend, I'm asking you to go back to your room and get some sleep. As your boss, I'm telling you that if you leave this hotel, you're fired."

Joseph shut the door in Natalie's face. She stood, fuming, staring at the cracked wood of the closed door as her rivals rushed around her.

As the Lt. Director walked up the highway, the lead Security Officer on the scene found him. Luna recognized the SO's face but couldn't place a name.

"Do we have any casualties?" Luna inquired.

"Negative. No GFN casualties. No civilian casualties."

"And in the vehicle?"

"At least one. He was the only one in the front of the van. We don't know if there were any combatants in the back."

"Tell me what happened."

"Perimeter security worked as designed. The van sped past the electronic checkpoint half a klick north of where it is now. Spike strips were deployed on the road and punctured the tires. The van came to a stop. An AR was deployed to check the van, but before it reached the vehicle, the driver exited the driver's side door with an automatic rifle. One of our snipers fired and hit him in the shoulder. As he was hit, the combatant squeezed the trigger of the rifle. He shot up the road in front of him, then fell backward, still shooting. The rounds hit the van and that's when the blast occurred. We are guessing the van was packed with explosives. We had a couple of bots out there earlier checking for signs of life. Unsurprisingly, they didn't find any. Now, we are waiting for the fire to calm down to make sure there are no remaining incendiary materials in the vehicle. We have the road blocked two kilometers north of the checkpoint and have rerouted incoming traffic to 591. That highway was previously closed, so we are performing manual sweeps. Luckily it's early so we haven't needed to divert too much manpower."

"When do you expect the road here to be clear?"

"Within an hour. Ninety minutes tops."

"Make it an hour."

"Yes, sir."

"Any idea who the combatant was?"

"Not right now, sir. Looks to be amateur hour."

Luna nodded in agreement.

"Good work," he told the SO, then started walking back to his sedan. He turned around and held up his index finger. "One hour."

From inside the car, Luna looked at the flaming van. *Idiots,* he thought. *These people are fucking idiots.*

Noah studied the manuscript. The text had been printed on stock paper. There was a hole on the top left corner and a piece of black ribbon tied the pages together. The ink on the top page was heavy and smudged. It read *For All Men of God.* Noah remembered the phrase from Harlan and Shelley. He was sure he must have "clearance" now. Noah bent the top page back and put the penlight in his mouth. He began to read from the beginning, whispering the words into the silence of the trunk.

> *This is the newest and last book of the Lord our God.*
>
> *Two millennia have passed since Jesus last walked the Earth.*
>
> *The Son's return is near.*
>
> *The message from the Lord our God remains the same. This book will not give the world new wisdom.*
>
> *This book is the final warning that the End of Days is here.*
>
> *The Earth is choking on human filth. The people are deaf, dumb, and blind.*
>
> *AWAKEN! OPEN YOUR EYES!*
>
> *There is no time.*
>
> *My name is Wade Barrineau. I am an American and I am a sinner and I am the vessel for the Lord's final message.*

Noah stopped reading and laughed, the penlight dropping from betwixt his teeth. He covered his mouth but could not stifle the laughter. He had read the lines two or three times before, but only now did he revel in the absurdity. Wade had always been a prideful, arrogant man, but this was a step too far. *To believe you were a prophet? Ridiculous. If Marie read this*—Noah stopped laughing at the thought of his wife. She would not read this. She was dead. The pain hit Noah with the force of an avalanche. He became embarrassed by his laughter. With the loss of his wife and kids, he had lost the ability to judge. Because he had been so wrong. He had been sure that he would grow old with Marie and watch their grandchildren start families of their own. That is what he had built his life around. And it was wrong.

Noah put the light back in his mouth and read, starting from the beginning.

> *This is the newest and last book of the Lord our God.*

The blast had awakened the hotel. Outside, people wore their robes and sleepwear and looked to the horizon, at the faint glow of fire in the predawn sky. Some recorded the far-off violence. Others were working to find transportation. Almost all were expecting to hear another blast or the rattle of gunfire. Natalie, furious with Joseph for denying her request to go to the scene, had marched to the lobby to look for a ride only to discover that the public transportation in Santa Fe was basically nonexistent and the GFN was not providing transportation to the blast scene. A pair of journalists had left the hotel and started down the road, their thumbs raised, hoping to hitch a ride.

Fuck Joseph, Natalie thought. *He won't fire me. He's been stuck behind a desk too long. And he wants me to join him.*

There was a hushed energy in the hotel lobby. Nearly all the tenants were on their APDs, searching for nuggets of information. The staff, reinforced with additional bodies after the explosion, was tense. There was talk of evacuating the hotel, but there was no action. They were frozen with uncertainty. Natalie approached a worried-looking employee with a tag that read "Assistant Manager."

"Do you have a car?" Natalie asked.

"What?" the assistant manager muttered. She stood by the reception desk watching the crowd while a voice on her walkie-talkie crackled near her hip.

Natalie spoke again. "Miss, I will pay you good money to use your car. Do you have one?"

The assistant manager looked at Natalie, her eyes narrowing and the creases on her temples deepening.

"What? No. No, I don't. Excuse me." She disappeared behind the desk and into an office.

Natalie slammed her hand against the desk and cursed.

Then, the lobby quieted, and the flow of people reversed. Guests started returning to their rooms. Natalie checked her APD and listened to the blinking report from the feed on her Reader.

"There was an explosion north of Santa Fe this morning. Federation officials are declaring that the source of the explosion was a foiled terrorist attack outside the perimeter of the city. There has only been one confirmed casualty. The casualty was an alleged combatant. There is no further threat of danger to the Santa Fe area."

Natalie retracted her APD and slid it into her back pocket. She felt like she had missed an opportunity. She had been in the wake of the devastation for months. Always following. Always behind. Now, she was here. She could add the first-hand experience her book so desperately needed. She needed to be in the action. To feel the heat rising from the concrete and breath in the smoke. But, there was no attack to witness.

There was no attack. Shame fell upon her as she realized that she, of all people, should feel gratitude for there being no tragic incident. There were families in Santa Fe this morning that wouldn't be weeping for the loss of a loved one. There were sons and daughters that would be sitting in their father's lap tonight instead of crying under the covers of their bed.

Natalie was disgusted by her selfishness. Her ambition and egotism had gotten the best of her; she feared it had become a pattern for her. The hotel's assistant manager tapped Natalie on the shoulder.

"Do you still need a car? I found one."

Natalie shook her head.

"No," she walked to the stairs, then stopped and reached into her pocket. She returned to the assistant manager and gave her a crumpled twenty-dollar bill.

"Thank you."

Natalie hurried away and started up the stairs. She still had an hour or two before she needed to get ready for the interview. She hoped she could get a little sleep but doubted she would. She hoped she could clear her guilty conscience but knew she wouldn't.

Lt. Director Luna rode from the blockade on Highway 285 to the Pueblo Bonito Bed and Breakfast where he had a smoke from his newly acquired replacement pipe and ate a Snack-Stat. He then walked to the Commission Building, wishing his morning run hadn't been interrupted. The night was turning to day and the thousands of people working and waiting around the capitol were waking up. The walk was calm, but Luna knew that the tranquil atmosphere would not last long. The journalists were drinking coffee and chatting idly; the protesters were emerging from their tents and preparing for a day of intense civil action—he expected the day to progress on edge. He needed his men and women to make sure the dormant emotion of the town did not erupt into violence.

Luna reached the HQ and walked to the top floor. The halls of the building gleamed with the efforts of the restoration team, but a fog of exhaustion had settled over the newly polished floors. The men and women roaming the halls smiled at the Lt. Director, but their eyes betrayed their fatigue. It had been a rough few days for NASO, but they would soon be home. Juan Carlos Luna would soon be home, this signing behind him. Luna found the room he was looking for and opened the door.

Inside the room, Deputy Amir Owens and a team of SOs stood over a large 3D topographic map. The map showed a landscape filled with foothills and creeks and swaths of trees. Owens moved his hands and the aerial view expanded its scope, showing two thousand square kilometers of land surrounding Santa Fe. The map was color coordinated. Gradients of red spread across the map; the dark pockets signified the areas under the heaviest surveillance and GFN presence. Shades of red rippled and streaked along the map as drones and units moved. A deep, dark maroon spot north of Santa Fe marked the location of the halted van. Luna looked at the clock at the corner of the holographic map.

"Is 285 opened yet?"

"Not yet, sir."

"Somebody tell those assholes to quit dicking around and get that road open, okay?"

Owens pointed at one of the SOs, then flicked his wrist to the door. The woman left the room to make the call. Luna looked over the map again. "Have we pinpointed the origin point of the van this morning?"

"Yes, sir. The vehicle had been spotted by surveillance outside Los Alamos earlier this week." The map zoomed in to the position described. "Today, a drone picked it up about six hundred meters from the compound and followed it." The drone footage appeared above the map. "The vehicle drove straight west. There were heat signatures in the back that were consistent with explosives. The drone team coordinated with the team on the perimeter and the call was made that the perimeter team would handle the situation."

"Good. Any other activity at Los Alamos?"

"Nothing unusual. It appears to be pretty sparsely populated."

"Petey's Ghost-town," Luna muttered to himself. He then took control of the map and studied Peter Whetstone's compound at Los Alamos. Three units marked by crimson blips staked out the compound. Luna played the situation out in his mind. *Whetstone had to know the driver would be followed and that the van had been ID'ed. Did the old man just not care? Was this all he had left? There wasn't even any solid evidence that man they called "the Atom Bomb" was still alive.*

"How many SOs do we have covering the compound?"

Owens looked at one of the other Federationists in the room, who found the number. "Thirty-five, sir."

Luna nodded and bit his lower lip.

"Okay. I want you to remove two of the units from the compound. Those pricks already blew their wad."

"Yes, sir. Would you like to bring the removed units in for the signing?"

Luna brought the view of the map back and again expanded the area shown. There were still huge gaps of white and muted red showing little GFN presence.

"No," Luna studied the map. He did not like what he saw. He leaned to Deputy Owens and whispered to him, "I fear this has all been rushed, Amir. I do not like being rushed."

We, as people from the loins of Adam, are killing the planet and the Lord our God has watched from above.

Because it is not the planet we need be concerned with saving. It is TRUTH. And we began killing TRUTH long ago.

TRUTH is pure. LOVE is pure. Neither can exist in a world with sin; they will each be corrupted over time. Both TRUTH and LOVE have each decayed so greatly that one day they will no longer exist. That day is nigh.

Let none of the Priests, or Rabbis, or Imams, or Reverends, or Apostles, or Sheiks, or Bishops, or Hakhams continue to spread one big lie. They tell us that the Lord our God is infallible. This is not true.

The Lord our God has made one mistake in all Creation.

He made man with free-will.

Since that point, man has corrupted God. And there has been no going back.

We, those who recognize God's fault, are given one job. Root out the corruption of the Original Sin that begot all darkness. The Human Race will never be good. The Human Race will never be pure. But, the Lord our God can be good and pure again.

Purity is the only state in which existence can be. Anything else rots all goodness until life is dark and mush and rank. Only when there is no more mankind can the Lord our God be pure. Only

*when the Lord our God is pure again can we hope
to bask in His ever-loving glow. The universal
mistake must be corrected. The purge must begin
with us.*

Natalie Kelley, the thirty-two-year-old senior correspondent for the *Chicago Tribune*, was showered and dressed when her editor, Joseph Kalani knocked on the hotel door. She wore a bice-green blouse under a tight, slim-fit grey vest. A single column of pearl-colored buttons lined the vest from the slip of the waistcoat to the throat. She wore the blouse and the vest with the top buttons unfastened, breaking with the fashion norm. Her slacks were a darker-grey color, tight around the waist, loose under the knee until they flared out below the shin. Her calf-high white shoes had two stilettos on each heel and tucked in nicely underneath the flare of the slack.

After the explosion this morning, Natalie had tried sleeping when she realized she hadn't packed anything for the interview. When she left Chicago, she hadn't known she would be sitting down with Antoine Dubois for an interview. While she had been preparing the substance for the interview, she hadn't thought about the aesthetics until she was teetering on the verge of sleep. There was no 3D printer in the hotel. It took Natalie half an hour to find an additive-manufacturing clothing machine in Santa Fe and another thirty minutes—as well as a $150 transfer for the owner to open early—for Natalie to use the printer.

Her hair was pulled back and she was applying some light foundation to her forehead when Joseph knocked on the door. She opened the door and went back to the bathroom mirror. Joseph sat on the bed.

"You know they'll have someone do that for you there, right?" he said with a smirk on his face.

Natalie hated sitting in the makeup chair. She made a guttural noise, put the pad back in the compact, and closed the lid. The bathroom light turned out behind her and Joseph opened the door, motioning for Natalie to pass through first.

"I like that outfit. I don't think I've seen it before. Is it new?"

Natalie laughed.

"Yeah, it's new," she said. She grabbed her editor's hand, stopping him before they moved into the hallway. "Joseph, before we go, I just want to apologize to you for last night. Er, this morning. I know—"

Joseph interrupted her, "Natalie, it's fine."

"No. I want you to know that you were completely in the right and I never should have pushed you like I did."

Natalie felt Joseph place his other hand over her own. It was warm except for the cool metal of his wedding band.

"Natalie, I know. It's okay. Really. Your passion makes you the person I admire. Now, dear," he opened the door, "let's go and interview the Secretary-General. Are you ready for the biggest story of your career?"

Natalie smiled and, as they walked down the hotel hallway, she placed her hand in the crook of Joseph's arm.

"What happened here?" Lt. Director Juan Carlos Luna pointed to the top of the map. Deputy Amir Owens zoomed in on the location. The map showed a red line shooting north, outside of the one-thousand-six-hundred-kilometer focus. The line stopped abruptly over Carson National Forest.

"Specialist Rivera?" Owens looked at a woman in the room who was scrolling through her APD.

"Just a second," the Security Office Specialist answered quickly. Her eyes narrowed, and her cheeks flushed as she looked for the information. "Here it is. Two days ago, we picked up some radio activity from the forest. We sent a drone to find the origin of the signal. It—" Rivera looked at the map, then back at her APD, "looks like the drone suffered an electrical failure and crashed. There." Rivera pointed to the spot on the map where the red line halted.

"Electrical failure? Have you reviewed the video stream from the drone before it went down?"

"I haven't personally," the SO replied. "But one of our analysts did. It appears the electrical failure cut out the footage and then crippled the navigation. So, the drone actually crashed a kilometer or so away from where the stream ended."

"Hm," Luna said, placing his index finger along his nose and covering his mouth with the three lower digits. "What did diagnostics conclude was the source of the electrical failure when we picked up the drone?"

"We—" Rivera fumbled her words, "we didn't pick up the drone, sir. There was the attack, then… our focus shifted."

Luna dropped his hand behind his back and frowned.

"Okay," he looked at Rivera and smiled. "Okay. Thank you, Specialist."

Luna turned to Deputy Owens.

"Amir, who is on point at the Los Alamos compound? McGregor?"

"Yes, sir."

"Okay. I want you to send Specialist McGregor and two others to Carson to retrieve that drone. I want to know what the hell downed that thing. That's the second one this month, that I'm aware of. Like I said earlier, leave one unit at the compound, but bring the rest back to Santa Fe. I want them working on geo-imaging."

"Roger, sir." Owens straightened his posture as the Lt. Director walked toward the door.

Luna turned around. "And Owens," he looked at Rivera, then back at his Deputy.

"Let me know if that drone came off the DefCorp line, okay? Better yet, let Arnie's assistant—" he frowned, remembering his friend was gone, "let Odyssey Thacker know."

Owens paused. He had never been asked to identify a manufacturer before. It was an odd request, but the Lt. Director was sure to have his reasons. "Yes, sir. We'll let her know."

Luna lowered his head and nodded. "Good. Okay. Keep up the good work, now."

Luna left the room. Rivera turned to Deputy Owens.

"Let him know if it's from DefCorp?" she asked, incredulous. "What does that have—"

Owens stopped SO Rivera before she could finish. "Just do as the Lt. Director asks, okay, Specialist?"

When man was created on the sixth day, each of us was to be divine, for God said, "Let us make man in Our image, according to Our likeness; and let them rule over the fish of the sea and birds of the sky and over the cattle and over all the earth, and over every creeping thing that creeps on the earth."

We were to be gods. And it was to be good.

The Lord our God told man: "You may surely eat of every tree of the garden, but of the tree of the knowledge of good and evil you shall not eat, for in the day that you eat of it you shall surely die."

Man ate from the tree of the knowledge of good and evil and man began to die.

When the Lord our God sent His only Son to be killed by the hand of man, He could still not stop the cancer of sin from growing within our polluted souls.

*The book we call the Bible is not the complete
Word of God; it has been tainted by man's will to
give optimism to the sinners.*

*The truth is that man is evil. And the only way to
fall back into the grace of the Lord our God and
enter the Kingdom of Heaven is to destroy that
evil.*

*Man must eliminate man. And we, who know this
to be the truth, must destroy ourselves.*

The car hit a pothole and Noah bounced in the trunk. He
hit his head on the metal roof and dropped the penlight. As
the car continued to drive over dips, the light spun and rolled
to Noah's feet. It illuminated a corner of the trunk, leaving the
rest in darkness.

Noah contorted his body and edged his fingers toward the
light. As the car swerved, the light slid and found Noah's hand.
Noah began to find solace in Wade's words. "The truth is that
man is evil." Everything Noah had loved had been ripped away.
By man. If that wasn't evil, Noah did not know what was. He
wanted to read more. To learn more. He placed the penlight back
between his teeth and the page glowed. On the page, the light
was interrupted by a slight, meandering break. Noah placed his
finger on the edge of the light and felt a small crack across the
lens. He dropped his finger and kept reading.

A white stretch SUV was waiting for Natalie and Joseph
on the curb in front of the Morning Cactus Hotel. A man
dressed in a black suit with a GFN Field Patch on the breast
pocket opened the rear door as soon as he saw the journalist
and her editor exit the hotel. The chauffeur said "hello" and
helped the pair inside. There were no captain seats. Backing

up to a mirrored partition was a bench of leather seats facing the rear, a mahogany table, and a second bench facing front. A portly woman in an amber pantsuit sat on the back bench, an iced drink cupped in one hand. She put the drink on the table as Natalie and Joseph sat on the rear-facing bench. As Natalie wiggled into her seat, the door closed and, for a split-second, the interior was pitch black. Then, lights on the roof and under the seats and table sparked on. No light came through the windows—they only reflected Natalie's face and the vehicle's interior back to her. Natalie thought she felt the car lurch forward. She did not feel like she was in an automobile. The atmosphere was closer to the small waiting room of a therapist's office.

The portly woman extended a welcoming hand to Joseph, then Natalie. Natalie needed to lift herself from her seat to meet the woman's hand. She was in her 60s, her jet-black hair was cut short, and she wore a mask of bold makeup.

"Mr. Kalani, it's a pleasure to see you again," she said. "How is your wife?"

"She's terrific, Miss Hernandez."

"Good, good," Miss Hernandez replied, then turned her attention to Natalie. "Ms. Kelley. It's a pleasure to meet you. My name is Isabela Hernandez, Director for The Federation's North American Communications Office."

Natalie smiled at Hernandez. She had met her a few years back when she attended a press briefing on Roosevelt Island, but she didn't correct the Communications Director. Natalie thought the woman looked much older now than she had in New York. Hernandez continued. "The press directive has been uploaded to your APDs. We require strict adherence to the directive. You will only be able to access the file in this vehicle, so I suggest you begin reading now. It should take you approximately eleven minutes to read the directive. Once complete, please submit your biosignature."

Natalie and Joseph each looked at their APDs. The file was already opened on their screens. It was a straightforward set of instructions regarding the process of meeting and interviewing Secretary-General Dubois. She would have exactly thirty minutes with the Secretary-General. The GFN would record the interview and give a copy of the recording to the *Tribune*. There was a long outline of topics that the Secretary-General would not discuss. The directive then stated that, due to security protocols, the journalists would not know where they had conducted the interview until the Secretary-General and his detail had departed. Natalie had heard that this was the case for Dubois's few previous interviews, but she found it unsettling as she sat in the car. She tried to look out the window, but again was only met by her reflection.

She didn't know how long she would be in this vehicle or where she would be when it stopped, but she did know that the reflection staring back at her would be a changed woman before the day was out.

Deborah Johnson found her boss on the roof of the New Mexico Commission Building. The Lt. Director was at the edge of the roof. He was talking with a group of snipers and pointing at the horizon.

"Sir," Deborah called, safely away from the edge. The wind blew hard three stories up and Deborah's words didn't reach Luna. She inched forward and called again, screaming. "Sir!"

Luna turned and looked at his assistant. She held up her index finger and Luna nodded in comprehension. He left the snipers and walked with Johnson to the exit.

"Only an hour 'til he lands, huh?" he asked.

"Yes, sir."

"Jesus," Luna stopped. "Debbie, you ever wish time would freeze and let you get things done right?"

"Every day, sir," she answered, dryly.

Luna chuckled and started walking again. They reached the exit and Luna opened the door for his assistant. "Or, have time speed up, just so you could be done with shit?"

Johnson was on the ladder descending from the roof to the top floor. "Also, every day, sir."

Luna laughed hard as he followed her on the ladder. When he reached the bottom, he wrapped his arm around his assistant.

"It's just a treasure to listen to an old man bitch, isn't it, Debbie?"

"Gold and jewels," Deborah replied. The pair walked down the packed hallway. Before reaching the stairwell, Luna recognized a young woman from the initial security detail, but he did not recall her name. She was in a wheelchair. The chair was currently vertical as she maneuvered the hallways. The woman had cuts carved across her face. Her neck was held immobile in a brace. Despite her physical state, the woman remained attractive and radiated a positivity that caught Luna's attention.

As Luna passed her, he held out the palm of his hand and the woman stopped the chair. She flicked a toggle with her finger and the chair backed up against the wall.

"Were you injured in the attack?" Luna asked, knowing the answer.

"Yes, sir," she answered sheepishly.

"What happened?" Luna asked.

The woman's gaze remained straight ahead. "A piece of concrete hit me in the back. It broke a few vertebrae."

Luna shook his head.

"That's terrible. I'm so sorry," then, "what are you doing here?"

Her face looked uncomfortable and the woman stammered her answer. "Sir, I'm a Junior Analyst—"

"No," Luna interrupted. "No, I mean why are you not at the medical center?"

"Oh," she said, relieved, "there were a few things I wanted to make sure were followed up on. I talked them into letting me out for a little bit."

Luna nodded his head, impressed. "You need to get back to the medical center and rest. We have everything covered here."

The Junior Analyst looked embarrassed. "Yes, sir."

Before Luna moved forward, he looked her squarely in the eye. "Thank you. For your service and effort. You really are an inspiration."

Luna leaned in and kissed the woman on the cheek. He tasted the salty tears rolling down her face.

Juan Carlos Luna and Deborah Johnson left the young woman and started down the stairs. Luna turned to his assistant. "Do you know that girl's name?"

"No, sir." Johnson replied. She had never seen the analyst before.

"Well, find out what it is, then get a hold of Hernandez. That's a face that needs to be seen. Have the world learn what those motherfuckers did."

Noah Bridger closed the book and clicked off his light. He was alone in the darkness, rocking in the trunk of a car while his fingers played with the ribbon which kept the pages together. Noah thought about the words on the pages he held. He wanted to dismiss them as pure rubbish, but, after reading them a few times, truth had seeped through the rubbish.

Noah felt the bleakness Wade detailed. He was a man who had lost everything.

My God, my family. I left my family. And now they are gone.

He wished he could see them again. One last time. He closed his eyes and summoned memories of his family—happy memories. He saw his wife. She was young, radiant, and smiling on their wedding day. They hadn't even known each other a year, but they both knew they would grow old together. After a month of dating, Marie had informally proposed to Noah. A week later, he had a ring and was down on one knee.

He saw his son, Samson, running onto a baseball field for his first game, his hat a size too big and falling down over his eyes. He waved to his parents in the stands as he stood at third base.

He saw his daughter, Priscilla, hiding under the front porch. When they were able to coax her out, she was holding two rabbit kittens, their eyes closed and their tiny bodies shivering in her arms. She said she found their dead mama a few feet away from the nest but didn't know what to do with the babies. Noah took them inside and showed her how to make a formula to feed them with an eye dropper. Priscilla raised the rabbits herself for weeks and she was devastated when the first kitten died. When the second was old enough, they let it run free on the ranch.

He saw all his children standing around his bed, singing to him to wake him up on his most recent birthday. They had made him breakfast in bed. Tabi, their youngest, was covered in cake batter. The kids were so proud that they had made the meal from scratch and Noah told them he could taste their love in the food, making it better than any automated meal. He said it was the best breakfast he ever had. And it was.

He saw them on the living room floor. All lying in a row, their faces pushed into the carpet, covered by hair and blood and God knows what else. He wanted to scream. He hadn't been there to protect them. Wade had given him a chance to deliver justice. Noah had never been a man of swift retribution, but he needed to be now—for his family. He clicked the penlight back on and read the first page, again. The words might have been rubbish, but they were giving Noah the strength to be a man of action.

The media directive was filled with minutiae and Natalie found it difficult to concentrate on the text. The second half of the directive was dense with legalese. Without finishing the document, Natalie scrolled to the bottom of the document and placed her thumb on the screen, submitting her biosignature. With her approval to the details of the directive, the document disappeared.

Natalie looked around the warmly-lit cabin. Joseph was reading the directive intently, his chin resting on his fist and his APD balancing on his thigh. Hernandez sat with perfect posture, her hands folded gently in her lap, and her left ankle crossed behind her right. When she saw that Natalie was done, she touched her Reader and turned off the news stream.

"Done already?"

Natalie nodded and fidgeted in her seat. The Communications Director stared at her, then leaned forward and spoke softly.

"I understand that it can be unsettling not knowing where this interview is taking place. No one likes to be taken so far out of control. I would just like to assure you that it is not a personal decision based on either you or Mr. Kalani. It is the standard operating procedure for all of these meetings. Ms. Farrelly is," she hesitated for the first time, "extremely concerned with these matters."

Joseph looked up from his APD at the two women, then continued to read.

"Yeah, it's fine," Natalie responded.

"I would just like to assure you that your safety, as well as the safety of the Secretary-General, is of our utmost concern. There are people—not many—but there are people that would do anything to get to Monsieur Dubois. As you surely understand, being one of the small number of individuals that meet with him at a one-on-one level, those that wish him harm may believe you have access about how to reach him. We make sure you don't have that sort of information and won't be able to answer any questions some of these people may have."

Natalie nodded her head. The Communications Director's explanation was designed to squash any doubts that she may have, but Natalie detected the underlying kernel of a threat in the words: *If you try to figure out any more than we want you to about the logistics of the meeting, you're going to be on your own.*

Hernandez placed her back against the leather and resumed listening to the media stream on her earpiece until Joseph finished and put his APD in the front pocket of his Windowpane jacket.

"Isabella, were you saying something about our safety? Sorry, I was busy reading the American Copyright Act of 1976."

Hernandez grinned. "Do you have any questions, Mr. Kalani?"

Joseph looked at Natalie. Her fingers drummed the leather of the bench and her eyes were zeroed in on the floor.

"Yeah, just one," Joseph looked around the cabin. "Where, exactly, are we going again?"

Natalie glared at her editor. He was smiling, and his eyes were wide with pleasure. A chuckle came from the opposite bench. Joseph nudged Natalie and put his arm around her shoulder.

"Hey, c'mon, kid. Loosen up a bit. I can hear your heart thumping from here. This is fun, right?"

Lt. Director Juan Carlos Luna was in the shower when a message came through on his APD. It was from Director Farrelly. Luna parted the shower curtain and looked at the message: the flight carrying the Secretary-General was early. It was landing in fifteen minutes. Luna washed the shampoo out of his hair, dried off, threw on his new Dante Wong three-piece, and ran to his sedan. He plugged the coordinates for the landing spot into the navigator and, as the car merged into traffic, he ran an electric razor over his face.

The sedan crawled through the Santa Fe traffic. Luna could hear the protestors yelling outside. He hit the steering wheel in frustration.

"Damnit!" he yelled into the empty car. Luna looked at the clock on the dash. He was going to be late. He hated being late. He tried to will the sedan forward, but it remained gridlocked.

"Call Jay," he told the car's computer system.

Luna's husband answered after one ring.

"Is everything okay?" he asked, his voice full of concern.

"Jay?" Luna responded. He hadn't expected the sudden tension.

"Yes, of course. *You* called *me*, Moon. Is everything okay?" Jay asked again.

"Yeah. Everything's okay. Why?"

Jay laughed. "Well, the most important man on the planet is landing in an hour and you are charged with protecting him. And you're calling me. And, honey, you never call when you're working."

"Yeah." Luna was despondent. "Yeah, I'm just stuck in traffic."

"You're stuck in traffic? In Santa Fe?"

"Yeah, it's crazy here. I'm running late to meet Dubois. Fucking traffic. Can't believe these Neanderthals don't have ERROW."

Jay was quiet for a second. "Are you nervous to meet him?"

Luna looked out at the traffic. He could see his turn ahead. "I've already met him."

"You have?"

"Yeah, I couldn't tell you. But I met him in New York."

"What's he like?"

"He's everything you would expect." The car moved forward. "I can't let him down, Jay."

"Baby, don't worry about letting him down. You're a man who does his job. Do your job and everything'll be fine."

The car found the turning lane and sped up.

"I wish you were here."

Jay laughed at this. "Bullshit, Moon. You wish Arnie was there."

Luna looked at the empty seat next to him. The car sped down the road.

"Yeah. I got to go. I'll see you tomorrow. I love you."

"Love you, too."

Luna was alone in the car. The road was empty, and the sedan flew. Jay had been a comfort, but the fact was that the call had been a momentary distraction; Luna's attempt to dam the sands of time. The sedan's speakers relayed an incoming message. It was from NASO Director Dierdre Farrelly. Their flight was landing.

Noah Bridger had never sought vengeance before. He thought back to when Wade had shown him the picture of his murdered family. After he wept, his brother-in-law had asked him a simple question.

"Do you want to bring justice to those that did this?"

"Of course," Noah responded. Rage buried his sorrow, but the pain was constant. "Where are they?" He looked back at the camp.

"Who?"

"The bastards that killed my fucking family, Wade! Where are they?"

Wade grabbed Noah. "They aren't here. But, I can bring you justice if that is what you want. Is that what you want?"

"Yes. More than anything."

"Good." Wade led Noah down the hill and to a shack filled with paper maps. A man Noah had never seen sat in the shack. Once the door was shut, Wade told Noah how he could capture his vengeance.

The plan was ludicrous, but Noah didn't care. It offered justice and that was all he wanted. It didn't matter if he lived or died. He told himself that all he wanted was retribution, but deep down he knew that wasn't true. He just wanted to be with his family. He wanted the pain to go away.

Crammed in the trunk of a jalopy, Noah recalled the last words Wade spoke to him before he left on his suicide mission.

"You are a lump of clay. You are soft. You have been beaten your whole life, but now, I am your sculptor. And God is the kiln. And, Noah, through the fire of Christ, you will emerge a work of art." Wade then gave Noah the Book and pushed him through the door.

Noah couldn't care less about becoming a work of art. His family was dead. And, before he went, he wanted others dead, too.

The car came to a stop and Natalie Kelley could feel her heart trying to break through her chest.

Joseph looked at his protégé. Her face was pale. "This is fun, right?" Natalie could hardly hear him over the sound of her pounding pulse in her ears.

"Any final questions?" Hernandez asked.

Natalie shook her head. Communications Director Hernandez then reached under the seat and removed two objects.

"Okay, then. Put these on," she said and gave one object to Natalie and the other to Joseph. Natalie looked at the black glasses in her hand, then put them on her face, per the instructions in the media directive. The lenses were dark, thick, and pixelated. Once sitting on her nose, the frames created an air-tight seal against her face, blocking all light. Natalie was blind. She heard the car door open and felt the breeze tickle her skin. Goose pimples sprouted across her arms. Natalie felt a hand grab her wrist and jumped back, startled. She heard a woman's voice close to her ear.

"Ms. Kelley, I'll be guiding you to the space where the interview will be conducted. Please follow me."

As she exited the car, she heard a different voice deliver the same instructions to Joseph.

With the woman's guidance, Natalie moved forward. Behind her, Joseph called out, "How you doing up there, kiddo?" Natalie held up her thumb, but then remembered that her editor could not see the signal.

 She called back, "Doing okay, Joe, but when we get back, I think I'll need to go to the eye doctor." Joseph's familiar laugh calmed her. Beyond the cackle, Natalie could hear activity all around her, but she found it difficult to pinpoint any specific sound. Her guide said something that Natalie didn't catch, then she felt her foot slam into something solid.

"We have just a few stairs now, Ms. Kelley."

Natalie lifted her right foot high in the air, then lowered it slowly onto the flat surface. She dragged her left foot up to meet its match on higher ground. Like a steady coxswain, the woman continued to guide Natalie, calling "Step! Step!" After six or seven steps, the woman announced, "Last one, Ms. Kelley. We're almost there."

The sun's warmth disappeared from Natalie's arms and she was ushered through a door. The air inside was still and the voices echoed. After a few meters, she felt fingers graze her cheekbones and the glasses were removed. She blinked her eyes to acclimate to the bright lights. She looked around the cramped room. The walls were made of long cedar logs stained dark brown. The floor was wood and scuffed and swept clean; the ceiling high and vaulted. Hanging from the ceiling ridge, a fan turned slowly. The room was wide, but a partition ran across the back of the room, cutting the length short. The windows were blacked out with a plastic glaze. The room was lighted by two hovering drone lights, which orbited the fan. In the center of the room, two women set up recording equipment. A bottle-cap-sized drone hovered five meters above the ground and projected a laser onto the floor, showing the women where exactly to place each piece of equipment.

Natalie heard a voice next to her. It belonged to Isabella Hernandez. "The Secretary-General is running a little early. We'll begin in about ten minutes or so. I suggest you find a seat over there to get a quick touch-up on your makeup."

Natalie sat in the makeup chair and looked in the mirror. Sweat and smeared foundation stared back at her. The makeup woman pursed her lips and began to wipe away the moisture.

She looked at Natalie's face in the mirror and said, "Don't worry, honey. In five minutes, you'll be drier than a Nashville Temperance Jam."

Lt. Director Luna's auto sped down the deserted highway. To the east, a small herd of pronghorn ran over the dry soil that was once Cochiti Lake. The Secretary-General's Landing Zone lay a few miles to the north and thanks to the traffic, Luna had not yet had time to inspect the finished LZ. To avoid tipping off the location, the preassembled construction materials weren't brought to the site until early this morning. With a fleet of ARs, the Landing Zone was constructed in just a few hours.

The sedan began to decelerate and pulled off into a parking lot that previously served as a boat ramp before overuse and drought dried the Rio Grande. The car's engine cut, and Luna sat patiently in the driver's seat. A few seconds later, a two-seat black-and-green Diamond ATV emerged from behind a cluster of Pinyon Pines. The vehicle's four wheels formed a diamond, which gave the vehicle its name. The car's double-wishbone suspension was flexible and extended forty-five centimeters away from the chassis. The wishbones met the chassis on a track, which gave them the ability to move to accommodate any terrain. A young man wearing green-and-brown fatigues and sitting under a fungi-molded cage scanned the parked car's registration. Luna noticed him sputter when he read the vehicle's security credentials. The Diamond pulled up next to the driver's side of the parked sedan. As Luna exited the auto, the driver lifted the cage and the Lt. Director sat next to him.

"I need to get to the LZ quickly, okay?" Luna said, but the guard didn't start moving forward.

"Before we go, sir, I need to scan your ID."

Luna, in his haste, had forgotten this portion of protocol. He rolled up his sleeve and the driver completed the IWC scan. The tardy Lt. Director heard the seconds ticking away in his head. Dubois and Farrelly would be deplaning any minute. After what seemed like an eternity, the Security Officer placed his APD in his combat vest. He pressed the big, black button on the center console between the seats of the ATV. He let his thumbprint linger on the button. Luna heard the bubbling of the water-based engine and the car hummed forward. Luna looked around and, perched in the evergreen trees, he saw silent snipers flanking the road. Overhead a drone followed the Diamond.

Luna looked at the driver and put his hand on the young man's shoulder.

"Can this thing go any faster?"

The young guard laughed, then placed his thumb back on the black button. On the dash a small, neon-green light flickered on, and the driver grabbed the gear shift. The Diamond's turbo-charged engine rumbled and the ATV sped up the hill. The rushing wind smacked Luna's face through the fungi-molded cage and whipped his Foulard tie into the air. The ATV passed through the ghost town of Cochiti Lake and, after a few minutes, Luna spotted the Cochiti Golf Course. The golf course served as the Landing Zone. On the eighteenth fairway sat a large aircraft, the tilt-rotors still spinning. Luna turned to the driver again, this time needing to yell to be heard over the gasoline engine.

"Right up to the bird, son!"

The driver nodded, jumped the curb, drove around a sand trap, and headed straight for the sky ferry.

The car stopped. Noah heard a rusted car door squeak open, then shut. Footsteps. The trunk flew open and there was a burst of sunlight. A silhouette stood above Noah.

"How was the ride?" the silhouette asked, extending a hand.

Noah grabbed the silhouette's hand and heaved himself up and out of the trunk. Noah exploded out of the cramped space. His body was stiff, but he managed to run across the road to a tall bush and relieve himself.

"Oh shit," the silhouette muttered and shut the trunk. He was a young man, no more than sixteen or seventeen years old. Noah had met him before being folded into the back of the Camry. He was told that the teen had a "clean" record and Federation credentials. The boy laughed to himself as Noah's stream trickled down. "I didn't even think of that, man. You must have really needed to go, huh?"

Noah zipped up and looked around. The car was parked on the shoulder of a mountain slope. There were no other cars in sight and no time to waste. With his back to his chauffeur, Noah waved and yelled, "Thanks for the ride."

After a few seconds of looking, Noah found the small wooden sign marking the trail and started into the brush. He walked for twenty minutes before he reached a steep slab of tan rock rising fifteen meters high. Noah stopped. There was no one around.

Tentatively, he called out, "Mardi Gras?"

There was a rustling from above, then a voice returned: "New Orleans!"

At the top of the slab, three men emerged dressed in camouflage. These were his contacts. He did not recognize them, but they responded to the code words he was given by Wade. One of the men threw down a kernmantle rope. Noah wrapped the rope around his waist and started up the slab, his leg aching. The slope was sharp, and the climb was slick. The men at the top helped pull Noah up, but when he reached the zenith his arms burned, and he was out of breath. Once he hoisted his body over the granite lip, he lay on the ground, panting.

After only a moment of recovery time, one of the men yanked Noah to his feet. Each man sported a sling which cradled a pristine assault weapon. Two of the men had sidearms holstered to their thighs. The third man had his sidearm removed. It was pointed toward the tree line. Noah followed the line of the muzzle with his eyes. There, tied to the trunk of a Douglas Fir with a gag in his mouth, was a middle-aged man. His face was beaten, and he wore the uniform of a Federation Security Officer.

The man who had jerked Noah to his feet smirked and said, "Santa's sleigh crashed right into the mountain and gave us an early Christmas present."

Natalie tried to sit still as Audrey, the makeup artist, readied her for the interview. She kept her eyes closed tight as the woman painted her face. Joseph crouched next to her and looked at the reflection in the mirror. He beamed as the artist swept the brush across her brow.

"You look beautiful, Nat."

Natalie opened her left eye, aimed it at Joseph, and responded with a huff. "I'm sweating like my great-uncle taking a *schvitz*." She closed the eye as the brush tickled the bridge of her nose.

The makeup artist broke in. "Don't worry, honey. This foundation I'm applying will divert any sweat on your face, so the camera doesn't pick it up."

"Can you divert the sweat that's cascading down my ass crack?"

Audrey stopped. "I don't think we—"

"I'm only kidding." Natalie interrupted.

"Save some of those jokes for Dubois," Joseph said.

"Great advice, boss."

The chairs and cameras were arranged in the center of the room. The lasered outline was gone. There were a few new workers in the room that hurriedly erected track lighting around the interview spot. Natalie, eyes still closed, spoke to Joseph. "Gonna give me a little pep talk before show time?"

He smiled and stood up, using her shoulder as leverage. He let his hand linger there, then gave her trapezius a firm squeeze.

"Nope. You don't need one. You were born for this, Natalie. You are going to be great."

Natalie looked in the mirror. The makeup artist was right—she could no longer see the sweat on her face. There was an announcement from the door: "Two minutes!"

A sense of calm washed over Natalie. She thanked Audrey and walked to the center of the room. The old wooden floor creaked under her feet. The track lights switched on, hot and bright. Natalie circled the space to get a sense of the domain. On the back of the far chair, there were white letters stenciled on that read "N. Kelley."

Secretary-General Antoine Dubois waved at the gathered crowd on the dusty fairway as he exited the sky ferry. He wore a navy-blue Nehru suit embroidered with the Ring of Light and white pants. He was flanked by two members of his security detail. A half dozen SOs had exited the massive aircraft first, teasing the group of nearly two hundred Federationists gathered for the arrival. When the icon emerged from the belly of the aircraft, the crowd erupted in applause: most had never seen Antoine Dubois in person before. This was a moment that many spent careers working towards.

Lt. Director Luna saw the still rotors of the Pelican P-190 looming over the crowd. He knew that, per security procedures, at this very moment five other Pelican P-190s were landing at faux LZs around Santa Fe. The luxury sky ferries sat 40 passengers and were popular among travelers who valued comfort above speed. The P-190 was a hybrid aircraft: it took off and landed vertically, like a helicopter, but once it reached a certain height, the blades retracted into the rotor and two turbo-shaft engines powered the craft. All six P-190s took off from Roosevelt Island this morning at 10:00 and were in the air for four hours before reaching Santa Fe. Although the sky ferry's journey was tedious compared to supersonic jet travel, it gave the Security team flexibility to choose Landing Zones in towns without functioning airstrips.

The Diamond ATV carrying Luna stopped at the edge of the crowd and the Lt. Director nudged through the clapping admirers. Dubois was standing at the bottom of the staircase helping Director Farrelly onto the freshly mowed dirt and weeds when Luna arrived at the front of the audience. As Luna met the idling Pelican, Dubois saw him and smiled.

"Lt. Director! Great to see you again!" he bellowed and thrust out his paw.

Luna wiped his clammy hands on his pants, then shook the extended hand.

"Secretary-General. An honor to meet you again, sir."

Dubois, with his hand on Luna's back, guided the Lt. Director toward the clubhouse. The crowd parted, clearing a path for the dignitary. Dubois's face turned grim.

"I would like to convey to you my deepest sadness and sympathy for the lost lives you endured the other night. I guarantee you that we will bring those who were responsible to justice and working with the AFG will be a great way for us to accomplish that." Dubois hung his head, then continued. His voice was coated with emotion and his French accent was more pronounced than it had been during their previous meeting. "I would also like you to know that, after reviewing the career of Chief Deputy Arnie Jones, The Federation will be posthumously honoring him with the Humanitarian Commendation Medal for his years of service to the BHS. I also spoke with President Wilson and he will be giving Chief Deputy Jones the Medal of Honor. We all owe him a debt of gratitude."

Dubois stopped and turned Luna, so he was looking the man in the eye.

"I also want you to know, Juan Carlos, that I, and the entire Federation, still carry the utmost confidence in your ability to do your job."

"Thank you, sir. That means a great deal coming from you. And I applaud the honor bestowed upon Arnie. He was a great man."

Dubois looked at Luna for a second more, then turned toward the clubhouse.

"Good," he said and walked away.

The Lt. Director stood still as Dubois entered the clubhouse and the crowd dispersed. Luna was relieved to hear the Secretary-General vocalize his confidence in him, but his uneasiness remained. He realized that, even after the treaty signing was over, the anxiety would persist. Antoine Dubois was a living legend and his assurance regarding Luna's job security and his proposed acclamation for Arnie Jones were welcome words, but Luna focused on something else the Secretary-General said. Luna replayed the statement in his mind, "Working with the AFG will help us accomplish that." On this point, Juan Carlos Luna was afraid that the most revered man in the world was wrong.

"This isn't what Wade and I discussed," Noah told the man, uneasily. The man had identified himself as Murphy and had spent the last fifteen minutes going over the details of a new plan with Noah. The second soldier, Temple, had his weapon trained on the beaten and restrained man while the third soldier, Gerhardt, had disappeared into the trees.

"Fuck Wade," Murphy said. "Let him stick to the scripture. We'll handle the military aspects of this operation."

"Fuck Wade?" Noah asked. He was taken aback. "You aren't—" he stammered, looking for the right words, "his followers?"

Murphy laughed. "Hell, no. We don't take orders from that delusional prophet. But his followers will do anything, and they're flush with cash, so Colonel Zobnin partnered with him after fucking Hill abandoned us."

"Colonel Zobnin?"

"Yeah, Colonel Zobnin. She was there to break you out, wasn't she?"

"You mean Sonya?"

"Yes, Colonel Sonya Zobnin," the man looked concerned. "Was she not with you?"

"Yes. She was. I—" Noah paused, "I didn't know she was a Colonel. She didn't mention it. I didn't even know she was a soldier."

Murphy laughed again. "She's a soldier, alright."

Noah thought hard. "And she would approve of this new plan?"

Murphy was confident. "Oh, yes. Absolutely."

Noah looked at the Gendarme secured to the Douglas Fir. His face was purple, and his eyes were swollen, but Noah could feel the hatred come through his shuttered gaze.

"And I would be him?"

"Yes."

"Okay. I'll do it. Let's do it."

"Good." Murphy clapped and walked into the trees. Noah followed him. A few meters into the wood, there was a large black plastic box sitting on a bed of dried brown pine needles. To the left was the dead body of a Fed. Noah stared at the corpse: there was a single bullet hole in her head. Next to the body, there was a path of bent grass and cleared floral debris. Murphy saw Noah taking in the scene.

"Gerhardt's lugging the other one deeper into the forest." Murphy held the black box with two hands. "You ready?"

Noah nodded, and they returned to the clearing. They sat on the grass in the shade of the firs.

"Have you ever undergone a cosmetic transformation before?" Murphy asked.

Noah swallowed hard, then spoke. "Just for costumes. For Halloween."

Murphy laughed. "This shit ain't for Halloween, brother. It's the real deal. This costs more than your house. And it's gonna burn like hell." Then, Murphy started the transformation.

The transformation procedure took twenty minutes. And it did burn; Noah struggled to keep still as the heat and pain spread across his face. The cooling process took another ten minutes and, as the cosmetics solidified, the pain abated. When Murphy finished, Noah lifted his hands to his face and felt the strange, foreign features.

"The cosmetics will begin to deteriorate in six hours. Now, remember, your name is Deputy D.P. McGregor. You are a Deputy for the North American Security Office. Your team was ambushed. The other two members of the team, named Betts and Ortiz, were killed. You escaped into the woods. You've been injured and need a medivac—"

Noah interrupted the man.

"I remember what you said."

Murphy stopped and studied Noah, then accepted his state-ment. "Just a few more things, then."

Murphy slid a case out from the bottom of the plastic box and removed a small AR. He placed the robotic device at the base of Noah's hand and it clamped onto his wrist. Then, the AR cut a thin laceration down Noah's inner forearm. Next, the AR used a small tweezers to remove Noah's Implanted Wrist Chip. Murphy removed the SO's sterilized implant from a small, liq-uid-filled jar, and placed it into the robotic tweezers. The robot placed the foreign IWC into Noah's muscle, then sutured the cut with a laser. A light scar blushed the skin as wisps of smoke rose from the arm.

When Murphy finished, he began to pack up the black box. As he did so, he turned to Noah. "You know, you'll be a legend for this, right? The name Noah Bridger will be in the history books."

Noah's hands continued to explore his new face. "Noah Bridger died with his family this morning."

His fingers tugged at his synthetic ears. Murphy shrugged and closed the lid to the box.

Noah proceeded to take off his clothes and don the uni-form of his enemy. As he examined his new attire, he caught the wicked Yellow Eye staring back at him. He pulled the cloth out and deposited a thick glob of sputum on the offending oculus.

During the IWC transplant, Gerhardt had emerged from the trees. There had been a single gunshot. Noah had heard a thud against the earth, and when he looked, Gerhardt was dragging the body into the trees. A few minutes later, while Murphy applied a plastic film on Noah's palms which would mimic the dead man's handprint, Gerhardt and Temple stood next to Murphy and studied Noah. Temple nodded his approval while he palmed his Glock.

"You look good, my man. Now, which leg was injured before?"

Noah answered him by raising his left leg from the ground.

Without pause, there was a loud crack and Noah fell to the ground. The pain was the same as it had been before, but Noah's mind blocked the rushing torment.

The men ran into the forest. The clock was ticking. Noah lay on his back and, as he fought the pain, opened McGregor's APD and requested an extraction.

Noah had been running from The Federation for over fifteen-hundred kilometers. Now The Federation was coming straight to him. And they couldn't get there quick enough.

CHAPTER TEN

14 May 2072

"That's it! That's all the time we have!" Communications Director Isabella Hernandez stepped between Secretary-General Antoine Dubois and the *Chicago Tribune* journalist Natalie Kelley. It had been exactly thirty minutes since the interview started. The lighting drones landed and The Federationists immediately began to disassemble the equipment.

Dubois rose from his chair. He removed the small wireless lapel mic and handed it to one of The Federationists nearby. He walked to his interviewer. He stepped directly in the path of the track lighting and his long shadow spread over the wooden floor and bent up the walls.

He startled Natalie when he spoke to her. She was seated. Her hands shook with adrenaline, failing to unclip the lapel mic, when she heard his voice.

"I would like to thank you for your time, Ms. Kelley. I hope my answers were clear." This last statement was almost a question. It was the first time Natalie had heard him speak without total confidence.

Natalie muttered a statement of graciousness, still fumbling with the mic. When she looked up, he was gone, walking out of the room, followed by a legion of workers. She was dazed. *Had the interview gone well?* She tried to think back but found her mind to be moving too quickly to grasp any individual thought; each idea streaked by as a blur out of her reach.

She stood up on wobbly, weak legs. One of The Federationists came over and unclipped Natalie's microphone. Natalie thanked her. Hernandez and Joseph approached as the track lights went out. Only the light on the overhead fan remained. The room was dark and nearly empty. Joseph hugged her and smiled.

Before they could say much, Hernandez pulled the two pairs of vision-blocking glasses from a pocket of her suit coat.

"We need to get you back to the hotel," she said and held out the glasses. Before Joseph or Natalie could grab them, another hand covered the glasses.

"Ms. Hernandez, if I could have some time with Ms. Kelley here, I would be much obliged. I can take her and Mr. Kalani back to town."

Natalie looked up and saw the face of Cooper Gates.

Lt. Director Juan Carlos Luna had been in the crowd watching the interview. Only fifteen Federationists had initially been permitted into the building, but the space had been crammed with over forty people. Luna had not cared to kick them out. He had been enchanted by the conversation before him. Antoine Dubois was intelligent, compassionate, and charming. Midway through, he felt a tug on his sleeve. It was Security Director Farrelly.

"I need to speak with you," she whispered in his ear as he bent down. She pointed to the exit. It was hard to walk away from a man so truthfully laying out his vision, but Luna followed his boss out of the clubhouse.

"I need your honest opinion," she said as she and Luna stood on a cement patio on the side of the building. Farrelly stared at Luna, serious as always. "How secure will the signing be today?"

Luna looked over the makeshift camp on the old driving range. A modular complex bustled with dedicated staff who moved with the sole purpose of making sure the signing was secure. In Santa Fe, there were more than two thousand men and women, each of whom would die to make sure The Federation's objectives were completed.

"The signing will be secure, ma'am," Luna said, giving his honest opinion.

"Give me a percentage," the Director commanded, analytically.

"One hundred percent, ma'am."

Farrelly turned her neck to the side, causing an audible cracking of her vertebrae. "Nothing is one hundred percent," she said. "We have seen that time and again. We saw that two nights ago."

Luna was tired of the woman's calculating demeanor. She had one of the finest brains on the planet, but little heart and no gut.

"The signing will be secure," Luna reassured her. "I put my job on the line for it."

With that guarantee, Lt. Director Juan Carlos Luna turned around and opened the door, wanting only to listen to Antoine Dubois speak. As he did so, Dierdre Farrelly's hiss stalked him inside.

"You bet your ass that your job is on the line."

Noah Bridger did not need to fake pain and anguish when the evacuation helicopter arrived. The dispatcher tried to keep him talking on the APD while the chopper came, but Noah was curt with her. He calmly lay on top of the granite slab, holding the throbbing leg, blood slipping down the rock face, when he heard the helicopter approach. There was a red cross on the side-paneling of the helicopter.

Watching the dark object grow on the vast, blue plane, he opened the block of his mind and let the pain in. The torment returned with a fury. He savagely yelled skyward at the medivac. Instead of landing on the clearing, a man rappelled from the aircraft, attached a series of carabineers to Noah, and the pair ascended into the cabin.

Through gritted teeth and wetted cheeks, he told the medics the tale he had rehearsed while he waited and bled on the mountainside. He and his comrades, Betts and Ortiz, had been ambushed while they followed a lead regarding potential insurgent activity north of Santa Fe near Picuris Peak. Their vehicle had been shot at and he, Ortiz, and Betts returned fire from the Humvee. The combatants disappeared into the mountainside. The Security Officers followed the assailants into the wood where they were met by an ambush. Noah—or Deputy D.P. McGregor to the evac team—was hit in the leg during the firefight and separated from Betts and Ortiz. He had been unable to reach them on their comms. He had found the clearing and summoned the evacuation chopper on his APD.

"Have you heard from Betts or Ortiz?" he asked, feigning concern. There were four individuals in the helicopter: the rappeler, the medic, the pilot, and the copilot. Inside the aircraft, Noah was placed on a black gurney and a medical AR slid down the rails of the gurney and measured his vitals. The cabin was filled with medical equipment. The medic, with the assistance of the robotics, began the operation to remove the lodged bullet.

"No. I must speak with Lt. Director Luna," he told the medic. "Immediately."

The medic shook her head. "We are taking you to the St. Vincent Med Center in Santa Fe. We need to fix your leg."

"No," Noah answered. He clutched the medic by the front of her shirt and tried to sit up. "I need to speak with the Lt. Director. In person. As soon as possible." He strained to make his face look serious but did not know how his cosmetic expression would appear.

The medic looked to the others in the open cabin. The rappeler opened an APD, certainly checking Deputy D.P. McGregor's clearance level. He spoke to the pilot. Noah could not hear the conversation over the whirling rotors. There was a gush of blood when the slug was removed, and the medic and AR quickly coagulated the flow.

The medic leaned close to Noah's ear. She told him that he needed to relax and that they would take care of him. The AR tried to administer an injection of the painkiller Buatetu to the wounded soldier, but Noah seized the arm of the bot. The medic tried to pry his hand from the AR.

"No," he said to the medic. "Not yet. After."

The medic looked at her patient. The artificial visage must have conveyed a sense of seriousness. She addressed the AR and the bot lowered the syringe without administering the painkiller. She spoke to the pilot through her headset. Again, Noah could not hear, but he felt the helicopter change course and bank west toward Cochiti Lake.

"Jesus Christ, Cooper. This is not the time!" Natalie hissed at her former lover. Joseph and Hernandez conversed a few meters away.

The strong young man grabbed her by the shoulders. The physicality of the act startled and excited the journalist.

"Natalie," he said sternly, keeping a tight grip on her. "This is important." He looked around at the room. "We need to speak somewhere private." Natalie, Cooper, Joseph, Hernandez, and two equipment technicians were the sole remaining occupants of the space.

Natalie was dumbfounded.

"This isn't private?" She gestured to the near empty room.

Cooper pointed at the recording equipment.

"For fuck's sake," Natalie cackled. "You think somebody cares about our soap opera bullshit?"

Cooper was tense. He kept Natalie close to him. "We need to go outside."

"I don't see that happening, Cooper. They led us here blind. Communications Director Hernandez was very clear that we would be leaving immediately."

He took Natalie by the arm and led her to a corner of the room, next to the newly erected plastic wall that had been constructed to compact the space. The corner was dark, lit only by the dim sunlight that spilled through the opaque window coverings.

"If I can talk to Hernandez and get her to put you under my guardianship for the duration of the day, will you listen to me? More importantly, will you believe me?"

Natalie looked Gates over. He wore a tan and orange tailored suit, separating him from other Federationists who wore professional, stoic dark colors. He was handsome and groomed as always, but his complexion lacked its normal color. Natalie could see that, under a layer of foundation, he had dark bags beneath his eyes. For the first time in their relationship, she worried about him. Natalie felt uneasy, but the opportunity that he presented was too good to pass on.

"And Joseph?" she asked, though she had already made up his mind.

"No, it has to just be you."

"Then my answer is no," Natalie bluffed and started to walk toward her editor.

Cooper held out his hand to stop her, but she was out of his grip, and he brought the hand back with a clap on the other.

"Fine," he called out to her. She stopped and turned around. "Fine. The old man can stay, too. Might be harder to swing..." he trailed off as she walked back toward him.

"And I can write about everything I see and hear? Complete clearance of the treaty activities?"

Cooper looked at Hernandez, then back at Natalie.

"That's fine. Obviously, per safety protocols, there will need to be a delay. But, I don't think the treaty will be what you want to write about after we have our discussion."

Lt. Director Juan Carlos Luna slipped out the front of the clubhouse ahead of the exodus of spectators. On the road in front of the clubhouse was a caravan of twenty idling black Suburbans. Luna walked around the log building to the back. Overlooking the Pelican and the dirt fairway, he packed his pipe.

Deputy Amir Owens slid next to Luna.

"He's something else, huh?"

Luna nodded. "I once saw Thapa conduct a one-hundred-and-ten-piece orchestra at Musikverein. It took me back there. *He* took me back there. I could hear Mahler's Second as he spoke. The man is a maestro."

"She was good, too," Owens added. "I'd never heard of her."

"She sure as hell didn't pull any punches."

"I think the Secretary enjoyed that."

"I think he did, too."

As the men spoke, a mass of people came around the edge of the clubhouse. They were led by Dubois. His Nehru jacket was off, and the sleeves of his white cotton shirt were rolled to just below his elbows.

Dierdre Farrelly approached Luna, her APD in the palm of her hand, pressed gently against her hip.

"He wants twenty minutes. Will that be fine?"

Luna checked his watch, then nodded. "Shouldn't be a problem."

"Shouldn't be?"

"It won't be, Director."

The woman walked off, hurriedly.

"Twenty minutes?" Owens asked.

Luna shrugged. They were already ahead of schedule. The treaty signing was not scheduled for another hour and a half.

"We have time." Luna looked around at the secured golf course. "Better to have him here than in the middle of that chaos."

Owens agreed. Luna smoked his pipe and the two men watched the Secretary-General. He tossed a quanco to his security detail and they ran through imaginary goal lines over the hard earth and crabgrass.

The ex-Olympian still moved gracefully in his advancing years and he looked utterly gleeful as he played. It had been forty years since the Casablanca Games. Due to the financial drain, that had been the last Olympics, but the Secretary-General almost single-handedly kept the sport of rugby alive. The crowd around the participants grew. At least one hundred eyes were trained on the man, but he did not seem to notice them. He had lived his life surrounded by people watching him and had grown accustomed to the world's gaze.

Luna watched and found himself wishing to play. He had never been a person who enjoyed sitting on the sidelines. He took off his suit jacket and holster handed them to Deputy Owens.

"Can you hold this for me?"

Owens laughed. "You play rugby?"

Luna smiled. "Nah, but I figured I could mix it up a bit."

Before he could leave the patio for the scrum, his APD beeped. Owens called him back.

"Sir! You have a message."

Luna retrieved the device from the inside pocket of his jacket. There had been an incident north of Santa Fe. Some Federation casualties were likely. Another good man was injured, and he was on an evac chopper. The injured man, Deputy D.P. McGregor, had requested to speak with the Lt. Director. The message claimed McGregor had urgent intel to deliver to the Lt. Director. *Urgent intel?* Then, he remembered. *North. Carson Forest. The drone.* He closed out the APD and frowned. He was glad that McGregor was coming straight to him and hoped he wasn't too badly wounded. He looked at the horizon. Deputy D.P. McGregor was in the air, on his way to Cochiti. And he needed to speak to La Frontera.

The medic had stopped the bleeding from the gunshot wound on Noah Bridger's leg. She asked if there had been some recent trauma to the leg, but Noah ignored her. He hadn't spoken since he refused the Buatetu; he had just closed his eyes and envisioned his mission. He began to believe he may very well be able to complete the impossible task. He would do it for Marie and for the kids. They would be proud of him. Wade would be proud of him. As would Sonya and the others at the camp. And millions around the world who had been victims of The Federation. And if he failed…

Well, then he would be with his family.

The medic had cut off Noah's pants just above the knee, but she left his sidearm strapped to his hip. Murphy had assured him that they would leave the 9mm with him, but Noah had been nervous they would remove it. He did not want to have to find a weapon on the ground. Luckily for Noah, the cosmetics and chip-implantation had given the evac team no doubt to question that the wounded man in their helicopter was D.P. McGregor.

Noah reflected on this new opportunity. It hardly mattered to him what the mission was. Originally, Wade had planned for Noah to enter the city of Santa Fe with the IWC and cosmetic blueprint of a stolen citizen. Murphy, Temple, and Gerhardt were to lead him to a vehicle that he would drive to the town. He would take the car as close to the capitol as possible. The car was to be lined with plastic explosives. Wade insisted that they would not be detected. When Noah reached the capitol, he was to detonate the bomb. Wade told him to abandon the car near the perimeter. Noah had planned to stay at the wheel.

The medic interrupted his thoughts. The helicopter was dropping.

"Are you sure we can't give you something for the pain, sir? It looks like the bullet cracked your tibia."

Noah kept his eyes closed.

"Yes. I'm sure," he said calmly, experiencing the strong sense of déjà-vu. He had had this conversation before with a GFN doctor in a helicopter like this one. It had only been ten days ago, but it felt like a lifetime. The last time he had been shot and in Federation custody, he had been terrified. Though the situation repeated, his emotions did not. Then, he was fearful, but now, he was resolute. Today, he knew he would die. Whether he would succeed or fail in his given mission was up to God. He would enter the Kingdom of Heaven as either a hero or a martyr. Either label suited Noah.

The helicopter jolted as it touched down on the ground. He felt his hand slide over the grip of the pistol at his side, then drop back to the metal flooring before the medic or rappeler saw the action. He was ready.

Cooper Gates left Natalie in the corner between the plastic partition and the wooden wall to speak with Communications Director Isabella Hernandez. Joseph Kalani walked over to his employee.

"What's up?" he asked.

"He wants to escort us for the rest of the day."

"At the signing?"

"I guess. And here. He said he needed to tell me something," Natalie shrugged. "Who knows."

"The day that keeps on giving."

They stood in silence and looked over the dimly lit room. Dusty footprints were all that were left of the horde of people and equipment which had filled the space only minutes before.

Cooper nodded his head vigorously, then left Hernandez. He walked to the door and put his hand on the push bar.

"Come on!" he called. Natalie and Joseph hurried to the door.

"Okay, here's the deal," Cooper started, keeping his hand on the closed door. "I will be your escort for the remainder of the day. There will be a ten-day moratorium on any reporting. There will be no recording. No audio. No visual. You will stay close to me for the duration of the escort. You will follow all civilian security protocols. Is that understood?"

"Yes," Natalie and Joseph replied in chorus.

"Okay," Cooper appeared nervous. "First, I need to talk to Natalie. Alone. Mr. Kalani, please stay next to the building while I speak with Ms. Kelley." Cooper pushed open the door. Sunlight flooded the room. The Federationist led the way outside, followed by Natalie, then Joseph.

They were on an abandoned golf course. There was a vast complex of modular buildings set up on the driving range to the west. Some flagsticks and netting remained, but the ground was mostly dirt. To the north was the battered 18th hole. At the start of the fairway was a Pelican P-190 sky ferry. A few hundred people were gathered on the hills overlooking the parched earth. A group of men were running between the mounds, playing a pick-up game of rugby. Natalie spotted Secretary-General Antoine Dubois playing the flank, galloping along the edge of the dry lakebed toward the overgrown green.

"Coop, this is incredible. You need to let me take footage of this. People are going to fucking eat this up—just look at him!"

Natalie had stopped on the patio with Joseph. Cooper walked toward the distant tee box, away from the crowd and the complex. He called to her.

"Natalie! Come on!" He moved his arm in a semi-circle.

Natalie jogged to catch him. "You gotta let me record that game, man. That's the shit people love to see. You know, some people are saying that the Secretary is getting old. This will shut that story right up. The PR for this is—"

"Natalie, I need you to focus."

She was reaching for her APD to record the game before her.

"Put that away!" Cooper hissed, swinging his hands downward. They walked into a wispy field of knee-high grass. When they reached the trunk of a dead evergreen, Cooper stopped.

"Did you get the box I sent you?"

Natalie was playing with the settings on the camera of her APD, hardly paying attention to Cooper. She had just conducted the interview of her career and was now seeing a side of the man that the public rarely had the chance to see. Ideas were what Antoine Dubois cherished and he tried to limit any attempt at humanization of those ideas. And that included humanizing himself.

"No, Cooper, I didn't get the box you sent. I don't need another necklace either, so when I do get it, I'll send it back."

"Goddamnit, Natalie, no!" He kept his voice low, but his impatience thickly coated the words. Natalie finally looked at him. She had never seen the man frazzled. He had always been cool, but now his face was red and sweat soaked through his silk suit. "The box from Oklahoma City. With the notes. The codes. The coordinates. Did you get the box I sent?"

Natalie put her APD back in her pocket. The gears in her mind began to click into place.

"You sent that box?"

"Yes."

The blush of anger had retreated from Cooper's face and it was now bleached white.

"Why? What is it?"

Cooper looked around again, ensuring that they wouldn't be heard by any physical or electronic ears.

"You need to listen to me very carefully, Natalie. You cannot record this. I'm putting my life on the line by telling you this."

Lt. Director Juan Carlos Luna was nervously watching the pick-up rugby game when he heard the approaching helicopter that carried his injured man. He was worried about Deputy McGregor. He was a good soldier. Luna had recruited him to join the NASO from the Navy SEALs six years ago and had closely watched him rise through the ranks of the GFN. Luna appointed him Deputy after he led a counterterrorism unit which dismantled the *Poigne de Québécois* on the Gulf of St. Lawrence. The medics stated that the injury was not life-threatening, but McGregor's urgent secrecy was uncharacteristic.

The medivac helicopter landed a hundred meters from the crowd between the old tee box and the sky ferry. Luna hurried over to the aircraft. The side door was open, and Luna could see movement inside. The copilot rushed around the nose of the chopper and grabbed the foot of a gurney. McGregor was on the gurney, his leg strapped to the board. As the gurney was pushed from the cabin of the helicopter, the medic at the head of the bed pressed a button and the gurney began to hover a meter and a half above the ground. Luna reached the gurney. The medic, still inside the cabin of the helicopter, tapped him on the shoulder and yelled into his ear.

"Like I said, he won't talk to us! Said he needed to speak with you alone! Try to make it quick, sir! He needs an operation!"

Luna nodded his understanding. He steered the Self-Levitating Gurney into a patch of prairie grass, away from the whirr of the blades. The gurney was easy to maneuver, designed to evacuate people out of the toughest terrains. McGregor kept his eyes closed. His shirt was drenched in sweat, but his brow remained dry. His lips twitched, but Luna could hear no sound emitted from them.

Blood had been cleaned from the injured leg, but wet redness still covered the bottom half of the bedsheet. Two thick plastic straps held the leg down; one across the ankle and the other above the knee. The leg was gnarled. At least one bone was visibly broken. The skin was red and looked stretched and pinched under the leg hairs. The entrance wound was covered by a small, clear dome which misted the hole with antibiotics.

Luna and the gurney reached the bank of a small ravine that a creek once coursed through. The Lt. Director stopped the gurney and bent down to face his Deputy. McGregor opened his eyes. They were wide and sharp and blue.

"How ya doin', D.P.?"

"We need to speak, sir."

"Yes," Luna answered. "The evac team said that. Go on. What happened up there? Has the threat been neutralized?"

His eyes fluttered, and the Deputy's mouth curled.

"No. No. The threat has not been neutralized."

This must be Juan Carlos Luna. La Frontera. Noah snuck a peek at the face above him. The man was speaking with the medic. Noah closed his eyes again quickly. He had never heard of "La Frontera" before, but Murphy had described the Lt. Director. Murphy spoke of him with abhorrence tinged with awe, but Noah was hardly impressed by his glimpse.

He felt the gurney move. The pulsing sound of the helicopter quieted. The breeze swept across his body, but he couldn't feel it on his face. Noah remembered his mask. *How long was I in that chopper? When did Murphy say the cosmetics would begin to erode? Five hours? Six?*

It didn't matter. Noah's mission would be complete by then. He would be dead before his true identity was revealed. He would be with Marie.

Marie.

Noah spoke to his murdered wife. Whispered to her intimately, the way he would as they lay in bed before the kids woke.

This is for you, my dove.

I never should have left you. I'm so sorry for that.
I hope that you and the kids didn't suffer.
I will be with you soon.
I am doing what I think God would want me to do.
But, more importantly, I am doing this for you.
A man must protect his family and I did not. I have failed.
I am going to right that wrong, my dove.
I love you. I wish and hope and pray I will see your smiling
face soon.

The gurney stopped, and Noah heard Luna breathing next to him. He closed his lips and opened his eyes. The sun was bright. An old, dark face hung over him. There was an echo in his ear.

"How ya doin', D.P.?" Lt. Director Juan Carlos Luna spoke to Noah Bridger.

Noah did not know Luna. He did not hate the man and he felt no rage toward him.

However, he was prepared to kill him.

"Natalie, you cannot record this and you obviously cannot use my name. This is the only time I will speak to you regarding this matter and if you try to question me again, I will feign ignorance, and if you quote me, I will bury you."

"You don't have to threaten me."

"Natalie, please!" Cooper Gates looked into the journalist's eyes and she saw fear staring back at her. He took a deep breath and blinked a long, poky blink. "I'm going to speak slowly, and you need to listen to me carefully."

Natalie remained silent as Cooper peered at her.

"Okay?" he asked.

She nodded, signifying her agreement.

"The GFN, or more specifically, members within the GFN North American Security Offices, have been using DefCorp

Dynamics to traffic arms to groups outside of the White Zone that have been labeled as terrorist organizations."

Natalie was stunned. She heard herself snigger at the claim. "Coop, that's absurd. There's no way—"

"Natalie, Goddamnit, just listen to me!" Cooper was shaking. "Let me finish, okay?"

She stared back at him.

He repeated himself.

"Okay?!"

She slowly came to the realization that the man in front of her was serious—more serious than she had ever seen him.

"Okay."

He bit his bottom lip and rolled his eyes, punching his thigh with a hard right fist.

"Fuck. I had this so well-scripted in my mind. And now... it's jumbled."

Cooper cleared his throat and looked around the grounds.

"Members of NASO are trafficking guns to multiple groups which have been labeled as terrorist organizations. At first, it was just a branch of the AFG. I think. There are still many murky areas concerning the dealings, but I do know that the original weapons provided were antiquated. I think they knew a signing was imminent. But NASO wasn't ready. So they needed to have an enemy.

"But things spiraled out of control. Greed took over and rumblings of a signing grew louder. More advanced arms were sold to more extreme terrorist sects. There was a concentrated effort to create chaos within the Grey Zone, as well as a bountiful financial field ready to be harvested. The documents I provided you with are a series of meeting points between a DefCorp employee and the buyers in the Grey Zone. The hard currency exchanged was staggering. It was supposed to be so... tidy. But, it—there was too much." He shook his head in frustration. "Do you understand what I'm telling you?"

Natalie's ears rang as if a shell had exploded right outside her foxhole. "Cooper. Christ. This is unbelievable."

"Do you understand?" he asked again. He appeared deeply shaken.

"Yes, I understand." Natalie began to comprehend the situation. "Dotson? Nejem?" she asked.

"Cleanup."

"Holy hell, Coop."

"Yeah," Cooper agreed. "I couldn't believe it myself. I'm still trying to make sense of it." His shoulders dropped and he rocked his head. Natalie could tell he was exhausted. "We only have a few minutes before we need to leave with the caravan. What do you need to know?"

A parade of questions flashed across Natalie's mind, but one remained bold and steady. *Who?* She was about to ask Cooper that question when a loud clap echoed from beyond the fairway.

"The threat has not been neutralized?" Lt. Director Luna was alarmed. There was a potential danger to the signing and his mission. His career was in danger. Lives were in danger.

"Speak, damnit!" he shouted at the injured man. McGregor was staring straight up. Luna followed his gaze but did not see anything.

"Tell me, D.P.!" he pleaded. "Tell me what's going to happen!"

Luna looked back to the fairway. More than a hundred-people continued to watch the rugby match. Others moved to ready the caravan. He scanned the crowd. There was nothing suspicious.

"Are they here?! Speak, you motherfucker! Speak!" He grabbed McGregor's collar with both hands and shook him.

There was a mutter from the Deputy, then Luna felt a grip on his wrist. The Lt. Director released the man's shirt and tried to back away but couldn't. McGregor had stretched across the gurney and clasped on to Luna. The self-levitating bed tilted.

"What are you doing, McGregor? What do you need to tell me?"

This man's lost it, Luna thought. He craned his head toward the chopper and shouted for the medics, but no one could hear.

"Deputy, let go of me. Now." Instinctively, he reached for his holster. There was nothing there. He had taken it off and given it to Deputy Owens earlier so he could join the match. His face turned hot with anger.

"Goddamnit, Deputy, unhand me. That, son, is an—"

He felt a prodding in his stomach. Then, a bite. Luna smelled sour cordite. He placed his hands over his midsection. He felt the hot blood slide through his fingers. Luna looked at his attacker, who looked surprised. Like an eclipse, the black pupils stared back at him.

"You shot me," Luna whispered, lacking conviction.

Then, with the swaying red fescue brushing against his knees, Lt. Director Juan Carlos Luna fell to the ground.

Noah Bridger's palm rested on the hip holster. The ID reader on the polymer frame scanned the latex film on his hand and the holster unfastened. The film worked; the pistol thought his hand belonged to Deputy D.P. McGregor.

The man was yelling at him. Noah didn't hear what he was saying. He didn't care. He felt he was moving in slow motion. As he brought the pistol out of its holster, the man grabbed his shirt. Noah was startled.

Did he see the gun?! Have I failed again? The man was closing in on him. He could smell his breath, sweet with tobacco.

Noah kept the pistol in his left hand and reached across the gurney with his right. He grabbed the man's wrist. The man released his hold on Noah and backed away. Noah held tight and jostled the man.

There was a spark of fear in the man's eyes. He looked toward the helicopter and called for help. Noah swung his hips and leveled the pistol at the man's stomach. He looked at the man named Luna. The fear turned to anger. Noah jabbed the muzzle of the 9mm into the man's gut.

He fired. It was easy. He lowered his sight from the man's face to his abdomen. A dark rose blossomed on the white shirt.

The air was still. Noah could hear the man's last words.

"You shot me." It was not quite a statement, but not quite a question.

The man fell to the ground. Noah felt the hovering gurney rock. He realized he was on his side on the edge of the bed. He tried to move his weight to the middle, but it was too late. The gurney flipped.

Noah hit the ground face-first. Unsettled dust billowed into his mouth and caked against his lashes. The shattered leg discharged a shock through his bones like lightning. He thought over his next move.

He could stay on the ground and wait for someone to arrest him.

He could try to run.

Or he could go straight to the crowd, fire his weapon, and meet Marie as a hero and martyr.

It was hard for Natalie to believe what Cooper Gates was telling her. The GFN, and Dubois personally, had worked tirelessly to root corruption out of The Federation. There was an anti-corruption clause in the original Montpellier Accords and an Anti-Corruption Force run by the GFN to monitor federal governments. If true, this would be the largest uncovered case of criminality in GFN history. Natalie evaluated her source to gauge the claim's validity. Cooper Gates was an ambitious career-climber and someone who leaked a story of this magnitude was putting their career in serious danger. He wouldn't risk his future for a limp rumor. There had to be something here.

Plus, he looked scared shitless.

Cooper stopped talking and stood at attention, like a skittish doe hearing a branch break.

"That sounded like a gunshot," he said to Natalie.

"You're just on edge," she responded. Her own thoughts blocked her from hearing anything. "Understandably."

"No, really," Cooper replied looking behind him. "I heard a gunshot."

They looked back over the fairway to the modular buildings. The rugby match continued, but none within had seemed to notice. Between Natalie and Cooper and the crowd, a helicopter had landed a few minutes before. To the east of the helicopter near the dry creek bed, there was an unoccupied self-levitating gurney. A man, using the gurney for support, began to rise from out of the tall grass.

"What the hell?" Cooper muttered and started walking toward the downed man.

Natalie grabbed his wrist.

"He's fine, Coop. Go on. I need more information. Dates. Names."

"He's not fine," Cooper rebutted, but just then the man waved at Natalie and Cooper.

Cooper again walked towards the man. Natalie harrumphed and followed. In the distance, the man stood next to the gurney. Seeing them approach, he shooed them away with his hand. He tapped his chest, then gave an "OK" signal using his fingers.

Natalie stopped. "See, he's embarrassed. Focus. If this is the only time we can discuss this, then we need to discuss this. I don't need to tell you how important it is."

Cooper stopped and turned around. "You're right. You don't."

They walked a few meters back, away from the injured man and the crowd.

"You have some of the dates on the notes I provided from Nejem. You can be certain there were other couriers involved at DefCorp. That is where you will get your information."

"What about those within The Federation?"

"I can't be certain of any names at NASO."

"What have you heard?"

"I need you to remember that these are good men, Natalie. Men that have fought hard for all of us. Men that have sacrificed more than either of us can imagine."

"Who, Cooper?"

"Again, nothing is substantial within NASO. The only concrete names I have are from DefCorp."

"Who, Cooper?"

"Arnie Jones was one name I've heard. And Juan Carlos Luna is another."

Darkness enveloped Juan Carlos Luna. His vision was a tunnel of black with a tiny spot of light at the center. And the spot grew smaller and smaller until it was the size of a pinprick. The blackness circled him like an Asmodean vulture.

Luna fought through the darkness and crawled out of the tunnel into the light.

He was lying on the ground. His head and arm hung in the open air. Below him was a lane of shattered earth. Luna rolled onto his back. There was blood on his stomach.

He had been shot. He remembered. He was dangling over the creek bed. He looked away from the dry ravine and for his assailant, but the fescue was thick. He needed to stand. He tried to rise, but the pain in his gut shook and reverberated throughout his body down to his marrow. The blood continued to dampen his shirt. He ripped it open and looked at his belly. It was sticky and crimson. He probed the flesh to find the entrance wound. It was ten centimeters to the right of his navel.

He needed to stop the bleeding. He reached over the ridge and picked a flake of dried soil from the dead stream. He put the dirt in his mouth and rolled it into a ball of mud with his tongue. He spit the mud ball into his hand and packed it into the bullet hole. *That would have to work for now.*

He tried to stand again. With his back on the ground, he tried to bend his torso, but the pain was too much. He rolled himself onto his front, then pushed his body into the air from his hands. From there, he tried to swing his leg up, but he was weak, and the action forced him back to the ground. As he hit the earth, his shoulder struck a buried object. His hands dug through the thick grass until he felt a metal rod. He pulled the object out of the floral web. It was a pole a meter in height. It was royal blue and on the top was the number "200". Luna dug the base of the pole into the soil and hoisted himself to his feet.

He saw his assailant walking out of the tall grass toward the crowd. The bastard was limping, struggling. The thought *why* flashed across Luna's mind, but he dismissed it immediately. He didn't need to know why. He just needed to stop McGregor.

The Deputy trudged forward slowly. He was only thirty meters away from Luna. The Lt. Director lunged forward, but the pain in his stomach buckled him and he caught himself with the pole. Although he was close to the traitor, he knew he would never catch him. Not like this.

Think, Goddamnit, man. Think!

He tried to yell, but as he drew his breath in, the air seeped out of the cavity like an unknotted balloon. Specks of dirt shot from the mud-packed hole and fluttered to the ground. Then, two meters to his left, Luna spotted the Self-Levitating Gurney.

"Luna? Bullshit." Natalie Kelley was stunned. "Luna?"

"That's a name I've heard."

"How sure are you Luna is involved?"

"I'm not sure. You pressed me. I needed to convey just how fucking serious this is." Cooper rubbed his eyes with palms, then brushed back his hair.

"So, who do you know that is involved?" Natalie asked.

"Nejem. Dotson. Start there."

"Not a great place to start since they're both dead."

Cooper shrugged.

"If you aren't going to give me names, why did you tell me this?"

"Because," Cooper stopped. He was befuddled, even though he had thought about this same question many times before. "Because, it was right."

Natalie looked at him sympathetically. She saw his turmoil and wanted to comfort him. Although she had been disgusted by the haughty prick after their Oklahoma City rendezvous, she was drawn to this exposed man.

"I know. I know it was right. Now, help me finish this, Coop. Who else was involved?"

Cooper sighed. "There's a woman named Thacker. Odyssey Thacker. She worked with Chief Deputy Jones. Try to speak with her." He shook his head. "I don't know. It's all rumors. Nejem and Dotson were involved. I can say that with certainty. Arnie Jones, probably. But he died here. In the attack at the hotel. So, if Arnie was involved then Thacker was possibly involved. I don't know."

"And Luna? Where does he fit in?"

Cooper shook his head again as if he were trying to shake off the unpleasant truth. "Arnie Jones never disobeyed Juan Carlos

Luna for four decades. I have nothing tying him, but I would be shocked if Jones pissed without telling Luna."

"Jesus," Natalie replied. The gravity of the situation settled on her with the weight of the Rockies. Juan Carlos Luna was one of the most powerful Americans alive. If you were to make a list, he would probably be on the first page. If there was some debate regarding who the most powerful American alive was, there was none regarding who the most dangerous was. That was Juan Carlos Luna. Natalie shivered.

"My God. Luna. He's here. Now."

"Yes," Cooper replied, lowering his voice.

"Why are you telling me this? When he's here? Jesus, Cooper..."

"Because, Natalie, you wouldn't *speak* to me. I had to do it here; there was nowhere else."

Natalie became suddenly frightened.

"They have to have this entire place under surveillance. They've heard you." She looked over at the buildings but saw no hostile forces approach. However, she did spot something unusual. There was a man staggering away from the creek bed and onto the fairway. He moved slowly, dragging his left leg behind him. It was the man from the gurney. He was not okay. As Natalie watched, he crumpled and fell to the ground.

Natalie brushed Cooper aside and ran to the injured man.

The leg hurt. He could put no pressure on it. Noah Bridger had to let the shattered limb trawl behind, heavy and loose like a burlap bag filled with stones. Murphy had told him to isolate and kill Luna. Noah had. It was easy. But he did not have instructions on what to do now.

With every laboring step Noah took, he expected to be gunned down—he *hoped* to be gunned down. But no one shot him. No one paid any attention to him. He was a ghost and he feared nothing. For the first time in his life, there was nothing he had to do. There were no chores. No commands. He had completed his final task and every step he took was stolen from fate, and fate made him pay for his theft with pain.

No one depended on him—at least, no one living. Marie and the kids still depended on him and, for the first time since their death, he felt singular, focused rage toward the people who took them away.

Noah's foot hit a sharp rock and he felt the leg freeze and stiffen. He could not keep his balance and he fell, landing on his side. He slammed into the ground with his shoulder, afraid the gun would accidentally go off. It did not. The injured left leg thumped onto his right and he felt the brittle bone splinter. Without thinking of surrender, he hopped to his one good leg and hobbled forward.

The crowd of people was distracted. They were still some distance away. They were watching something. A rugby match. This disgusted Noah, but he didn't know why. He recognized a large man gallop toward the scrum.

Antoine Dubois. That bastard. The French fuck that ruined America. Noah heard himself repeating words in his mind that were never his own, but he felt the conviction. The man called Luna had been an emotionless objective, a conduit to reach his family in heaven. But this man. Dubois. Satan incarnate. Noah felt that *he* was personally responsible for murdering his family.

Noah knew what he needed to do. He clenched the gun in his fist and moved it behind his back.

Suddenly, he heard a noise. Someone yelling. From behind. They were screaming at him.

"Hey! Hey! Are you okay? Stop!"

Noah peeked behind him. A woman was running toward him. She was coming straight at him. She would stop him before he reached Dubois.

"Hey! Stop!" The calling came closer.

Noah wheeled around and fired the pistol.

Lt. Director Luna reached the gurney by using the pole to prop him up. He was drenched in sweat. He could taste the salty beads on his tongue. He wheezed, shallow and quick draws of air. He hoisted himself onto the gurney; the floating bed bobbed as the hovering slab's magnetic field adjusted to Luna's weight. He felt his stomach. The packed mud had slowed the blood loss but had not stopped it.

Luna looked at McGregor. He was still stumbling forward. He was nearly halfway between Luna and the crowd. Luna saw the pistol in his hand, stapled tightly against his rump. There was a large crowd gathered on the far sideline of the rugby match. Luna saw Antoine Dubois. He was hard to miss, and he was isolated, no more than one hundred meters from McGregor.

Why hasn't he fired yet? If he wanted to get Dubois, he could get him from there. It would be a difficult shot, but not impossible. A soldier of McGregor's caliber could make that shot.

Again, Luna needed to remind himself not to question the motives of the gunman. He just needed to stop him.

Lying on his stomach, he looked at the control panel on the Self-Levitating Gurney. The panel blinked red. The gurney's battery was running low. Once the battery was depleted, the magnetic field would disappear, and the bed would fall to the earth. Luna would be stuck. He dismissed the panel's battery warning and went to the navigation menu. He commanded the SLG to move forward, then turned it to face the treacherous Deputy. He started for him. Within seconds, he was gaining on McGregor. The battery warning began to flash faster.

Luna, piloting the SLG, was fifty meters away from Deputy D.P. McGregor when the traitor spun around and fired a single shot.

The man needed help. He was alone and struggling and no one had noticed him. Only Natalie. Momentarily, she forgot about what Cooper had told her. She was in action mode, moving on a combination of instinct, training, and adrenaline. When her father was killed, she had stood by helplessly. She vowed to never be helpless in an emergency again. She enrolled in CPR and first-aid classes. She studied text and diagrams of basic medical education. And she spoke constantly with first responders who had careers in crisis. Before, when the man had seemed okay, she didn't want to intervene. Now, she knew she had been wrong and that this unknown limping man needed help.

He was back on his feet quickly. Natalie waved. He did not see her. If he was calling for help, Natalie did not hear him. He was moving slowly, taking small hops on one foot, dragging the other useless leg behind.

He didn't need to keep walking; Natalie was coming to help. She slowed her sprint to a jog and yelled to him, "Hey! Hey! Are you okay?"

His head turned slightly, trying to identify the noise. He kept limping. Natalie kept jogging. She was only thirty meters away now.

"Hey! Stop!" She called again, certain the man could hear her. He whirled toward her. Natalie saw the gun a split second before she heard the distinct, chilling pop.

There was an old sand trap a few meters to Natalie's left. She sprinted to it and dove in. Safely beneath the lip, Natalie pulled out her APD and commanded the camera to start recording.

The gunshot was loud. The amplification of the noise surprised Noah Bridger. The first shot must have been stifled by Luna's flesh and muscle. This shot echoed across the open range. Noah knew he only had a few seconds left. He turned toward the rugby match. Antoine Dubois stood stoically as his guards ran to cover him.

Noah raised the gun. The man was still so far. His hand shook. He would never hit him from here. He closed his eyes and his finger slipped into the trigger guard. If he was going to kill Dubois, it would be with the guiding Hand of God.

Noah squeezed the trigger. Then squeezed again. The trigger was oiled and swung with ease. As he tugged for a third time, there was a mechanical ringing in his ear. A moment later, there was a swift crack against his skull.

It's done, Marie. I'm coming.

He had no more thoughts.

McGregor had fired on a woman to Luna's left. When the shot rang out, she fell to the ground. She was moving on the dirt. Luna did not think she had been hit. Even better, Luna did not think McGregor had seen him on the SLG. The Deputy pivoted to face the crowd gathered to watch the rugby match.

The control panel on the gurney flashed red at him, then began to emit a high-pitched beeping. The charge was nearly completely depleted. Luna was fifteen meters from McGregor. The SLG slowed.

McGregor fired at the crowd. The SLG schlepped forward. Five meters away. A second shot. Two meters away. The gurney stopped. McGregor hesitated. The SLG, out of battery, began to drop to the ground. Luna, with the blue yardage marker in hand, lunged off the gurney and into the air. He swung the pole in a wide arc and felt it crash down on McGregor.

Luna landed hard on the dirt and let go of the pole. There was a fire in his gut. The entry wound had ripped open when he stretched in the air. Blood gushed onto the earth and Lt. Director Juan Carlos Luna closed his eyes.

CHAPTER ELEVEN

Three days had passed since the attack at Cochiti Lake. The world had watched the excitement and aftermath in New Mexico through *Chicago Tribune* journalist Natalie Kelley's broadcast. Her cool, concise narration of the event, coupled with her interview of Secretary-General Antoine Dubois that morning rocketed her into stardom.

Once Communications Director Isabella Hernandez discovered that Natalie Kelley had been broadcasting live, she capitalized on the situation. The world's eyes were on Ms. Kelley and, consequently, the strength and resilience of The Global Federation of Nations. Once the threat had been neutralized, Hernandez provided Natalie with the North American Communications Office's staff and equipment for the duration of the day. The broadcast was picked up by streaming services across the planet. The live peak viewership of Natalie's broadcast was 2.5 billion people.

She had been the only journalist interviewing those present at the attack. She had been the only journalist broadcasting from the GFN motorcade from Cochiti Lake to the New Mexico capitol. And she had been in the front row as American Freedom Group President John Hill signed the Basic Human Standard. Natalie had tears glistening in the corners of her eyes as she reacted to Secretary-General Dubois's speech after the signing.

"We will not be stopped by those who prefer terror over peace. Destruction over prosperity. Anarchy over justice. We will not be taken down by those who prefer despair over hope. Cowardice over bravery. Dominion over equality. Despite their best efforts, we are here today. We stand united with those who opposed us because every single person, even our enemies, deserves the opportunity to live a long, happy, fruitful life. Every person that charges at us with savagery in their eyes will be met by a wall of humanity, a billion deep, with love in their hearts."

Capturing the momentum of the tumultuous day, Natalie's one-on-one interview with Dubois was published the evening after the signing. In twenty-four hours, recordings featuring Natalie Kelley outnumbered the global population, topping ten billion views. Soon, however, life marched on and the news cycle's attention shifted. Phillip, Prince of Wales, proposed to his girlfriend, the singer DiDi. In Nepal, an earthquake with a magnitude of 7.2 rocked the city of Lalitpur. In Kahului Harbor, a ship suspected of poaching the near-extinct humpback whale was sunk by a group of militaristic environmentalists.

Natalie was relieved when the spotlight started to dim. She had always dreamed about becoming one of the globe's foremost journalists, but she had always envisioned it happening due to her merits, not because she was at the right place at the right time. After traveling to New York, London, Paris, and Hong Kong over the previous forty-eight hours to appear on a variety of news programs, Natalie was back in Chicago. Her editor Joseph Kalani gave her the day off to rest, but, unable to relax, she found herself in his office.

"I'm sure you know this, but I am extremely proud of you, Natalie," he said beamingly as they sat on the couch in his office and sipped Scotch.

"I couldn't have done it without you," she replied, clinking glasses with him. She was physically and emotionally drained and her words fell flat as they left her mouth.

They sat silent for a few moments and drank, trying to organize the events of the past few days, when Joseph spoke, gazing at the ice in his glass.

"As your boss, I try to stay out of your personal life," he started. An awkward preface for a question Natalie had anticipated since the day of the attack. Joseph took a drink, then finished. "What exactly did Gates need to talk to you about?"

Juan Carlos Luna lay in a medically-induced coma for three days. The assailant's bullet had ripped through the Lt. Director's stomach, tearing open his ascending colon. A loop colostomy was performed at the modular triage at Cochiti. Luna was then flown to the Naval Medical Center in San Diego where, after an eight-hour surgery, his colon was fully repaired under the supervision of Dr. Anaya Sai, RDML. During the surgery, Dr. Sai used additively-manufactured cells to repair the damaged organ. Once the surgery was complete, the naval medical staff kept Luna under and battled a blood clot at the entrance wound and peritonitis for two days. Dr. Sai relayed this information to Luna once he woke from his coma. Dr. Sai told Luna that he may need to be in the hospital for at least a week. Luna scoffed at this, but the doctor ignored his displeasure. After she delivered her summary, she asked her patient if she could "shake the hand of the bravest man she'd ever met."

Luna obliged.

He felt groggy and weak. He let go of the doctor's hand.

"Why?" he asked her.

"Excuse me?"

"McGregor. Why?"

The doctor looked at Luna, confused, then seemed to grasp what he was asking.

"I'm not at liberty to discuss any of that with you. In fact," Dr. Sai moved toward the door, then opened it. Luna heard applause erupt from the hallway. In the midst of the applause, Director Dierdre Farrelly entered the room.

Dr. Sai stood by the open door.

"I will be back to check on you very shortly, sir," she began to walk out of the room, closing the door behind her when she stopped, wiped her hands on her white coat, and turned around. "Again, thank you for your heroics. It has been an honor to meet you, sir."

The doctor left, and the door closed. Luna could hear the muffled clapping and hollering through the walls. Farrelly stood next to his bed. She was smiling.

"Well, Juan Carlos, I think it's safe to say your ass is no longer on the line."

In the month of May, night did not come to Nunavut Deradicalization Center. A period of twilight lasted a few hours, but daylight reigned supreme. Noah Bridger did not experience this marathon solar path. He had been left isolated two stories underground for six meals.

Noah reflected on his arrival to the Arctic. Having lived his entire life in North Texas, Noah Bridger had never experienced such bone-chilling cold as he did when he was led out of the hold of the cargo plane. The sweat on his back froze to the metal stretcher beneath him. Snow and ice filled the gaps between his restraints and skin. He did not remember being apprehended and did not remember being loaded onto the plane. He woke once on the plane. He was groggy but felt no pain. He had been drugged. He was pinioned to the metal floor of cargo plane, surrounded by a dozen rifle-toting Gendarmes. He was muzzled, unable to speak. The plastic gag dripped with his breath's condensation. There was an IV tube in the crook of his right arm and a fresh suture on his left wrist. Noah was disappointed that he was not dead and, with the realization that he would not be ascending to heaven and his family, he began to cry. The tears came quietly at first, but soon the sobs were loud and violent, muffled by the mouthpiece. An SO cranked up the dosage on the IV and Noah drifted into a dense fog.

When the plane landed and the cargo doors opened, the wind blew snow into the hull. The snow swirled and nipped at Noah's face and the cold's bite brought Noah back to consciousness. He remained supine, the floor of the hull released, his wrists and ankles bolted down. Two SOs carried him down the ramp on the metal stretcher. A large man with a thick orange beard looked down at him. His fiery face jutted into the stark whiteness above.

"Noah Bridger, you have been deemed a danger to humanity by The Global Federation of Nation's North American Security Office. In accordance with provision 46-C2 detailed in the Treaty of The Global Federation outlined in the Montpellier Accord signed by your federal government in acceptance of the Basic Human Standard, all of your civil liberties have been suspended."

The man walked away. That was it. Noah was taken into the complex, then down an elevator. He was placed in a small, dark holding cell with a mat on the ground and a hole as a toilet. He had been given food and water and drugs for the pain. Noah spent his time in captivity curled on his mat. He did not speak. He did not think. He did not pray. His mind was as empty and bleak as the landscape above.

Then, some days later, as Noah stared at the cold concrete wall beside his mat, the thick metal door swung open.

Natalie Kelley had anticipated the question. She had dreaded it. She had hoped that her editor would not ask her about Cooper Gates, but she had always known that he would. He had to.

She played coy.

"Gates? When?" she said, knowing that she was unconvincing.

Joseph smiled and took a drink of his Scotch. His thin lips retreated.

"I hate this shit." He tilted his glass and the brown liquid and ice tumbled into Natalie's highball which was now filled to the brim. Joseph laughed. "Careful, now," he said as he moved to the office bar cart. The cart was beneath a large window which gave view to the Chicago skyline. Joseph looked out the window as package drones buzzed by and he poured a belt of gin. He then moved behind his desk. "Is Gates leaving his wife for you?"

Natalie looked at Joseph. His mouth curled into a smirk. She had never told Joseph about her relationship with Cooper Gates; she obviously didn't give the old Hawaiian enough credit for his investigatory prowess.

"No. It had nothing to do with that." She took a deep drink and placed her glass on the table in front of her. "You're going to have to trust that I can't tell you what we discussed, Joseph."

She hoped that would end the conversation. She wished she could tell her mentor about the conversation she had with Gates regarding the NASO's involvement in trafficking arms to the AFG and other terrorist organizations, but she hadn't figured out what she wanted to do with the information yet. This revelation wasn't something one could just blurt out—those who knew had their lives at risk. If Cooper was right, then factions both inside and outside The Federation had been killed to keep this story silent.

Joseph was studying Natalie's face and knew that she was uneasy. "You would tell me if it was something serious, right?"

Natalie didn't want to lie to the man. She picked up her glass again but didn't take another drink. She stood up and dropped the full glass off at the bar.

"I'll tell you what Gates and I discussed when I can tell you what we discussed," she said to her editor. She leaned down on his desk, so she was looking at him on an eye level. "Is that okay?"

Joseph took a second, then nodded. "I trust you, Natalie. But right now, you need to trust me."

Natalie felt the story of the scandal rise up inside her. She wanted to unburden the weight of knowledge to a man she thought could handle it, but she suppressed it back into her gut. It was not yet that time.

"I do trust you, Joseph. And I'll tell you all about Cooper and I's discussion. Soon," she leaned toward him and kissed his cheek, then walked out of the room. Instead of going to her apartment to rest on her day off, she hopped in a SinCab and headed to O'Hare.

"You're a global hero, Juan Carlos." Dierdre Farrelly had pulled a chair next to Luna's bedside. She sat like a debutante. Luna lay on his side as an AR cleaned the post-op incisions. Coarse, silver whiskers speckled his dark cheeks and neck.

"A mint?" he asked the Director, his voice scratchy and deep.

"Excuse me?"

"Do you have a mint? My breath. It stinks."

"Um, sure." Farrelly replied. She stood, walked to the door, and called to the congregation in the hall. She gave the spearmint disc to Luna and lowered herself back into the chair. Luna placed the mint on his tongue and sucked.

"The signing?" he muttered. The mint cracked.

"I'll tell you everything you need to know." Farrelly pulled out her APD and read from the GFN press release. "Yes, the signing still occurred due to your leadership and courageous actions."

"McGregor?"

"Deputy D.P. McGregor was found tortured and murdered north of Santa Fe along with two of his team members. The man you stopped had McGregor's ID implanted in his arm and a cosmetic procedure to impersonate McGregor. The impersonator's name is Noah Bridger."

"One of the escapees."

Farrelly was impressed by Luna's recognition. The GFCoJ was not under Luna's jurisdiction. "Yes. He was one of the fugitives from the ambushed transport on the road from Forrest City to Memphis. He has since been transported to Nunavet."

"Accomplices?"

"We have yet to find his brother-in-law, Wade Barrineau, but there is an intensive manhunt underway. We'll find them all. Or, more aptly, you will."

Luna laughed, then stifled the laughter as the pain rocked his gut.

"I'll get right on it," he jested. He didn't expect to be in the field any time soon.

"When you catch Barrineau, La Frontera, it will be the triumphant dawn of, what is sure to be an illustrious career as the Director of NASO."

At the cell door stood the same large, orange-bearded man who had met Noah as he was carried off the plane. He was flanked by two stern SOs, each with a TS-33 strapped to his back. A bright light sparked on overhead. Noah remained laying on the stiff mat, his eyes staring at the cement wall. The lead man crouched next to the cot. He spit a thick stream of tobacco juice on the bare floor, then wiped the dribble from his chin with the back of his hand.

"In the old days," he began, "when I got my hands on a piece of shit like you, I'd put a couple of electrodes on his boys and zap him 'til he started to puke blood." The man looked around the cell, then back at Noah. "And that wasn't even to get him to talk. That was just to pay him back in some small way for all the years he'd spent on this Earth being a piece of shit. Now—" the bearded man didn't finish. He stood up and headed back for the door. Noah kept staring at the wall, his body shaking.

As the burly SO reached the door, he turned around to face Noah.

"You're going to end up begging to help me. Everything you know right now is wrong. You'll figure that out soon. You're just a dumbfuck from Bumfuck, Texas, that's been used, man. Soon, I'm gonna use you. And you're gonna let me."

Noah heard the bearded man and the two armed guards leave the cell. He heard the door shut and lock behind them. The overhead light turned off and Noah Bridger remained staring at the cement wall, though he could no longer see it.

Natalie Kelley was nervous when her flight landed at General Rodriguez International Airport in Tijuana. As she walked across the Cross-Border Xpress, she carried no luggage—only the box containing what she now knew to be the clandestine notes of Samir Nejem. She had spent the flight trying to concoct a plan to arrange a meeting with Juan Carlos Luna, but was not confident in any of her ideas. Mid-flight, a press release announced that Luna had been named the new NASO Director. Dierdre Farrelly, the woman he was replacing, would become a Special Advisor to the Secretary-General. Natalie was relieved to hear this news since it indicated that Luna was conscious. At least she hoped that he was conscious.

Natalie had debated using her professional relationship with Communications Director Isabella Hernandez to schedule a sit-down but needed the meeting to be off the books. She knew that if she could arrange the meeting, Hernandez would want it recorded and published but Natalie knew making the meeting public was not an option.

In the sunlight, beneath the palm trees, she summoned a single-seat passenger drone and headed straight to Bob Wilson Naval Hospital. The passenger drone dropped her off at the entrance and, before she had come to determine her course of action, the naval guards recognized her. They rushed her, asking for photographs and autographs. Natalie spent thirty minutes appeasing the mob. The crowd, in their excitement at encountering the budding celebrity, had led her past the guardhouse and into the lobby of the medical center. She did not need any of her excuses to enter the base.

Once the frenzy of attention subsided, Natalie found the admissions desk and inquired after Juan Carlos Luna.

The woman behind the desk stonewalled Natalie and told her "unless you are a spouse or blood relative, I can't give you any information about the Lt.," the woman corrected herself, "about the Director."

As Natalie began speaking again, the admissions clerk looked up. "Oh, my God! It's you!" she exclaimed. "Are you here to interview the Director?"

"Yes, something like that," she said uncomfortably, then added, "I wanted to express my gratitude to him in person. He's a hero." Natalie found it difficult to characterize the man as such considering what she had recently learned about him but found that the lie fit the narrative.

"Of course, of course. I thought you were great. A real voice for the people." The woman blushed. "The Director's in Room 786."

Natalie began to walk away, then the woman called after her.

"Didn't they give you a pass?" she asked.

"A pass? No. I guess they forgot."

"Well, here," the woman grabbed an electronic card and handed it to Natalie. "That'll give you access to the Director's floor. They won't let you take that upstairs though." The woman pointed at the box. "I can keep it for you here." Natalie paused, then reluctantly handed her the box and she placed it underneath the desk. "God bless you, Ms. Kelley. It'll be here when you get back."

"Thank you," Natalie muttered, unable to believe her luck accessing the man she traveled to question. With a pass in hand Natalie headed toward the elevator to confront a global hero.

Director Juan Carlos Luna had spent the last hour in a hospital bed with his husband, Jay, at his side. The man had always known how to comfort the wounded soldier. Jay was the innocent light in Luna's dark, corrupted world. As they held hands and talked, a naval MP came to the door.

"Sir, you have a visitor."

"Not now," Luna replied and turned back to his husband.

"Sir, she says it's important and she has the proper ID."

Luna was not expecting anyone and had been told that access to him had been restricted. He was curious to see who the visitor may be and told the MP to let her in.

A young, dark-haired woman entered the room. Luna recognized her from the interview with Secretary-General Dubois.

"Can I help you?" he asked, confused why the journalist would be at Bob Wilson Naval Hospital. Communications Director Isabella Hernandez had ensured him that he would not be speaking to the press until he was ready.

"Director," she started, standing in the door frame, "I would like to congratulate you on the promotion and I would like to say thank you for your heroic actions the other day."

Luna vaguely remembered a lone woman being shot at before the gunman opened fire on the crowd. He surmised that this journalist was that woman.

"Ah, well I appreciate that," he replied. "How are you? Are you okay?"

Natalie blushed. The man seemed sincere and she did not expect warmth from him. "I'm fine, sir. Thank you."

The room was silent, but the woman remained in the doorframe.

Jay recognized the tension and rose from his seat at the side of the bed. He whispered in Luna's ear, then kissed him. As he walked out the room, he stopped and shook Natalie's hand.

"I hear you're a big star now. Congratulations."

Natalie dipped her head and muttered thanks. The door closed, and she was alone with the Director. He spoke first.

"You aren't here to simply offer gratitude, are you?"

"No, sir," Natalie walked across the room. Her heart dribbled against her ribcage. She stopped at the foot of the bed.

"I need to be blunt."

Luna laughed. "Just a few days ago, my colon was shredded by a terrorist's bullet. I'm sure I can survive the candor of a reporter." He gestured to the empty seat next to the bed. "Please, sit down and be quick."

Natalie sat in the chair. The smell of iodophor was strong beside the bed. She drew in a deep breath and began.

"I have evidence of what I am about to suggest, Director, and I came to you as a courtesy, to give you a chance to confirm or deny this report. I am going to publish a story stating that the GFN, under your guidance, has been selling arms to the AFG and other American terrorist groups. I also have evidence to indicate Federationists' involvement in the murder of at least two people, though I suspect I will find more." She stopped. Luna's eyes had narrowed to black drills which bore into her. Natalie steadfastly kept eye contact. "Do you care to make a comment?"

The food slot on the door opened and a sliver of light spilled in. Instead of a meal, a thin manila folder slid through the slot and landed on the concrete floor with a flat smack. The overhead light flickered on.

Noah rolled over on the mat and looked at folder on the ground. The staggered corners of white paper jutted out of the folder. He stared at the folder for a few minutes, then reached over and plucked it off the cold floor.

Noah opened the folder. The first page was titled, "Potter County, Coroner's Report: Investigator's Narrative." Noah read on. The document came from St. Paul's Hospital in Amarillo, Texas. Then he saw a name: "Marie Bridger." He quickly closed the cover of the folder and threw the file across the cell. The papers within flew out and fluttered onto the concrete floor. Noah could not look away from the strewn documents.

One of the pages showed two black outlines of a faceless, sexless person. The outlines stood side-by-side and, between the outlines, were a pair of black-outlined profiles. On each of the outlines, there was a red dot on the top of the head.

Noah closed his eyes. He crawled off the mat and, without looking, attempted to gather the loose documents and put them back in the folder to hide the truth. On his hands and knees, he moved across the cell, grabbing, crumpling, and bending the papers as he gripped them in his hands and shoved them in the collar of his bright red jumpsuit. In his haste, he banged his head against the solid wall. Instinctively, he raised his hands to his forehead, dropping the papers, and rubbed the tender skin.

He opened his eyes.

He saw a twenty cm by twenty-five cm photograph. Noah instantly recognized the porch of his house. The photo was taken from the air. In the photo, three men appeared to be walking up the steps of Noah's porch. Two of the men kept their heads down, their faces out of view. But the third man had his head turned and was looking up at something.

Noah immediately recognized the man. It was Murphy.

"You're not going to publish any of that," Luna answered. He was sitting up in bed, staring at the young journalist seated next to him. This woman had named the thing that he had hoped to ignore. As she spoke of his right-hand's corruption, the newly appointed Director knew that he needed to snuff this thing out.

A smirk crept across his still face.

"So, you don't deny the claims?" she asked.

"I don't need to. You won't publish that story."

Natalie was taken aback. "Why not?"

"Because you have too much to lose. I'm sure you're some kind of hotshot now after the interview with the Secretary-General, yeah? I haven't seen the news, but I'd guess that's how you got in this room. Do you really want your second act to be to try to take down the people that gave you the acclaim you're enjoying?"

"This story is bigger than—"

"Sure, it may be. But I don't think you understand what you're dealing with, hotshot."

"You provided arms that terrorists used to kill people. *Your* people," she spat accusingly. She was annoyed at this man's condescending tone.

"I provided nothing," he replied.

"Fine. Arnie Jones and Odyssey Thacker provided—"

"Miss, you can accuse me of any heinous shit you wish to think of, but if I hear you mention that good man's name again, you will surely regret it." He readjusted his position in the hospital bed. "And in the future, if you even think the name 'Odyssey Thacker,' that will be the last neuron your brain ever fires."

Natalie could see the man was deadly serious and she was afraid. "The fact remains that people, again *your people*, provided weapons that killed many innocent lives, lives you have been charged with protecting."

"They were never meant—" Luna's voice rose before he cut himself off. He calmed himself, then spoke as he looked out the hospital window. "Do you believe that we've been good?"

"Excuse me?" Natalie was confused.

"Do you believe that The Federation has been good?"

"I don't see that that has anything to do with this scandal."

"It's a simple question: Do you believe that The Federation has been an overall good? Do you think humanity is better off with the Basic Human Standard put in place?"

Natalie decided that she needed to play along. She answered truthfully. "Yes. I do believe it's been good."

"Alright. On that, we agree." Luna stopped, closed his eyes and gathered his thoughts. "The thought of some was that allowing the Freedom Group into the prosperity and protection of the GFN was a mistake. Those men, John Hill and all the others, cannot be trusted. Peace, unfortunately, is still far off. Those weapons were used to prove that point. To expose the wolves and let them claw each other to ribbons. To show this treaty signing was premature."

"Jesus," Natalie said. "That was not your call."

Luna chuckled. "It was partly my call. Now, even more so. You're not going to publish this story. You don't have the facts and you don't want to ruin your reputation. And you don't want to put any more lives at risk. Think of the ammunition you are giving to these bastards if you put this information out there. You will find that being a journalist, it's often the stories you don't publish that will advance your career opposed to those you do."

Natalie looked at Luna. "You're a monster."

"A monster? Young lady, I saved your life. Maybe not directly on that golf course, but I saved it long ago, far away from your cozy office. Monster. You know nothing of true monsters. Those that lurk in the shadows and attack your very freedom. You enjoy the comfort of your cushioned bench and try to belittle the men and women that let you sit there and cast blame. Fuck you, you know nothing of monsters. I'm no monster—I'm a soldier. And I know my enemy. And I have a duty to protect the people living here. And I am going to do that any way I can."

Natalie began to walk out of the room, when she heard Director Luna call after her. She turned to look at him.

"If you publish this story, young lady, the blood on your hands will never wash away."

Natalie ignored him and started to close the door. She heard his voice, pillowed by laughter, follow her into the hallway.

"Out, damned spot. Out, I say!"

EPILOGUE

17 May 2072

Natalie Kelley grabbed the box from the admissions station and hurried out of the Naval Medical Center. She was confused; she had expected Luna to completely deny the accusations or to confirm them and show remorse. She did not expect him to stand by the scandal with such conviction.

She knew that what had been done was wrong, but his analysis of the situation was right. When she had first mentioned the situation, she thought she saw a flicker of confusion or even terror in his eyes, but he had quickly regained his composure. After their meeting, Natalie believed that the newly appointed Director may have had nothing to do with the original sin, but he was not going to let the transgression see the light of day. He had seen through her bluff of having strong evidence supporting the story. She had a box full of coded notes from a dead man and the statements of two men who would deny any involvement. She knew that she needed more to even begin writing such an article or he would destroy her world.

She walked the streets of San Diego, following the setting sun. She knew that she may be famous now, but she didn't have anywhere near the clout to take on a war hero, let alone one of the most important people on the continent. It could be career suicide, even if she had airtight evidence to back up her accusations.

More importantly from a global standpoint, she knew that Luna's assessment of the terrorist reaction was correct. There would be attacks attempting to exploit The Federation's corruption across the planet. She could do nothing to save the lives that had already been lost. Was she prepared to have the blood of innocent men, women, and children on her hands because of words she penned? *That is, if I lived to see the publication.*

Natalie stopped walking and found herself at a railing, a dozen meters above the Pacific Ocean. The waves crashed against the rock below. A herd of harbor seals barked at diving gulls. People paced the walk behind her, taking pictures and holding hands. Natalie looked out at the seas, the white caps tumbled across the horizon. The wind blew in from the ocean and Natalie smelled the stinging salt.

She raised the box filled with notes over the railing. She held the box of proof, hanging above the coastline, with her finger on the lid's latch. Inside were documents that would indelibly print her name in the history books, but at what cost?

Natalie Kelley, the newest rising star of journalism, felt small crushed between the vastness of the Pacific and the threats and mockery of America's most dangerous man.

As she leaned against the rail at the edge of the shale cliff, she closed her eyes and prayed.

Made in the USA
Columbia, SC
30 July 2020